THE Queen OF Junk Island

ALEXANDRA MAE JONES

annick press

toronto · berkeley

Cover and interior art by Nikki Ernst
Interior designed by Paul Covello
Edited by Claire Caldwell
Line edit by Adrineh Der-Boghossian
Copy edit by Mary Ann Blair
Proofread by Doeun Rivendell

We thank Elijah Forbes for his contributions to this work.

Annick Press Ltd.

We acknowledge the support of the Canada Council for the Arts and the
Ontario Arts Council, and the participation of the Government of Canada/la
participation du gouvernement du Canada for our publishing activities.

Library and Archives Canada Cataloguing in Publication

Title: The queen of Junk Island / Alexandra Mae Jones.
Names: Jones, Alexandra Mae, author.
Identifiers: Canadiana (print) 20210328843 | Canadiana (ebook) 20210328908 | ISBN 9781773216355
(hardcover) | ISBN 9781773216348 (softcover) | ISBN 9781773216379 (PDF) | ISBN 9781773216362
(HTML)
Classification: LCC PS8619.O5245 Q84 2022 | DDC jC813/.6—dc23

Published in the U.S.A. by Annick Press (U.S.) Ltd.
Distributed in Canada by University of Toronto Press
Distributed in the U.S.A. by Publishers Group West

Printed in Canada

annickpress.com
alexandramaejones.com

Also available as an e-book. Please visit annickpress.com/ebooks for more details.

for all the girls who grew up feeling too
many things, in too many directions

A note:
This novel is set in the mid 2000s and contains
terminology and attitudes from the time which may be
outdated. Take care while reading.

Part One

THE COTTAGE
and CHRISTOPHER

Chapter 1

We drove out to the cottage with all of our things in June, a week after the phone call came and two weeks after Christopher Smith ruined my life. Mom didn't say it like this, but it was clearly a "two birds, one stone" kind of deal. I could read the plan in her jittery eyes like she was screaming it out loud: get this girl far away from this school, this mess, this city. Bury her in the earth, under work and distractions, so I don't have to look at her.

Mom and I have lived in the city for most of my life: first in a cramped apartment with two sad-eyed ladies and a baby who wouldn't stop crying; second in a building with crooked stairs where there was a man with a crinkled face always smoking outside who I was Not To Talk To Ever; and third in the apartment we've got now, where I have my own room. For the most part, I like the city—the rush and the cluster and the way the sky never truly goes black at night—but I've always known that it's not where I started out.

When I was a toddler, "the cottage" was home. I've only ever heard it called that, but it's really just the house where my mother grew up and where my grandparents lived until they died. I haven't been back since I was really little, not until this summer.

For the past five years, Mom's been renting it out to the same guy, but now he's gone, obviously.

Maybe this all happened because Mom didn't have you around for advice anymore. But it's too soon for that. I didn't know you existed at the beginning of the summer. And if you want to hear about this summer and how I got stranded out here, at the end of everything, this is where it starts.

✳

I was in the bathroom, ostensibly taking a shower, when the phone call came. There's no landline at the cottage, so when the government needed to call someone about the mess, they rang our apartment. Over the running water, I heard my mother answering, then her voice ticking up like a skier going off a sudden and unexpected jump. "I'm sorry?"

Sometime later, I became aware of a pounding on the bathroom door.

I must not have responded fast enough because it felt like I'd only just registered the sound when I was pulled out of a deep, sunken daydream by the shower curtain being ripped open.

"What are you doing?" my mother said, staring down at where I was sat in the far end of the tub.

"Get out," I said. I really wanted to yell it, but I was feeling all mush-mouthed and hazy in the steam, and it wouldn't come out louder than a mumble.

"Dell, you're fully dressed, and there's water all over the floor. What were you thinking?"

A hand landed on my shoulder and I jerked back violently, sending a tiny wave sloshing from one end of the tub to the other. I searched for a quip. How was I supposed to explain something I couldn't quite explain to myself? I remembered putting in the plug and stepping into the tub. I remembered the sound of the spray changing from a hiss to a roar as the water level rose. But the reasoning behind it all felt elusive.

Since I was a kid, I'd been afraid of water—not of rain but of sitting water, water in wait, water that can envelop. While I waited for the shower to warm up, trying to breathe through the panic that had clapped its arms around me the second I tried to undress, it had seemed like the only way to forget a new fear was to retreat into an old one.

"I mean, the laundry machines downstairs are still broken, right?" I said. "Thought I could multitask."

Mom didn't laugh. She bundled me out of the bathroom and told me to get into fresh clothes. I changed as fast as I could into a tank top and sweatpants, trying not to look at either myself or the spot in my bedroom where a boy had stood the week before. Once dressed, I went out to sit in the kitchen and listened to my mother wring out my wet clothes in the bathroom, water slapping thickly into the tub.

"I can do that myself!" I yelled.

"You're not coming anywhere near this bathroom right now."

"Stop freaking out," I said. "God, you make a big deal about everything. I was in the shower—is that it now, you've just decided I don't get to have privacy?"

My mother's face appeared around the doorframe, white and drawn.

"You stopped answering me," she said. "You can't do that. You've made a disaster out of this bathroom, and we've probably leaked through to the floor below, and I'll get yelled at by the landlord again and I can't—"

She pressed her forehead to the wall, the line of her throat shuddering like there was something living underneath the skin. I could almost feel her disappointment like a physical force pressing me down into the floor.

"I'm sorry," I said.

"There's been a report that someone's been dumping garbage on our property," my mother said.

"What?"

"At the cottage. And I have no way to contact Roger because he doesn't have a phone. I can't deal with this right now on top of—" She waved a hand at me. I was a thing to be dealt with now, I guess.

"What about what's-his-face?" I asked. "Doesn't he live in the area? Can't you ask him to go check out the property and kick Roger's butt?"

"If you're referring to Joe, his son is visiting. I don't want to bother him."

Joe was my mother's new boyfriend. I guess "new" implies there were other ones, which really isn't the case. Mom hadn't dated for years, or at least, she hadn't told me about a boyfriend in years. She didn't even tell me about this one at first. Sure, I knew something was up—she'd been wearing her Celine Dion perfume and biting her nails less, staying out for "evening meetings" and coming home late for a while now. She hadn't had a boyfriend since I was thirteen, but I knew what it looked like on her.

When she finally let slip a couple weeks ago about dating Joe, she told me he'd lived in the town by the cottage since they were kids. She'd reconnected with him in the winter when he was in the city for a business trip.

"You've met him before, but you wouldn't remember it," she'd told me. "You used to play with his daughter when you were both very little."

So I'd known there was a daughter involved. But this was the first time I'd heard of a son. Did this guy also have a wife and seven dogs squirreled away somewhere?

"You could just go to the cottage. It's not that long a drive, right?" I asked.

"I'm not leaving you here alone right now," Mom said.

She sat down across from me on the other side of the kitchen island, rubbing a hand over her jaw as if it had slipped out of place. Once after I came home bleeding from a fight with the girl next door, she went over and yelled at the girl's parents so loud that her jaw kept clicking for hours afterward. I remember getting scared that her face would never return to normal. After I apologized and apologized, I took her cheeks in my hands, feeling for the seam where the bones had gone wrong.

Right now, she didn't look like a different shape than the one I knew. She just looked tired.

I got up, put on the kettle, and found the chamomile tea in the cupboard. We both probably needed something calming.

"Is he grown up?"

"Sorry?"

"The son, if he's visiting, does that mean he's, like, an adult?"

Mom looked at me.

"What, I can't ask questions about them?"

"He's not an adult," Mom said stiffly. "He was the product of a relationship that Joe had years ago. It's his business, Dell, and not something I'm really comfortable getting into right now. I haven't been focused on Joe these past few days, given recent events with you."

She went very still after that, or maybe I did. There was a soft pop, and when I looked down, tea leaves were stuck to my palm—I'd squeezed the tea bag so hard that it had burst. I hadn't felt it happen. The kettle broke the silence with a thin little scream.

"Then why didn't you tell me about him earlier?" I asked in a singsong voice.

"It is not the same thing and you know it," Mom snapped.

Sixteen-year-olds don't get to have secrets like adults do.

I switched the kettle off. The idea of pulling out another tea bag seemed like a lot of effort all of a sudden. I imagined what would happen if I took the kettle and poured the water out over my hand instead. The skin would flush as red as my mother's face; she would scream and lunge for the first aid kit. It was a weirdly satisfying image.

I got another tea bag out, filling the mug in silence. I set it down in front of her, and she thanked me softly.

"We could go to the cottage together," I said. "Then I wouldn't be alone, would I? I'm on summer vacation, so it's not like I need to get up early tomorrow."

I expected a no. It had been "no" my whole life, after all, whenever I asked about her childhood or about our family. It had been "Later, Dell," or "That's too long of a story for right now," or, back when they were alive, "Ask your grandparents."

"Okay," my mother said. "Get your coat."

*

When people think of the word "cottage," they probably picture those summer homes my richer classmates visit periodically when they want to feel rustic for a weekend. The house on the lake wasn't a cottage in that sense. It was where my grandparents had lived all year round, and it was in the boonies of rural Ontario, where nobody cared to vacation.

I don't remember actually living there with my mother and grandparents because I had been too little then. The first time I realized that the apartment Mom and I had shared with the two ladies and the screaming baby wasn't the first place I'd lived was when I was seven years old, and Grampa had given me the photos.

It's my first clear memory of my grandparents. They had come for Thanksgiving to the building with the crooked stairs. Grampa had been tasked with amusing me while Gram and Mom made the food (this was before we got a VCR and the adults could keep me happy with old episodes of *Pokémon* during holidays). Grampa told me that our family had lived on the same property for generations, and brought out a set of seven photographs to prove that I was included in that.

"There's the lake out the back of the house," he said, finger tracing the strip of dishwater blue on one picture. He flipped to the next one—me as a toddler, holding hands with another little girl. "And here's you by the lake! With your little water wings. That was when we tried to teach you to swim. You hated it."

"I don't like water," I told him. "It's scary."

"Even more reason for you to learn how to swim. Water doesn't care how afraid you are when it's angry."

"What are you two talking about?" Mom called sharply from the kitchen side of our one-room apartment.

"Just showing Adele some of the pictures we have of her when she was little," Grampa said.

Mom looked all pinched for a moment, but Gram touched her arm and Mom turned away. I don't remember a lot of conversations with Gram—she never bent down when she spoke to me, so my predominant memory of her was of the stressed elbows of her sweaters, always jutting out from her sides like little chicken wings.

"Why don't I live with you now?" I asked Grampa.

"Well, sweetheart, you and your mom only lived with us until she could get a job," Grampa said. "And then she got one here, so you were able to move out. It's normal for you and your mom to live somewhere else." He made a grumbling sound like a radiator kicking on, and when he spoke again his voice was louder than before. "Though usually, when one's daughter moves out with a grandbaby, there's a father in the picture—"

"Dell," Mom said. "Why don't you come help your gram make this salad?"

That was the end of that conversation.

But I got to keep the photos, all seven of them. I kept them pinned in the center of the corkboard in my room, these days in among pictures of my best friend, Paul, and drawings my mother made. Imagining life at the cottage was the quiet obsession of my childhood. I was sure I would have fit in better there, with the trees and the hush and the stained earth. Space to run. Mom didn't let me go out by myself very often, worried about things in the city that could hurt a girl, suspicious of friends whose parents she hadn't met, strict about wasted time and potential.

I once asked her why we didn't simply move into the family home when both of my grandparents were gone, especially since I knew how much she struggled to afford our shitty apartments.

"You wouldn't have really wanted to live there," she'd said, laughing off the suggestion. "In a town with no Booster Juice? Don't you like it here? I swear we'll get a better place soon. Before you go off to university, how's that? You'll get a huge room. Seventeen corkboards so your pictures aren't crowded!"

We made that first hour-long drive mostly in silence. I watched the boxy lines of the city crumple down like Tetris levels into a flat, open plain of grass and darkness. My hair was still wet at the ends, but as we sped down the road, I could feel all of it—the shower, the fight, everything—falling behind the wheels.

Eventually, the grass turned into huge black rows of trees crowded up against the road. It started to pour, the kind of rain that turned the windshield into a rippled gloss in between wiper swipes. I hollered when I spotted a driveway, and the car skidded into it, my mother clutching the steering wheel for dear life. We idled next to a red mailbox overflowing with wet newspapers. My mother wrenched open her car door to grab the stack.

"I guess Roger doesn't read the mail," I said as she slid the pile into my hands. The letters and flyers were so soaked that they felt soft, like feathers instead of paper.

The driveway was incredibly long. As our car pitched through a tunnel of trees, I tried to pick out animals or demons or mountains of garbage through the flat blackness. A tingling feeling rose up my arms, my body recognizing the setting even though my mind had lost those toddler memories. The moon cut through an open patch in the trees above, a burst of light as sudden and blinding as a camera flash—I squeezed my eyes shut, and when I opened them again the car was curving around one last twist in the driveway and the house was there.

It was a dark, blocky shape, stationary among the blowing trees. No lights on. Two main stories and what looked like a tiny attic were visible in the moonlight, a triangular peak rising above its narrow window. Mom's chest sucked in at the sight, like her rib cage was trying to retreat further inside her. The car rolled to a stop, the headlights cutting two round spots through the dark, outlining a peeling wooden porch with several posts on the railing snapped clean in half.

We sat in silence for a moment. I felt like I might vibrate out of my skin.

Mom blew out a sharp breath and laughed. "What do you say we go to the town, get some gas, and go home?"

"We can't go back now!"

"I didn't think this through," she said. She sounded kind of scared, which was weird because my mother got tense all the time, but she didn't get scared. "I was just so worried—I don't know why I drove you all the way out here. This really can be dealt with tomorrow. And I called Joe to tell him about this before we left, so I could still ask him to have a look. I'm sure it wouldn't be that much of a bother."

I hadn't seen the cottage in over a decade and now she wanted to take back my first chance to actually go in? I popped open the glove box and grabbed one of my mother's emergency flashlights.

"If you want to stay in the car, I understand," I said. "I got it."

I darted out of the car, sprinting away from my mother's furious shriek toward the porch, the flashlight beam wavering crazily on the ground in front of me. Something heavy in my coat pocket bounced against my hip. The rain was colder than the shower had been, but it felt cleaner.

The headlights shut off as I reached the bottom step, and I almost face-planted into the sudden darkness. By the time I scrambled up onto the porch and out of the rain, my mother had reached me, the wet mail bundled up in her arms. She had another flashlight in her hands.

"When we get back, you're grounded."

"I thought I was already grounded for—you know. Is this kind of rain typical around here?"

"No," my mother said. "There's supposed to be a drought on right now."

"Farmers are happy, I bet."

When I knocked on the front door, it creaked open by itself; it hadn't been locked. We shared a nervous look before ducking inside. Mom slammed the door shut behind us, and the pound of rain was cut down to a muted buzz. I stood frozen in the darkness by the door.

"What if Roger's dead?" I whispered excitedly. "And we stumble on his body?"

"Adele, don't say things like that!" Her flashlight beam wobbled a bit as it cut along the floor and swept over the walls.

"There," she said, her flashlight illuminating the light switches. I reached out and flicked the nearest one on.

The room flooded with light. We were standing in what looked like the kitchen, except there was no table or chairs, just scrape marks on the floor. It wasn't completely bare—a counter and upper cupboards were built into the far wall. One of the cupboard doors dangled from a broken hinge, revealing the emptiness inside. Hanging from the center of the ceiling was one of those old, fancy light fixtures, with three tulip-shaped glass heads and a wooden ceiling fan with flowers painted on it. One of the rotors was missing, and it was revolving slowly, as if someone had just tapped it to get it going.

I flicked the second switch and the ceiling fan picked up speed. I flicked it off and watched it slow again.

"Maybe Roger's been a ghost this whole time," I said. For all I knew, he could've been, frankly. I'd never met him. My only reminder of his existence was when I would pick up the mail and there was a letter from him with the rent.

When I'd asked Mom why she'd chosen him to rent the place after Gram died, she'd just said, "He knew your father," which gave Roger one over me.

"He's not dead; he's just done a runner," Mom said, walking briskly to the counter. "Probably moved out the second someone reported what he was up to. You'd think after five years he'd at least let us know he was leaving."

"Maybe he's being chased by the Russian mob," I offered. "Are these the same cupboards and stuff from when you were growing up here?"

She slapped the stack of mail down on the counter. "Yes."

"I thought it would've been a bit dirtier," I muttered. "I mean, a hoarder level of dirty. Something to justify being called 'an illegal dumping site.'"

It was hard not to flood her with questions, but I didn't want to spook her. I'd gotten us in the house. That was a step forward. "There's acres of land on this property," Mom said. "He wouldn't have needed the house for it—the forest would've been a good spot. But we're not going out there tonight. I just wanted to speak to him and clear this up, but apparently that's not an option. I'll have to come back in a couple days to figure out what to do."

"Can I come next time, too?"

My mother didn't respond—she was staring at the broken cupboard, her mouth twisted down. I felt vaguely like I wasn't supposed to be looking, and I turned away.

There were two doorways to my left. The bigger one opened into a wider room, while the other led into a narrow hallway heading toward the back of the house. I moved through the first doorway, down a couple steps into what had probably been a living room, which was revealed to be just as empty as the kitchen when I flicked the light on. Slowly, I walked to the center of the room. The floor had small indents in the wood, too, pale streaks skidding away from each dent, like speed lines. The afterimages of furniture, of life.

I tried to imagine myself standing in this room when I was younger. I'd expected to have a rush of nostalgia or excitement when I got inside—something like what I'd felt while we were driving up. But a huge feeling of loss welled up in me. Everything was gone.

My mother slammed a cupboard in the kitchen. In the wake of the noise, it was suddenly clear how quiet it was.

"I think it's stopped raining," I said.

"Sorry?" Mom said.

"It's not raining anymore!" I yelled.

I waited, but she didn't say anything else. I caught sight of a staircase, the last steps just visible through a doorway in the far corner of the room. I crossed over to it then paused, gazing up.

"That was what, a fifteen-minute shower?" I said. "If there's been a drought on, that won't have helped much."

I waited again. The air was still and silent. I missed, for what seemed like the thousandth time this week, the easy way my mother and I used to talk to each other.

"Mom, I'm going upstairs," I called.

There was a small flurry of noise from the kitchen, then silence.

"Be careful," she said. "I don't know what Roger's done to the house. Call for me if you see anything out of the ordinary. And keep an eye on the ground; there could be nails. Or you could get a splinter."

"Through my shoes?"

"Maybe you should just wait until I'm done here, and I can come with you."

"It's a house, Mom," I said. I tested the first step. "Not a death trap."

"Adele—"

"I'll call if I need you!"

The top of the stairs looked like a mouth above me. When I aimed my flashlight up, the menacing throat of it disappeared, flattening out into nothing more than old steps and a cracked wall at the top.

I could say that my mother wasn't always this overprotective, but it simply wouldn't be true. Overprotectiveness was a weapon she wielded well. The whole Christopher thing had just made it sharper.

Of course, that was the reason I'd had to keep him under wraps. The day I invited Christopher Smith into my room, during the last few weeks of school, I'd triple-checked that my mother would be staying late at work. Somehow, she seeped into the house with us anyway. While I gave him the grand tour, I ended up talking about her, about the cottage where my family used to live. He stood in front of my desk, his shoulders huge in my small room, and looked at my corkboard.

"Did you draw these?" he asked, pointing at a spray of penciled flowers I'd pinned up.

"My mom did. I'm useless at art."

"Is she, like, an artist or something?"

"I think she wanted to be when she was younger, but then— then she had me, so."

"Who's this?"

He'd pulled one of my photos right off the corkboard, tearing it from the pin. It was the one of me with the other little girl beside the lake.

"Me and someone I knew when I was a kid. The daughter of a friend of my mom's. We lived in the country when I was a toddler."

"You look so cute," he said. "Always knew you couldn't be a city girl."

"Why's that?"

"'Cause you've got something wild about you," he said.

I was sprawled back on my bed, propped on my elbows to look up at him. My legs dangled off the bed, and he came forward to stand between them, gazing down at me. There was light all around his face where his head blocked the window, creating a dazzling haze at the edges.

"And you make such a good model, too," he added.

I tripped.

Suddenly, I was back in my own body, climbing that dark staircase in the cottage. I caught myself on the steps as I fell, my windbreaker crackling angrily around me. Something clunked hard on the stairs as the left side of the jacket swung forward.

The windbreaker, two sizes too big, was handed down from my mother. The last time I'd worn it was on a date (that we didn't call a date) with Christopher in the park after school. He'd brought his whole camera setup—the big professional-looking one with lenses that he could swap out, the little point-and-shoot, and the beat-up Polaroid he said his parents had given him as a gag gift. He stuffed the last one into my pocket at the end of the afternoon and told me it was a loan.

"Shoot me something good," he'd said.

The camera was still there now. I could feel it, huge and bulky, impossible to ignore. I'd known it was there when I put on the jacket back at my house; I just didn't know why I hadn't picked another jacket until this moment.

Halfway up the steps, I took the camera out, driven by the same weird impulse that had sent me slamming out of the car into the rain. It wasn't the one he'd used, that afternoon in my bedroom, I told myself. And it was in my hands now, not his. Two contrasting urges gripped me. Smash it on the floor, make dents of my own in the wood—or make it mine in a different way.

I raised it to my eyes and turned to look behind me, at the path I'd just blazed up the steps. The flash bleached the narrow staircase white. When a picture popped out of the top, I stuck it and the camera back in my pocket without looking at it. The choice had been so quick I couldn't deal with it now.

But somehow, I felt stronger. I kept climbing.

When I reached the top of the stairs, the first thing I saw, to my left, was wallpaper peeling off the wall in long curls. To the right was a narrow hallway with two doors. Watery moonlight filtered in through a window at the end of the hall, outlining squares of embellishment on one of the doors in a faint blue. The other door was open, a tall rectangle of black in the wall.

I couldn't hear my mother anymore, couldn't hear anything. The hallway felt like its own bubble of space and time, completely separate from my regular life. I swept my flashlight back and forth, and mundane details stuck out like new discoveries in an alien landscape: the layer of dust sitting on a decorative ledge; the pattern of the floorboards, short and almost square, like cobblestones; the smell of the stale, wooden air.

I raised the camera for another shot, a miniature blast of lightning in the hallway. It felt easier, using it the second time, and the thought cheered me.

The fear was gone. The city and Christopher were gone. I could feel myself in the floor under my feet. The photo and camera went back in my pocket.

And then, two steps later—a sound from the open door on my right. A distinctive creak.

I froze.

"Hello?" I whispered.

Nothing.

A raccoon, I told myself. Or just the house adjusting to having people in it again.

Holding my free hand at the ready in case I needed to defend myself, I slowly crossed to the open door. I'd flunked out of karate as a kid, ironically for being "too violent." Would that count in my favor if Roger was actually still here, just waiting for someone to come investigate so he could go all Jack the Ripper on us?

The door led to another empty room. I aimed my flashlight over a crisscross of heavy beams on the ceiling and what looked like a closet door on the right wall.

This room was darker than the hallway; the two small windows on the opposite wall weren't at the right angle to properly let in the moonlight.

I was just about to step back into the hallway when I saw it.

There, in the crack at the bottom of the closet door—a sliver of white, glowing when my flashlight caught it. Something Roger hadn't thrown out?

I crossed to the door and threw it open.

A face hung in the blackness. Two wide human eyes met mine.

Something hit my chest, driving the air out of my lungs. The room pitched viciously, and I was slammed back onto the ground, one leg twisted underneath me. My head met the floor and bounced up into a strange, sweaty palm. It pressed down over my mouth; skin stretched against my teeth, and I tasted salt. For a moment, I couldn't see anything at all, my vision gone static like a television in a storm.

"Oh," said a voice. "You're just a kid."

My eyes refocused. The face was there above me.

It was a girl, a teenage girl, I thought. Her hair cascaded down around us, soft on my collarbone.

I yelled something like "What the fuck!" into her hand and tried to buck her off, arms flailing ineffectively. Her face shifted, and I felt her straddle me, knees clamping my body in place.

"I'll take my hand off if you don't yell, okay?" she offered.

I nodded. She took her hand away. I screamed, and she clapped her hand back down, cutting off the sound.

"Jesus Christ," the girl said. "I ask for one thing."

The flashlight, still clutched in my nerveless fingers, lit up a bright streak across her body, sweeping over a T-shirt and a red windbreaker and one bare shoulder that had slipped out of the fabric.

I pitched my head to the side violently enough to dislodge her hand. Anger had beaten out fear.

"What the fuck?" I said again.

"Who are you?" the girl asked sharply.

"Who am I?" I said incredulously. "You're the one hiding in a closet! In the dark!"

"Because I heard a car coming up to an abandoned house and I didn't know if it was murderers or not!" she shrieked.

"If it's an abandoned house, what are you doing here?" I demanded.

"My stepmom owns it."

I stared, my response caught in my throat.

"What's going on up there?" Mom shouted from downstairs. The space between us distorted her voice, making her sound unfamiliar.

"You came with someone?" the girl asked, her profile swimming back into view. I couldn't decide whether she looked scared or simply intense.

"No," I said, letting a tremor come into my voice. "I have no idea who that is."

"Are you serious?"

"Dead serious. Maybe I was followed."

Teach you to call me a kid, I thought. She couldn't be much older than me, and yet she was going all James Bond on me for opening a closet?

Mom was hurtling up the stairs now, making an awful, panicked racket. The creaking steps made it sound like a monster was approaching, not a thirtysomething woman. The girl was no longer bent over me, her head turned instead toward the door. All at once, she swung her leg over me, releasing her knee-hold on my hips.

"You should hide," she said suddenly. "Get in the closet."

That wasn't what I'd been expecting. "What?"

Shoes squealed at the end of the hall. The girl swore under her breath, rising higher in her crouch to block the doorway from my eyes—she'd put herself between me and the hall. There was a sliver of movement past her shoulder, and she made an aborted movement, half lunging off the ground before she came to an abrupt halt.

"Anne?"

"Ivy?" came Mom's voice from the doorway. She sounded winded. "What are you doing here?"

The girl shot fully to her feet, and my mother was suddenly visible, standing in the hallway with her flashlight pointing at the ground. When she spotted me on the floor, she rushed forward to pull me to my feet. I immediately noticed that the other girl was taller than me then felt stupid for caring.

"You aren't hurt, are you?" my mother asked. "What happened?"

"I'm fine. She just jumped out of a closet and surprised me," I replied. "Ivy?" I knew that name somehow.

"You were hiding in the closet?" Mom said, rounding on the girl.

"I was checking out the house for you," Ivy explained. "I overheard my dad on the phone with you and, I mean, he's all distracted with Jamie, and Jamie's mom doesn't want me in the house when he's there anyway, so I thought I could come over and talk to Roger to help you out, and then it started to rain and the door was open . . ."

She trailed off, shrugging uncomfortably.

With the second flashlight and the moonlight from the hallway adding an ambient glow, Ivy's features were starting to come into focus. She had long hair tucked up in a high ponytail, and a pointy chin that stuck out, her first line of defense. It was a face I had seen before, I was sure.

"She said you were her stepmom," I said to my mother.

Ivy twitched slightly, a half step in my direction.

"You said you didn't know who else was in the house," she hissed at me. Then, loud enough for my mother to hear, she said, "I said that only 'cause I didn't know it was you downstairs, Anne. I was just trying to make my story sound more believable because I thought she was breaking in."

"It's fine," Mom said, hands out like she was soothing a pair of fussy cats. "It's all right. Ivy, this is my daughter, Adele. Adele, this is Joe's daughter, Ivy. I've mentioned her, remember? I think she's actually in one of—"

"My pictures," I said. The ones from Grampa, the little girl holding my hand. I felt a dragging feeling, like my lungs were descending into my legs. I had a burning desire to shine my flashlight directly into Ivy's face so I could see her properly and temporarily blind her all at once. I slid my hand into my pocket instead—the camera didn't feel like it had been damaged in my fall.

Mom was already talking to Ivy again.

"Does Joe know you're here?"

"No."

"And you came out here by yourself? In the rain?"

"I like going running out past here. I know the area, and it's not that late. Joe's fine as long as I'm back by eleven."

Mom's face was tight with disapproval, like it had been a few days ago, when I was trying to explain what I'd let a boy do. I knew that look—she was definitely about to start yelling. I braced myself, hoping I wouldn't get dragged into it.

My mother sighed.

"Okay," she relented. "Okay."

I waited, but nothing else seemed to be coming.

"Mom?"

My mother ignored me.

"Why don't we get you two downstairs," she said.

"She broke into our house!" I exclaimed.

"The door was open," Ivy said defensively. She wasn't even looking at me, and something about that rankled me even more than my mother not listening.

"It's still trespassing!" I cried. "No matter who your stupid dad is!"

"Adele!" Mom snapped. A flush of embarrassment lit up my skull.

Mom turned back to Ivy. "We'll get this sorted out, okay?"

"Yeah," Ivy said. "All right." A pause, and then she stepped forward into Mom's outstretched arms and hugged her quickly.

"It's good to see you," Ivy said, her voice muffled.

My mother blinked and hugged her back, slightly stiff but looking pleased. An intense resentment suddenly threatened at the back of my throat, like acid reflux.

"Joe was always doing reckless things when he was younger, too," Mom said softly. "Gosh, it's dark up here. Dell, no wonder people think you're creeping up on them if you don't turn the lights on."

She paused, reaching a hand out toward me. "You're sure you didn't hurt yourself when you fell?"

The final injustice. There was no way I could admit that my ankle hurt in front of this new girl, especially when she looked so cozy cuddled up against my mother. How could Mom not understand that there was no dignified way for me to answer her question?

"I'm not made of tissue paper!" I retorted, flapping a hand to dismiss my mother's. Which, okay, wasn't very gracious, but I was low on options.

"Well," Mom said, clearly taken aback. "I apologize for asking then."

She blew past me with her arm tucked securely around the other girl's shoulders. Just as they passed through the doorway, Ivy looked back at me, and for the first time, as the moonlight in the hallway caught her fully, her whole face was visible.

I had stared at that face again and again while growing up—held it in a square in my hand and wished to be back there beside those dark eyes and that dark hair—but now that she was here in front of me again, time had made her unfamiliar.

This girl wasn't the friend I'd always envisioned, couldn't be, not when she was looking at me like that, a hint of a triumphant smile leaking out over Mom's arm.

They turned toward the stairs and were gone. I was alone again, but the feeling I'd grasped in the hallway before was gone completely. If there was anything of me up here, Ivy had trampled over it.

Chapter 2

Did you ever have a rival or archenemy when you were a kid? I used to carefully select my rivals out of the prettiest girls, the smartest girls. I'd watch them obsessively, trying to learn everything I could in order to understand how they'd ascended to their position of social power.

When you're a teenager, though, a rival finds you. And at first, that's what I thought was happening here.

Ivy sat on the kitchen counter and fiddled with the broken cupboard door while she talked. Her face was unconcerned, her eyes sharp. She was wearing tiny shorts and had very long, smooth brown legs. She was beautiful; Christopher would have liked her.

She and my mom explained that they'd met in person last month—Ivy had accompanied Joe to the city as part of a school visit to an art gallery and they'd had coffee during Mom's lunch break. I remembered the day. Paul and I had gone to the park after school and spread out on the grass while I told him I thought I was in love with Christopher.

"I'd always been curious about this place," Ivy was saying now. "Sometimes I bike past here, and Creepy Roger used to have signs up at the end of the drive saying 'Private Property' and stuff." The capital letter on "creepy" was obvious in her tone. "Sometimes these big rusty trucks would drive through town and go down his lane, so we all wondered what was up with this place, especially after I met you, and my dad said you owned it. But I only came inside tonight because it was raining, I swear. I wasn't trying to do anything dangerous." Turning to me, she said, "And I didn't mean to scare you."

Around a month ago, I'd lost track of time while out with Christopher. He'd wanted to go dancing, even though I had an 8 p.m. curfew on the rare evenings Mom let me hang out with friends after school without planning days in advance. Christopher found a place that didn't card, and my phone vibrated again and again against my thigh as his hands dug up under the back of my hoodie and failed at unhooking my bra.

When I got home at 10:30 p.m., I opened the door to my mother's face, which looked broken up with anger like a landscape after a flood—eroded down to sharp points, unrecognizable.

I'd been grounded for two weeks (the first for the infraction, the second for not telling her where I'd been), and even after that, it had taken what felt like a month of my best behavior—volunteering to make supper, keeping my room spotlessly clean, studying at the kitchen table after school instead of spending hours burning mix CDs on our computer—before my mother decided I was forgiven.

All Ivy had to do was say "sorry" and shuffle her heels against the cupboard, and Mom said, "It's all right. As long as your dad knew where you were."

It was the kind of unfair that digs right under your skin and makes you bubble with disproportionate, righteous fury.

I pretended I wasn't listening to their conversation after that, flipping my phone open and shut against my palm. My mother learned when Jamie (the brother, I gathered) had shown up to visit (two days ago), how long he would be staying (Joe would be driving him home tomorrow morning), and how someone named Elizabeth was doing.

"I mean, she never tries to talk to me," Ivy said. "I guess she's in a better mood if she let Jamie come stay for three whole days when she knows I'll be around."

My mother insisted on giving Ivy a ride home, and Ivy went off to find the bathroom first, heading into the small hallway off the kitchen. As soon as she left, the warmth drained from the room.

"Surprised you didn't go with her to hold her hand," I said after a moment.

Mom pressed a palm to her forehead. She closed her eyes.

"Dell, don't make this a big thing. She apologized for scaring you."

"You would've—you would've crucified me if I did something like go into an abandoned house at night. It's bullshit."

I knew I'd gone too far the second the words left my mouth. Mom snapped her head up, leveling me with a look of disbelief.

"Excuse me?" she said. "It's what, exactly?"

"Sorry."

"Tomorrow you're taking those tests I bought," Mom said. "First thing in the morning."

My stomach dropped.

"I told you there's no chance," I said. "We didn't do that, Mom, I told you."

"Then you should have no problem putting my mind at ease."

"I'm not lying." My voice sounded weird, a wobbly dam against tears. A sick, hot panic that had been living in my head for days now was waiting to spill out. Mom wasn't even looking at me anymore, her gaze fixed on the dark window over the sink, staring like the sun was going to suddenly rise and illuminate everything.

"So you're all right with your boyfriend's daughter breaking into our cottage, but I do one stupid thing and you won't believe anything I say ever again?" I wailed.

"Ivy is not my daughter," Mom said.

I kicked the wall as hard as I could. It hurt all the way up my leg. Mom finally looked back at me.

"This house is over one hundred years old," she said, her voice clipped. "It didn't ask for that kind of treatment!"

"Well, *I* didn't ask for someone like you as a mom." Being angry was always better than crying.

There was movement in the doorway to the hall; Ivy was back, one hand on the doorframe. Her eyes flicked from mother to daughter, and I wilted all at once, the anger retreating inside me like a defeated army.

"He only left half a roll," Ivy said. "So if you guys want to go, don't use too much."

Mom took a deep breath then smiled at Ivy. She'd gone all porcelain-doll pale.

"I'll just be a minute," she said, brushing past Ivy.

There's nothing like being alone in a room with someone who just witnessed your temper tantrum to make your sweat glands start working overtime. I shoved my hands in my pockets and the edge of one of the photos scraped against my palm. Ivy was watching me.

"Kind of disappointing," she said.

"What?"

"The house," Ivy said. "I've biked past this property so many times and always wondered what it looked like. Half of my high school is obsessed with it because of Creepy Roger. Not as interesting when you're actually inside, is it?"

"Maybe you just think that 'cause it's not your house," I said. "My family's lived here for generations."

"My dad basically lived here when he was a kid," Ivy said. "Our parents have always been super tight, apparently. Your mom told me about it."

I gripped the Polaroid still jammed in my pocket, and Ivy's eyes flicked down at the movement. The ceiling fan was still slowly spinning above us, even though it had been at least ten minutes since I had turned it off.

"Were you listening to us?" I asked.

"Do you want to see something?" Ivy said as if I hadn't spoken.

She waved for me to follow her and then backed out of the room. I hesitated, imagining Mom coming out to find me gone. Ivy stuck her head back around the corner.

"Come on," she whispered.

Flashlights abandoned on the counter, we crept down the hallway past the bathroom, our feet glowing in the thin strip of light from underneath the door. We reached a room at the end of the hallway with glass windows all along the walls, then stepped through a door that led outside to a short row of steps and a wall of black trees. The air was cooler than before, and it was brighter outside than inside, the moon setting the ground aglow with blue. Ivy hopped down the steps.

"We're going to get lost," I warned, following her.

"You were all 'screw you, Mom' a second ago, but now you're scared?"

"You don't know what you're talking about."

"Then prove it."

The ground was soft from the rain, shifting underneath our feet. It was too dark for me to have any idea where we were going, the shadows sunken and inky blue in a way they never got in the city, but Ivy's shoulders still stuck out, moving in front of me. We were following some sort of path, and as Ivy sped up and started to jog, I pulled alongside her. We kept glancing over at each other. And then somehow, we were both flat-out running, neck and neck.

For a short, heart-pounding stretch it was almost fun, like racing my friend Paul down the side of the fence in the schoolyard. But then, as we rounded a corner onto the bottom of a hill, Ivy shoved me. My left foot caught my other ankle—the one that had already been hurting—and I slipped sideways, stumbling off the path right into a tree.

"Hey!" I shouted. Ivy jogged to a stop at the top of the hill. She was laughing, barely winded.

"Oh shit, I'm sorry," she called down. "I seriously didn't mean to do it that hard. You okay? You weigh, like, nothing!"

"What's that supposed to mean, you bitch?" I said, feeling stupid and more than a little angry. My arm stung from the whip of a branch. "What was that for?"

"Bitch?" Ivy said. "Okay, you really are nothing like your mother described."

I lurched back onto the path and stared up at Ivy. Her body was bleeding into the night sky, but I could still see her eyes, her mouth. She was grinning or snarling, I couldn't tell which.

"Come and see," Ivy said.

"Not sure I'm all that interested anymore."

"Three more steps to see it and you're going to give up?"

I tripped just before I reached the top, and Ivy caught my wrist and pulled me up the last few steps, her fingers pressed hard into the soft skin over my pulse. I yanked my arm away and put space between us.

Ivy pointed past my shoulder. "There."

I turned.

The lake I had only seen in pictures was spread out before me like a pool of oil, somehow both bigger and smaller than I'd imagined, with a distant line of trees on the opposite shore and the sides extending out beyond my frame of view. The water was black at first glance, but I could see deep blue shapes shivering on the surface, muted light trying to find a reflection. The whole thing moved, pushing and pulling in a soft rhythm, except for one spot right in the middle. The tiny thread of moonlight went sharp over this spot, this aberration.

I took the camera out.

"What is that in the middle?" I asked.

Ivy made a noncommittal noise. I took a picture of the lake, the flash briefly lighting up the ground and trees. I had the peculiar feeling that the lake was swelling, getting closer, while the solid patch of darkness in the middle, edged in moonlight, remained motionless. The photo joined the growing pile in my pocket.

"Kids at my school used to talk about this lake," Ivy said. Her voice was low—she'd inched up beside me while I was looking out, and her face was too close. "Used to say that they heard things when driving past here. Odd sounds, like things were being torn apart, or ground up. Most everyone brushed it off—'Oh, it's just Crazy Roger, just Creepy Roger'—but there were others who believed it was something else. People who knew this house from when your family still lived here. Even my dad couldn't give me a straight answer about it—just said that there was a reason your mom left town."

"Maybe to get away from a town filled with nosy people?" I snapped. Ivy continued like I hadn't said anything. Her eyes were enormous now, paralyzing me.

"There's something in the lake, they said. Something that shouldn't be there. Something huge and dark. Something that has a taste for . . ." She paused, leaning closer, then suddenly yelled, "Shitty children!"

Ivy grabbed my shoulder and yanked me forward, as if she was going to throw me down the slope and into the water. I shrieked something that was a combination of "Get off!" and "Screw you!" before wriggling out of her grip. She started laughing, and I stared at her, my heart pounding sickly.

"You up for a swim to check it out?" Ivy asked. "Come on. Could be fun."

"Shut up," I said, pushing her away.

"Why are you so angry? You know, your mother talked about you so much when I met her," Ivy said. "'My daughter Adele is just so nice. Such a good kid, so smart. Always looking for a way to help me out.' I didn't expect you to be such a brat."

"You don't know what you're talking about." I shoved her again, and she stumbled, but it didn't feel like enough. I needed revenge for more than just the prank. I surged forward again, and we were grappling suddenly, a strange shuffle back and forth on the top of the hill.

"She didn't tell me anything about you," I said.

"Maybe she just doesn't trust you with important things."

The truth of it stung worse than the push into the tree. I couldn't find my footing with Ivy's hands yanking me closer and pushing me away. I couldn't see the lake or the thing that was in it anymore, just the shadowed sway of Ivy's face close to mine. My feet slid, and I realized I was at the edge of the hill. My stomach swooped horribly.

I got my fist in Ivy's collar and pulled myself forward. With my other hand, I swung the camera up from my pocket and blindly pressed the shutter, a white bomb of light going off between us.

Ivy shoved me away, staggering back with a hand to her face.

"Fuck," she spat.

"Why don't you go for a swim?" I suggested.

My heart was pounding. Bizarrely, I felt more alive than I had all week, exhilarated by the fight. Ivy rocked on her heels, grinding her palms into her eyes. Below her wrists, I could still see the glint of her teeth.

"Don't have my bathing suit with me," Ivy said, finally dropping her hands. "Did you at least get a good shot?"

She made a swipe for the photo sticking out of the top of the camera, but I got there first. I flapped the square in the air and pretended to squint at it.

"Looks like shit," I said.

"So much for my modeling career," Ivy mused. "Geez, my eyes hurt."

"You wanted to push me in the lake!" I yelled.

Ivy laughed. "God, you're easy."

I went very still.

"What did you say?"

"That it's easy to piss you off," Ivy said. "Another thing your mom didn't mention. You cannot take a joke. I wasn't actually going to shove you in the lake. I was just getting back at you for earlier."

She was standing at the peak of the hill, the lake bright behind her. As we stared at each other, the edges of the thing in the water seemed to stretch out her shoulders, blending with her body until she looked like a part of the landscape. She looked broad enough to be someone else entirely. I could remember Christopher standing in front of me like Ivy was now, except then he was the one with the camera.

I was suddenly very aware of my body—my legs still tacky and damp under my sweatpants, my chest expanding and contracting into the tight fingers of my bra, my wrists poking out from the sleeves of my windbreaker. It felt like all my limbs were on the verge of crumpling inward, sucking into the tiny black hole that had opened up somewhere just below my breast-bone.

"I'm not easy," I said.

"We should head back," Ivy said.

The bathroom light was off when we crept back into the house, and I sped up, terrified that my mother had been looking for us and was frothing with anger and worry. But when I came around the corner into the empty kitchen, it became clear very quickly that we were far from her mind.

She was standing in the center of the living room, half-hidden by shadows. If I hadn't recognized the shape of her shoulders, I would've thought she was a statue, she was so still. Her hands were over her eyes.

Ivy hurtled into the kitchen so fast she slid into me. I caught her automatically as we swayed off-balance, and my mother turned toward the noise.

The look on her face settled so quickly into annoyance that I figured I must have mistaken the lost emptiness that had been there before. I was always searching for parts of myself in my mother that weren't there.

"I've been calling for you two. Where were you?" she bristled, marching into the kitchen.

"I was just showing Adele something I found out back, sorry!"

"It's Dell," I said. I was still too rattled to put my thoughts together.

Mom grabbed the mail and gave the room a scan. On her tip-toes, she stilled the wobbling ceiling fan and then ushered us out the door.

I had assumed Ivy would want shotgun, but apparently she assumed the same about me, because we both ended up in the back of the car. I could see Mom's eyes in the mirror, watching us straining to keep our limbs from accidentally touching.

"Sorry again about running off," Ivy said. "I didn't mean to make you worry."

"It's the woods around here," Mom murmured. She turned the car on and the headlights blasted the forest into view, trees lunging out of the blackness. "They make you want to go exploring. Julie and I used to get up to so much trouble out here when we were young."

I glanced sharply back at the mirror, but Mom's eyes were lowered, focused on pulling the car out. The name was familiar, but I wasn't sure how. A childhood friend of hers?

Like she was aware she'd let something slip, my mother rushed to say, "Seeing you two next to each other, you can barely tell Ivy's a year older. I'm sure you two have loads in common."

Ivy's eyes flicked from my feet up to my face before she looked away again. I had thought nothing would ever feel so humiliating after Christopher, but a tiny scan and dismissal from someone who looked like Ivy could apparently still burn.

The car rocked down the driveway and Ivy's knees swayed into mine, touch and go.

"What were you two investigating before?" Mom asked.

"I was just showing Dell what Roger did to the lake."

My mother's knuckles whitened on the steering wheel.

"You went down to the water?" she said. "By yourself, without telling me?"

Ivy had stepped into the danger zone, and even she could tell. She scrambled for a casual tone.

"We didn't go down close. Just enough to see the stuff in the middle of the lake."

The tunnel of trees unwound into open sky. We paused at the lip of the driveway before turning right, heading the opposite way we'd come in. I craned my neck, trying to catch one last glimpse of the house through the trees, but it was too late—it was out of sight.

"What do you mean, in the middle of the lake?" Mom said slowly.

"By the island," I said—because whatever had been out there, it had to be on something, right?

"Dell, there isn't an island," Mom explained. "It does get shallow near the center, but even with a drought, that wouldn't be enough to call it an island."

"Wait," Ivy interjected. "You haven't seen it yet?"

"Seen what?"

Ivy hesitated, suddenly not so bold.

"There is something in the middle of the lake," Ivy said slowly. "It's the trash Creepy Roger's been dumping there."

Mom's eyes flicked up to the rearview mirror.

"No," she said flatly.

"Yes," Ivy said. "I've seen it during the day, too. I can show you." She paused. "I thought you already knew. I'm not lying."

Those three words sounded different coming from Ivy than they had from me—version 2.0, the upgrade.

"Anne," Ivy continued. "I'm sorry, but it's true, I swear."

"I'm not saying it's not," Mom said. I stared hard at my pale knees, feeling the pull of that little black hole again, the threat of collapse.

"But it's late," my mother continued. "Let's deal with what is or isn't in the lake later."

She switched the topic to some sort of art project Ivy had been telling her about the past few weeks. I stared out the window at the forest blurring past. How had my mother pushed down her anger so fast?

I checked my phone; Paul had texted me seven times since that morning. The preview of the last one was "heard the creep is probs gonna go 2 jail for . . ."

I thought about opening it, but Ivy shifted suddenly in my peripheral vision, and a surge of fear stiffened my entire body. I shoved the phone between my thighs and slumped back against the door, pretending to doze. Ivy and Mom went on talking.

In less than five minutes, we were in town. It wasn't even that late, but there was no one outside and we only passed a few other cars. One solitary traffic light blinked red at the main intersection. The car hesitated there for a moment before continuing.

We turned onto a side street stuffed with cute little houses, the kind with gingerbread trim and fences that probably led to actual backyards. It looked like something out of a picture book for kids.

Ivy's was a two-story redbrick house at the end of the road, a bay window at the front. We inched into the driveway and stopped at a side door with a fat yellow light shining above it.

Instead of letting Ivy out, my mother parked the car. Panic swelled. I couldn't take any more socializing with Ivy, and I definitely wasn't ready to meet my mother's boyfriend like this. I jammed my eyes shut.

"We aren't going to stay, but I can walk you to the door," my mother said, presumably to Ivy. Then, "Dell, do you want to come up and say hi, or stay here?"

"I think she's asleep," Ivy said quietly.

My mother made hushed noises of understanding, and then I heard the matching cracks of two car doors opening. The car dipped as the weight shifted when they got out.

"Would it be all right if I came up, with Jamie here, you think?" my mother asked Ivy, her voice muffled. "He'll be in bed already, for sure."

The driver's side door was closed carefully, with a clean snick of the lock catching. I waited to feel the back door close, but even though I heard footsteps crunching on the gravel, I could tell that Ivy hadn't left. I made sure my breathing was even, calm, deep.

The air to my left changed, narrowing like something was taking up the space.

"We'll see each other soon, I'm guessing," Ivy whispered. Her voice was thoughtful, like she had bought the ruse and was speaking more to herself than me. "You know, it's weird. There's something about you that's really familiar. Something other than the whole toddler-friend thing. It almost feels like I've seen you somewhere else before."

My chest sucked inward, black hole dark, and I fought not to react. Ivy hummed out a note. Then, there was a rush of air and her presence beside me was gone. My mother called out in the distance, and the back door slammed shut so abruptly that the impact bounced my head up off my own window and back.

My eyes stayed shut. I wanted to open them, but my head wouldn't allow the movement without feeling like it was going to burst; everything that had happened that evening was flooding in at once, and I was afraid one prick to my water-balloon skin was going to make it come rushing out.

I don't know how long it was before my mother came back, but it had been long enough that I'd slipped into a real doze. There was a scraping pop—the door coming open—and the car rocked to the side, jolting me out of my stupor.

In the rearview mirror, my mother's eyes found mine.

"I didn't mean to wake you," she said quietly. "Want to sit up here with me?"

Once next to my mother in the front seat, I buckled myself in, limbs heavy.

"We don't need to leave right away if you wanted to dash up and say goodbye to Ivy."

I was looking at my phone, fingers hovering over the button that would open my messages. Baffled, I glanced up to see my mother fixing me with this strange, hopeful little expression.

"No," I said. "I want to go home."

Her face fell a little. She opened her mouth, and suddenly I was rushing to speak, needing not to hear whatever she was going to say.

"Can we please just leave?" I asked. "Please, Mom, I just need to be out of here—"

"Okay, okay. It's all right."

Everything was spinning. The car shifted around me, swerving in one direction, jerking to a stop, and then kicking up again, the momentum pressing me back. I wondered how fast we'd have to go for me to be completely flattened into my seat, to disappear into the fabric and stop hearing the word "easy" over and over again.

"I didn't mean to spend so much time up there," Mom began. "I know it's late, and—"

"She knew," I interrupted. "Mom, she'd seen it, she knew, everyone knows."

My mother faltered.

"Don't be ridiculous," she said after a moment. "Where's this coming from? It's already all taken down, and I made sure the police are handling it. There's no way a girl who doesn't even go to your school—"

"I'm telling you she knew," I insisted. "I hate her, I hate her, I hate everybody."

"Dell . . . Dell, stop that. You don't. Honey, please."

I had seen my mother cry only once, when I was ten: I'd been in the room with her when we'd gotten the call that Grampa was dead. My mother looked pretty when she cried, like a painting. It was not a trait I had inherited—as I felt my face crumple up, I hunched forward, trying as hard as I could to disappear.

"If only you hadn't gotten yourself into this situation, Dell."

"I know. I know."

"Crying does no good."

"Shut up."

"I'm sorry, sweetie."

We drove the whole way back in silence. At some point I fell asleep and dreamed that I was in a forest, with nothing but poison ivy covering my crotch and chest. It wouldn't come off, and the itching pain of it grew deeper and redder. I scratched and scratched and scratched. Somewhere, someone was laughing.

A few days before, I had been scratching and crying in my mother's arms because a boy I had fallen for had taken pictures of me that ended up on the computer screens of everyone at my school.

("talk to me if you wanna see more ;) trust me she wont mind. she was easy," the caption said.)

My mother held me silently while I cried and explained, and then she made me tea in a travel mug, wrapped me up in her coat, and took me to the police station two blocks down from us. As soon as the police were done taking my statement, my mother brought me home, told me to stay put, and went back to the station.

I begged Paul to come over because I couldn't take being alone, and when Mom came back hours later, she kicked him out and screamed her throat raw over a boy in the house without her permission. Didn't matter that she'd known Paul for two years and knew that we were just friends—that wasn't what she was screaming about, and I knew it.

It escalated quickly once she started screaming about Christopher. Red-faced intensity like I'd never seen from her before: "This could be on your record for the rest of your life"; "One Internet search and employers think they know what kind of person you are"; "You cannot be stupid like this, Adele, life doesn't give you that kind of luxury"; "I did not raise you to be the sort of girl who acts like a slut"; "You were supposed to be smarter."

And most of all: "Why didn't you tell me a boy was pressuring you? Why didn't you come to me when he started asking you to do these things? Why didn't you tell me about him earlier?"

I'd said, "I know, I know, I'm sorry," over and over until she'd stopped talking, kissed my forehead, and bundled me up in her arms the way she so rarely did. She told me that she would take care of it—the pictures would be pulled off the site they'd been hosted on, and the police were handling Christopher. The best thing I could do for the moment, apparently, was to get a good sleep and try to forget about it.

It felt like forgiveness at the time.

I'd woken up later that night with flashbulbs and hands strobing in front of my eyes, my feet itching to run. I got up to go to the bathroom, but when I looked through the crack of my door, I saw a light on in the kitchen and my mother sitting at the table. The grooves at the corners of her mouth looked like they'd been carved into her skin. She was drawing wide, looping strokes of her pencil on a page in front of her. I couldn't see what the picture was, but I watched as she drew and started over, again and again, until my feet grew cramped and numb. The table was covered in crumpled balls of paper and Mom was still drawing when I crept back to bed.

The next morning, the paper was gone, and Mom was stiff and awkward, barely able to look at me, never mind talk to me. When she went out to the drugstore to buy eggs and came back with the tests, it was clear to me then that forgiveness was far from her mind.

*

The pregnancy tests—three of them because my mother apparently thought I was so slutty I'd gotten pregnant three times over—had been sitting untouched on the kitchen table since she bought them. The day after we got back from the cottage, she placed the boxes in my hands and told me to go to the bathroom and complete not just one but all of them. I smiled, locked the bathroom door behind me, and did nothing of the sort.

"You're not coming out of there until you've taken those tests," my mother yelled through the door twenty minutes into our stalemate.

"Guess I'm not coming out," I said. "You think we could fit a futon in the bathtub? I think it might be a squeeze."

"Your refusal to take them is not making me believe you, Dell. In fact, it's making me more suspicious that you are lying to me and the two of you did engage in—"

"Moooom!" I shrieked. "Maybe I just don't need to pee!"

"If you're not mature enough to hear the word, you're definitely not old enough to do it!" my mother shot back, as if the topic hadn't made her own voice as thin as an elastic band stretched almost to the breaking point.

"I told you, we didn't!"

"That's what teenagers always say. Especially ones who think they're more adult than they actually are!"

"Fuck you!"

The doorknob rattled, and I skittered a few steps away.

"You do not speak to me like that," my mother said, sounding dangerous.

"Why can't you just believe me?"

"Because I can't."

I almost opened the door at that. Mom didn't sound like Mom. She sounded like she was speaking from under a pile of rubble, crushed by the pressure.

It tugged at a memory buried in the back of my mind: six years old and waking up in the middle of the night to find my mother shuddering in her sleep in our shared bed. I touched her shoulder and said, "You're having a nightmare, Mommy. It's okay, it's not real," because that was what she had always done for me. It had been too dark to see my mother properly, but the sliver of wobbling chin that I could make out didn't look like the person I knew, as if my mother had slipped out of her body and left nothing but the loose flesh behind. It scared me, but she was more scared than I was, so I told myself to be brave.

My mother's nightmares had stopped when we moved to a

place where we didn't have to share a bed anymore. I hadn't really ever thought back to them. They didn't match up with the picture I'd built of her as this titan who crushed mean teachers and bullies and knew me better than anyone.

"Adele, I'm not going to ask you again," Mom snapped, and I amended my thought: she used to know me better than anyone.

"One test," I heard myself say. "I'll take one of them, okay? I'm not taking three. That's stupid."

Silence. I saw something move out of the corner of my eye, and I glanced over to see it was only an arm—my arm—shifting in the mirror above the sink. I'd thrown a towel over the mirror to hide my reflection, but part of it had slipped, leaving a sliver peeking out. Carefully, I pulled the edge of the towel so it hung straight, covering the whole surface.

Ever since Christopher, I didn't look in mirrors.

"You show me when you're done," Mom said. "You understand me, Dell? You bring the stick out here and show me."

It was another thirty minutes before I could get my body to cooperate, one hand holding the test awkwardly in the toilet bowl under my spread legs while I stared up at the ceiling and tried not to cry loudly enough for Mom to hear it. The test was negative, of course: I wasn't pregnant. My mother stared at the stick long enough I thought she was going to cry herself, and then she said "okay" and threw it away and asked me if I wanted to get ice cream. It was so similar to a move she would've pulled when I was six years old that I could only laugh.

That night, I dreamed there was a girl in the lake and

she was naked, unashamed. She was waist deep and walking backward, her eyes on me standing on the shore.

"Shoot me something good." It was Ivy's voice.

I raised the camera.

Chapter 3

You're probably wondering when you come into this whole thing. I didn't find out just how much my mother had kept from me about our family until we got to the cottage the second time, but I can try to tell you now about when I first saw your face—the night before we drove back up.

You already know, of course, that Ivy was telling the truth about the island of trash. You knew about it before anyone else did (except Roger, I guess).

Mom had gone back to visit in the daytime without me and actually saw the giant pile of garbage sticking out of the water. Sure, there was trash scattered throughout the forest, but a big part of it was in the lake. It was much more than one person could make, my mother said. The trucks and moving vans Ivy had seen in town must have belonged to people Roger knew—friends or clients—people he had let dump things on the property. My grandparents hadn't owned the lake itself because lakes don't belong to people, but since they owned all the property around the lake, no one else could access it unless they, or in this case, Roger, let them in.

"I guess he thought he could get away with it because I haven't visited in a few years and the water would hide it from prying eyes, but with the drought the level has gone down," she told me later that night, after she came home.

She didn't tell me at first what we were going to do about the whole thing—just spent days ferrying herself back and forth between the city and the cottage and talking on the phone with various people in official-sounding tones.

And I was stranded, stuck with my own thoughts.

The weird part about having your entire life flipped upside down in the space of a few camera flashes is that there's really nothing you can do afterward. Going to the cottage had been a good distraction, even though I'd had to suffer through all the strangeness with Ivy, but in the days that followed, I didn't have anything to take my mind off the recurring realization that my entire school, and my mother, had found out that I was—

You know.

So I would go to sleep in the middle of the day and wake up three hours later, feeling like I'd been turned inside out and run over. I'd sit at the table with a mug of lukewarm tea, staring at the cupboards. The stiller I was, the more it seemed like everything else was moving, just out of the corner of my eye, as if the furniture was creeping away, but afraid to be caught at it.

The feeling made me think of when my mother and I had bought a used box set of season one of *ER* from Blockbuster when I was eleven or twelve and marathoned it over the weekend on our crappy VCR. I thought of all those scenes with doctors running around and yelling "We're losing her!" right before the heart monitor quit its steady beeping. How the quiet would set in then, the slow motion, as the camera zoomed in on that straight line running across the screen, the drone of it swelling until it was the only sound.

That was me, post-Christopher. Straight flatline.

*

"Are you gonna, like . . . talk to someone about it?"

It was a few days after my visit to the cottage, and Paul had called me from school. It was still exam period for him, and he had his last one in an hour—I could hear the bustle of the hallway echoing tinnily through the speaker.

"I'm talking to you," I said.

(All of my exams had been done early in the exam period, luckily, so I wasn't at school when everything went down.)

"Like a shrink. A therapist or something."

"You kidding? I can't even talk to my mom about it! You think I'm going to tell some stranger about how shitty I am?"

"Listen, Christopher's the shitty one. Anyway, it's not like you ever talked to your mom about any real stuff before this, so I don't see how that's a reason not to talk to someone."

"I talk to my mom about stuff all the time."

I did. Or, at least, I used to. When I was a kid, I wanted to be exactly like her—walk like her, talk like her. I wanted to be good at drawing and art like she was. I wanted to stand up to teachers and principals and mothers of mean kids with the cold aggression she seemed to wield so easily, standing in front of me like a knight in hard, thick armor.

So, yeah, I talked to my mother about everything. When I met Paul in drama class the first day of Grade 9, I'd told her all about how I made a new friend. When Cora and Karoline, my friends from elementary school, ditched me a couple of weeks into that school year, I had blubbered to Mom for hours, and had to talk her down from phoning their mothers to yell. And when Paul had taken pity on me and invited me to have lunch with him and his friends a week later, I had gushed about it to her, too.

I talked to my mother all the time. It had just changed a little when I hit puberty and realized I was a changeling trickster in a horribly made human suit, with a million creepy, gross fixations that my mother would never understand.

"Okay, Dollface," Paul said. He didn't sound like he believed me.

Paul was tall and big, but it was more in the way a carnival teddy bear was big than the way a linebacker was. He had soft hands, and his mouth was always open, even when he wasn't speaking. He was loud and weird; I was mostly quiet and weird. We were a strange pair. But we liked the same things: Deadpool and Scott Pilgrim comics, Gorillaz and Death Cab for Cutie (okay, that last one was more my thing than his), and doing dramatic stunts in the name of environmentalism or embarrassing our parents.

I was a bit of a charity case for him at first, but our friendship became real a month after we started hanging out, when I backed him up while he was faking an injury to avoid running laps in gym. In high school, lying for each other—especially to adults—was the best way to cement an alliance. But we had always sworn not to lie to each other.

"What does Facebook say?" I asked. In the immediate aftermath, when Paul texted to warn me that people at school were talking about pictures of me, I had seen a barrage of mocking posts. I'd been avoiding all social media since.

"Nothing," he said. His voice had changed. "Facebook is absolutely dead. MySpace, too, but I know you don't have that. Today, my aunt posted a LOL cat meme on Facebook, and that was the peak."

"If you won't be honest, I'm going to check myself."

My head was very heavy—I bent down and pressed my forehead to the kitchen table, closing my eyes. The cool press of wood gave me the strange image of lying in one of those medical scanning machines, a cold line sweeping over my body, searching for problems.

"I'm typing it in right now," I said. "F-A-C—"

"No one we know is saying shit about you," Paul said, suddenly serious. "No one from drama class, no one we actually care about. June, Daysha, Kelsi, Mark—they're all, like, cool with it. Well, not cool, they think it sucks for you, but what I mean is that they aren't being assholes."

An image flashed in my mind—Ivy, standing on the edge of the hill above the lake, grinning mockingly at me. I forced it away.

"None of them have texted me."

"It's not that they don't want to; they just don't know what to say. You didn't tell them you guys were a thing."

I hadn't known what to say to them. Never had, really. They had always been Paul's friends first and foremost—people I sat with at lunch and texted about homework but never quite connected with one-on-one.

"You didn't mention what Natasha thought about it," I said.

Paul was silent for just a little too long. "I don't know. I haven't really talked to her recently."

There was a reason he had needed me to back him up in gym class—Paul was no good at lying.

I opened my eyes and the floor below me was blurry. I thought of Natasha with her long, straight nose and her immaculately curled hair and the way rooms seemed to tilt toward her whenever she spoke. Of all the people who knew Paul first, she was the one whose approval I wanted the most when Paul brought me into his friend group. She carried herself like she'd already figured out the world, like she was years ahead of us. I'd thought she was starting to like me, that the way she laughed whenever I said earnest things was a sign that she found me funny, at least, but maybe I'd been wrong and Natasha just thought I was a joke like the rest of the school definitely now did.

"She thinks I'm a slut, doesn't she?" I said.

"No! Seriously, Dell, barely anyone actually saw the photos, so anyone who is talking shit is talking out of their ass."

"So there are people who are still talking shit. What kind of things are they—"

"I've unfollowed half the school on Facebook, so I wouldn't even be able to tell you what they're saying."

"Half the school?"

"Most of them are dumb, so really, the unfollowing spree had nothing to do with you," Paul said. "Not everything is about you, Dollface. Self-centered much? I've got an exam in, like, ten minutes. We should all be worried about my ability to retain anthropology and sociology facts. People forget things super quickly—what year humans evolved to use tools, what the hell *Homo erectus* is, whether someone's boobs were spread online or not, you know."

"I could give you a pop quiz if you want. You know I took that class first semester."

"I think I'll be fine. Are you going to be fine?"

I could go on Facebook. See for myself whether anyone had tagged me in horrible posts or messaged me to make fun of me. That site was probably where most of my classmates had seen the photos—the link sent through their messages, or even posted on each other's walls if they were stupid enough. (Did you know that kids can get in trouble for having naked pictures of other kids? It's still considered possessing child porn even if you're a child. That's something I learned recently.)

"Sure," I told Paul. A lie for a lie, making us even.

After Paul ended the call, I went into the hallway. Our two-bedroom apartment didn't really have a living room, just a bit of extra space between the bathroom door and my mom's bedroom, but it was just big enough to fit a tiny desk, a chair, and our boxy gray computer—our version of a "computer room."

Standing behind the chair, I looked down at the black screen of the monitor, crouching menacingly on top of the computer tower where it lay flat on the desk. When I touched the monitor, my fingers tingled, like the surface itself was trying to suck me in. A light-headedness clutched at me, and I had to sit down on the floor and count to ten, again and again, like I did when I was a kid, panicked in the principal's office for the millionth time, waiting and dreading and longing to see my mother's face.

∗

But when she got home that day, it didn't come with any sort of relief.

My mother presented the idea to me like she was giving me a cake: "We're going to spend the summer at the cottage!"

And then the knife went in, cut out a slice, and revealed the trick center full of oozing, toxic sludge: "And Ivy's going to stay with us!"

"What?" I managed.

"Well, we've got to clean it up," my mother explained. "And you get to spend time in the family home like you've always wanted!"

I couldn't believe I wasn't thrilled to actually live in the cottage for a few months, but—"You invited Ivy to stay with us?"

"She needs something to do for the summer and Joe wants to keep her out of trouble."

"So she's a disappointment, too?"

"Adele, you're not a disappointment."

I stared at my hands, focused on peeling off a chunk of hanging skin by my thumbnail.

"When you were younger, you always used to have a girlfriend over who you could run around with," my mother said softly. "I miss seeing you happy like that."

I winced. My mother could sound so old-fashioned sometimes.

"There's something to be said for girls having girlfriends," she continued. "Paul's a sweet boy, but I think Ivy could be a good influence. She's had some difficulties, too, but she's got her head screwed on straight now."

"Why didn't you ask me about it first?" I said. "Maybe I don't want to be around people right now."

My mother pressed her hands to her temples. "Dell, can you please just give this a try? I thought staying at the cottage would be good news."

"It is," I said. "But—"

"I know you two didn't get off on the right foot the other night, but if you just try, I know you'd like each other," Mom said. "She said she was excited about getting to know you. Please?"

I'm not entirely sure what she said after that because the only thing I could hear was Ivy saying, "You're easy."

Easy peasy, easy sleazy, easy lemon squeezy. I told myself I wasn't going insane—just went to my room, pinned another bedsheet over the mirror on my desk, and set about packing.

＊

At 11 p.m. the day before we left, my mother stepped out to buy last-minute groceries and matches.

I'd already stuffed summer clothes and the odd sweater into

a duffel bag, but the job of packing felt unfinished. I didn't know what was missing until I came out of my bedroom and spotted the despondent tilt of my jacket on the coatrack by the top of the stairs.

There it was in the pocket—the Polaroid camera. When I pulled it out, the photos I'd taken earlier that week fell to the floor, and I stooped to pick them up. The dark shots of the inside of the cottage were mostly impossible to read, the hallway reduced to one glowing blue window floating in a sea of black.

The one of the lake was almost pitch black, except for a weird white streak in the very center, brighter than moonlight, a tiny speck perched close to where the island would've been.

Bizarrely, the picture that had come out the best was the split-second shot of Ivy—a smeared blur of her neck and shoulder, and then the crystal-clear snarl of her mouth and one surprised eye, lit by moonlight. It almost made me laugh. I drifted down the hallway, camera and photo in hand, looking for my mother to show her.

It was only when I was standing outside her bedroom door that I remembered she wasn't in there. The smallest of things crushed me these days. I sank forward and tipped my head against the door—and it moved.

She hadn't pulled it completely shut.

I walked into the dark room and stood there for a moment. Since we moved to this apartment, both of us had taken advantage of finally having personal space, and I had rarely been in my mother's room, and never when she wasn't there—she always closed the door securely when she was out, a clear sign to stay away. Her bed was neatly made, pillows snuggled together at the top. The corkboard on the wall at the foot of her bed, matching the corkboard in my own room, was completely empty apart from one rectangle—a photo?—pinned to the bottom left. I briefly contemplated climbing into her bed, swaddling myself so deeply in the center that it would be impossible for her to untangle me.

When I turned to leave, something rasped against my bare ankle, and I looked down to see that a crumpled piece of paper had fallen out of the garbage can half-hidden behind the door. The can was overflowing, paper crunched into balls and forming a precarious pile that appeared to defy gravity.

I bent down to pick up the fallen scrunch of paper, but before I put it back on top of the stack, something made me smooth it out.

It was a drawing—no, a series of drawings, crowded together on the page. The same face, over and over, the same girl from different angles.

For a second, I thought it was my face. But although the girl looked eerily like me, something was off, as though I'd been distorted ever so slightly. I was shot back into the previous week, seeing my own face and body through a camera lens, through someone else's eyes, so unfamiliar and horrifying that it had woken within me the kind of primal fear I imagined the Neanderthals must have felt when they first met *Homo sapiens*—the feeling of "me but not me," recognizing an alien quality in the other and yourself all at once.

I dropped the drawing and reached into the garbage can. Slow at first, then in a fever, pulling out pieces of paper and uncrinkling each one until the images became clear. Every single drawing was of the same girl, my pseudo-doppelganger. I dug deeper, sinking my hands into used Kleenexes and gum wrappers, grasping.

And then I looked back up at the photograph pinned to my mother's corkboard, just a few feet from the garbage can, and there it was. The true model for the sketches.

The photo was of a teenage girl standing in front of a lake—a lake I knew I had only been to once at that age, in the middle of the night with Ivy at my side. The girl in the picture was smiling, closemouthed. She was pretty at first glance, and then less so as you looked longer, skinny and too tall for her round white face. I could recognize my own big front teeth and weak chin in the picture.

I'd never really seen any photos of my mother as a teenager, but I look so little like her now that people sometimes don't believe we're related at all—I'd never have thought she looked this much like me when she was my age.

But standing in front of that lake, who else could it be?

The girl wasn't smiling in the drawings—she had her eyes closed in most of them, like she'd been caught by a camera mid-nap. Drawn from memory, not from the photo. I picked up one page that held a huge, close-up portrait, smoothing my thumb along the line of the girl's neck. Remembered my mother hunched over the kitchen table in the middle of the night, sketching in big, desperate lines and then crumpling every piece up.

"I was going to tell you about him," I said softly. "I wanted to tell you."

The neck under my thumb moved, and the girl's eyes opened, meeting mine.

"No, you weren't," the drawing said.

I dropped the paper and jerked backward so fast that something ripped, audibly. The room tilted around me, the ceiling dropping down in front of my eyes.

When my vision cleared, I was a meter away from the garbage can, my back against the bed. The drawing sat on the floor in front of me. It looked exactly the same as when I first saw it, except now there was a rippled half-moon torn from the top of her head. The missing piece was stuck to my hand: a strip of white, strands of pencil-drawn hair, and one single eyebrow.

Just a drawing, I told myself.

I shuffled back over and started stuffing the paper back into the garbage can, suddenly paranoid. As I put the last piece into place, I caught sight of something scrawled underneath one of the drawings, a word.

And there it was, in my mother's handwriting: your name.

Julie.

Part Two

THE ISLAND
and IVY

Chapter 4

We arrived early afternoon. The front of the cottage blazed white in the sun, Ivy barely visible in the glow where she stood on the front steps.

"You're late!" she yelled when the car had rolled to a stop.

"We are not," I said.

I went for the bags in the trunk and Mom went to greet Ivy, who swept her up in a hug. The trunk wouldn't open without the keys that were in Mom's fist, so I stood by the car and watched my mother's face get swallowed up in Ivy's dark hair.

"Mom," I said.

The two broke apart, smiling.

"Oh, forget your stuff for a second, Dell, you've gotta see the island in the daytime first," Ivy said. A week had left her looking somehow taller than before. "Come on."

She took off around the side of the cottage, waving to indicate I should follow.

"Ivy, you are not to go near the water!" Mom yelled after her. "Ivy!"

Before I could take more than two steps to follow her, my

mother cut me off with a "tch, tch, tch," her hands fluttering at her sides like distressed birds.

"You don't know how to swim," she said. "I'd feel better if you stayed where I could see you."

"I wasn't planning on jumping in the lake," I retorted.

"Dell," Mom sighed, like I was the one being unreasonable. "Ivy's got her lifeguard certification, so she's a little better equipped if something goes wrong, but really, I don't want either of you to go too close to the water's edge. We probably shouldn't be within twenty feet of it. We don't know what contaminants Roger might have dumped in there."

"We've been here for ten seconds," I said. "I just want to see the island. Can you let me go do that without it being this huge deal? I'll tell Ivy not to break out the breaststroke yet, okay?"

Mom threw up her hands. "All right."

I took off toward the spot where Ivy had disappeared. Mom called, "You come back here in five minutes, okay?" but it was too late. I was out of sight.

A trodden dirt path wound around to the back of the cottage before it disappeared between the trees; I realized it was the same one I'd taken with Ivy in the middle of the night. Her dark hair was visible as a flicker of movement farther down the path.

"Hey!" I called.

Ivy looked back for a second and then kept on, vanishing from sight. I ran faster. The path curved, the dirt crumbling closer to sand under my feet, as it sloped into the hill I remembered from before.

I came out through a break in the trees at the top and stopped.

The path and the ground fell away all at once, slanting down to a short beach, half sand, half stony earth. It ended in dark mud just before the water. The lake stretched out in front of me, and there it was, slightly off-center, two hundred feet away: a heap of garbage.

The island was smaller in the daylight. It rose uncertainly from the lake like an alligator, something that belonged out of sight. The main bulk of it seemed to be made of the rounded cab of a truck, one tire visible where the front axis protruded from the water. I thought I could see a bed frame and a lamppost to the right, making up one shoulder of the beast. The rest of the island wasn't composed of anything instantly recognizable from the shoreline, just a slow landslide of stacked rubble tapering down and disappearing below the surface. The water sucked at the sides, and some of it rocked slightly, but the core of it was solid; this was a tip of a mountain.

My foot slid and light flared in my eyes—there was something shiny out there, to the left of the truck, catching the sun.

"Shit," I said, ducking forward to clear my vision.

Ivy was at the edge of the water, ankle deep, her shoes dangling from one hand. Various pieces of junk littered the shoreline around her. A broken dollhouse lay directly to her left, the rooms flooded. She glanced over her shoulder.

"Right?" she said.

"There's no way," I said. "We'll need a boat. We'll need a boat with a crane."

"There actually is a little rowboat out there," Ivy said excitedly, and when I squinted, I thought I could see what she was talking about—the brown bulk of something curved and wooden peeking up over the back of the island. "I don't know if it's intact, but if it is, all we'd need to do is go out there once to get it, then we could use it like our own little ferry."

"You can't get a car frame out of a lake in a rowboat."

"I'm not saying that."

She took another step into the lake and her foot sunk fast—she wobbled, tipping toward the dollhouse, then windmilled herself upright again.

"Are you okay?" I said, trying not to laugh.

"Don't be dumb," said Ivy, looking flustered. "Anyway, I just thought you'd want to see the island before Mum figures out how we're going to dismantle it, or whatever."

"Mum?"

"Yup," said Ivy.

"She's not your mother. And you're not British."

"Oh, come on." Ivy smiled. She pulled her foot free of the water with a sharp, sucking noise; it was black with mud when she started up the hill toward me. "It makes a nice difference between what you and I call her, right? You get Mom, I get Mum. It's cute."

Her face dropped when I didn't respond.

"Your mom told me you were also sorry about how weird things were with us last time," she said after a moment. "If you guys are good, I don't have beef with you, so I'm just trying to be normal."

"So you're saying you're sorry?"

"Not if you're not."

We squinted at each other. I frantically tried to tally who was more at fault the first time we were both in this same spot—me for yelling at my mom in earshot of Ms. I-want-to-call-her-Mum or Ivy for trying to scare me by the shore like she was my mother's personal knight in shining armor—taunting me about photos I was sure she'd seen, no matter what my mother said.

"We could swim out there and get the boat together," Ivy said at length.

"My mom says we're not allowed in the lake because it could be dangerous or contaminated," I said. "Also, I can't swim."

"Sure, but—" She cut herself off with a sigh. "You're still pissed. Got it. I'm going to go help your mom empty the car."

I watched her stomp away down the path, her muddy foot leaving a lopsided trail behind her. When I glanced back at the lake, a cloud was bringing a wide patch of shadow in from the right, heading toward the heap in the center.

It still seemed an impossible thing, even though the island of trash was in front of my eyes. And I knew there was even more to it that I couldn't see.

"Does the name Christopher mean anything to you?" I said.

Ivy stopped just before the curve in the path ahead.

"No?" she said. "Unless we're talking about Winnie-the-Pooh."

"What?"

"Christopher Robin? You didn't read those books as a kid?"

"No, I did, I just—"

I fell quiet. At this distance, I couldn't measure the honesty in Ivy's face and tell if she was hiding anything. I felt stupidly off-balance, like I was back in Grade 9 gym, changing in the bathroom stalls instead of the locker room because I was scared of being in my underwear around the pretty, popular girls. I'd never known how to act around beautiful girls. Their appearance was a weapon I couldn't guard against, revealing all my own flaws and strange, internal urges to impress, to fight.

"Okay," Ivy said slowly, when I continued to stand there silently like an idiot. "I'll see you back up at the house."

I turned back to the lake, closing my eyes so I didn't have to see the water mouthing menacingly around the island. I listened until Ivy's footsteps faded to nothing and all that was left was the sound of the trees talking and the suck of the water against the shore. I counted to sixty in my head and then turned and headed back up the path.

My mother's boyfriend had brought over some basic furniture from the charity shop in town the day before we arrived—a kitchen table, a few chairs, a mini-fridge, one sour-green velour armchair. Mom told me this as she wiped down the insides of the kitchen cupboards, the cloth turning slowly brown with grime under her hand. Our luggage was piled in the empty living room like a campfire in the middle of a loose circle of folding camping chairs.

"Joe is in Kingston today," she said. "So he wasn't able to help us move in, but he's going to bring over a couple of friends' old beds in a few days. We're on air mattresses until then."

Joe—a blank, gray, man-shaped space standing between me

and my mother in the kitchen. The fact that I still hadn't met him but had met his daughter left me feeling prickly every time his name came up. It sounded too normal in Mom's mouth, like he was a fact in our lives, instead of a new development.

"Ivy's just brought some of the bags upstairs," my mother continued. "Do you want to give her a hand? The two of you are staying in the room where you met the other week. The one with the closet?"

"Can't I bunk with you?" I asked. "I'm sure she'd love to have her own room."

"Come on, it'll be fun! You used to love having sleepovers with your girlfriends when you were younger."

"Ivy's not—"

"You can help me clean the kitchen or you can take the bags up and sort out the air mattresses," Mom cut in sharply.

I grabbed Mom's duffel bag and a deflated air mattress and headed for the stairs. When I was halfway up, Ivy appeared at the top.

"Coming through," she said, barreling down the steps. I pressed myself against the wall as far as I could to let her squeeze past.

"I took the left side of the room," she called over her shoulder. "We can switch if you want, but you better not want."

I heard her clamor into the kitchen, saying something about "Oh, you shouldn't have to put those away by yourself! Let me." My mother's voice kicked up high and happy in response.

Mom's room had three windows that overlooked the back of the house. Through the trees I could see the blue-and-white shine of the lake and a mishmash of color that was probably the island. I looked carefully at the floor, trying to spot where the bed might've sat. This had probably been my grandparents' room.

It struck me again just how weird it was to stand here, after over a decade away.

When my grandparents died, I knew I should've been sad, but all I'd felt was a big blankness. Death to me meant raccoon guts spread across the middle of the road or a pigeon lying on its back at the foot of a glass skyscraper. It wasn't Gram and Grampa just slowing down and stopping one day, with Gram on a one-year delay.

One of my mother's old friends from high school who still lived in the area—a blonde lady named Lucy—watched me both times while Mom took care of whatever needs to be taken care of when your parents suddenly die one year apart. I remember sitting in front of the strange luxury of a flat-screen television, watching Much Music videos and Nickelodeon shows I would've been thrilled to have the chance to see on any other day, hearing nothing but my mother and Lucy talking in the kitchen about finances and renting and other things I didn't quite understand at ten and eleven.

I didn't see the cottage either of those two times—didn't see anything more of my mother's hometown than Lucy's pink guest bedroom and the town hall where the funeral receptions were held.

After Gram went, Lucy sat out on her porch with me and told me it was okay if I wanted to cry.

"I know you're trying to be strong for your mother," she'd said. "But it's hard, losing family. Especially when you have so little of it left."

She told me about her own family and how she'd lost both her high school crush and her grandparents as a kid, too, but I admit that I don't remember much of that—I'd been too lost in my own head to take it in. I did cry a bit, but I didn't let Lucy hug me. How do you explain to a stranger that you're crying because you're mad? I couldn't be sad at having lost something I didn't even know. I guess I'd thought that those holiday visits from my grandparents would someday start to take place at the cottage, and we'd talk more about real things, about family history and the lives they'd all had before me. But now that possibility was gone. Why had my mother kept this place—these people—from me? I'd felt suddenly like my whole past was this big, empty black hole.

Mom found Roger to rent the cottage and that was the end of that. No more visits from Gram and Grampa on holidays, no more stories, no more house by the lake.

But now I was finally here. And maybe I could start filling things in.

I set Mom's bag down in the middle of the empty room and knelt down to spread out the air mattress in what seemed to be the cleanest corner.

"Hey," said Ivy from the doorway. "I brought the pump thing."

"I thought you were helping my mom in the kitchen."

"Anne wanted me to make sure you were good." She plopped down on the floor next to me. "Here, move over."

She knocked her shoulder lightly into mine and I stood up.

Ivy hunched over the air pump, bringing it under the cradle of her body. I stared down at her; her hair was in a ponytail, like it had been when we met. Short, wispy pieces escaped at the nape of her neck. My fingers cramped.

The machine kicked to life and an overpowering thrum filled the air. The air mattress began to plump up slowly. Ivy turned to me and said something too quietly for me to hear.

"What?" I said.

"Are you going to stand there all day?" Ivy yelled. "Go look at our room!"

She seemed excited, almost friendly. Happy to spend her summer rooming with a freakshow? Maybe her friendliness always came with an edge of challenge.

The room with the closet looked nothing like it had the night I met Ivy. She had apparently fully moved in and decorated in the time she'd been in the house before me. Her mattress was still deflated, but she had a bedside table with knick-knacks on it, a little chest of plastic drawers, and three different All Time Low posters splashed on the walls. One of the posters was definitely cutting into my side of the room, which was completely barren, except for the crumpled air mattress with my bag thrown on top.

None of it felt like there was any room for me. At least, I thought to myself, there was no Internet here, so I wouldn't be tempted to escape Ivy by checking Facebook.

When I glanced back, I could see Ivy testing out Mom's mattress with one hand. She seemed compatible with the cottage in a way I wasn't, like she was a doll who had come with a set, and

I had been found in a thrift shop. Making us play together didn't make sense.

I was about to head back downstairs when I caught sight of what looked like a trapdoor to the attic in the ceiling at the opposite end of the hallway. When I walked over to stand underneath, I saw that a thick silver ring protruded from the center. I reached as high as I could, but my middle finger only brushed the bottom of the metal loop.

The entrance to the attic?

Downstairs, the kitchen was empty, a cloth lying abandoned inside the now doorless cupboard. The bag of food Mom had been unloading was still half-full.

"Mom?"

"In here!" came a voice from the hallway.

She was standing in the sunroom by the door that led out to the forest behind the house. The whole room was golden with light, twice as bright as the rest of the house. The door was mostly glass with a thin wooden frame; the bottom pane had been shattered, and a flap of ripped cardboard was taped loosely over it. Another thing I hadn't noticed when I followed Ivy out into the night.

"I felt a breeze," Mom said distantly. "I guess this is where it was coming from. There's more to do than I thought. Even just on the house."

"Was that your room when you were a kid?" I asked, hoping to distract her before she spiraled. "The one you've put me and Ivy in."

My mother made an agreeing hum. She was staring out the

window. I craned my neck to look around her, but all I could see was trees.

"You saw the big mound of trash in the lake earlier, right?" my mother said. "Horrible, isn't it? The fine for an illegal dumping site this large could have been astronomical. We're lucky the municipal government gave us the summer to clean it up ourselves, but I have to admit, I'm not exactly looking forward to wading into that problem."

"We could always just assign Ivy to do all the really difficult cleaning," I joked. When she didn't respond at all, I gave up and said what was really on my mind. "So does the attic open?"

My mother blinked, as if just registering my presence, and swiveled to look at me. "Sorry?"

"There's a trapdoor in the hallway ceiling upstairs. Does it open? Can we go up into the attic?"

She looked more flustered than I expected from such a simple question.

"It can open," Mom said. "But I think we'll deal with the things up there later in the summer."

"Wait, there's stuff up there? Did Roger fill it with trash, too?"

"No!" she said, her tone strangely sharp. "No, I haven't—I haven't looked, but he didn't keep his own things up there. Part of my arrangement with him was that I could keep some family knickknacks and furniture in the attic. Just things I didn't want to donate but"—she half-raised her hands, fluttered them, and put them down again—"things that wouldn't fit in our apartment."

Excitement surged through me. A treasure trove of information about my past, just hovering above our heads?

"What kind of things?"

"Things, Dell," Mom said. "Memories, you know, nothing of immense value. We're not going up there yet. We have so many other priorities."

"But don't you want to make sure it's all still there?"

She hesitated, eyes back on the window again. For a moment there was a strange air about her, like I was seeing the child who spent years running around this house.

"Anne!" Ivy yelled from somewhere upstairs. "I think one of the air mattresses has a hole!"

The spell was broken. My mother shook herself.

"We have all summer," she told me. She gave me a distracted smile and went to find Ivy.

We set out into the forest carrying garbage bags after supper, when the sun was pricking itself on the tops of the trees, and the light had gone slanted across the driveway. Everything outside of the forest seemed to disappear as soon as we were five feet in, a narrowing of the world like a microscope focusing. Picking through the trees, light scattered like loose change on the ground, felt like clarity. I wished that I had brought my camera with me to capture it.

As we moved through the forest, I trailed behind, searching for and snatching up every piece of trash that dared to cover up the green. Ivy kept pace with Mom, their shoulders brushing, and begged for stories about her dad as a kid.

"You must have some dirt on him, right?" Ivy said.

"Mountains high," my mother said. "But I can't just go and reveal all his secrets just like that."

"I'm sure Dell wants to hear, too," Ivy said. "I mean, she hasn't even met him yet."

"More reason not to ruin her impression of him right off," Mom said.

I jogged a few steps to catch up, moving along my mother's other side.

"No, I wanna know," I said. "Were you guys in the same class in school?"

"He was a few grades above me," Mom said. She paused for a moment. "He used to get called Jumps because he was so easy to startle."

"Jumps!" Ivy crowed. "Please tell us all the times you've scared him, right now."

"Joey Jumps was his full nickname," my mother said, grinning.

"Have you ever scared him while he was . . . sitting on the toilet? Halfway up a tree?"

"Up a tree? He's nowhere near that acrobatic."

Ivy waggled her eyebrows. "What about during sexytimes?"

Mom tripped, and all threat of a smile was gone when she straightened up.

"Not appropriate, Ivy," she said, her voice clipped.

I could sense Ivy glancing over at me, but I kept my gaze on the trees, scanning for garbage. She was on her own with this.

"Sorry," Ivy said. "I was just joking."

Halfway up a hill and seven pieces of shredded newspaper

later, Mom said, "I did scare him once at a mutual friend's farm and he fell into a goat pen."

"Oh my god," I blurted.

Ivy said, "Were there any goats in the pen?"

"They had around fifteen goats, including the babies," Mom said. "Joe had the bad luck to fall into the pen of the one goat they kept separated from everyone else because he was so ornery."

"The goat or my dad?"

"Very funny. He got chased for a harrowing few minutes before he managed to get back over the fence. We teased him about goats for weeks."

Ivy threw her head back when she laughed, her gums visible in a pink, shiny line above her teeth.

"I'm going to ask him leading questions about goats when I see him," she said. "See if he's been scarred since the incident."

"Has he ever said anything about goats to you before?" Mom asked.

"No," said Ivy.

"There you go. Clear avoidance."

"Because goats as a topic comes up often?" I said.

I was just trying to find a way back into a conversation that seemed like it was rapidly becoming a two-person club. But it came out too sharp. The smile Ivy shot me was all lips and no teeth at all, never mind gums.

"You'd be surprised, city girl," she said. "All anyone does around here is talk about their farm animals."

As much as I wanted to pretend that my mother wasn't dating anyone, I did kind of want to hear about Joe—my mother had let slip only a few things in the car on the way up to the cottage. I knew that he was shorter than her. That he was a high school principal, only in his second year at the job. I knew that he was Native, and that growing up in an overwhelmingly white small town hadn't been the best experience. My mom hadn't exactly gotten into all of that on the drive up, but I could read between the lines.

The idea of meeting him at some point was still scary. I mean, I wanted to meet him, if only to try and understand Ivy more, but confronting an aspect of my mother's life I never saw was definitely going to be weird.

As we wove through the forest, we found ourselves on a path that had been widened by tire tracks at some point, probably from a four-wheeler. Foot paths split off from it occasionally and disappeared into the undergrowth. The garbage seemed to come in waves—a pile of plastic chairs and beer cans and newspapers would appear suddenly, and then there would be nothing for several minutes. I kept falling behind because I was picking up too much—every few minutes I'd look up from my swelling bag to see my mother and Ivy waving for me to catch up.

Farther down the path, we found a teal metal filing cabinet resting against a tree, dented on top and at the side, so it looked like a person bent at the hip. Its two drawers still seemed intact, but they were stuck so fast they didn't even rattle when I pulled. I tried to pry one of the drawers open with a branch, but it snapped in my hand. My mother fussed over splinters, and I shook her off.

"We'll need a crowbar," Ivy said dismissively. "And I can ride a four-wheeler if we need one to drag stuff out of here."

We walked on. We hadn't seen any garbage for around ten minutes when the path with the tire tracks stopped abruptly in a mess of confused grooves at the foot of a wide maple tree. Somehow we'd wound toward the shore, or the shore had wound toward us, because the lake was suddenly visible through the trees. There was no beach here—the ground just dropped away sharply to the water below.

Mom set a hand on the maple tree and leaned against it to catch her breath.

"Should we head back?" I suggested carefully.

"Not yet," my mother huffed. "I was trying to find the water hole."

"Oh!" Ivy exclaimed. "I know where that is—we should be close!"

My mother and I looked at her, and she instantly realized her mistake.

"I mean, I haven't been there before, but some kids from school talked about sneaking onto the property when Creepy Roger lived here so they could go swimming," Ivy said. "Not often, I don't think. They probably only did it a couple times last summer."

"Really."

Mom's tone had flattened to that "I'm disappointed in you, but I'm not going to say it until you've already apologized a million times" sort of monotony. This time, surely, Ivy wasn't going to get away with it. I found myself perversely excited, ready for the playing field between us to level.

"So you would swim unsupervised on a stranger's land while

no one knew you were there?" my mother said slowly.

"Not me," said Ivy. "I wouldn't be that dumb."

"You just said that you knew where it was," I said.

Ivy threw me a poisonous look. "Because I was told how to find it."

"Then why don't you show us where this pond is? I want to see it."

"Girls!" Mom had straightened, her energy seemingly replenished by the chance to boss people around. "Maybe we should just head back for now. We've got a lot of trash collected already, and it's probably best I just find it on my own another day. But when we get to the house, I'd definitely like to hear about how teenagers were sneaking onto this property, Ivy."

"Of course," Ivy said. "I'm sorry if I sounded excited when I brought it up. Obviously it was a super reckless thing for those kids to do."

Super reckless? How was she so good at slipping into "parent-speak"?

"No," I said, surprising myself with the vehemence in my voice. "I want to see it. You said it was close. Is it this way?"

I stepped off the path into the tree line, pushing past a curtain of leaves.

"Dell!" my mother called, clearly exasperated. I could hear the two of them scrambling to follow, twigs and underbrush folding underneath their feet. I picked up my pace, crashing through a tunnel of thin, prickly plants.

"This is the way, right?" I yelled over my shoulder, exhilarated. Ivy was closer behind me than my mother, and I could feel the thrill of the chase fueling me through the forest. The ground arched up into a hill, rocks starting to protrude like fists from the earth. I was faster than the other two; I let their voices push me right to the top.

"Dell, slow down!" my mother shrieked.

The trees opened onto a rocky plateau and then the world suddenly disappeared. I skidded to a halt only a few feet from the edge of a drop. Below, maybe two or three meters down, lay a wide circle of water, surrounded by dark gray rocks. For a dizzying moment, I thought I was tipping over the edge. I could almost feel the water closing over my head, suffocating me.

I stepped back and almost bumped into my mother.

"This is why I didn't want you running off out of my sight," Mom said shortly, shuffling me slightly behind her. "What if you fell? You can't even swim!"

The end of the sentence got a little lost in her mouth. She stared down into the water.

"Oh shit, this is awesome," Ivy said. "I know you wanted to go back, Anne, but can we go down for a second? I heard it was deep enough to dive."

"No one is diving from here," Mom said. "And you watch your language."

Ivy walked casually up to the edge of the short cliff, the toes of her shoes lined up with the break between rock and air. I shrank back, afraid that I was going to lunge forward and push her—or worse, pull her to safety.

"We've got to go down, just for a minute, Anne!"

"All right. A minute to rest."

There was a sort of half staircase, half ladder of old wooden boards set into the soft ground where the rock gave way to earth again, and it took us down the curved side of the water hole, our garbage bags left behind at the top. Once we'd reached the bottom and circled around, I could see that the water hole was about the size of a public pool, flat as a sheet of glass. The highest part of the rock surface was where we came in, forming a small cliff-diving spot. The whole thing looked a bit like a giant had pressed its thumb into the forest to make a depression in the earth.

A line of discoloration on the rocks indicated that the water level was usually much higher. My mother crouched beside a dried-up trench winding away from the water hole into the trees. She reached out slowly, brushing the tips of her fingers over the cracked, dried mud.

"This used to connect to the lake," she said quietly. "It was where the outflow led; everything that fell into the lake would wash up here eventually. This was our favorite spot."

The pond was clear, and there was no garbage visible anywhere, just tiny, smooth stones collected on the lip before the water got deep in the center. Ivy started to kick off her shoes.

"Isn't this too small of a lake to have waves and, like, a direction where things wash up?" I said.

"That's what I mean by outflow," Mom said. "The lake is fed by some creeks way on the other side, and since the ground is lower here, it all slowly flows from the lake through this stream down to the water hole."

She pointed to the opposite side of the pond, where the rocks ended and lush green plants went right up to the edge, mired in mud. "The ground is more porous there, so the water soaks into the soil, and into little underground streams between the rocks. I've never seen the water level so low that the pond was cut off from the lake."

"The water looks so nice," Ivy said. "Roger didn't get any garbage over here. Come on, Anne, I'm sweating buckets."

"We didn't bring anything to swim in," my mother said.

Ivy stripped off her shirt, revealing the smooth expanse of her back, split by the baby blue straps of her bra. Her spine pressed eagerly against her skin when she bent forward to work her pants down her legs. She kicked them off and glanced back over her shoulder, standing in nothing but her underwear like it was no big deal.

"So?" said Ivy. "We're all girls here."

She splashed into the water so fast it almost looked like the pond rose up and swallowed her. My chest went tight with fear before she surfaced again, shaking her wet hair back from her face.

"That wasn't very smart," Mom said. "You're going to have to walk all the way back in wet clothes."

"That's fine," Ivy said. "Don't be mad. I'm fine."

She dove back underneath, her feet flicking out, and popped up again a moment later with a showy splash. I made myself look away from her wet skin and sat down on a wide, flat rock.

My mother had tried to get me to learn how to swim when I was twelve. She'd recently gotten a new job as a secretary at a high school at the other end of the city—where she still works today—and I guess that meant we could afford an extravagance like swim lessons. I'd cried in the car on the way there.

"It's a good idea for your future," Mom kept repeating.

The instructor was a teenager with a tuft of dyed bright red hair on the top of their head, who towered over me and just said "nope" when one of the kids asked if they were a boy or a girl. When I was too afraid to go down the steps into the pool, another kid pushed me in as a joke. I sunk straight to the bottom, survival instincts going right out the window, and the instructor had to fish me out, their grip around my waist as sure any I'd ever felt.

I remember them pushing my wet bangs out of my face, swaddling me in a towel. "She's having a panic attack," they told my mother. I don't really remember what that felt like. I was busy staring at the teenager's arm tucked around me so I wouldn't stare down their swimsuit at their boobs. They had a tattoo of a vulture on their upper arm, and when their bicep moved, the feathers fanned out toward my cheek, on the edge of flight.

Mom had seemed almost as eager as I was to get out of there. She didn't mention swimming lessons ever again.

It was strange watching Ivy swim so confidently. It looked like she had no fear at all, like she was in complete control of how her body moved, even when caught in the hand of something much stronger than herself.

I wished again that I'd brought the camera. Maybe if I could capture the walls of the cliff and Ivy's black hair in a manageable two-dimensional box, I'd be able to squash my fear down into that. But then the thought slid uncontrollably to the idea of myself squashed down by a camera, the image flooding computer screens, and I had to shake it away.

I focused instead on my mother, who was pacing around the far edge of the clearing.

Something seemed different about her here, by the water—even more so than at the cottage. It felt a little as though I was watching her step back into a memory version of herself, recognizing a familiarity that she hadn't felt in years. She'd never looked less like me than she did now, standing a foot away from the pond with her features drawn in on herself.

"Mom," I said. When she didn't react, I said it again, then, "Anne?"

She jolted and looked over at me. For a moment, I knew she was seeing someone else, and then her eyes refocused.

"You said this was 'our' favorite spot," I said. "Did you come swimming here with friends when you were a kid?"

"Julie liked swimming more than I did," she said slowly. "I would try to draw her, but she moved around too much." She half waved an arm, as if to sketch a person out of the air beside her. "It's been so long since I thought about any of that."

I stared at her, my heart kicking up double-time.

When she didn't add anything else—explain the name and the drawings I'd seen—I said, "Julie?"

"My sister."

"What?"

My mother glanced at me, clearly confused by my confusion. "My older sister."

"You don't have a sister," I said. "You never told me you had a sister."

She was facing me properly now. "I did. We did. Your grampa

told you about her when you were six or seven, didn't he? I remember him bringing her up because it was so rare for us to actually talk about her. My mother would always avoid the topic."

"I don't remember this at all." A distant image of Grampa hunched over the dinner table at our first apartment pushed at the back of my brain.

"I was sure you remembered. Julie was four years older than me."

"Was?"

"She died the year before you were born."

I felt like I'd been clubbed over the head, crouched low and scrambling to catch up with what was happening before the next blow came. It all made sense, so it shouldn't have been surprising. The girl in the drawings in my mom's garbage can had looked so much like me—more of a family resemblance than my mother and I had. But I hadn't wanted this to be the answer, I realized, because it meant my mother had kept yet another thing from me.

"Even if you thought Grampa had told me, we only saw him and Gram maybe twice a year. You've never mentioned Julie yourself," I said, trying not to let my voice betray anything. "Not once. And when I was a kid, I used to ask about the cottage all the time."

"Are we talking about your aunt?"

Somehow, I'd forgotten that Ivy was there.

She was bobbing in the water a few meters away. There was no surprise on her face, just a bright, lively curiosity.

"I wasn't trying to interrupt," she said cheerfully. "I just heard Julie's name. That was your older sister, yeah?"

She was talking to my mother, but the words felt like arrows with my name on them.

"You knew I had an aunt?" I said.

Ivy's head swiveled back and forth between me and my mother. Her smile faltered. "Well, yeah. She and my dad were friends; they were the same age. That's why he was over here all the time when you guys were kids, right?"

The ground was unsteady—I clung to the rock I was sitting on like it was a raft in the ocean.

"How did she die?" I asked my mother, too shaken to be anything but blunt.

It was Ivy who answered.

"My dad said it was an accident. At the lake."

There was nothing Ivy did not know about my family, apparently. Joe told his daughter about a childhood friend he'd lost, and yet my mother couldn't trust her daughter enough to tell me about her own sister? She thought I knew? That didn't explain why she'd never even mentioned this person, even in passing, within my living memory.

Julie had my face, and I hadn't known she even existed.

I stood up, swaying. My mother moved toward me, arms out, and I waved her off. I was giving away too much in front of Ivy. My face was shudderingly hot—I can't imagine how red I must have looked.

"Adele," my mother said, hushed, like she, too, was trying to pretend there wasn't a third person there with us. "By the time I felt you were old enough for me to talk to you about her, there never seemed to be a right time. My parents never recovered after she died—my mother made her a banned topic—so she didn't come up when we were all together as a family, and when you never asked me about her, I just thought you were aware it was a difficult subject for me."

"Maybe we should head back," I said.

"Adele."

Did dating Joe make my mother miss her sister and this place she never spoke about? Was that the real reason that we were here now, watching this girl neither of us really knew swim around in her underwear, instead of at home in the city while someone else took care of cleaning up here?

I couldn't trust that she would answer any of my questions.

"It's Dell," I said.

When I made for the stairs, my mother moved as if to intercept me. Ivy said, "Wait, wait," and when my mother hesitated, I slipped past her, hopping over the old, dead stream.

As I reached the bottom step, Ivy was swimming to shore and clambering gracelessly to her feet, squeezing water out of her hair. I couldn't help but keep glancing over at her even as I moved away. Her bra had wet wrinkles along the bottom swell of the cups, and water dripped steadily from the drooping center of her panties. I missed a step.

My mother called my name again, just as I scrambled to the top of the cliff, and I looked down one last time. She was standing next to Ivy as she wrestled her shirt back on, but I was caught by another flicker of movement, directly below me.

Shimmering on top of the water was a face. And though it was familiar, I knew instantly that it was not my own.

I did a double take, and the second time I looked, there was nothing there but a few leaves drifting serenely on the surface.

I took off into the forest, leaving my mother and the usurper behind.

*

The sunlight was scraping the earth, my shadow thrown out long and thin behind me like the tail on a comet. I tripped and stumbled sideways into a tree. When I started running again, I was no longer on the path. I kept going.

The memory that had threatened before was starting to trickle into my head, the recollection I should've had when I first saw your name on my mother's drawings.

I had heard the name Julie before—my mother was right. But the moment had been so brief that I hadn't understood the significance.

Grampa had accidentally let slip your name while he was telling a story at some holiday when I was a little kid. I was the only one who'd caught it. "Julie? Who's that?"

I could see the claustrophobic walls of the kitchen now, the glances shared among the adults. Gram had tried to rush us along, and Grampa said, "Susan, for god's sake, does it hurt to tell the child her name?" and my mother sat there looking absolutely miserable and frozen and so, so young, like she'd been transported back to whatever age she'd been in the story Grampa was telling.

"Lord knows I don't want to think about it any more than

you do," Grampa said in a quiet, seething voice to Gram, "but can I please occasionally say her name?"

Gram said all this stuff I don't fully remember about "shame" and us being "better off" and something like "sometimes I think she was taken for a reason," and my mother swooped me up into her arms the way she hadn't in years (because I was a big girl by then) and carried me out of earshot so that "your grandparents can finish their discussion."

When Gram called us back to the table, all Grampa said after that was, "Julie was your aunt, honey," and I said, "okay" because I didn't want them to fight anymore, and having an aunt was a loose enough concept for me that I wasn't interested in pursuing it.

Maybe if I'd fully grasped that "aunt" meant my mother used to have a sister when she was my age, I wouldn't have let the memory slip from my mind so easily.

I was still running. I didn't know how long I'd been running.

*

Just as my knees were starting to shake, I came to a small clearing where I could see the purpling sky through the break in the canopy above. When I tested one of the branches of the tallest tree with my hand, it seemed strong enough. I began to climb.

Five minutes later, I wedged myself into a crook of the main trunk near the top of the tree and fished my phone out of my pocket.

"Dollface!" Paul said loudly. "Are you dead yet?"

It was good to hear his voice.

"Almost," I said. "I'm in a tree right now."

"Of course you are. Is your mom shitting her pants down below?"

"I sort of ran off. It's been a weird day."

"Boyfriend's daughter?"

"Yeah. How was Sugar Wreaths?" I asked. It was the coffee shop where Paul worked in the summer. He'd tried to get me hired there last year, but Mom had wanted me in summer school because I'd done shit at math. It was ironic how hard Paul worked, since he got an allowance and I was the one who was poor as dirt. He hated giveaways though. "It doesn't mean anything if I got it from them," he'd say.

"Oh god, don't ask," Paul groaned. "Tool Coworker wasn't in, but that didn't mean I was free from weird-ass comments. Today I had this white lady order a tall black while giving me this weird look and I was, like, 'Do you think this is Starbucks, or are you hitting on me in a vaguely racist way?'"

"My guess is the vaguely racist option."

"I mean, I am pretty good-looking in my uniform."

"The perpetual coffee smell just makes you more attractive."

"How have you resisted all these years?"

"Sheer willpower."

I shifted in the fork, shaking out my free arm before wrapping it around a different branch for stability. This high up, the air was moving more, pulling the top of the tree into an aimless sway.

But with Paul's voice in my ear and my feet planted firmly, I felt safe.

"Steven's been weird lately, too," he said. "It was his three-year anniversary with Annabeth a couple days ago. It must be freaking him out or something."

"Ah, my nemesis," I said. "When will they break up and grant me my prince?"

Paul laughed loudly enough that I had to pull the phone away from my ear briefly. Steven was his older brother, now in his third year of university—I had a huge crush on him back in Grade 9.

"Maybe soon," Paul said. "He keeps muttering about color schemes. Clearly his mind has cracked. He asked me what I thought the most romantic sex position was the other day."

"So that's what brothers talk about. I've always wanted to know."

"It's not," Paul said sharply. "It's just what he thinks brothers should talk about."

I hummed into the phone, unsure what to say to that. Paul loved his sisters to death, but he and Steven had never gotten along the way I'd imagined brothers would. I always thought it would be like having a built-in ride-or-die friend, someone you could tell everything to. I wondered if my mother never talked about her sister because they had been so close that losing her hurt too deeply or because they'd been distant and my mom had just forgotten about her.

For a second, I considered not telling him—it seemed humiliating all of a sudden to admit that I knew so little about my mother's actual life, especially after I spent so much time defending her to him. Paul had always thought my mother was weird and overprotective.

"Did I ever tell you my mom had a sister?" Then, I rushed on before he could answer: "I wouldn't have because I didn't know about her. But Ivy did."

I filled Paul in on everything I'd learned at the water hole.

"Jesus," he said. "So your mom just tried to tell you that you knew about Julie even though you didn't? That's screwed up."

"I mean, she was right that my grandparents told me about Julie once, but it was so long ago that I literally forgot until today. She said she thought I was respecting it as a difficult topic by not bringing it up." There it was. The "defend my mother" impulse. "Ivy said her dad told her she'd died in an accident here."

"Like a car accident?"

I gazed out at the lake beyond the treetops. Remembered my mother's face in the car on my way home from my first, and last, swimming lesson.

"I think she might have drowned," I said.

Paul let out a low whistle. "No wonder your mother's never wanted to go back there."

That hadn't occurred to me yet. I tried to imagine if I would've done the same—wanted to avoid part of my life so badly I would keep my daughter away from my hometown for years, even though we lived relatively close. I thought of my grandparents, who willingly drove their tiny Volkswagen Beetle up to the city every Thanksgiving and Christmas instead of making us come to them, always talking about the loons on the lake and never about the past.

"What if that's the real reason I'm so afraid of water?" I said. "Maybe I got it from her."

"Like you were born with the memory in your body of someone in your family dying that way? That's dark, dude."

"It's Ivy knowing that pisses me off more than anything, honestly. Like, why does she get to have that? She's always sucking up to my mom, too."

"She probably also feels weird that she's spending the summer with you guys."

"She looks at me like—like I'm the gum under a desk that she accidentally touched," I confessed.

"Really?"

"Yeah, 'cause she's obviously seen the pictures."

A sharp intake of breath cut through the line. Finally, someone was taking this as seriously as me!

"What, she told you she'd seen them?" Paul said. "Like, she mocked you?"

"Well, not exactly," I said. "It's more how she looks at me."

A pause.

"Don't tell me she can't have seen them," I snapped. "I know she goes to a different school. In a different town. But Christopher's on the track team, and he has friends from tons of schools. *And* he posted them publicly. It would take one person from Ivy's school finding them and thinking they were funny enough to share. They were up there for hours before you warned me. Anyone could know."

"Okay, okay."

A thin layer of sweat had coated my entire body, leaving me clammy. I tried to breathe.

"You could be right," Paul said. "But—let me just say this—it's more likely that things are weird between you two because you don't know each other. You can be . . . intimidating sometimes with girls you think are prettier than you, or whatever, 'cause you assume they're out to get you."

I tried to focus on the careful sincerity in his voice, but all I could see was Ivy's long black hair plastered to her wet back. It was like a scab on my brain that I kept coming back to, picking at, until my body shocked with heat, hurt.

"It all just seems so easy for her," I said. "Earlier, she stripped to her underwear to go swimming. Like it was nothing. I can't even—after, you know—I can't even look at myself—"

"Hey, what did we say last week? What did we say?"

The tree rocked slowly, and I sighed. The wind sounded alive.

"No thinking about Christopher stuff."

"Wrong! No thinking about King Trashbag stuff," Paul said firmly. "You're away from all that, okay, and you don't have to see him again."

What if I wanted to? I didn't say it out loud because that would be ridiculous. Of course I didn't want to see him ever again. But there was something I wanted back from him, a feeling I'd captured for just a moment in my room, with his eyes on me.

I blew out a noisy breath.

"Maybe Ivy's a bitch, or maybe she's just awkward. Either way, you can't let her ruin your family home for you. Especially now that you've just found out you had an aunt. Dead or not, she's your aunt, not Ivy's."

"Okay," I said. "Sorry I was being shitty earlier. It's not your fault my summer's going to suck."

"It doesn't have to! Just don't forget about me over here, suffering through being related to the weirdest dude on the planet."

"I'll see if Mom will let me have you over for at least a weekend or something."

"As if my parents would take time out of their busy lives to drive me somewhere."

I closed my eyes, trying to pretend he was there with me, but all that did was turn everything seasick and scary—I opened them fast, staring out across the treetops.

"Paul," I said, "what if my mom never really forgives me for Christopher?"

There was a long moment of silence.

"Are you still in the tree?" Paul asked.

"Yeah."

"You should go higher. Go as far as you can."

I put Paul on speakerphone, shoved my phone into my shirt pocket, and wound my way up through the branches. The sky lowered to meet me, clear dark blue, a few stars breaking through above my head.

"You at the top yet?" I steadied myself and pulled the phone out of my pocket. The branches were too thin for me to risk going farther, but I was planted surely, the dark canopy spread out around me. "I'm here, Paul, I'm right at the top."

"You feel better at all?"

His voice was tinny and small but still there above the wind. I could twist the wrong way and fall to my death or drop my phone and lose him. But this was still something my body knew how to do.

"Yeah," I said. "I do, I—"

Something flashed out beyond the trees. I swung around the side of the trunk, bending until I could see the dark lump of the island in the middle of the lake. The light came again—a tiny blink, like someone was flicking a lighter. A cold, electric shiver went through me.

"Dell? You still there?"

"Yeah," I said distantly.

I watched, but the light didn't come again. The island was dead, a black silhouette against the water. I thought about telling Paul, explaining, but the island was watching me.

"I just thought I saw something," I said. "That's all."

When I climbed down and made my way back to the house, following the sound of my own name being called, I found my mother sitting on the steps to the sunroom. She shot to her feet so quickly when she saw me that for a second I thought she was actually going to run down the steps and hug me. But her fluttering hands settled at her sides.

"Good to see I don't need to organize a search party."

"Sorry," I said, pausing just before the bottom step.

"I told you before we even got here that I needed you to stay near the house and not run off in the forest. You used to listen to me. You could've fallen in the lake, you could've—"

"Drowned?"

I know. That was harsh. I regretted it as soon as I said it.

She drew up short, breathing hard.

"Bringing you here was clearly a mistake," she said quietly.

"You had a sister you never even talked about," I shot back. "You don't get to be mad at me right now. I just wanted to call Paul."

"Oh great," she groaned, throwing her arms up. "So he can tell his parents even more about how your mother is a screwup."

Paul's parents had met my mother only once. I don't think it went well, but she's always been overly concerned with how she looks to other parents, worrying about her salary, her age, about being a single mom, like anyone cares.

"I'm not going to not talk to him just because you think his parents don't like you," I said. "I wasn't lost, okay? I didn't go near the lake at all. I'm not stupid."

"You used to talk to me," Mom said. "We used to tell each other things, like when you liked a boy at school."

There it was. Her only effective weapon against my anger about Julie. Christopher was suddenly standing on the second step in between us, and I couldn't see my mother's face past him.

"You said Joe was bringing over the beds on Thursday, right?"

"Yes," Mom said hesitantly, clearly bracing for some sort of jab. "I was thinking he could stay for dinner."

"He can't be worse than his daughter."

"If you don't want to meet him yet, that's perfectly fine."

"It's weirder that I haven't met him yet. Do you want me to meet him?"

Mom didn't say anything.

"You just don't usually tell me when you're dating someone,

much less introduce me," I said. "I wonder where I learned it from." Before she could react to that, I continued, "He was friends with Aunt Julie?"

"He was. When we were younger."

"What if I didn't want to meet him ever?" I said. "Would you break up with him?"

My mother was silent for a long moment before answering.

"We're starting early tomorrow. You should get ready for bed."

Chapter 5

Okay, so it's important you know that the thing with Christopher didn't start with him. Not really.

The closest I can figure is that it started with me sitting on the cold floor of the bathroom, somewhere between four and six years old, holding my mother's hand mirror between my legs so I could see what Mom called my "private area." It looked sort of like a neat little line, like a really puffy closed eye, until I poked at it a bit, and then it turned out the inside was pink and fleshy and gross. It looked nothing like the other private parts I'd seen—another kid, Trevor, had pulled down his pants in front of the whole class a few days before and gotten yelled at by the teacher. I didn't know whether mine was supposed to look like his, or whether there were a bunch of things people could have between their legs. All I knew was that his stuff had looked like a weird noodle. Mine just looked like a wound.

Poking at it made me want to pee, so I peed, and then tried to forget about it, because private parts were weird anyway, and Mom had told me many times that I wasn't supposed to touch there outside of the bathroom.

I had always liked my body, liked the things I could do with it. I liked climbing stuff, liked running off and exploring and making a mess of things. I was what teachers called a "disruptive influence." I liked being in charge of myself, of where I was going and what I was doing. I might not have had many friends, but I could tell my arms and legs to move a certain way and they would obey and then I'd be halfway up a tree and far away from the other kids anyway.

My private area was the only part of my body I didn't understand. It itched sometimes, and felt good when I went to the bathroom, but it was fiddly and weird and smelly and I couldn't move any part of it with my brain, which was stupid.

In Grade 1, my school had a big bathroom with a row of huge square cubbies attached to the wall next to the stalls. When the bathroom was empty, I would climb to the top of the cubbies and push at the loose ceiling tiles. I used to hide stuff up there in the ceiling, magpie-like: wrappers and a little notebook and pens I stole from my classmates.

One day I had just sat down at the top when the bathroom door opened. There was a whole row of stalls between the cubbies and the door, so instead of climbing down I just froze. The other girl was small, a year younger than me at most. She kept her eyes on the floor all the way to the last stall, the one right next to the cubbies.

She disappeared into it. I could hear the rustling of her clothes, the sharp sound of unzipping. I scooted carefully along the top of the cubbies. When I got to the edge, I could only see a little into the girl's stall—there was the top of her head and the toilet paper dispenser but not the actual toilet bowl or the girl's lap or the space between her legs. She started peeing, tinkling loudly, and I leaned over as far as I could, trying to see.

I slipped and caught myself on the top edge of the stall. The girl looked up and screamed. The stream of pee cut off abruptly.

"Shhh!" I said frantically, but the girl kept screaming. She didn't stop until a teacher barged in and found me halfway through climbing back down the cubbies.

I waited outside the principal's office for half an hour before Mom got there. I was very glad to see her.

"Sweetie, are you all right?" Mom asked.

"Yes," I said.

"They told me on the phone that you were spying on another girl in the bathroom. Is that true?"

"Yes," I said.

My mother didn't look like she'd expected that.

"Why would you be doing that?" she asked.

For the first time, I had the sense that maybe I was in actual trouble, not the kind where the secretary let me color in a coloring book until I was allowed to go back to class. Usually when my mother stormed in to talk to the principal on my behalf, she was firmly on my side. She didn't look so on my side this time.

Then the other girl's mom showed up, and she and Mom were ushered into the principal's office. The other girl, who'd started crying when she saw her own mom, sat as far away from me as she could. I wanted to tell her to stop being such a baby, but the last time I'd tried to speak to the girl, the secretary had yelled at me.

I could hear yelling from inside the office, too, but I could only make out a little bit of it.

". . . fault that you're raising a pervert!"

"She's six years old!"

"My daughter's the same age and she definitely knows better!"

The principal cut in sometimes, but his voice was too low for me to hear most of the words.

"Ladies, please, can we . . ."

". . . and frankly, I don't know why I'm surprised, considering how young you look," the other mom said, talking over the principal. "What were you, twelve, when you had her?"

"I was twenty, and that kind of comment is uncalled for . . ."

". . . if I had my way, you'd be declared unfit to . . ."

The secretary was giving me a weird look. I sank down in my seat until my feet could touch the ground and put my hands over my ears.

When Mom came out of the office, she took me by the hand and pulled me out into the hallway.

"You are never to do something like that again," she whispered angrily. "What were you thinking? We've talked about how people have their own space and you do not invade that."

"I just wanted to see if she had the same stuff as me," I said. "If hers looked like it was a hurty."

Mom put her hand over her own mouth for a minute. I knew she was very, very angry, and I felt like I might start crying.

"Adele, your private parts look exactly as they're supposed to," she said. "And they're called private for a reason. Do you understand?"

I didn't say anything.

"I asked you if you understood," Mom snapped. "Say it with me: private parts are private."

"Private parts are private," I said quietly.

"You are not to go around looking at your classmates' privates," Mom said. "Girls who do that could get hurt, or people could think badly of you and that reflects on me, which could be bad for both of us, okay? I don't want anything bad to happen to you."

"Okay," I said.

Mom had to go back to work after that, and I had to go back to class. By the end of the day, everyone knew what had happened. Mom had been right—my classmates called me mean names and some of the girls I ate lunch with decided they didn't want to be my friends.

That night Mom wasn't mad anymore, and she hugged me and told me that if I had any questions, I could ask Mommy. But I'd gotten the message: private parts are private, and if they aren't, Mom will yell at you.

*

Christopher Smith had big gray eyes and a smile just crooked enough to charm. He moved to my school at the start of Grade 11 and somehow slid into the cool groups like he'd always been there. But unlike most of those kids, he seemed nice. We got assigned to do a science project together and when I said, "Call me Dell," he scrunched up his nose and said, "Like the computer company?" I deadpanned, "Yeah, I invented those," and he actually laughed. His friends all squinted over at us in confusion. It was like winning a trophy—someone so far out of my league finding me funny.

We were meant to look for examples of different types of local plants in city parks, but instead of splitting up the work, we went together because Christopher wanted to take all the photos himself. Our shoulders touched when we crowded around his camera to see the results, and I almost lost my mind. Boys didn't stand close to me ever, apart from Paul, who didn't count because he was my best friend.

"This is my favorite photo," Christopher said, pointing at a plant with a crown of wispy white flowers displayed on the tiny screen. "What did you say it was called?"

"It's just a weed," I said. "Queen Anne's lace. Grows everywhere; it's really common. You must have seen it before."

"Maybe I have," he said, looking at me. "But I didn't notice how pretty it was before."

It was an obvious line. No one had gone to the effort to use one on me before. I let out a stupid giggling snort and shoved him. He gaped for a second then burst into laughter.

He seemed different away from his friends, who definitely would've made fun of him if they'd seen him cuddled up around a camera with me, weirdo extraordinaire. He seemed more like a human being. He made me feel like a shaken-up can of pop, fizzing and sweating anytime he looked at me. It was the best thing I'd ever felt.

The problem was, I wasn't allowed to feel it.

When I turned thirteen, my mother had implemented one important rule.

No dating until university.

Dating led to distraction, she said. Distraction led to poor grades, which led to not getting into university. Dating was not what I should be focusing on right now.

Before Christopher, this rule had always felt abstract. I happily told my mother about new crushes because there was no universe where the boy would like me back, so there was no risk whatsoever.

With Christopher, I could sense things were different, even before he made a move. I had this impossible feeling that someone actually might like me, even though I didn't have pin-straight hair or DC shoes or the big boobs I'd gone to bed hoping for every night when I was younger. Every time I thought about telling my mother how I felt, how excited I was, I pictured the questions and the lectures and the rule reminders, and the suspicion I'd face every time I left the house—and the glow in my stomach would turn into cement.

I'll put it off, I told myself. I'll wait until Christopher and I have been dating for a while. Until we tell all our friends. Until we're serious. Then I can let her know. She'll understand then. She'll forgive me. Surely she's felt like this before, right?

*

After my mother ushered me inside the cottage, I locked myself in the bathroom until Ivy hammered on the door, yelling about brushing her teeth. When I came out, I ran back upstairs and slammed our door so I could get changed into my pajama top before she came back.

Ivy had propped a full-length mirror against the wall that I hadn't noticed before. I wasn't standing where I could be caught in its reflection, but I still crept around the edge of the room to turn the mirror around before I felt safe enough to try and change.

The air mattress had deflated partially since it had been blown up, air leaking out through some unseen hole, so it was awkward climbing onto it. But I had to get in bed before Ivy got back. The sleeping bag would protect me. It was like a game, all of it, and once I had my shield up, Ivy's scrutiny couldn't touch me.

Five minutes after I safely cocooned myself in my sleeping bag, the door creaked open.

"Are you not going to brush your teeth?" Ivy asked.

I stayed silent, my eyes closed. I heard the door shut.

"You're not asleep," said Ivy.

"Maybe I brushed them before you." I hadn't.

Ivy's footsteps came closer and then retreated, soft on the floor. I shifted onto my side, my back to her. I opened my eyes and stared at the wall, listening to Ivy shuffle into her own sleeping bag.

"Is this the part where we have girl talk?" Ivy said. "Never had many sleepovers, so I wouldn't know."

I said nothing.

"Your mom was so worried earlier," Ivy said. "Like, she could barely get back up the steps out of the water hole, she went so weak. I swear she was going to call the O.P.P. or something until I convinced her you just needed to cool off. But honestly, I don't get you."

"Excuse me?" I said, rolling to face her.

"Do you even care that she was freaked out?"

"Of course I do!"

"It just doesn't seem like you respect her very much."

"And you do?"

"She's not my mother."

I know, I wanted to say. So what gives you the right to comment?

"But yeah, I do," Ivy continued. "Sure, she's a little uptight and kind of a prude sometimes. Stiff about things—" Ivy broke off to laugh. "Sorry, didn't mean to do that—stiff about things, but she's really nice. She seems like she cares a lot. Maybe you should think about that."

The injustice wasn't just that she was poking her nose where it didn't belong. It was that I could tell she thought she was right. Even if she knew about the pictures, she didn't know how my mother had reacted. And she didn't know how much it hurt to see her talking with my mother so easily when I'd spent so long just running at my mother's heels only to ruin everything between us over a boy.

"I wanted to call my friend Paul somewhere where you weren't hanging around all the time," I said softly.

"A friend? Do you mean a boyfriend?"

She stretched out the word like there was no way that could be the truth. Paul would probably have just found it funny if I lied to Ivy about us. His parents were always jokingly calling me his girlfriend, especially his father, who refused to believe we weren't secretly in love. But somewhere in the space between Christopher's shoulders and Ivy's bare back, that kind of stuff had stopped being funny to me.

"No," I said. "He's just my friend."

"Sure."

We both fell silent. My throat had gotten that gross, penny-tasting tackiness of held-back words, and I prayed she wouldn't say anything else. Ivy sighed.

"Look, I know I got pissed at you earlier on behalf of your mom, but we should probably try to get along a little. At least for her sake, right?" She sounded almost sincere. I didn't know how to trust it. By the time I worked up the courage to open my mouth, it was too late because Ivy was speaking again.

"Okay. Just trying to be nice. 'Night then." The softness was gone. Maybe I'd only imagined it.

I rolled to face the wall again. Shut my eyes and tried to fall asleep.

*

But it had been years since I shared a room with another person. I'd forgotten the way that the small shifts of another body only emphasized how quiet a dark room could be at night, when you were meant to be shutting off your brain and all your brain wanted to do was scream.

I tried not to think of Christopher, but an idea once summoned doesn't like to leave. I could hear his voice, could hear the click of his camera. I cast around desperately for another thought, another image—but all that would come was the creeping urge to find relief the way I normally did at night.

Usually, when I was feeling this anxious, I would use touch to get myself to sleep: it was easier to shut off my mind once I was tired and loose. But Ivy was right there in the room.

This part is gross, sorry. I know it's gross, but I swear it's relevant.

When I was twelve, I'd kick-started an addiction, hiding inside the buttoned-up yellow world of my duvet with my fingers cramped and finally successful between my legs. It was one of those moments that solidified for me just how messed up I was. One second, I was jolting like a Looney Tunes character struck by lightning, all frozen and lit up, and then I was back to reality, lying in my own ooze and sweat, feeling colder and more disgusting with every breath.

You know that panic when you've done something wrong and you think you're going to get in trouble for it? Except no one knows you did The Bad Thing, so you just sweat and flinch every time your mother looks at you for the next month? Yeah, this was a particularly twitchy part of my childhood.

It wasn't like I could ask my mother about masturbation—the idea was laughable. Back in Grade 6, she'd demanded to see all the worksheets and to hear exactly what we'd been told in sex-ed class, as if my teachers might have slipped state secrets into anatomy discussions.

"They shouldn't be teaching you this stuff so early," she'd muttered, flipping through notes on reproductive organs and diagrams I'd copied from the board. "It'll just give you the wrong idea. Did you feel comfortable hearing about this stuff, hon?"

"No," I said.

"Exactly," Mom said. "I was still trying to figure out how to put my hair up in a ponytail by myself when I was your age. They need to let things go at their own pace."

I knew I couldn't ask my mother all the questions I had that I was too afraid to bring up in class. Even back then, I was clearly going faster than I was supposed to.

Ivy rolled over in her sleeping bag, the material crinkling on the air mattress. I chanced a look and saw that her back was to me, her pointy shoulder slipped out of the neck of the sleeping bag.

Was she sweating like me? Was she wearing just a T-shirt and underwear to bed like I was? She wouldn't be wearing more than that, not with the heat up like this, but less? No, surely not with me in the same room.

Another memory surfaced: a "girl's night" sleepover almost as strange as this one.

A few weeks before my jerking-off revelation, I'd spent the night at my friend Karoline's house. Karoline had a big house and pink inflatable furniture in her room and a mom who asked us to call her Joanne and to tell her "all the gossip about the boys!" which made her a lot cooler than my mom. When Karoline invited me and Cora—the third part of our trio—over for sleepovers, we were allowed to stay in the basement, where there was a pullout bed and a huge TV with hundreds of channels.

The three of us were lying in a row on the pullout bed in our pajamas, heads propped on pillows so we could see the TV screen.

It was pitch black in the room otherwise, and a clock radio next to the TV was searing 2:18 AM into my eyes in red. I'd wanted us to have the deep conversations that only happened once all the lights were out and we couldn't see each other, but the other two wanted to watch TV because they were boring.

It happened very fast. Karoline was flicking through the channels when suddenly there was a close-up of what looked like a pink column being pushed into a red mass of ground meat. I froze. Cora squeaked. Karoline changed the channel back to a period drama.

Our breathing suddenly sounded very loud.

"Sorry!" Karoline said, and when I looked over, they were both turned toward me.

"It's fine," I said. Why was Karoline apologizing just to me?

"We don't have to watch that," she said.

"I want to watch it," Cora said.

"Dell might not want to."

"I don't care," I said. It had looked violent. Violent and gross. Sex. That had definitely been sex. I felt all shaken up, like every atom in my body had done a flip in the space of one second.

"Dustin was saying the other day that he, like, jerks off every night watching this stuff," Cora said. "His parents don't care 'cause they're never around anyway."

"Dell?" Karoline said.

"Don't ask *me*," I said. "Do you guys think I'm some sort of innocent flower? I'm not."

"I want to watch it," Cora insisted.

Karoline flicked it back on.

We lay in silence. The couple on the screen were very loud—the woman made high-pitched gasping noises and the man kept grunting. It was bearable on a wide shot, one where I could see their whole bodies and their faces; with the camera zoomed out, sex looked jerky and frantic but at least populated by human beings. But then it would go to a close-up of where the man's penis was shoving in, and suddenly it was an alien horror movie. Everything there was mottled red and glistening and it looked like it hurt, like the woman was being turned inside out, and I had to look away. I felt like I was going to vibrate off the bed—or throw up or something. All I could think of was when I was little and thought my private parts looked like a wound. The thing between the legs of the woman on the screen definitely looked like a wound. It looked gross.

Cora shifted, and her leg touched mine. I flinched away. "Sorry," I hissed.

The scene changed eventually to one with new characters. Everybody had their clothes on, so I relaxed. A tall blonde lady with huge boobs told her pretty redheaded friend that she didn't feel sexy enough for the man she liked. They went to a place that looked like a weird massage parlor and met up with a third woman, who introduced herself as "Vivienne."

I was starting to get tired again; the strange adrenaline of the last sex scene was fading. I closed my eyes. After a moment, the sound of voices on-screen cut off, replaced with the soft suction of kissing. I opened my eyes.

The blonde lady was sitting in a chair in a T-shirt and panties, Vivienne kneeling between her legs. Vivienne's mouth was on the blonde lady's stomach. The friend was hovering beyond, watching the other two women with a calm smile that said that this was all right. This was good.

I lay as still as I could. On-screen, Vivienne moved lower and licked up the center of the blonde lady's panties. Lesbian, lesbian, LESBIAN porn, this is LESBIAN porn, my mind screamed. The blonde lady moaned. The friend smiled.

I was terrified either Cora or Karoline were going to change the channel, but it didn't happen. The three of us lay there in silence through the entire scene. The lady's underwear stayed on the whole time, and when she pulled her shirt up, her boobs were big and soft and perky in her own hands. It seemed so much gentler than the scene before, all round edges and clean blue underwear. The characters all smiled at each other a lot. It was so dark in the basement, and so late; the images on the screen seemed to waver in front of my eyes.

"Do you feel sexy now?" the friend asked in a knowing tone of voice. "Do you?"

I felt like my stomach was melting.

The show ended with the blonde lady having sex with the bearded man she really liked. The credits came quickly, and then the image went to static.

Karoline sat up and started flicking through channels again.

"Maybe that was the only one on right now," Cora said.

"Maybe," Karoline said.

"I need to pee," I said quietly.

"Me too," said Cora.

"Yeah, me too," said Karoline.

We all lined up outside the bathroom, hands hovering somewhere around our thighs. I was last, and I had to listen to them both peeing, loud and wet. When it was my turn, I sat on the toilet for a long time. I didn't need to pee. I didn't know what I needed, though, so I just went back down to the basement and went to sleep.

After I figured out how to get off on my own, I wanted to ask Cora and Karoline if they'd ever done stuff like that, but we'd never talked about what we saw that night. Not even when we had another sleepover at Karoline's and watched a bootleg copy of *American Pie*, where a teenage boy tried to masturbate with an apple pie.

"God, boys are gross," Karoline said afterward. She'd spent the whole movie squealing in a shocked, disgusted way that struck me as kind of theatrical. "I am so glad we're not like that."

Everyone knows boys are obsessed with sex. It's normal.

"You know how boys are," adults would say when their sons said gross things about girls. After Cora's chest ballooned overnight, the Grade 8 boys snapped her bra straps until her shoulders were striped red, sure—but they just had a crush on her, according to our teacher. They couldn't help it.

When boys in high school joked about jerking off, the other girls would wrinkle their noses and laugh, all superior, feminine disgust. And then there was me. Me with my body going hot and sticky in the middle of the day, in the middle of class, in the middle of supper. Me logging on to the family computer to read gross stories on DeviantArt anytime my mother worked late, rereading my favorites until I had the sentences memorized and could play them back in my head later while perched on the edge of the closed toilet lid in the far stall at school, trying to work as quickly and quietly as possible.

Everyone knows it isn't normal for girls.

I know this because other girls don't talk about it, Mom doesn't talk about it, and it really hadn't been talked about in sex ed at all. The teacher tossed off a quick summary—"masturbation is normal for teenagers"—during our single week of sex ed in Grade 9 gym, but with the whole class snickering, it wasn't like I was going to raise my hand and ask, "Sure, boys jerk off, but girls don't . . . every day? Multiple times a day?" That would be humiliating.

And surely if another girl jerked off as much as I did, she would've asked the teacher about it, so I didn't have to, right?

Christopher was the only person who'd seen me for exactly what I was.

I could see his face behind my eyes now as I lay in bed. Could feel the heat of my palms against my thighs. Ivy was only a few meters away, and her soft breathing seemed to fill the room. A phantom tunnel of open mouths raced through my head, swallowing me one by one—Christopher's, Cora's, Ivy's, my own—in some ouroboros nightmare.

I lay there awake for an impossible time, wishing desperately that I was alone. That the events of my life so far had somehow added up to a different person entirely.

A dream was finally starting to take me—wispy images of trees and arms and camera tripods reaching for me out of the darkness behind my eyelids—when I heard it.

A scrape from the other side of the room, hushed and short.

My whole body went tense, and I was back in the room, in the melting heat of my sleeping bag. The sound came again, a little louder.

I rolled over as slowly as I could.

At first, I couldn't pick it out in the darkness, but then something shifted in the black and I could suddenly see Ivy's air mattress. It was rocking like an unsteady rowboat, scritching rhythmically on the floor. There was a lump in the middle of her sleeping bag, moving slightly. My body flushed red hot, jealous and disbelieving.

Ivy had to think I was asleep. There was no way she'd be—if she knew I was awake—

Ivy blew out a shaky breath and turned her head on the pillow, her face suddenly visible. Her mouth was open, forehead crinkled up. I slammed my own eyes shut. My heartbeat was so vicious I could feel it pulsing all through my body.

The noises stopped after a while. When I chanced a look, Ivy's eyes were open, looking in my direction.

Ivy rolled over before I could figure out if I'd been caught. She let out a small, satisfied sound and then went silent.

I turned my face into my sleeping bag and breathed in the musky cupboard smell. *You're asleep, you're asleep*, I told myself, trying to get the panicking buzz of my blood to settle down. I felt like fresh dough, waiting for firm hands to knead me into shape.

It took a long time after that to get to sleep. I couldn't see Christopher anymore.

Chapter 6

The next morning, I woke up covered in a layer of stale sweat, panicked from a horrible dream that immediately slid from my mind.

Ivy was gone, her open sleeping bag baking in a square of sun. Her air mattress was slightly crooked. I stared at it, trying to figure out if the images in my head were memory, dream, or fantasy. Ivy had looked at me, after, hadn't she? After she had—

I closed the door to get dressed for the day then walked carefully over to Ivy's sleeping bag and stared down. It was hot to the touch, and when I lowered my face to the center, where Ivy's hips would've been, it smelled only of sweat and mothballs. I stayed on my knees for a moment longer then shot up, shuddering. My skin itched all over; it was the only thing on me I couldn't shake off.

"why am i the creepiest person alive" I texted to Paul.

His answer came as I was pulling on my socks.

"scientists have been looking for that answer for years Dell. Years"

When I finally made my way into the hall, I heard voices coming from downstairs. I could see through the open door that my mother's room was empty. Green leaves flickered in the window above her air mattress, and I found myself walking into her room, crossing to the panel of three windows at the far wall.

At first, I could only see the lattice of branches, waving slightly with the breeze. But when I moved to just the right spot, the lake burst forth from the foliage. And in the middle: the island, lit up with bright morning sunlight, this bizarre hunk of faded wood and metal and color in the middle of the water like some bulbous, misshapen lily pad.

Seeing it again felt like an electric shock. All at once, I remembered the light I had seen last night, from the top of the tree, glinting in the center of the island where there should have been nothing but blackness. The image felt like a signpost in fog—something to latch on to amid the chaos of the past few weeks of my life.

From this distance, nothing stood out enough to pinpoint any logical explanation for the light (not that I had any idea what exactly I should be looking for). But one thing did catch my eye.

The blurry edge of the rowboat Ivy had pointed out, tipped just at the far side of the island.

And as I squinted through the window, my dream from the night before suddenly burst into my head.

I'd been somewhere dark, and I could hear the sound of water all around me. There had been a light blinking just above my shoulder, faint, and with each pulse I could see a flash of my surroundings—the empty cab of a truck, a bent coat stand, a heap of metal siding.

I had been on the island. I had been on the island and I hadn't been alone.

*

I crept down the stairs, trying not to make any noise. Edging my way along the wall of the living room, I paused at the corner, just out of sight.

"—if you could just bring the plate over here. Thank you." My mother's voice. The sound of something sizzling. "If I'm remembering right, I think I made you French toast the last time you were here. When you were just a little girl."

"I barely remember any of it," Ivy said. "I was maybe five, right?"

"Yes," Mom said. "Dell would have been four. You two got to be quite good friends on your little playdates. You were always holding hands."

"Sounds adorable," Ivy said. "Was I good or, like, an evil child?"

Something clunked on the table. I could hear them moving around it, could imagine Ivy ducking past Mom as comfortable as she was in water. As comfortable as she was rubbing one out with no care for who else was in the room.

"You were very loud," Mom said. "Dell followed you everywhere, and you were a bit bigger, so you would try to give her piggyback rides."

Ivy made a pleased noise.

"One night you stayed over, and you, me, and Dell all stayed in that room the two of you are using now. You two shared the bed and when I woke up you were all cuddled together. It was so sweet."

"I bet," Ivy said. She paused, and when she spoke again, it was quieter than before, and I had to strain to hear. "So, what's her deal now?"

A sigh. A pause.

"She doesn't have a 'deal.'"

"Sorry, I just—I just meant that she seems . . ."

Ivy trailed off. I stared across the empty living room at a stain on the windowsill.

"You know, you weren't just her first friend," Mom said. "For a while there, you were the only friend she'd ever had—when she started going to school, she had a really hard time relating to other kids."

Ivy made some sort of understanding noise, and it hit like a branch whipping across my chest. I pushed away from the wall and stepped into the kitchen.

"Morning!" I said. My mother was leaning on the counter. Ivy stood over the stove with a spatula in hand, and a piece of French toast already sat on a plate between them. The sight of her was almost a physical shock.

"Did you sleep well, sweetie?" Mom said. As if she cared—I hadn't forgotten our fight yesterday, the revelation of Julie. I made a noncommittal sound.

"That piece is for Anne," Ivy said, pointing at the toast. "No taking it. Last person up has to cook their own."

"Fine," I said. "Give me the egg stuff."

She handed over a small silver bowl. A wave of gelatinous yellow slopped up the curve and kissed the lip before retreating. I couldn't tell if her expression was as strange as my own, because I couldn't bring myself to look at her for longer than two seconds.

I dipped a piece of bread, flipped it, and then slapped it down on the frying pan so it spat butter up the sides.

My mother had already turned back to Ivy and was saying something about the house. She'd forgotten me already.

"I want to learn to swim," I said loudly.

My mother sputtered mid-sentence, grinding to a halt. I resisted the urge to smile.

"You want to what?" Mom said.

"Ivy's a really good swimmer, right?" I said. "You don't want us in the lake, sure, but what if she taught me how to swim at the water hole? Didn't look like there was any garbage there or anything dangerous."

My heart was pounding just from saying the word *swim*. They were both staring at me. I fixed my gaze on my mother.

"I know you got mad when I went off into the forest last night because you were worried I might fall in the lake or something," I said. "Maybe if Ivy taught me to swim, you wouldn't be so nervous."

I risked a glance at Ivy. "It could be fun."

Her face was studiously blank.

"That's—that's actually an excellent idea," Mom said. "You're right; I think it really would put me more at ease around here if I knew you could handle yourself in the water. It might be a good idea to get a start on that today since we did make some progress with cleaning yesterday evening."

"I'm happy to help, Anne," Ivy said immediately. "I taught my brother to swim when he was just five, so I think I can deal with Dell."

Of course she was on board as soon as my mother showed any interest.

"I thought it might be a good way for us to spend time together, too," I added, gesturing between Ivy and me. "You know, so we can get to know each other better."

My mother beamed. One point to me.

"Of course, this would only happen at the water hole," she stressed. "The lake is still far too dangerous for any of us to be splashing around in. Agreed?"

Ivy and I nodded.

"Cool," I said. "You want to head out now?"

"I think you might want to flip your French toast first," Ivy said. "It looks like it's burning."

I didn't own a bathing suit, but my mother had brought extra. While Ivy changed in our bedroom, my mother ushered me into hers so she could rummage through her duffel bag.

"Are you going to swim with us?" I asked her awkwardly. "More than one teacher might be a little much." Now that we were alone, the fight from yesterday felt very present in the room, almost like a third person.

"I'll just be there to keep you girls company," Mom said. "I'll bring a book. I'm not trying to get in the way of you two, you know, bonding and—" She made some sort of complicated hand gesture, like that was supposed to end the sentence.

Silence fell. After Christopher, the distance between us felt like it held this huge weight of disappointment. Disgust. If one thing made me feel better, it was that now we were equally wary of things the other person had kept secret.

My mother, wrist deep in fabric, took a deep breath. For a split second, I thought she was going to actually apologize for bringing up Christopher last night—or maybe, just maybe, ask me about the photos.

"You know, I might have some things of Julie's up in the attic," she said.

My disappointment was overtaken by a swell of excitement.

"Yeah?"

"I thought that at some point this summer, we could go through all of it together."

"Really?"

Maybe I seemed too enthusiastic, because she almost took it back—I could see her face fighting the urge to turtle into a frown, her shoulders creeping toward her ears.

"I don't see much point in dredging up things from the past," Mom said in a rush. "You know that. What's done is done. I'm interested in focusing on the future, on making that good." She tossed a tangle of denim over her shoulder with a scowl. "But I did know you were interested in the cottage and all of that, so the fact that you never asked about Julie should've let me know that you didn't remember Grampa telling you about her."

She took another deep breath. Had she rehearsed this part so it would come out without her snapping at me?

"I know I was taking the easy way out by waiting for you to ask about your aunt," she said carefully. "And yes, my parents wanted to pretend she never existed, but I didn't have to be that way when it was just the two of us."

Something clicked in my brain, two puzzle pieces coming together.

"Wait, I assumed they were just too sad to talk about her," I said slowly. "What do you mean, they wanted to pretend she didn't exist?"

My mother hesitated. Across the hall, Ivy dropped something, the thump of it reverberating in the floor at my feet. I could feel this rare moment with my mother slipping away.

"Your gram had a complicated relationship with Julie," Mom finally said. "They'd fought right before . . ." She trailed off with a shoulder shake that I took to mean *before she died.*

Had my aunt been the problem child, like me? Enough to erase her from family memory?

My mother made a triumphant sound and pulled out a fistful of horrible yellow. A one-piece, with a bow in the front. She plopped it into my hands like a dead fish.

"What about you and Julie?" I asked. "Did you guys get along? Were you friends?"

"Oh, Dell, does it matter right now?" Mom blurted. "We found you a suit—shouldn't you go put it on?"

I stared. Her shoulders trembled, sank.

"We were very close," she said, quieter. "She was my sister. Of course we were very close."

*

(Here's a super fun fact: I can remember every second of that little "photo shoot" Christopher and I had. I could pick out the exact paint chip color of the afternoon sunlight on the walls. I could tell you the time on the clock across the room before and after the first flash.

I know that when I took off my pants that day, I stepped out of them with my right leg first.

Now, when I get undressed, I do it with my eyes closed. Left leg first. Whether I'm going to change into pajamas or a hideous bathing suit.

I'm trying to break patterns. I'm trying to break fears.)

*

"How much do you think people were paying him to dump their stuff here?" Ivy said as we walked through the forest. "I bet he made a lot."

"Well, there's a dump about an hour down the road, so that's what doesn't make sense to me," said Mom. "I guess maybe it meant a shorter trip for some? I know it costs more to dispose of some things at the dump, so he could have also been offering cheaper disposal. It's baffling. I didn't know him well, but I'd spoken to him before, and he seemed sincere when he talked to me about renting this place. Joe mentioned that Roger didn't show up in town often, but I never heard about his little nickname until you said it."

"Only the kids at my high school called him that. Adults are too polite for that stuff."

I hung back and let them talk, fiddling with the strap of the bag my mother had given me to protect my camera. It was hard to feel bitter about the two of them getting along so well when my stomach was churning with five thousand things: swimming anxiety, questions about Julie, thoughts of Ivy and wherever the hell we stood. My discussion with Mom had almost made me forget the whole "did Ivy catch me watching her last night when I didn't mean to be watching her" thing, but it was definitely creeping back to the forefront of my mind with her forging ahead of me through the forest, her jean shorts inching up her thighs with every step.

As we circled down the stairs coiling around the water hole, Ivy asked me, "So how much experience do you have? Do you at least know how to float?"

"I live on the fifth floor of an apartment building and my high school doesn't have a pool. What do you think?"

"I don't know," Ivy said. "If I had been scared of something since forever, I'd want to face it and get over it, so I'd have made a point to learn how to swim."

"Oh, so you're some superhero with no fears?"

Ivy mimed shooting lasers from her hands and almost tripped down the last few steps. I reached out automatically to steady her, and she aggressively ignored my outstretched hand as she regained her footing.

Mom, taking up the back of our single-file procession, piped up. "We've all got things we're a little wary of."

My mother had brought a tote bag with her, and as soon as we got to the bottom, she pulled out a blanket, spreading it on a flat patch of ground, far enough back from the water's edge that the earth wasn't damp. She pulled three water bottles and a small red lunchbox out of the bag, lining them up meticulously on a rock before digging deep and producing—as promised—a book.

"When you need them, your towels are over here, girls," she called. "You just get to it. Don't mind me, I'm not even here."

She showily unfolded her book in front of her eyes and lay back on the blanket.

Ivy was already stripping down to her bathing suit. I set my camera bag on a rock that wasn't too close to the water and self-consciously pulled off my shorts.

"You know you won't get sunburned with all these trees around, right?" Ivy said. "You don't need to keep the shirt on."

Ivy's white bikini was covered in black roses, petals curved and distorted over her chest. I smoothed my T-shirt, making sure it covered as much of me as possible.

"You don't know," I said. "I burn really easily."

Ivy made a weird face, almost like she was insulted, then spun away from me. She marched into the water until she was waist deep and spun to face me again.

"Now you, T-shirt wonder."

"Isn't there something you're supposed to teach me before I go in?" I asked. "Like, how to stand or something?"

"That's surfing," Ivy said. "If you want to learn to swim, you have to at least be in the water. We're just staying in the shallow bit right now, so you don't have to worry about the drop-off."

"Drop-off?"

Ivy smacked her hands against the surface, sending up a spray of water.

"Come *on*, Dell, don't back out on me now! It won't even be up to your shoulders, you coward."

"Ivy," my mother called from behind me. "Let her go in at her own pace."

I'd almost forgotten she was there, and the overattentiveness rankled.

"Mom, you said you'd leave us alone!" I reminded her. "I'm fine." Whipping back to Ivy, I lowered my voice and snapped at her. "I'm not a coward."

Ivy shrugged, but when she spoke, her voice was quieter, too—a tacit agreement that, yes, this was not something parents belonged in.

"I don't think your boyfriend would be very impressed," she said.

"Paul's not my boyfriend."

"Obviously. Who would date someone who can't even take five steps?"

I opened my mouth to retort again, but suddenly there was coldness tapping against my foot. I'd been moving slowly forward with each dig, and now my toes were resting on smooth, slick stones, the edge of the water nudging against them. I stared, fear rushing back in.

"Hey, hey, don't stop," Ivy said. "Look at me."

I looked at her.

"I'm annoying you, remember?" she said. She smiled, and bizarrely, it looked genuine. "You want to get out here and punch me in the face. Just think about that."

"Are you encouraging the idea of me punching you in the face?"

"I think I could take you in a fight."

I took another step, consciously this time, and water sloshed around my calves. I froze, feeling stupid and shaken. I hoped desperately that Mom wasn't looking at us, that she really was reading her book.

"I can't do this."

"Yes, you can," Ivy said. "It was your idea to come out here. You're not even in as deep as a bathtub. I've had glasses of water deeper than what you're standing in right now."

"Shut up."

"And are you seriously going to keep wearing that T-shirt?" she asked. "It's not like you have anything I haven't seen before."

That familiar, yawning black-hole feeling opened up in my chest. I fixed my eyes on her grin and surged forward. Water splashed away from me like it was the one afraid, and the cold rushed up my legs, claiming my knees, my thighs, my stomach. I was slowed, my fury cushioned and muffled; I tripped the last few steps, falling forward into Ivy's outstretched arms.

"Gotcha," she said softly.

I swung out, aiming for her chin. She jerked back. My arm shot through the air by her face. Her hand around my back dropped—my feet skidded out from under me on the stones, and suddenly the world was cold and blue.

I was hauled back upright, hacking up my lungs. It felt like I had swallowed the ocean, even though I'd barely been under for a second.

"Is she all right?" my mother shrieked. I heard splashing getting closer.

"I'm fine!" I wheezed. I wormed out of Ivy's arms, tugging a strand of wet hair out of my mouth. I closed my eyes. The only thing I was capable of registering was that everything was too much. "Just give me a second!"

"Maybe this was a bad idea," my mother said. "Or we could take you to proper swimming lessons, how about that?"

"No!" I said. "Ivy's great. This is fine. I just tripped. I'm okay."

I flashed a thumbs-up toward where I thought the shore was. "I'm okay."

When I peeled my eyes open again, everything had a cheap plastic film. My mother was standing at the edge of the water hole, her book dangling from her hand, looking about eight years old. I gave her a thumbs-up again, and she seemed to jolt out of some sort of trance.

"All right. But be careful, you two!" she yelled.

Ivy smiled, waved at my mother, and yanked my shoulder around so she couldn't see our faces.

"I was joking about fighting, but if you want to recreate *Fight Club*, we can do that," she said through her teeth. "I just figured we weren't aiming to murder each other in front of your mother on the second day."

"Why the hell would you say that shit about having seen all of me before?" I said. "What is your problem?"

Ivy blinked.

"I was messing with you so you wouldn't think about the water," she said slowly. "And look. You're here."

I looked down at my waist, disappearing into the clear clutch of the rippling water, my feet seemingly miles away.

"Oh," I said.

"You get set off by the weirdest things," Ivy mumbled. "But see? You're fine. Just give it a minute and get used to it."

I breathed carefully and closed my eyes, settling into the feeling of the water floating up under my shirt. Ivy was still holding on to my arms. Her hands were warm, grounding. I tried not to feel embarrassed for overreacting. This morning, she'd told my mother she didn't know my "deal," which seemed to imply that she hadn't seen the pictures, but every time she said something even the slightest bit snide, I couldn't get it out of my head that she knew. That anyone who walked by me on the street might know at a glance where all my moles are underneath my clothes. The thought of it made me want to claw out everyone's eyes. My own eyes.

"Okay," I said. "Sorry. I'm good."

When I opened my eyes again and looked at her head-on, Ivy's face so close was a shock. I got a flash of her face last night, tipped on its side in bed, and had to look away. Ivy cleared her throat.

"The next thing you're going to do is stick your face in the water for a few seconds."

I took a step back, almost slipping. "No way. It'll go up my nose."

"You just breathe out through your nose," Ivy said. "I'll show you."

She bent forward so quickly that I didn't have time to move: the top of her head brushed the front of my shirt, and then her face was in the water. I stared down at her head almost touching my stomach, the back of her neck with water pushing around it.

Ivy popped back up, shaking off water. She swiped her hand over her face, slicking her hair back.

"See?" she said breathlessly. "Nothing to it."

"What if I start choking?"

Light was shining off a chunk of hair plastered down her chest. I kept getting distracted.

"Then you pull your face out and try again."

I closed my eyes. Before I could think about it any more, I shoved my face down into the water.

The world went muted and soft, pleasantly cool; water flooded my nose and I shot back up, sputtering. There was a hand at my back, solid between my shoulder blades.

"Breathe out through your nose while you're under," Ivy said. "Try again."

There was no scorn in her voice, and I took a deep breath. I was shaking slightly, but it felt like it was happening to someone else. I could do this. I nodded, flexed my fingers out against my thigh, and let Ivy guide me back down into the water.

I didn't inhale this time. Ivy's hand had slid up to cup around the back of my neck, like the clip on a leash, simultaneously soothing and terrifying. I imagined that pressure growing, forcing me down—but when I pushed back, Ivy's hand went with me, letting me straighten up again, gasping.

"Good," Ivy said.

I ran a shaking hand over my own face, rubbing water away from my eyes.

When I glanced back at the shore, I caught my mother peering at us around the corner of her book, looking kind of scared. I had barely made eye contact before the book fluttered over her face and then lowered, revealing nothing more than a sheepish smile.

"You girls are doing great," she called. Her voice seemed a little wobbly.

I hesitated then sent her another thumbs-up in response.

"You can be honest if you think I suck," I told Ivy. "I know you're only going along with this because my mother wanted it."

"You can't suck at something you haven't even done yet. You put your face in the water twice, but don't get ahead of yourself. Besides, I've got ulterior motives."

She smiled. It was disorienting, a split of sun through storm clouds.

"Yeah?"

Ivy flicked a glance at my mother then leaned in close.

"Once I teach you to swim, we go get that rowboat," she said. "I want to know what's on that island, and I'm not swimming out to that potential death trap by myself."

I could still picture the light I'd seen from the top of that tree. My dream flashed in my head.

"You think there's more out there than just trash?" I said. I didn't want to let on that I'd had my own plan to investigate the island with the help of these lessons.

"It's never just trash. My dad took me to the dump once to get rid of some shingles and stuff," Ivy said. "He let me explore a little and I found a wedding dress on a mannequin, right on the top of one of the piles."

She swept her hands through the water, and a tiny wave lapped up my stomach. "There's nothing cooler than the things people want to get rid of."

"What did you do with the wedding dress?"

"Nothing," Ivy said. "I was ten. I didn't want to get married. I'm not like my dad—he's been ready for marriage since he was born, I think. Your mom better watch out."

Ivy spent the rest of the lesson trying—mostly fruitlessly—to teach me to float. There was a lot of yelling—her yelling instructions and corrections, me yelling panicked almost-swears while trying not to sink the second I took my feet off the bottom. My mother yelling stuff from the sidelines I tried my best to ignore.

We sprawled out on the rocks beside the water hole to dry off before hiking back. Ivy found a rock large enough for her to lie on her back with her legs and arms spread every which way. She didn't seem to have any concept of being ashamed about looking weird, about the damp strands of hair curling just out of the sides of her bikini bottoms and sticking to her thighs. Mom handed us our water bottles and packets of goldfish crackers she'd brought in the lunchbox.

Above us, the canopy cut out dark green silhouettes against the blue sky. The air smelled sweet, despite the garbage I knew was lurking around, and I let myself relax. I took a few photos of the sky, and then of the water hole itself, Ivy's legs just barely making it into the last picture. Snuck one of my mother pouring crackers into her hand, framing it so the hand appeared to be floating in a contextless mass of green foliage, blurry orange raining down on her palm.

I had nearly dried off completely when Paul texted me.

"Tool Coworker hit on me again today. like really explicitly. was kind of gross."

"what did she say?" I typed back.

"she compared my dick to a large coffee? i think? there was weird comments and eye contact wile she was making one in drive-thru. i dont get it."

I had visited Paul at work many times, and he'd pointed out the coworker in question before—a tall white girl with blonde hair that somehow still looked good even twisted up into a bun in a hairnet. She was the kind of beautiful that usually held a lot more currency with boys than personality. I didn't like that she was making Paul feel uncomfortable at work, but a small part of me was confused by his complete disinterest. Maybe it was a "Good Christian Boy" thing? His family didn't seem strict about that stuff, but they were pretty big into church.

"maybe shes just trying to connect with you on the guy level," I suggested. "sex is the common denominator. or so i hear"

"lol i guess. i don't get what the big deal is tho. id rather drink that large coffee than spend even one minute in heaven with Tool Coworker. its all kind of gross."

Ivy slapped my rock without getting up.

"Is that the not-boyfriend?" she asked.

"Yes," I said. I snapped my phone shut.

"He answers pretty quickly for someone who isn't dating you."

"He's my best friend," I said.

"How terribly romantic." Ivy's voice was syrupy.

I shrunk in on myself—I thought we'd been making progress toward being friendly. When Paul made a joke, it was obvious because he always started laughing before he'd even gotten it all out. With Ivy, it was impossible to tell whether I was included in the warm circle of the joke or whether I was its target.

"It's not like that," I said. "He's practically my brother."

"Yes," my mother interjected, not quite hitting the nonchalance she was clearly going for. "They're very good friends. He's a lovely boy."

Oh, now you think so, I thought bitterly, remembering her yelling at me for inviting him over after the Christopher fiasco.

When all the goldfish crackers were gone, Mom called for us to pack up, and I wriggled my shorts back up over my thighs.

"So, is Dell a good student, Ivy?" Mom asked.

"I don't know if 'good' is the word I'd use," Ivy said.

"Hey!" I said.

I swiped at her—jokingly this time (I think)—and my mother laughed.

"No, she did way better than the last person I taught to swim," Ivy said. "My friend Mackenzie said she wanted to learn and then cried for half an hour 'cause she got a tiny bit of water up her nose."

When I'd suggested the swimming lessons, I hadn't really thought through the impulse. I just knew I wanted to start feeling more in control. But even after years of avoiding lakes on field trips and telling Paul I was fine on the sand when we went to the beach with our friends, I'd done kind of okay today. I didn't know whether that was down to Ivy's strangely abrasive tactics or my mother's admittedly reassuring presence, but it was a nice thought.

Ivy leaned into me as we walked back through the forest, my mother forging ahead through the trees.

"I bet he likes you."

"Who?"

"Paul."

"You don't even know him. Or me."

"In the movies, the best guy friend always likes the girl. It's one of those unspoken rules of society."

She was smiling. Was she making fun of me? Why did she even care?

"Not in this case," I said. "Honestly, I think he might be gay."

The word sounded like an engine backfiring in the woods—out of place. I had never said that out loud about Paul. It felt weirdly like a betrayal, and I glanced up to make sure my mother hadn't heard any of this before I looked back at Ivy. Her face was blank, and I felt more afraid than when I'd been waist-deep with Ivy's hand at my back.

"Would that be a bad thing?" she asked. Zero inflection.

"No," I rushed to say. "I'm not, like, homophobic. It's just a vibe I get."

My phone buzzed in my pocket.

"If he's gay, fair enough," Ivy said. "It's better than your siblings theory."

She lengthened her stride, pulling ahead of me on the path, and I tried not to think of the feeling in my stomach as disappointment. I watched her back swaying in front of me for a solid minute before I could bring myself to look back at my phone.

"how are things going with the Demon Daughter?" Paul asked.

It took me a long moment to reply.

"just trying not to drown"

It was just a thought I had sometimes. Paul didn't act aggressively into girls the way all the other guys seemed to. He only really talked about celebrity crushes. I carefully asked Natasha once if he'd ever dated anyone, because Natasha had known him since they were little, and she laughed at me.

"He had a thousand girlfriends in middle school," she said. "And then he shot up three feet and stopped asking anybody out."

She'd come up with the theory of Paul's hypothetical gayness and told me only because I asked the right questions while tagging along with her to the Dollar Store one lunch period when Paul was off school sick. But unlike me, she wasn't burning to be told. "If it's true, he'll tell us when he's ready," she said. "I'm sure he knows that we'd all be good with him being whatever, as long as he didn't flip-flop and be, like, 'Oh, I'm bisexual,' and then, 'Wait, no, I'm definitely gay.' You know? Like, figure yourself out and then talk to me, I have no time for wishy-washy people."

"For sure, I get that," I remember saying back. "But we would still be there for him while he was working through that stuff, right?"

"I wouldn't be an asshole, but I'd lose a little respect for him," Natasha said. "Like, everyone knows being bi is just a phase, so it would be like, 'Come on, you're smarter than this,' you know? It's scary, but people gotta just be honest with themselves."

Natasha had a way of saying things that made it sound like she was dispensing an ultimate truth that no one else was brave enough to say—even if her bluntness came off a little harsh sometimes. That was what made her so cool in my eyes.

I didn't have that clarity of vision, that certainty. If Paul really was confused and wanted to come out as bi, I'd probably be too scared of hurting his feelings to find the right words to reassure him that he could just come out as gay, that he didn't need a stepping stone. We couldn't all be as confident as Natasha, so I understood why it would be scary for him to come out if he really was gay. Even though gay kids were way more accepted now than when we'd been in elementary school, there were still assholes who treated them like a punchline—the "no homo," "that's so gay" kids who ruled the school.

Once, in chemistry class, Garett Anderson had announced that he was "experimenting with bisexuality now," but when Connor had tried to go over and kiss him as a joke, Garett shoved him off and theatrically pretended to vomit into his Bunsen burner.

"I was obviously kidding," he yelled. "As if I'd be gay—that's so gross!"

That had been the cause of one of my first fights with Christopher. He'd laughed the loudest in the room at Garett's so-called joke, and I'd told him later it was a dick move.

"He called gay people gross; that's a shitty thing to say," I'd said, hot and scared all down the back of my neck at the idea of fighting with him, saying such blunt words.

"It was just a joke," he'd said. "That's the weird thing about you, sometimes. It's like you have no idea how normal people act."

I mean, he wasn't wrong.

Natasha still hadn't texted me since school ended, since Christopher.

*

I changed for bed while Ivy was still brushing her teeth downstairs, but she burst into the room before I was done— luckily, I'd already gotten my sleep shirt over my head and just had to yank it down around my thighs. I swore I could feel her eyes on me, but then she was stripping out of her clothes, and I quickly busied myself with putting my own dirty clothes in the fold-up laundry hamper I'd brought from home.

Swimming together should've taken away some of the tension. But being back in our bedroom, at night, with her, had my heart going double-time.

Was it going to happen again? I felt like a scientist, looking for a replication of an experiment to prove a hypothesis.

"I'm not gonna bite if you change in the same room as me," Ivy said quietly.

"I can do what I want," I said, which, as a response, wasn't exactly the sharpest.

"Right. Got it. You and your mom have the prude thing in common."

"What?" I said, turning. "Wanting privacy has nothing to do with . . ."

I caught a glimpse of the bottom of Ivy's breasts as she pulled her sleep shirt on and lost the rest of my sentence. Her head popped out of the shirt, and I looked away again.

"Ugh," Ivy said, flopping down on her air mattress. "I can't wait until my dad brings over actual beds. These are the worst."

"Can I turn out the light?" I asked, heading over to the switch.

"They're so noisy," Ivy pressed on. "Every time you move, you can hear it."

My hand was on the switch. When I looked back, Ivy was staring at the ceiling. "I'm turning it off," I said.

"Like, every movement," she said slowly. "If someone so much as rolls over, you can hear it."

Her eyes fell on my face, like the sweep of a lighthouse, and I was suddenly caught out, aware of rocks on all sides. I switched the light off and fumbled over to my sleeping bag, heart pounding with guilt. There was no sound from Ivy's side of the room.

I lay down and turned my back to her, staring at the wall. I didn't move once, not when my shoulder got numb and my arms went tingly. Not when Ivy whispered, "You awake? Dell? Are you awake?"

She'd waited long enough that it was plausible I could've been asleep. Was she just making sure that she was safe to proceed without anyone listening? Did she want me to respond, tell her no, tell her yes?

I squeezed my eyes shut and said nothing.

This time when the noises started they were a tiny bit louder. If I had been asleep, they wouldn't have woken me up, but since I wasn't asleep, they were unmistakable. Ivy let out a little sound when she was done—too quiet to be called a moan, really, but too obviously sexual to be anything else. I stayed still. I had given permission through my silence to her question earlier. I only had myself to blame.

I flattened my palm carefully to my thigh, digging my fingernails in. If I was supposed to share a "prude" trait with my mother, my body certainly hadn't gotten the memo.

After an eternity, I sat up. Ivy breathed evenly on the other side of the room. I crept downstairs to the bathroom through the blue darkness of the house. I slumped on the lid of the toilet with my hand between my legs, running through tried-and-true narratives and images in my head until all of my jittery tension peaked and withdrew.

I washed my hands with my head down, finally tired.

But I'd forgotten to open the mirrored doors of the cabinet above the sink, to make sure I couldn't see myself.

When I raised my head, a face was reflected in the mirror—a girl with flat, shoulder-length brown hair, a soft chin, and staring eyes.

It wasn't me.

When I came back to myself, I'd somehow ended up on the other side of the bathroom, crammed into the corner to take myself out of the range of the mirror's reflection. I groped for the door and made my way out.

Out, out.

Out down the hallway and out the back door. I took the path through the forest at a run. My feet fumbled when the lake—and its island—burst into dark, shimmering view as I mounted the hill, but I didn't stop. I half ran, half slid down the slope until the ground under my bare feet turned cool and began to sink, clinging to my skin like it wanted to climb up my legs, swallow me whole.

Wrenching one foot out of the mud and then the other, I came to a stop on a wide rock at the edge of the water, gazing out.

I took a deep breath of fresh, clean night air, and looked down at the still water where my face should have been reflected back up at me.

She was there, the same girl from the mirror, the same girl I had glimpsed over the edge of the cliff at the water hole, the same girl I had seen in endless drawings pinned up in my mother's room.

Julie, you were there with me.

Chapter 7

When Joe arrived with the beds late Thursday afternoon, I locked myself in the bathroom.

"Dell?"

My mother knocked tentatively on the door.

"I'll just be a minute, Mom."

"He doesn't need to stay for dinner if you're not comfortable, but we need to get the beds in."

"It's fine, Mom. I'm just going to the bathroom! Leave me alone!"

I stared at the roll of toilet paper, trying to memorize the design. Even though I'd ripped open the doors of the bathroom cabinet as wide as I could, I could see the flash of my pale shoulder in the sliver of mirror tilted toward the toilet. It made me nauseous.

"Dell," Mom said. Her voice sounded closer, quieter, like she was leaning into the door. "I'd like for you to come say hello."

"I'm trying to pee!" I shouted. "Can you please leave?"

"We'll be out front when you're ready," she said.

*

My mother had introduced me to only one boyfriend before, when I was thirteen. Gary was forty and had been divorced twice, and he always wore hats, even indoors, which I found out on month three was because he was developing a bald spot.

"I think you and me are close enough now that I don't need to hide this from you," he said, ceremonially hanging up his fedora on the coatrack.

Mom smiled a lot when he was around, going soft-footed and nervous in a way I had never seen before. Gary taught me how to play Crazy Eights and played it with me until I got good enough to beat him. His shoulders could fill a doorway and he took up half the table by himself. He made our little apartment seem smaller but in a good way.

Halfway through month six, Gary started staying overnight in Mom's room sometimes. I stayed up late, listening for sounds, but I could never hear anything. I was both disappointed and relieved that my mother didn't seem to be having sex with him. It would have seemed wrong in some fundamental way for my mother—who flinched at a "shit" and had never really given me "the talk"—to actually have sex, but surely adults had sex at this point in a relationship, right?

Once, he made pancakes in the morning for me before school.

It didn't last long after that. I never found out why they broke up. Mom was sad for a long time afterward, in that quiet way adults are when they're trying not to let you see.

"We had different priorities," she said when I asked what happened.

My mother was tall and blonde and pretty, and there was no

reason anyone would break up with her except for the girl-shaped ball and chain around her ankle. I'd taken him from her without even trying because there was something in me that ruined things.

As bad as I'd felt about Gary, I still wasn't ready to share her with anyone yet—not Ivy, not her dad. Not until I'd made up for Christopher and made my mother like me again.

When I came out of the bathroom and made my way to the porch, Ivy was standing in the bed of a black pickup truck, holding up a tarp to look underneath. Mom was around the front of the truck with a dark-haired man a couple inches shorter than her. He was wearing slacks and an unbuttoned dress shirt over a T-shirt. His sleeves were rolled up over his forearms, and he looked very strong.

"Hi," I said when they all looked over. I waved then felt immediately stupid for it.

"Joe, this is my daughter, Adele," Mom said. She beckoned, and I crossed to her side. Mom squeezed my shoulder. "Adele, this is Joe. The two of you have met before but you were a lot smaller then."

Joe smiled. He had heavy features that pulled his whole face down in a solemn sort of way, but he was attractive. He looked a lot like Ivy.

"It's good to meet you, Adele," he said, a bit awkwardly.

"Everyone calls me Dell."

"That's appropriate," he said. "Out here in nature and everything." He glanced around, taking in the blank faces. "*Dell* is an old word for a valley. Covered with trees and—"

"Dad," Ivy groaned, appearing at his shoulder. She was almost the same height as him. "If you have to explain your joke, it's not very funny."

There was something strange about seeing Ivy next to her father. I had grown used to thinking of Ivy as a force unto herself—seeing her as someone's kid didn't make sense.

"Are you girls getting along so far?" Joe asked, looking between Ivy and me.

"Oh, we're basically best friends," Ivy said. "Where's Jamie?"

"He's staying over at a friend's house tonight," Joe said.

"Did Elizabeth have to sign off on that?"

"Why don't we just start moving the beds in while it's still light out?" Mom suggested.

Ivy and I deflated our mattresses and dragged them into the hallway, leaving them in a heap at the far end.

"You said Jamie was your brother, right?" I said.

"Yup. Half brother. He's staying with my dad this summer."

Her voice had gone clipped.

"Is that why you're not at home?" I asked. "Is there not enough room for both of you?"

"I'm not at home because I knew Anne would need at least one competent person to help her out here," Ivy snapped.

We piled our belongings in the corner of the bedroom, my half-open duffel bag slumped against Ivy's plastic drawers and the tangle of sheets my mother had brought up for the beds. Joe and Mom carried the bigger pieces up together, and Ivy and I brought in the slats.

Ivy had a cut in the middle of her bottom lip, a thin red split like she'd smiled too wide. She kept tonguing at it absently, an occasional flicker of pink.

"Jamie used to always spend summers with Joe and Ivy," Mom told me in a moment alone in the stairwell. "But this is the first summer in a couple years that he's able to be here. It worked out best for him to come if Ivy stayed with us. She was the one who suggested it to me and her father. Which was a win-win because we sure need extra hands around here!"

"Do Ivy and her brother not get along?" I asked. I vaguely remembered Ivy mentioning him the night we first met. "Is Elizabeth Jamie's mom?"

"It's a bit more complicated than that," Mom said. "And yes."

"Is she what's stopping Ivy from living at home?"

"Dell, I really don't think that's any of our business."

Once we'd carried all the pieces and Joe's toolbox up to the room, Ivy and Mom worked on putting together Ivy's bed and Joe and I worked on mine. Joe asked me questions about school and my friends and what it was like living in the city. I answered as best as I could, but I kept getting distracted by the heat of him hovering so close. He'd discarded the dress shirt pretty quickly, but he perspired a lot anyway, huge damp patches growing under his arms.

"This was your mother and her sister's room when they were kids," Joe said as we put the last screws in the bed. "Did she tell you that?"

"Yes," I said. Across the room, Ivy and Mom were huddled together over a corner of Ivy's bed, heads bent close.

"The walls used to be covered in her drawings," Joe said. "I asked her to draw me once, but since I forgot to specify what style I wanted, she turned me into a caricature."

I laughed, and Joe looked suddenly relieved, like he'd passed some sort of test, which was annoying; I wasn't supposed to let him feel at ease this quickly.

"Did you have a crush on my mom when you guys were kids?" I said bluntly.

Joe laughed and shook his head. "I was eighteen when I met her, and she was fourteen. It wasn't until we ran into each other when I was in the city for some meetings last winter that I ever thought of her like that."

I nodded along like I'd heard this story before, even though Mom hadn't told me the actual details.

"I knew her the second she stepped into the room," he said. "Your mother is not someone you forget."

My mother and Ivy slipped out to grab extra tools from Joe's truck, and I took advantage of being alone with him at once.

"What about my aunt?" I asked. "My mom said you guys were friends first."

He stilled, then seemed to deliberately relax.

"Ah, are you wanting to know if I had a crush on Julie before your mother?" he said.

"No, I just . . ." I shrugged. Lowered my voice. "Mom hasn't really talked about what happened when she died."

"Right."

Joe sat back on his heels, and I thought for a horrible moment that he was going to yell for my mother to come back and tell her what I'd asked.

"I know she hasn't spoken much at all about her sister with you," he said quietly. "But things like that—it hits you hard when you lose someone that young."

She would have been older than me, I wanted to say petulantly. If Julie died the year before I was born, my mother would've already been well into university. She was already an adult.

"Your mother and Julie were attached at the hip, despite the four-year difference. I used to get frustrated, actually, that Julie always had her kid sister tagging along." He smiled. "That was before I got to know Anne."

"Ivy said you told her it was an accident," I said. "When she—" I gestured vaguely with my screwdriver. "Does that mean drowning?"

My dream last night pushed at my consciousness, like waves against the sides of the island. I had been there again, and the water had seemed higher, closer. This time, there had been someone rowing away from me, their face hidden. I had woken with an intense, clawing fear of being left alone.

Joe hesitated. "Yes. It was devastating for your mother."

"What about my grandparents? I got the impression from my mother that they didn't really get along with Julie."

I was trying very hard to adopt a casual tone of voice.

"That's an understatement," Joe said, letting out an uncomfortable little laugh. I could hear footsteps in the hallway outside the room. "But I don't know if I should be getting into that with you."

After both beds were successfully set up and the mattresses maneuvered through the halls with great difficulty, Joe volunteered to help Mom make supper downstairs while Ivy and I got our things sorted. Mom was going to have to stay on an air mattress for a couple more days because he hadn't been able to find a bed for her yet and hadn't been able to convince her to take his from his house. They bickered good-naturedly over it as they left the room, and I could hear my mother's laughter carrying up the stairs behind them.

I turned to my new bed and flopped down on the bare mattress.

"Damn, he must really like Anne if he's volunteering to cook," Ivy said. "Does he pass inspection?"

I grunted. "It's not up to me if they date or not."

"What? You think he's not good enough for your mom or something?"

I sat up. Ivy was lying on her back on her bed, head tipped to the side so she could look at me. The light in the room suddenly slipped sideways, a pale darkness crawling up the walls; the sun had moved below the trees, and we were abruptly halfway to night. Ivy's eyes were bright, like when she'd caught me watching her that first night.

"I didn't say that," I said, though obviously an honest answer would've been that no one was.

I went over to the bedding Mom had dumped by our stuff in the corner. The sheet lying on top had red roses all over the fabric—at a glance it looked like it was covered in blood.

"I like the flowers," Ivy said. "Are you okay with the kittens? I'm more of a dog person."

I hadn't even noticed the other sheet set. The kittens were adorable.

"You're not one of those dog people who hates cats, are you?" I said.

"You know they'll eat you if you die in your apartment and your body is left alone with them, right?"

"If I was dead, I don't think I'd care all that much." I paused then remembered I shouldn't care about Ivy's opinion of me. "Do you believe in ghosts?" I asked.

She didn't say anything at first. I stared down hard at my arms sunk in the sheets.

"Why?" Ivy asked. "Are you looking for some?"

"Just—" I shrugged. "You know."

The bed creaked, and I looked over to see that Ivy had propped herself up on her elbows.

"Is that why you're carrying around that big camera half the time?"

"What?"

"The Polaroid," Ivy said. "The whole 'ghosts show up on film' thing."

I froze, trying all at once to catalog the things that I had pointed the lens of my camera at over the past two weeks—the trees, the ground, the island, all caught in the square fist of a photograph.

"I hadn't actually thought of that," I said slowly.

Ivy put her chin in her hands. She lowered her voice. "Do you think your aunt might still be around here?"

The face I had seen in the water last night seemed like it should've been part of my dream. But it had been real, hadn't it? This stumbling, translucent memory from the half-awake hours of who-knows-how-long-past-midnight.

"I don't know," I told Ivy. Truest thing I'd said to her so far. I tried to gather the kitten sheets up into my arms, but the fabric resisted, forcing me to tug harder.

"It's a cool concept," Ivy said. "That we could leave imprints of ourselves behind when we die. I don't *not* believe in ghosts. But honestly, until I've seen one, I'm not going to go around saying I do."

"Because it's stupid to believe without proof?" I shot back, stung.

"Jesus."

She laughed, flopping over onto her back hard enough that the mattress popped down into a corner it hadn't been pressed properly into. Her hands were over her eyes.

"You take everything I say as some sort of dig at you," she said. "Listen, we're going to be stuck out here for most of the summer. Anne wants us to get along and be friends, or whatever. It would definitely make swimming lessons easier."

"So you're trying to pretend you haven't been all weird to me since we got here?" I said.

"Pot, kettle," Ivy said. "I get that there's tension. Our parents are dating. It's weird. But can I say I want to try without you jumping down my throat?"

The sheets had gotten caught on something somehow—when I pulled harder, Ivy's plastic drawers fell forward, and a box came crashing off the top, popping open and spilling a flood of photos and papers onto the floor. Ivy sat up and swore.

"Sorry!" I dropped the sheets and knelt, trying to scoop it all back into the box. Ivy's knees knocked into my shoulders, and she was leaning down, trying to push my hands away. She yanked a photo out from under my hand and it flew away from us, flipping over to land faceup on top of the rest.

Ivy scrambled to pick it up but not before I saw it. The photo was worn, the edges gone as loose as fabric. In it, a young woman stood smiling in a denim dress, with blonde hair, fair skin, and crinkled eyes. Her face disappeared into Ivy's palm.

"Who's that?" I asked.

"None of your business."

"My mom had a dress like that when she was younger, I think," I said absently, trying to pull up the memory of a photo Grampa had shown me years ago.

"It's not your mother!" Ivy snapped. "She's my mom."

For a second, I had no idea what she was talking about, ready to spit fire at Ivy claiming Anne. Then I realized Ivy was looking at the photo in her hands.

"Oh," I said. "Sorry, I didn't . . ."

Ivy turned back to the box on the floor as I trailed off, hunching over it. She was bent hard enough that her spine stuck out even through her shirt, a dotted line leading up to her shoulders.

"That's a picture of your mom?" I said.

"Why is it so hard to imagine she's my mother?" Ivy said.

"I didn't say that."

"I just look more like him than her," Ivy said. "Mom was white, Dad is Native, not that hard to understand."

"Right, yeah, I wasn't . . ." I abandoned the sentence, aware I was floundering. Sure, I was white as white could be, the kind of kid you assume is anemic at first sight, and I knew the kind of unfair advantage that pasty glow brought, but being aware of that didn't mean I had to act weird around Ivy about this and make her uncomfortable (something I was pretty sure I had already failed at).

Ivy threw the papers and photos haphazardly into the box, leaving the photo of her mother for the top, and then clapped the lid on hard.

"What was her name?" I asked.

Ivy pushed out a sharp laugh and stood up. "She's not dead. Might as well be, though. She just took off as soon as she realized she didn't want a toddler dragging her down."

She carried the box to the closet in the other corner, the one she had jumped out of that first night, and tucked it into the corner of the top shelf, far out of my reach. I wanted to say sorry again but didn't know how. Sorry for seeing the photo? Sorry for her mother being awful and leaving them?

I thought of my mother downstairs and how Ivy always tried to find a way to be nearest her in a room.

"I get it. My dad left us, too, before I was born," I said. "I don't have any photos of him at all."

When Ivy finally spoke again, all she said was, "Are you going to choose a set of sheets or what?"

The fact that I didn't have a dad usually didn't bother me. I had always been partial to the phrase "the father's not in the picture." It brought to mind a cheery sort of image of me and my mother marching out of the house and down to the local Sears to pose, smiling, for a photo, some anonymous lump of "father" left behind in bed. Like we'd just up and chosen to make our own picture without him, or maybe he once was in the picture until Mom took a pair of scissors and neatly cut him out. "The father's not in the picture" didn't say "because he left my mom pregnant at twenty years old." It implied that my mother and I were separate from him, and that was always how it was supposed to be.

I had collected only a handful of details about him over the years. I knew he and my mother met when they were kids. I knew he was still alive (probably). The last time I had gotten any details out of my mother was when I was eleven. I'd been over at Cora's house for the weekend, and Cora's father had helped us choreograph and record a "music video" in her backyard, so the idea was on my mind. Cora's dad had sung along with us and danced, too, badly. I liked him.

"Why do you ask?" my mother said when I mumbled out a question about how she met my dad. "It's not very interesting."

I shrugged.

"He was my high-school sweetheart," she said shortly. "Who followed me to college."

"Have you ever . . . I don't know, tried to contact him?"

My mother barked out a sharp laugh and, in a voice very unlike her own, said, "No. I don't know where he is now, and that's probably a good thing for everyone involved. He didn't deserve you, honey."

If they met in high school, that would mean they met when Mom was living at the cottage. So my father was one more thing to add to the list of why my mother didn't like thinking about this place. One more thing that kept Mom from trusting me with knowledge about my own life.

Watching Ivy and Joe didn't suddenly make me care about this dad-shaped cutout in my family picture. But maybe it did press on some sort of bruise, the kind you forget is there because the color hasn't reached the skin.

We ate dinner at the table, with Joe and Mom—and me and Ivy—sitting opposite each other, like some sort of strained family sitcom. The other three talked about how Ivy had gotten into a fancy art school in British Columbia, which she would be jetting out to at the end of the summer. Ivy squirmed in pleasure at being the focus of attention. I wanted to text Paul under the table about how annoying it was, but I was afraid the tapping of the keys would be too loud. Paul's phone had nicer keys—he had one of the fancy ones where the keyboard slides out of the side, but I have pretty much one of the cheapest flip phones on the market. If we didn't live in a city, my mother probably wouldn't have sprung for me to have a cell phone at all when I turned fifteen. I knew Ivy didn't have one.

Joe asked where I was thinking about going after Grade 12. I shrugged.

"Haven't thought about it."

I had, but the idea of it all was too big to really grasp.

"You said you were thinking about being a science major," my mother said. "Maybe studying more about plants."

"Yeah, I guess. I'm still thinking about it."

It sounded so small next to Ivy's plans. I didn't have a niche.

The whole botany thing had been my mother's suggestion after she saw how excited I was over the pictures of garden flowers I'd taken for that project with Christopher. The idea was more than a little soured now.

"No art for you then?" Joe asked. "You didn't take after Anne?"

My eyes snagged on Ivy's across the table, and I looked down at my plate instinctively.

"No," I said. "I'm useless at art."

"I'm sure that's not true," Joe said. "Probably for the best though. Raising a teenager is hard enough without them being an 'artist.'"

He made air quotes with his fingers. Ivy whacked him in the arm, but she was grinning the same way he was. I liked him and felt mildly resentful about it.

"What's your favorite medium?" Ivy asked Mom. "Do you just draw with pencils, or . . ."

"I used to like charcoal," Mom said. "Back in high school. I wouldn't necessarily call my little scrawls these days 'art.'"

"We should draw together!" Ivy said. "Or paint or something. I've been trying to get into watercolors, but I find them so much harder to control than acrylics."

"Actually, I might want to go into photography," I said suddenly. I kept my eyes on Joe, pointedly not looking at my mother. "I've been doing some of that lately."

I waited for his expression to flicker—betray some sort of knowledge of my "experience" in that field. It didn't happen. "Well, if you ever need any pointers, I was a bit of a photography buff in my youth."

"I figure it's a lot easier than going to all that effort with paint, right?" I said.

Joe laughed.

"That was my thought exactly," he said. "We're clearly the smart ones, taking a shortcut to being artists." His face changed when he laughed—he looked lighter, and the lines on his face lifted and brightened. It was weird to think it of an adult, but he was young still, no older than the actors I used to google pictures of when I was twelve and crowded around a library computer with Cora and Karoline.

I found myself growing hot. I looked back at my plate.

Joe spent the rest of the meal politely aiming questions my way while my mother sent me encouraging looks. He didn't ask about boyfriends.

After supper, my mother and I did the dishes together while Ivy took Joe outside to show him the island. Mom asked what I thought of Joe. She sounded soft, hopeful. I was elbow deep in hot, soapy water, my knuckles burning. Something turned queasily in my stomach and prickled over my skin, like sunstroke. Joe had large hands, like Christopher. My mother wouldn't be looking at me like this if she knew what I was thinking.

"He's cool."

*

Joe was staying the night.

"is that fast?" I texted Paul while I was holed up in the bathroom, door locked. "that seems fast."

"dell most adults fuck, or so iv heard"

"not my mom"

"oh my god, u were an immaculate concepion? u nvr told me!"

They weren't going to do that tonight, I told myself. After I've met him once? With their children in the other room? My mother—who's dated one person in all the years I've known her, never stays over at other people's houses, and who balks at even the hint of sexual innuendo? No.

I got into my pajamas in the bathroom this time. Ivy had flipped her full-length mirror back around in our room again, and it was easier to avoid reflections when they were on cabinet doors that could be opened. I thought about peeking, just to see if it would be you looking back at me, but the risk of it being The Thing I called me was way too high.

"What's with the pants?" Ivy asked when I got into our room. "My dad's not going to judge your hairy legs if he bumps into you in the hallway, you know."

"I was cold last night," I said.

"It's summer and there's a drought on, so I doubt that's true," Ivy said. "Hey, do you think they'll actually do it on an air mattress? Personally, I would be too afraid that it would pop."

"Speaking of not true," I muttered.

When I glanced over, Ivy was giving me a strange, inscrutable look.

"Okay," she said. "So are we actually . . . talking about that?"

My body flushed cold.

"Talking about what?"

It hung in the air for a moment between us. Ivy smoothed her hands over her bedspread, looking down at her lap. She seemed almost nervous, but I had to be reading that wrong.

"You don't sleep with your eyes open, right?" she said.

"No."

"Okay, good, that would be super creepy." She let out a wispy, semi-panicked laugh.

Another pause, thick as soup.

"So you know I know you were looking the first night," Ivy said abruptly. "At me."

"Don't know what you're talking about."

"I thought you were asleep. But then. You were looking. I saw you."

Camera flashes. Christopher's greedy eyes. My throat grasped at a breath; I struggled to stay in the moment.

"I said I don't know what you're talking about." My voice was too loud. She was looking at me too much. She was seeing me. Slime coated my body, leaking out of my pores, and any second now she was going to recoil from the monstrosity in front of her.

"I'm not getting mad," Ivy said quietly. "I just wanted to say that we could talk about why you were watching me."

And suddenly, the flip—I was Christopher, I was the nameless people behind the view count on the photos he took, I was the thousand eyes.

"Watching?" I said. "Watching what? I'm not interested in whatever weird shit you get up to. I don't want to be here, I don't want you around in my house, okay? Do you get that? That—that's gross. You're gross for even, like—saying . . ."

The words piled up, like railway cars colliding in a wreck,

falling right off the mountain. Ivy's face was coldly blank, the openness gone, her surprise shown only through how wide her eyes had gotten. I wanted to apologize, but I didn't know how. Why did I keep messing up like this?

"Gotcha," Ivy said finally. "I'm going to bed. You can get the lights."

I knew what was going to happen as soon as I settled into bed in the dark, but somehow I was still surprised when it did. It wasn't like the nights before—this time Ivy didn't wait, or even check if I was asleep. I lay with the blankets pulled up to my nose, staring at an orange kitten playing with a ball, and listened to her body sliding on the sheets, the sound of her shuttered breathing.

How was she able to be so whole with her body after what I'd just said to her? It wasn't fair.

The pants had been a mistake. I started out clinging on to the waistband for something to hold, but soon I was rocking down against my own grip, the seam running between my legs pulled taut, pressing in. Push and pull and clench and release—I forced myself to let go of the waistband, flipping onto my stomach and pressing my face into my pillow.

I risked a glance at Ivy and saw she was looking up at the ceiling, her head tipped back. She was getting louder, like she wasn't afraid of my mom or her dad busting in and seeing her, like she owned this room, owned me and my every reaction. It wasn't fair, I thought, and it became a mantra in my head, a rhythm. It wasn't fair, it wasn't fair—I was rolling my hips down. The bed squeaked on the floor.

Ivy's head lolled on the pillow to face me, her eyes open. I squeezed my own shut, fear racing through me instinctively, anger right on its heels. It wasn't fair.

I pushed my hand down my stomach and into my underwear.

I couldn't open my eyes, but I made it obvious as I moved against the bed, against my hand. Ivy fell silent for a moment then started again. I didn't let up—to do that would mean letting Ivy win, and I may not have been able to make art like my mother, but I was just as stubborn as she was. It felt like a fever, like I was sick, even more than it usually did, and I was making the kitten sheets damp, rubbing my own sweat into them. Our parents were a room away, cuddled up on an air mattress. *Our* parents. I could barely breathe.

Christopher flashed into my head, his crooked smile against my shoulder, his fingers digging bruises into my side, and my fear spiked so high I couldn't separate it from everything else. My eyes flew open and found Ivy's fixed on me from across the room. If she had already been looking, that meant I was allowed to. A sort of shock passed between us, visceral, and Ivy's mouth dropped open—we were watching each other, and that was it.

I shook out against the mattress, wrung dry. As soon as I could move, I flipped onto my other side, staring at the wall with my head ringing and empty. There was no room for anything but relief.

Ivy cleared her throat.

"Good night," she said, her voice a low rasp. It scraped across my shoulders and I shook again.

"'Night."

*

In the morning, for the first time, I would remember my dream in full.

I was tied to the truck on the island and yelling for my mother, wrists rubbed raw against rope. The sun was going down, and tiny lights were sparking around my head, a welding torch impact of sun on skin against the falling darkness.

There was a boat, and I'd been wrong before. There were two people there in the dream with me—a presence somewhere behind me on the island itself that I couldn't see, and a naked woman sitting in the boat. She was leaving, rowing slowly away from the island. When she glanced back, she had my mother's face.

Chapter 8

I ran into Joe coming out of my mother's room at 7 a.m., wearing nothing but boxers. At the sight of me he jolted, feet very clearly leaving the ground an inch, and then skittered to a halt.

Finally, I thought, a person with an accurate nickname.

"Morning," Joe said softly. His hands twitched at his sides, like he was resisting the urge to cover himself—clearly he hadn't been expecting to see anyone up yet.

"Yes," I said inanely, keeping my eyes determinedly on his face.

"Early riser?" Joe asked.

"No," I said. "Need to pee."

"Oh, well." Joe spread his hands, backing into the doorway of Mom's room to give me space to pass. "Ladies first."

When I came out of the bathroom, Joe was waiting, wearing sweatpants and a T-shirt now—he'd come prepared for a sleepover.

"Dell," he said seriously. "I wanted to check with you—was it all right that I stayed over?"

I shrugged. Trying to look him in the eye was weird. He was too sincere, so unlike his daughter.

"You're dating my mom, not me," I said.

"Look, I've been a single parent as long as your mother, and I know that a parent dating can be more than a little weird," Joe said. "I want you to know that I'm serious about your mom."

"You've only been dating for a few months."

He laughed nervously. "Right, well, I'm not about to propose tomorrow or anything, but I'm not just going to show up for a couple months and mess up your life, all right? I'd like this to work, so if there's anything you need to ask me or tell me, I'm here anytime."

"Okay," I said. "I'll remember that."

Joe nodded for a moment before he turned away awkwardly, with the air of a man who needed escape but had no real destination. He paused halfway through the movement and looked back at me.

"You and Ivy getting along?" he asked shrewdly.

I didn't know what to say to that, but my silence apparently offered enough of an answer.

"Can I share something with you?" Joe said. "I think she's angry with me right now. So, sometimes, she might aim her bad mood at the wrong person."

"Yeah?" I said, trying not to sound too interested.

"I wasn't as relaxed about her going into art when she was applying for schools as I maybe seemed at dinner last night, so I think she's still carrying a little bit of bitterness about that. If she's standoffish, just ignore it and let her sort herself out." He paused. "Unless you two are actually fighting."

I saw Ivy hunched over her mom's photograph, looking small. I saw her as she'd been the night before, in bed. I imagined telling

Joe, Your daughter's out of her mind. She's horrible and confusing and I never want to see her or you ever again.

"No," I said. "We're fine. I just don't know if she likes me yet."

"I hear you're letting her practice her swim teacher skills," Joe said. "Trust me—she likes anyone who lets her be the boss once in a while."

He didn't look so much like Ivy when he smiled. Her smile had come from somewhere else.

*

Because he wanted to set a good example or something, Joe suggested the four of us go into the forest with garbage bags for a quick comb before he had to go. He'd brought over these fancy spiked sticks, so we could poke pieces of garbage like troubled teens in a movie doing community service. I watched Ivy's shoulders shifting through the foliage ahead of me and tried not to stab myself in the foot.

"Do you want to do some more swimming today, hon?" my mother asked, sidling up to me with a magazine speared on her garbage stick. "You and Ivy made great progress the other day. It's good to see you two getting along. You seem a little more cheerful."

Compared to what? I wanted to ask. Make her acknowledge the whole Christopher thing outside of random digs at me.

"Actually, I thought that maybe we could look in the attic later today?" I suggested. "I want to see all of the family stuff you said is up there."

Mom bent to pick up a plastic six-pack ring, her face hidden by a curtain of hair.

"Well," she said as she straightened up, "I don't know if today is the right time for that."

Joe couldn't stay very long because he had to pick up Ivy's brother from the sleepover. Mom was heading into town with him to go grocery shopping and grab a chest freezer from her librarian friend to set up in our kitchen.

"So are we coming along?" Ivy asked as the two adults dithered on the porch, checking their bags. "I bet Jamie and I could lift a freezer all by ourselves."

"I'm not set to pick him up until after I drop Anne and the freezer back here," Joe said.

"Gotcha." Ivy's tone was normal, but when her dad looked away, her face twisted up. I blinked, and the sour expression disappeared.

"It can still be a good little errand run," Mom cut in. "What do you think, Dell, you want to see the town in the daytime?"

I did want to see the town. But after having my suggestion for the day shut down so clearly by my mother, I had the self-destructive urge to disagree. I didn't have the energy to watch her and Ivy pal around while I tried to awkwardly navigate conversation with Joe.

"I'm kinda tired," I said, ignoring my mom's look of disappointment. "Can I just stay at the house?"

"Yeah, I'm actually a little tired, too," Ivy piped up. Joe looked slightly confused at her sudden flip—I understood the feeling—but my mother just smiled, seeming way too pleased.

"I understand, you girls just want to hang out," she said.

Of course, before she could go, my mother left us with the usual rules, repeating the "don't go down to the lake" one too many times. Joe laughed and said, "I think they have it at this point."

After Joe's truck disappeared down the driveway, I said, "You want to go to the water hole?"

"Didn't your mom say she wanted us to always let her supervise?" Ivy said.

"Thought you didn't care about those rules."

I finally looked her in the eye for the first time that day. She didn't seem disgusted or dismissive, like I'd expected. Instead, she had a strange smile on her face, as if I had somehow impressed her.

"Fine," she said. "But if she gets mad, I'm throwing you under the bus."

*

I thought we were still in the "staying in the part of the pond where I can stand" phase. Ivy had other ideas.

"Just take my hands."

"Then I'll definitely sink!"

"No, you won't. I'm going to tow you around."

Ivy was calmly bobbing in the deep part in the pond, holding out her hands as if it wasn't absolute witchcraft that she wasn't already drowning.

"How are you even doing that?" I asked.

"I'm treading water," Ivy said. "It's like riding a bike. They do have bikes in the city, right?"

I opened my palms and let Ivy drift close enough to close her cold fingers around mine. She looked steadily at me as she eased backward in the water, pulling me toward her. I had a flash of watching *Peter Pan* with my mother as a kid, seeing the mermaids grab at Wendy's arms, urging her into the water.

"Just keep your eyes on me, okay?" Ivy said. "And for god's sake, remember to kick! I'm not going to drag your dead weight around!"

The water is not a mouth that will swallow you, I thought nonsensically. Ivy is not one either.

I relaxed enough to be drawn into the deep water. When my toes left the rocks at the bottom, I swallowed against the lump of panic in my throat and kicked, my legs feeling wobbly and terrified.

"Hey, look at me," Ivy said. "Just look at me."

Ivy's face was the only consistent thing in the world. I was aware of us moving, water unfolding against my shoulders as we cut through, but I couldn't think about it if I wanted to stay calm. Ivy's eyes wavered from mine only by centimeters, glancing around my face and then darting back. I wondered what she saw, and almost dipped in the water at the anxiety of the thought.

"Remember to breathe," she said. "You're so tense. You can still breathe while you're swimming, just in and out."

She took exaggerated breaths and I copied her. I hadn't even realized I was holding my breath before.

"We do have bikes in the city, by the way," I said belatedly.

"I know," Ivy said. "I've been there on school trips before, obviously. And my dad takes me sometimes if he's got to go in for something—that's how I first met your mom."

I wasn't interested in hearing about how Ivy had swept my mother off her feet. "Did your dad come on the school trips, too, or do principals not get to do that?"

"Oh, he made sure to come on every single one." Ivy rolled her eyes. "He and your mom have overprotectiveness in common, I guess. I have to say, riding the subway isn't as cool as you city folk seem to think it is."

"City folk?" I sputtered. "Suddenly you're a farmer in an '80s movie?"

My foot brushed against something underwater. I shrieked before my brain placed the sensation as a stick. Ivy let out a burst of laughter.

"Like you can make fun of me right now," she said.

"Maybe you just haven't been on the subway on its cool days," I said. "One time on my way home from school, I stood next to a man in a banana suit who was carrying a sausage dog."

"Yeah, well, my school has a Tractor Day."

We'd made our way under the silken shadow of the cliff face. I almost stopped kicking when I laughed, so used to the glide through the water that I'd forgotten I was propelling myself. As Ivy laughed with me, the fear stayed back, even though my body fought to sink, and Ivy's fingers pressed hard into my arm trying to keep us both up.

"What the hell is Tractor Day?" I asked once my legs were moving again.

"Kids who own tractors drive them to school and compete in, like, tractor-themed events," Ivy said. "Don't even try to tell me you have something that strange in the city."

"We have Build a Skyscraper Day."

"You definitely just made that up. I can spot a liar from a mile away, and you are the biggest one in this pond."

I had been looking into Ivy's eyes for too long to tell if there was any malice there. She sounded like she was joking still, and my life was literally in her hands. I could only kick my feet and trust her. I smiled and rolled my eyes, and Ivy smiled back. The palms of her hands were warm against mine, so different than the cool water. Maybe that was why I kept shivering.

"Last night," I said.

"Yeah?" Ivy said. "You want to talk about how much you snore?"

"I don't snore."

"So there's something else you wanna talk about?"

She sounded pretty calm considering the way I had exploded on her the last time she had asked the same question. I strove to look at something, anything other than her face.

"In case you're wondering, no, I don't rub one out every single night—it just helps when I'm stressed or have insomnia," Ivy said when I stayed silent. "That's why I wanted to wait until you were asleep. Creepy of you, by the way, to listen to me during."

I gaped at her.

"We share the room," I said.

"I had to share a room with my brother for a month when I was fourteen, and he fell asleep way faster than you do."

"That's gross."

"Don't try to tell me you were planning on going the whole summer without, because there's no way I believe that."

I wanted desperately to yank away from her grip, but I couldn't lose its safety. Embarrassment churned viciously in me, which wasn't fair, since Ivy seemed completely fine apart from her words coming out a little fast. Girls didn't talk like this.

"Sorry I don't pass out as fast as your brother," I said. "Or—he's only your half brother, right?"

"It's not 'only' anything," Ivy snapped. "You don't have any siblings, so you don't know shit. No wonder you're so bad at this stepsister thing."

"We're not stepsisters."

"If you think this summer isn't some sort of warm-up to that, you haven't been paying attention."

I pictured Ivy and Joe squashed into the tiny apartment in the city with me and my mother, knocking elbows in the kitchen and sharing beds—Ivy next to me on the subway, stealing Paul away with her smile and her sharp laugh. I felt something like panic.

"Hey," Ivy said.

"What?"

"You realize you've been in the deep end for like ten minutes now."

"So?"

"I'm just saying, good job. It's easier than you think it is. I could probably let go, and you'd be fine."

I clung hard to Ivy's hands. "Do not let go of me."

Ivy had been joking again. I watched the amusement unfold

on her face. I had the strange, sudden feeling that maybe Ivy was like me in a way that other people weren't.

"Don't worry, I'll teach you how to use your arms properly before I toss you in the deep end alone," Ivy said. "I'm not that much of a dick."

"I didn't think other girls did it."

"What? Swim?"

I shook my head. Then nodded. For a split second, we were back in our dark bedroom, meeting eyes across the impossible chasm between our beds.

"You did say your best friend was a boy."

"I had friends who were girls when I was in elementary school."

"Elementary school?" Ivy said. "It took me longer than that to get there."

It didn't sound like she was condemning me, almost like she was impressed.

"All the boys were already talking about what they did way back in grade six," I said. "I've never heard another girl talk about it, except to be, like, 'Oh, boys are weird, I don't do that kind of stuff.' I don't even remember hearing about it in sex ed—I thought girls just didn't."

"Well, I don't know about all other girls, but I do," Ivy said. "And I know other girls who do, too."

"One night I jerked off six times in a row," I blurted.

A wave of humiliated heat crashed over my head. I waited for her to let go of my arms in disgust, let me sink to the bottom of the pond.

Instead, she just raised her eyebrows.

"I don't think I can beat you there, but it's not, like, a bad thing," she said. "Like, why would it be fine for a guy to brag about that, but not girls? Of course, society doesn't teach us it's okay. There's nothing more frightening to adults than girls who know what they want. Gotta keep us stupid so we'll marry the first guy who chances a look at us, whether he sucks at sex or not. Whether he cares if we get off or not. How would we know the difference?"

We'd bobbed closer together, and Ivy leaned in farther still, like she was sharing a secret. "If we know we can opt out of that kind of shitty life and only accept what we actually want and deserve, their whole precious, normal society of marriage and babies comes crumbling down, and I bet most of the old people in this world don't want that, do they?"

"That's not fair." Other girls, Ivy had said. It wasn't just me and her who were messed up?

"No shit. I kind of assumed sex ed would be better in the city, though."

"Nah, it was still like what was in *Mean Girls*: 'If you have sex, you'll get pregnant and die. Here, take some condoms,'" I said. "When I was fourteen, my teacher made the girls write letters to our future husbands explaining why we were going to abstain from sex until we met them."

Ivy let out a wordless shriek. "What? Even my teachers weren't that bad. But, hey, at least you had a mom you could ask stuff if you needed to. I had to ask the librarian."

"Are you kidding?" I said. "I don't think my mom has, like, jerked off or—ever. She'd think there was something wrong with me. She already does."

Ivy went quiet, and I wished I hadn't said anything. Here, in the water, kept safe only by Ivy, I'd forgotten somehow that the rest of the world existed, that I'd have to stand next to my mother in a couple hours with Ivy seeing it all.

"I wish I'd figured all this out when you did," Ivy said. I could feel her words on the cold, water-pricked flesh of my neck, and it brought up goosebumps. "I didn't get it fully until I was fifteen."

"Doesn't matter what I thought I figured out," I said. "It's not like it improved my luck with boys any."

"Boys," said Ivy after a moment. "Right." She drew in a breath and looked up at the sky. The break in our eye contact felt almost physical, and I lurched forward with an anxious push of my feet, not wanting to lose her hold.

"We should head back," Ivy said. "Anne'll be home soon."

We dried off on the shore side by side. I bent double trying to squeeze as much water as I could out of my T-shirt without taking it off, but I shouldn't have worried; Ivy was crouched by the pond, not even looking at me.

"I'm sorry," she said abruptly. "I really did think you were asleep the first night. Wasn't quite sure the second, but I definitely knew you were awake last night. It was pretty gross of me to keep going with it."

My instinct was to apologize, too, but I had done nothing wrong. Not when it came to that, at least.

"Thank you," I said finally. "I shouldn't have called you weird when you tried to ask me about it."

Ivy nodded.

"Last night, I guess I thought, well, you'd already heard me before, so if you wanted me to stop you'd have said so," she said. "And you'd just been such a dick to me. But then today, I was thinking, if some guy tried to jerk off in the same room as me when he knew for sure that I could hear, I'd feel . . . I dunno, scared, I guess. Freaked out."

Ivy? Scared? I gaped at her back, curved still over the water.

"I wouldn't want to make someone feel that way," she said quietly.

"You didn't," I said. "I've felt like that before and—you didn't."

I knew she looked up at that, but I was staring down at my feet. For some reason, my body was flashing hot on and off, and I felt a little like I was going to pass out. Or throw up. But it was the truth. I'd been something last night, but it wasn't scared.

Maybe it was the relief of finally being sure: Ivy had never seen me through Christopher's eyes. She couldn't have and still looked at me like she did last night. Like I was some sort of revelation.

"We were never told how to talk about any of this," I said. "Was it weird that I—you know, also . . . ?"

"Don't think I'm really in a position to say if that's weird or not," Ivy said.

I finally looked up, meeting her eyes again, and all of a sudden the sheer awkwardness of everything crested over into hilarious. I burst out laughing—after a split second, Ivy followed.

"We're so fucked," she said.

"Life is so fucked."

"Oh, very profound."

"Shut up!"

*

When we got back to the house, my mother and Joe still hadn't gotten back. As I rounded the top of the stairs to the second floor, the attic door caught my eye, taunting me. I thought of my mother's dismissal that morning, and—bolstered by the strange new camaraderie that had followed me and Ivy back from the water hole—I suddenly knew what I wanted to do.

"I'm not tall enough to reach that ring to open the attic," I told Ivy. "My mom said there are family things in there, but she keeps putting off actually showing me the stuff. I know it's only been, like, a week, but I just want to take a peek."

"Couldn't you just stand on a box to open it?" Ivy said. "Why get me involved?"

"If you're part of it, you're not going to tell on me."

We changed back into dry clothes, me muttering about needing to use the bathroom so that I could change there, then reconvened under the attic door, assessing the silver ring in the square above us.

The moment felt weirdly monumental, and I was pretty sure Ivy, with her shifting feet, was feeling it, too.

"So if you're going behind your mother's back, you must still really be pissed that she didn't tell you about your aunt," Ivy said.

"Wouldn't you be? Everyone I know has big, extended families, and I've only ever had four people at Christmas," I said. "It would've meant so much to know that I used to have an aunt. And she literally never talked about her."

For a second, I considered telling her about the face in the water. But Ivy would just think I was crazier than she already thought.

Ivy stood on her tiptoes and made a swipe for the trapdoor. On the second try, she got her fingers in the silver ring and managed to pull it down. There was a click and then a hiss as the door popped open an inch, a curl of dust unfurling from the edges.

"Yes!" I crowed. Ivy pulled harder, and a set of wooden steps started to unfold. I grabbed the edge of the bottom step and coaxed it down until a full set of stairs stood in the middle of the hallway, leading up into a dark hole in the ceiling.

With Ivy on my heels, I started to climb. At first, as I rose head-first into the blue darkness of the attic, I couldn't make anything out, but as my shoulders cleared the lip of the trapdoor, my eyes slowly adjusted, and I froze.

"Shit."

"What is it?" Ivy demanded from below me.

"It's been, like, ransacked," I said. "Someone's definitely been up here."

The attic was much bigger than I'd expected and had clearly once contained much more than was left in it now. A triangle of blinding white cast from a high window lit up a cascade of ripped paper in the center of the floor. Some of the paper was trapped under two tipped-over filing cabinets, one of which had clearly gotten damaged in the fall, the top drawer dented inward. There was a pile of sagging cardboard boxes stacked at the back; a couple with "FRAGILE" scrawled on the side had fallen open, and shards of porcelain teacups were dotted across the papers. A tiny desk missing all but the bottom drawer was leaning against the right wall with a thick leather book sitting on top—and that was it.

Nothing else but the dust in the air.

I climbed up a little farther, just enough that Ivy could fit her head through the opening.

"Somehow I feel like this isn't how your mother left it," she said quietly. "We shouldn't be here."

This was supposed to be where my mother told me about Julie and her parents. But it had all been torn apart.

But before the sickly boil in the pit of my stomach could spill over, far below us, there was a distant scuffling sound then a distinctive creak: the front door swinging open.

"Girls?" My mother's voice.

Ivy backed down the attic steps so fast it was like she fell. I heard her race down the main stairs, heard the breathless sound of greetings on the first floor—and all I could do was look around at the disarray of the attic and try not to feel like I'd destroyed it all myself, just by daring to open the door and look.

With Ivy gone, I had no hope of folding the attic stairs back up. I headed down to join everyone instead, panic making my skull prickle. When I reached the kitchen, Joe was plugging the freezer in and Ivy was standing like a statue in the middle of the room, her shoulders up by her ears.

"Did you two have a good time while we were gone?" my mother asked.

"Yes," Ivy and I said in unison.

After a few minutes of small talk, Joe headed out, giving Ivy's forehead a quick kiss.

"I'll tell Jamie you said hi, all right?" he said. Ivy smiled, but only her mouth showed it.

We put away the groceries. My mother made noises about going up to her room to grab something, and I stepped in front of her automatically, like an idiot. She looked from my feet to my face, and something slipped in her expression.

For the second time in a month, I was about to hurt my mother very deeply.

"We should probably tell you something first," I said.

My mother took the stairs two at a time. We scrambled after her, but by the time I was rounding the corner into the upstairs hall-way, she'd already climbed halfway up the attic steps, her body cut in half by the ceiling. A low, unearthly cry came from the opening.

"It's all gone," my mother moaned. The knees on the stairs shuddered, as if on the verge of buckling.

"Mom?" I said. Her legs drew up the final few steps and disappeared into the attic.

Ivy pushed past me toward the stairs, and I pulled myself out of my stupor to follow.

Inside the attic, my mother was on her knees, her body hunched over. Ivy hovered a few steps in, her arms folded over her chest. Crossing the threshold of the trapdoor fully into the attic felt like shifting into another realm—the air had a different weight.

"I should never have left home," my mother said.

"Why would he even go up here?" I said quietly. "If Roger was just throwing his own shit out, or letting people dump their shit on the property—did you tell him he could keep his stuff up here, too, or did he just get his junk mixed up with our things?"

"No." Mom's voice was hoarse. "He knew he wasn't to go in here; that was the agreement."

She traced a pale beige skid mark in the wood, her eyes following her hand as if mesmerized.

"How much was in here before?" I asked.

"It looks like half of it is gone," Mom replied. "My parents donated most of their things to charity before they went. But there was this rug, and a dresser that had years of things in it, and this used to be my father's study, to keep him out of your gram's hair, and Julie used to keep him company, sitting at that desk, while he sat in this godawful green armchair over there . . ."

She was looking over at an empty corner of the room, her face heavy with regret.

"I shouldn't have just left all of it here."

Her hand flew from the floor to her face, pressing hard enough that I could see the tendons straining against the skin. She hit herself in the forehead with the ball of her palm, once, twice. All my thoughts flew out of my head. I'd never seen her like this.

"He didn't throw out all of it," Ivy said quietly. "There's still . . . there's still some stuff."

Mom shook herself. "You're right," she said. "You're right. We should clear this up."

She got up and strode to the center of the room, pulling a dangling string to turn on the lone bulb in the ceiling. It barely made a dent in the overall gloom.

I went over to the box of smashed teacups and carefully righted it. Apart from the broken ones on the floor, there were four others still inside the box, shiny white with flowers lacing their way around the brim. Two had large chunks bitten out of their tops by the impact with the ground, but the other two were wrapped in tea towels, completely intact.

I turned to show my mother, but suddenly there was a scraping sound to my left: Ivy dragging out a huge black portfolio case from behind the little desk. She unzipped it and took out a wide sheet of thick, cream-colored paper.

"Anne?" she said. "Did you draw this?"

Ivy held up the page, and my mother and the drawing met eyes. I could see it instantly—Mom's hand in the sketchy pencil strokes of a black bird. A smile flicked on her face for the first time since we'd entered the attic.

"I was fourteen when I drew that," she said. She crossed the room carefully to stand by Ivy. "My mother kept everything from my art classes. I forgot I'd stashed these here when I was cleaning up after she died."

I joined them by the desk. The burgundy leather book on top of the desk looked like a photo album, but I didn't want to pick it up and distract my mother from the art, which seemed to have calmed her. Ivy was already looking through the rest of the portfolio, her eyes all bright in a way I hadn't seen before.

"This is amazing," she said. "You couldn't have been fourteen—that's just not fair."

She pulled out another drawing, this one clearly a step up from the last—it was a charcoal portrait of a woman bent over a windowsill box of flowers. It took me a minute to realize it must have been Gram when she was younger, Gram as the mother of Anne the teenage girl.

"My final piece for art class in grade eleven," Mom said, taking the drawing. "I sat outside on the steps and watched her gardening until it got dark, week after week. My father used to bring me grape juice while I worked because he'd read that it was good for concentration."

"Why didn't you go to university for this?" Ivy said. "How could you just leave it if you were this good?"

The sun had crawled across the floor and was hot on my back; I had chosen the wrong place to stand. Ivy pulled out a new drawing, a sweeping one of the lake, no island, no garbage, drawn in thick, luxurious black on soft, textured paper. I knew it was beautiful—knew also that I was the reason that my mother now only drew on computer paper or in the margins of newspapers.

"Sometimes things like that just don't work out," my mother said finally. "Let me show you my best work."

Mom took the portfolio from Ivy and began to flick through it, casually at first, and then with increasing urgency.

"I had drawings of my parents and Julie," she said. "They were part of my grade-twelve senior project, so I know they should be in here. I remember looking through them before I closed up the attic after my mother's funeral. They were here."

"What was your final project?" I asked.

"It was six drawings that went together," she said. She lay the portfolio out flat on the floor and began taking each picture out and restacking them, searching. "They were in a smaller red folder. Red. Do you see one?"

We tried to help her sort through the drawings, but Mom's hands were too frantic for us to do much good. When she reached the end of the stack, she started flipping through them again, faster.

"The project was six portraits of people I loved, mixed with imagery from nature. My mother and father and Julie and my art teacher and Scott and—"

She sucked in a breath, and her hand clenched on the drawing she was holding. A sheet of clumsy watercolor flowers pinched in toward the center of her palm.

"Why would Roger do this?" she said. Her voice started to rise. "I give him a place to live, fair rent, don't bother him for years—it doesn't make sense. If he was angry, why wouldn't he destroy everything? Why would he only take parts of it? If he wanted the one drawing, where are the others? Where is my sister?"

Her hands left the art now, patting at the floor, at the china shards and loose buttons and other scraps of paper. Her eyes were feral, unfamiliar. I looked away, frantically cataloging the room, the emptiness where years of possessions should've been boxed up, the way the filing cabinets had been knocked over—there were marks on the floor that I recognized, leading toward the trapdoor.

The filing cabinet we'd found in the woods had been exactly the same color, I realized.

"Maybe he didn't take it for himself," I said quietly. "Maybe he ignored you and put some of his stuff up in here, too, and then he accidentally grabbed some of our things when he was throwing the rest of it into the lake and woods."

"Or maybe he wanted to get everything out of the house before he took off but got interrupted midway through," Ivy said. "Leave a clean slate so he could just disappear."

There was a second window on the other side of the room, through which the lake was reflected. My mother followed my eyes to it, to the misshapen island of trash gleaming in the distance.

"Anne," Ivy said, and then Mom was thundering down the attic stairs.

Ivy and I followed at a run, the whole house shaking under our feet. My mother pitched down the hallway to the sunroom and out the door. Our bare feet sounded like dull fireworks popping on the steps, one after the other, Mom and then me and then Ivy, all running down the path to the lake.

Mom splashed into the water and kept going, darkness surging up the legs of her jeans. She went deep so quickly it looked like she was being eaten, her arms moving side to side in an arc above the surface of the water.

"Mom!" I yelled. She didn't turn.

When we reached the lip of the water, Ivy plunged into it without slowing. I jerked to a halt. The water around my mother's hips wasn't as clear as at the water hole—it looked darker, like the oil slicks that coated birds and pulled them under. Panic swelled.

No, I thought. You just did this earlier; this should be fine! Move! Move!

But I didn't have Ivy as a guide. She was splashing her way forward without even a glance back.

My mother stopped with the water more than halfway up her torso, leaning toward the island as if she could see from here whether her drawings and her parents' things were mixed in among the truck and bed frame and floating junk.

"Mom, you were the one who said it might be dangerous to go swimming here!" I yelled.

She didn't even look at me. "Adele, get back to the house!"

I didn't move. Ivy had just about reached her, a V-shaped trough flowing behind her. The water was almost at her shoulders—it would have been collared around my neck if I was out as far as them.

Ivy said something quiet to my mother that I couldn't hear, and then, "Your kid's right. Got to set a good example."

"He put it out there," Mom said, still looking at the island. "I know it. I thought maybe all this trash was just him working out his own issues, but no, it wasn't. He went into that attic, and anything he took, he put it out there, where it would be hardest to get."

"I thought he was just an acquaintance," Ivy said. The two of them were getting quieter. Going against every instinct I had, I forced myself two steps deeper into the water. "Why would he need revenge or something? He probably only put super big stuff in the lake to hide it. Your family's stuff is probably just in the forest somewhere. Come on, let's go back to the shore."

Ivy reached out to Mom and stopped, her hand hovering awkwardly in the air. My mother didn't move for a long moment.

"This place was supposed to be passed down to Julie," she said suddenly. "Julie loved it here, she wanted to settle down here, and I wanted to leave." At this distance, her words almost melted into the sound of the water pushing lightly on my legs. "I never wanted this place, I wanted to grow up and move away. So once all of this fell to me, what did I do? I pushed it off onto a man I barely knew."

"You had a life of your own, you couldn't just up and move here," Ivy said.

"None of this is really Roger's fault." My mother was still looking out at the island, her back to me, but her body was tilted enough that I could see her mouth move as she spoke again—this time the words were lost completely. Ivy's face changed in reaction to whatever it was, a tiny shift sadder.

"Mom, come back to the shore!" I called. "Maybe the folder is still in the attic!"

Finally, my mother looked over her shoulder. When our eyes met, I had to take a step back—for a split second, blonde hair bleached white in the sunlight, she looked as pale and wide-eyed as a ghost. As she caught sight of me, a transformation came over her, the distant expression shuttering inward as she visibly tried to pull herself together.

She tried once to speak. Across the distance, I saw her mouth pinch in for a "J" and then stop. Regroup.

"Adele, you shouldn't be in the water!" she shouted. "You can't swim. I'll just be a moment. Could you just give me a minute?"

She turned to Ivy, seemingly registering her for the first time as well, and made a "you too" sort of motion, pointing her back to shore. Ivy shook her head and finally put her hand on Anne's shoulder, saying something I couldn't hear, which slowly brought the color back to Anne's face.

*

What seemed like a million years later, Ivy got my mother to turn around and wade back toward the shore where I was waiting.

"Get the fold-up chairs," Ivy told me. "Now. Put them on the porch."

I ran into the living room and hauled them outside. I could hear wet fabric being wrung out in the bathroom, like my mother had done for me what felt like so many weeks ago.

Ivy ushered my mother out into a seat on the porch. She got a stool for a table, set a glass of water down, and handed my mother a sketch pad.

"We're going to draw some trees, okay?" she said.

"Mom—" I started. Ivy glared at me and made a cut-throat motion.

"I'm tired of thinking about serious stuff," she said, turning back to my mother. "We're just going to draw for a little bit and sort things out after. I personally want to relax, and I could use some company."

My mother took the pad and pencil she was handed. She looked at them like she wasn't quite sure where she was, then made to stand up.

"I'm fine," she said faintly. "I should make us something to eat. We have new. New. There are things in the freezer."

"I'm going to make some food," I announced, surprising even myself. "You don't worry. You just—" I looked at Ivy. Her eyes said she had it under control.

And she did, didn't she? More than I did.

"You just stay out here with Ivy," I finished.

*

The house was quiet that evening. My mother had gone up to her room to rest without eating any of the macaroni and cheese I'd made after she and Ivy had come back inside. When I'd tried to speak to her, she'd smiled and waved me off.

I texted Paul and ignored Ivy while we ate in silence.

I wanted to ask Ivy what she'd said to my mother to convince her to get out of the water, but I didn't know how to start that conversation without letting my jealousy come through. It was petty and stupid to feel sad that Ivy had been able to help her when I couldn't, but the feeling kept rising up, this yawning sense of uselessness. I kept thinking of when I was small and my mother would wake up gasping from nightmares, clinging to me.

Back then, keeping each other going was simple—I would tell her she was safe, and she would bring me back to earth. Now, when the roles were flipped, neither of us knew what to do.

Chapter 9

I woke up in the middle of the night.

I had turned in before Ivy and hadn't heard her come to bed, but when I sat up in the darkness, she was curled up on the other side of the room, sleeping soundly. The house breathed quietly around me.

Once awake, I couldn't simply go back to sleep.

I climbed out of bed. Got my camera. And headed out into the blue-black forest.

The filing cabinet we'd seen had been off the path on the way to the water hole. Maybe I couldn't swim out to the island or stand beside my mother in the water or calm her down by making art together, but I could try to find a cabinet for her.

The path wavered under my feet. Trees stabbed out at unpredictable angles, like they were trying to keep me out, keep me from going farther. It was cool outside. I felt it on my bare feet. Felt it deep in my throat like the press of midwinter fingers.

I kept imagining I heard things—creaks and shudders and

footsteps. I swiveled back and forth, pointing my camera at anything, blindly hitting the shutter so the whole forest flashed stark black and white for seconds here and there.

When I looked at the top of the camera, I saw I was almost out of film. Only a couple photos left.

I could barely see where I was going, but I felt sure I wasn't straying from the path we'd taken before, filled with the confidence of someone still half in a dream.

Once when Christopher and I had only just started hanging out—after he'd started kissing me and before he told me "Yeah, sure, we're a thing"—we'd gone to this weird store near our school during lunch and I'd gotten lost in the maze-like aisles in the basement. I had left Christopher looking at a rack of T-shirts to follow a glimpse of movement between two racks and into another room that was almost invisible from where we'd been standing. When I returned a minute later, he wasn't by the T-shirts anymore.

He didn't respond when I called his name lightly, so I searched for him through the shelves until I was so turned around with panic that I didn't even know how to get back to the stairs.

He found me just as I was starting to cry, and as soon as he saw my face, he wrapped me up in a hug.

"Hey, you're okay," he said. "Sorry, I thought it would be funny if I hid for a minute. But you're okay, right, you're okay, come on."

And he kissed me on my forehead, casual and sweet, like we were the kind of couple who did that all the time. Like we actually were a couple. Standing warm in his arms, I felt completely whole and treasured, the whiplash of happiness coming so fast it almost made me dizzy. I wanted someone to appear at the end of the aisle and see the two of us together the way he never allowed us to be at school, to see how much he really did like me.

"You're so cute when you cry," he told me. And then when I smiled a little bit, he took my chin in his hand and said, "But that's better."

The path wobbled and a tree trunk rose suddenly to catch my left shoulder. I came back to myself, leaning against the bark, the camera swinging from my neck. I was somewhere deep in the dark forest, halfway between the water hole and home.

Why had that memory burst into my head like that? I was supposed to only remember bad things about him, wasn't I? Or no—I wasn't supposed to be thinking about him at all. King Trashbag, Paul had called him.

After my mother saw the photos of me that Christopher had posted, she had looked at me with an expression way worse than the one she'd aimed at me today, standing lost in the middle of the lake. But the core of it was the same: a complete lack of recognition.

When I reached the huge maple where the path ended, I knew I had gone too far. I backtracked, keeping my eyes wide open, but the cabinet was nowhere to be seen. All I had as proof of my mission was numb feet and a handful of half-developed photographs.

The house was just as dark and silent when I got back as it had been when I left. The attic staircase was still swung down, and Ivy was still asleep in our room, huddled on her side.

I climbed up into the attic, shoved a loose slat of wood over the opening in the floor to block any light, and turned on the lone bulb. I tried opening one of the filing cabinets, but it was locked.

I sifted through the papers on the floor, but my eyes refused to focus on any words.

I crossed to the desk where the burgundy leather book still sat. When I opened it, I found that I'd been right—it was a photo album. The first page was a single picture of a squash-faced baby wrapped in a pink-and-white blanket.

The name "Julie" was scrawled underneath it.

I flipped through the first few pages. There was Julie as a chubby baby smiling up at the camera, caught mid-laugh; Julie as a toddler in a yellow dress; Julie crying with her feet in the water at the edge of the lake. I recognized the spot—one of the pictures Grampa had given me of my childhood showed me sitting in the exact same place. The trees looked the same.

I could barely breathe.

I flipped ahead until I found a picture of Julie as a teenager. It was unmistakable—this was the face that had been following me since I'd gotten here, the face that was my face but wasn't. Was she trying to tell me something? Did she know how to help my mom, how to help me?

I wanted to know what you wanted from me, Julie.

A scraping sound split the air, and I whirled around to see two hands pushing away the wood over the trapdoor opening before my mother's head appeared. When her eyes fell on my face, she breathed out a long sigh then sucked herself back up again. I wondered if she'd been expecting to see a ghost.

"Dell, it's the middle of the night," she whispered. "What are you doing up here?" Her eyes lit upon my feet, still streaked with dirt. "Tell me you didn't go outside."

"I was trying to find the cabinet."

"Cabinet? What cabinet?"

"The filing cabinet we saw in the forest the other day. It's the same color as the other ones up here. I thought—"

But my mother was staring at me blankly, even as she pulled herself up into the attic properly.

"We saw it the first day we went into the forest," I said. "Remember, we couldn't get it open? And then we went to the water hole?"

"Maybe there was a cabinet, I don't recall," Mom conceded. "But it doesn't matter right now. You can't run off outside like that, especially alone, especially at night! What were you thinking?"

"You ran into the lake," I countered.

My mother ducked her head, nodding slowly. "Okay. That's fair. I—I overreacted. You shouldn't have had to see that."

She seemed about to say something else but stopped, spotting the photo album in my hand.

"Is that mine or Julie's?"

"Julie's," I said. I opened the cover so she could see the photos. "Is there one for you?"

"My mother made albums for both of us," Mom said softly.

She came closer and urged the album from my hands to hers. When she tipped it away from me, I could see that the leather on the cover was rippled strangely, looking stiff and brittle.

"Why is it burned?" I asked.

"I don't remember." That expression had returned, the one that had sent her straight to the water, and somehow I knew that wasn't the truth.

"Mom?"

"Yes?"

"Are you—" I had to swallow a couple times before I could get the words out. "Are you okay?"

There was a hovering, suspended moment where my mother didn't react, and I thought this was going to be it. She would close the trapdoor, sit me down here, and tell me everything I'd always wanted to know. The two of us would be alone in our family's space, and she would paint the ruined room with words, and finally I would be able to glimpse the other side of my mother's life and be asked in return if I was okay.

Mom raised her chin and smiled.

"Don't be silly! Of course I am," she said. "Earlier, that was . . . nothing you need to be concerned with. Like I said, I overreacted. We should probably clean the attic later in the summer. Work on the forest more and then come back to this."

At least, I think that was how her sentence ended. I missed the last bit of it because a strange, droning pressure had started up in my head, pressing against the backs of my eyes. When my mother set the album down on the desk, I picked it back up.

"It's time to go back to bed, sweetie," my mother said.

"Who is Scott?" I blurted out.

"I'm sorry?"

"Scott. You said one of your grade-twelve portraits was of someone named Scott. You said they were all of people you loved."

I waited for her to say something true: admit that he was my father. He had to be, based on the little she'd told me about meeting my dad when they were kids. Mom took a sharp breath.

"Love means something different to a teenager."

The words slid neatly between my ribs, right where Christopher's arms had curled around me.

"I didn't love him, okay!" I burst out. "Sorry I didn't stay pure and innocent with my high-school sweetheart until we were both adults at college, okay, but I wasn't stupid. I didn't love him. I didn't."

"Excuse me?"

I kept my gaze fixed firmly on the photo album in my hands.

"You brought that boy into our house and put yourself in a dangerous situation on—on a whim?"

"What? No!"

"That's what it's starting to sound like! That's real stupidity. I can understand making mistakes for . . . for what you think is love, but—"

Mom sounded too thin and shrill, like there wasn't enough space in her lungs. She was waving her arms now. I looked away from her and back down to where Julie's face had gone all blurry.

"I thought you'd be happy to know I didn't love him," I said.

"Happy? I believed that at least you were selective in who you would engage in that kind of behavior with, and now I'm hearing differently. You're supposed to be better than that!"

I flipped the page. My aunt even looked like me when she was a baby.

"That wasn't what I meant," my mother said. She had moved closer, but I couldn't look up. "You know I love you. I don't know what to say."

I'd thought I wanted to have this conversation, but this wasn't what I'd pictured at all. Everything was coming out wrong.

"So why are you up, anyway?" I asked. "Couldn't sleep?"

"Dell, don't just change the subject."

"You were perfectly happy with that for the last two weeks!" I shouted. "You keep pretending everything is fine with us and bringing stupid Ivy into every conversation! I swear, you've said more to her than you have to me since we got here!"

Mom faltered, a half-formed word dying as a huff of air.

"I'm sorry I'm not perfect like you," I said.

A wispy laugh squeezed out of her. "That is the last thing I'm looking for from you."

I tore my gaze away from Julie's face and gaped at my mother. She wasn't even turned toward me anymore. Standing beside the trapdoor with her arms crossed, she was looking at the window that pointed to the lake. She was taller than ever, an effortless skyscraper person. I had the sudden, very clear thought that I was tired of trying to climb up to her heights.

"If I'm a disappointment," I said, "maybe I got it from Scott."

I slammed the photo album shut and stood up, tucking it under my arm before I headed toward the trapdoor. My mother blocked me.

"That stays up here," she said. "I don't want you misplacing it."

A surge of bitterness made me strong, and I locked my elbow into my body, holding tight to the album. Mom grabbed the cover and pulled; I stood my ground. Footsteps reverberated up through the hole in the floor, inches from both of our feet.

"You had her for nineteen years, and I never even got to meet her!" I said. "I'm not going to lose it! Why can't you just trust me, for once?"

"You are not going to risk one of the last things I have of my sister," she shrilled.

"Anne?"

A head of black hair flashed at the bottom of the stairs. Mom glanced down, seemingly registering for the first time just how close we were standing to the edge of the hole. Her hands fluttered open, and I staggered back, album clutched securely to my side.

"Careful—"

Mom reached out to urge me away from the trapdoor, and I shied away.

Ivy pulled her shoulders up into the attic, a hand braced on the floor between me and my mother. Mom dropped her arm all at once, looking down at Ivy.

"Are you guys good?" Ivy asked.

"Of course. We didn't mean to wake you," my mother said. "Dell just couldn't sleep."

Her voice sounded rough, not quite managing the pleasant tone she usually aimed at Ivy.

Ivy looked between us, her eyes lingering on the photo album.

"Okay," she said.

"Can you move back?" I asked. "I'm going to head down."

Ivy ducked away. My mother said my name, but I ignored her, tucking the album firmly against my side. Once I made it down the stairs, I headed for the bedroom door, where Ivy waited, casually curious. The stairs thumped as my mother came after me.

"Dell," she said. Caught my shoulder. "I'm sorry, I'm just—I just want it to stay safe. You can take it to your room for a couple days if you want. Please just be careful with it." To Ivy, she said, "Make sure she doesn't stay up all night looking at it, okay?"

Ivy gave a little salute.

"Did you hear me and Mom upstairs?" I asked once we were alone in our bedroom.

"No," Ivy said. She seemed softer, sleep-rumpled, with her perfect, silky hair gone bristly and tangled on one side, like one of those plants covered in burs. "I don't know what woke me. I just knew you were gone."

"Oh," I said.

I waited for a snarky follow-up, a joke at my expense to cover up the weird vulnerability of that statement. But Ivy only stepped closer.

"Breathe," she said. Her voice seemed to come from the bottom of the lake, the bite of it softened, muddled.

"What?"

"You're freaking out. Come on, I know you can breathe. I showed you."

She reached up suddenly. I flinched, but her hand didn't form a fist, or deliver a shove. She just brushed a chunk of sweat-sticky hair out of my face.

"I'm breathing," I said.

Ivy just kept looking at me, eyes shifting from her hand on my temple to my eyes. The darkness in the room had formed a cocoon around us. Something in her face changed, an up, a down. Then her hand was gone, and she was stepping away, leaving me cold.

She crawled back into her bed as if nothing had happened—not that anything had, of course.

"I'm going to look through this a little," I said, gesturing with the photo album.

"I don't care what you do," she said.

"You won't tell?"

"I. Don't. Care. What. You. Do. I just wanna sleep."

In the daytime, her apathy would've felt like an insult. Here, it was a gift. I was almost touched.

"Okay."

In bed, I pulled the covers up over my head and turned on my flashlight, the burned leather shining fierce under the beam. I opened the cover, and Julie smiled up at me.

In photos alone, you seemed more alive than anyone I had ever met in real life.

You were always in action—jumping, climbing, streaking out of the frame as a blur of motion, caught mid-laugh or mid-sentence. There were photos of you with your track and baseball teams, photos of trophies with your arms raised in triumph. It looked like you liked moving around as much as I did, Julie.

As I flipped through, I remember a thought appearing like a lighthouse in the darkness in my head: maybe it was okay that

I was nothing like my mother if I was like someone else in my family. Maybe this was why I kept seeing you everywhere—maybe this was what you wanted to tell your niece.

There were a lot of pictures of you with my mother, grinning and swimming and posing together. I paused at one where you were looking at the camera, your arm around Mom's shoulders. Mom's head was turned up toward you like a flower searching for sun. I wanted to reach inside the photo and pluck you out, steal you away for just a moment so I could know how you made my mother look that happy.

The photos cut off as you got older, with none showing your early years as an adult. Was that just a product of you ducking away from the camera in Grampa's hands, protesting the embarrassment of it? Or was that when my grandparents had decided you were a shame to the family, someone they didn't want to document? There were no photos of you with dyed hair or piercings or the usual teenage trappings that parents got mad about. So what had you done to warrant being erased from all future retellings of the past?

A spread near the end contained photos that had clearly been taken on the same day, by inexpert hands. Joe was in most of them, sandwiched in the middle of a pile of teenagers, you sprawled by his side and laughing. He looked strange as a teenager—somehow less like his daughter, as if he'd changed to match her only once she was born. One picture took up a whole page—you tucked in between a redheaded boy and a blonde girl whose right arm ended at the elbow. It was the same woman I had been left with as a child—Lucy—those two times my mother and I were in town for my grandparents' funerals, but I didn't recognize the boy. The three of you grinned at each other, not the camera, and the shadow of the trees above you cast shades of blue and purple over the whole thing. In the corner, someone had written "Verne, Lucy, and me" in clumsy block letters.

Across from the big photo was a smaller one of the same three, you smiling at the blonde girl and redheaded boy as they cackled at some unknown joke. I pulled it out, running my fingers around the edge. Trying to picture what kind of camera took the photo. One of those big-lensed ones that Christopher carried around? Did these pictures have to be hung in a darkroom like laundry, dripping and pinned? On a whim, I turned the photo over.

Cursive writing this time. Scrawled at the bottom, hasty.

I want, all the time, way too much. I'm going to hell I'm going to hell I'm going to hell.

Part Three

THE APPARITION
and ANNE

Chapter 10

It kind of puts things into focus—stumbling through a forest in the dark, chasing redemption and ghosts and love gone misshapen like paper left out in the rain. It makes things clear. Makes a person realize that they need to stop ignoring what's really going on and actually deal with stuff.

"So, I think I'm being haunted."

On the other end of the phone, Paul made a distracted hum. Then, "Say that again?"

I was in my room, supposedly taking a bathroom break from garbage duty in the forest. Cross-legged on the bed, I fanned out a semicircle of photographs, all taken by my hand. Square cutouts of forest, sun, faces. Snatches of my mother and Ivy with water and leaves shining in the distance.

"I keep seeing my aunt everywhere," I told Paul. "Like, glimpses of her in the water and stuff. And I've been having the same dream almost every night, where I'm stranded on the island by my mother."

I had so many photos of the island, but it was impossible to tell if my dreams had gotten the layout right; there was the cab of the truck and something that could've been a coatrack near it, but mostly it was a mishmash of color and shape, bubbling under the sunlight.

I inspected the photos one by one, looking for white streaks, smudges, unexplainable glows.

"A spirit only sticks around if they have unfinished business, right?" Paul said. "Do you know what that could be?"

I thought of my gram refusing to speak of her, of Joe and my mother's awkward avoidance of Julie's relationships with her parents. I thought of my mother running into the lake, convinced that our family's things had been dragged out and abandoned on the island.

"Not yet," I said. "But I'm going to figure it out."

The morning after the lake debacle, Ivy and I had woken up to find the trapdoor folded neatly back into the ceiling. Two hours into forest cleanup, my mother had casually dropped that she didn't want us to get "distracted" and that it was more important to clean and learn to swim than to go through old things.

I hadn't pushed back. I'd gathered garbage and followed Ivy and my mother down to the water hole as they chatted like best friends. I'd let Ivy demonstrate different arm strokes and leg movements under the silk of the water while my mother occasionally yelled pointers from the sidelines. I had played along with all of this over the past few days. And all the while, my mind was elsewhere, chasing after a girl in baseball socks, who looked so much like me.

"Has your mother or Ivy seen the ghost, too?" Paul asked.

"No," I said. "I think if she's trying to send a message, it's for me. I just don't know what it is yet."

The problem was, if I was going to solve this mystery, there was another mystery I needed to crack first.

Ivy.

*

You'd think that jerking off in the same room as somebody while they're also jerking off, and you both know that both of you know about that, would have to fundamentally change something. Either make things so uncomfortable that you never look at each other again, or bond you together as best friends for life in some sort of weird, bodily fluids pact. But somehow, it hadn't done either of those things.

We hadn't talked about it again after the first time. Like the swimming lessons, it happened some days and some days it didn't—though, unlike the swimming lessons, it was just for me and her, the only thing my mother wasn't involved in. There was an unspoken rule that you didn't ask or try to set it up—that would be weird. But if someone needed to touch to sleep, the other person could do the same, and there was no need to hide it. It was strangely freeing in a way I knew I would never be able to explain to Paul or any of my other friends from school.

In the daytime, nothing was as simple. Ivy still seemed to want to be my mother's best friend, and my mother still wanted me and Ivy to be best friends, and those two things didn't really go together.

But we'd made a deal. If Ivy taught me to swim, we would go out to the island together. And I had a feeling that whatever we found there would be the key to unraveling what had really happened to Julie all those years ago, and why she was sending me these clues. Was that something I wanted Ivy to be part of?

How do you trust someone with a ghost-hunting mission if you don't understand who they are?

*

I met Ivy's little brother the first time Mom and Ivy and I all went into town together. The trip was ostensibly to get more garbage bags and gloves, but then my mother casually said, "Why don't we duck into Terry 'N' Raider's, give Dell a taste of that free pie on Sundays deal," and there was Joe, with a pint-sized, skinny little growth at his side, clinging to his hand for dear life.

The trip into town started off with my mother narrating everything as we drove down the main road. I hadn't been in my mother's hometown in daylight since Gram's funeral, and Mom had been too quiet then to show me around. This time she kept pointing things out through her open window.

She made sure we noticed the bowling alley and the skating rink and the town's single pizza place, where a man was crouched outside, nailing new boards to the staircase leading up to the door. She pointed out an old gas station that was now a restaurant and told us that the Foodland used to have a deli section but had since become more of a "glorified convenience store."

"And there's the library," Mom said as we passed a tiny brown building with a rusted O.P.P. sign. "Used to be a police station, but now it has books in the basement."

"I remember," I said, so faintly I didn't think my mother heard me. I'd spent a lot of time with Lucy, the librarian—who I now knew had started out as Julie's friend, not my mother's—back when the funerals were going on. The curtains on the library were still the same pale blue as they'd been the day Gram was put in the ground.

We passed two churches, one on the edge of town, and one smack dab in the center, towering over everything around it.

"That's the Pentecostal church," my mother said. "So many Sundays there."

"Wait, you were actual, church-going Christians?" I asked. We did Christmas and Easter and stuff, but when it came to actual religion, my mother had always been staunchly agnostic.

Her shoulder jerked up and down. Her hand eased up the side of the steering wheel. "I suppose."

"So what, Gram and Grampa were, but you were never really into it?" I said. "What about Julie, was she super religious?"

"Ah, here we are," my mother said, pulling the car over. "We can chat more about that later, Dell."

We stopped in at a general store where the store manager recognized Mom, called her "Susan and Anthony's girl!" We picked up garbage bags and more cleaning spray and the right film for my camera—Mom placing it on the counter with a smile sent my way, back in "appease Dell" mode after our fight.

"Spitting image of her aunt, isn't she?" the manager said as he rang us up, gesturing to me. "What a shame that was."

I glanced at my mother. She kept her gaze on the shopping bags, smiling vaguely.

"Yes," she said.

We put everything into the trunk of the car and walked down the main street, under the single, blinking traffic light, toward a white gabled building in the distance, the only place where there seemed to be any cars in the parking lot. As we crossed another dead intersection, the edge of a huge building came into view around the corner of a house.

"Is that your school?" I asked Ivy.

"Yup," she said. "Good old West Central. It looks like a shithole, doesn't it? Sorry, Anne."

It did kind of look run-down—a brick-red box with gray windowsills and some gray pillars visible at the side.

My mother had explained that the high school served a bunch of little towns spread out across the county, dotted in between open farmland and factories. That was how some kids had grown up in the town and some hadn't, how the town's population doubled between 8 a.m. and 3 p.m. during the school year, and how the local Dairy Queen cut their staff every summer because they didn't have packs of teenagers for the lunch rush anymore.

As we passed the front of the school, a yellow bus pulled up behind us. My mother had gotten ahead a little—I'd been lingering by the gate, trying to picture Ivy there. Ivy groaned and ducked around me so my body shielded hers.

"Summer school kids," she explained. "Can we walk faster?"

A pack of students oozed out of the wheezing bus doors. A boy with a snout-ish nose and a red baseball hat caught sight of us and paused on the sidewalk.

"Hey!" he called. "Little Principal!"

Ivy gave him the finger. "Hey, asshole!"

My mother slowed, realizing she'd lost us. She turned around.

The boy laughed, his mouth open and throat moving up and down like a deployed jack-in-the-box.

"You here for some extra learning?" he said. "Your dad didn't make sure you passed?"

"Oh, no, he did," Ivy replied. "I'm just here to watch you losers arrive. Bet you failed math on purpose 'cause you're too much of a wimp to help your dad kill pigs."

She made a confusing but clearly obscene gesture, snarling. Another boy snorted, elbowing the one who'd spoken. "Ouch, Parker."

"It's a pig farm, not a slaughterhouse," the boy said. "We raise 'em. Wouldn't expect you to know the difference, though; don't you guys just eat, like, raw meat?"

"Excuse me?" My mother stepped in front of Ivy, and Parker's face changed—he clearly hadn't registered that an adult was in earshot. Mom still looked shockingly young until you met her eyes. "What did you just say to her?"

"Nothing," Parker mumbled. "Gonna be late."

He and his friend hustled into the school.

"Do people talk to you like that all the time?" my mother asked Ivy.

"No, he's just a dick," Ivy said. "Sorry, sorry, I didn't mean to swear again."

A group of girls got off the bus and waved at Ivy. They looked like they were about to start heading toward us when she made a quick throat-cutting motion and turned away from them. "Can we keep going?" she said. Her friends shrugged and followed the pack into the school.

Ivy didn't seem happy that my mother had stepped in. In a way, I got it. Ivy could've come out on top if she'd just been allowed to finish the fight herself. But now she'd been made the victim, someone who needed to be defended. It felt weird to understand that while also knowing that I could never understand what it was like to have racist shit thrown at me, to have to learn how to fight back against that kind of viciousness. I thought back to when we first met, the assessing look in her eyes. Maybe she hadn't been measuring me to see if I passed an imaginary coolness test, as all my insecurities had screamed at me—maybe she was just assessing whether I was going to treat her like a person or the way people like Parker did.

We continued to Terry 'N' Raider's, a low-slung country house that had been turned into a combination gift shop and bakery. Colorful scarves and tiny bottles of perfumes and boutique cleaning supplies adorned the shelves for a cluttered, warm atmosphere. It looked like a witch's shop run by a witch who listened exclusively to Shania Twain and knitted in her spare time.

Ivy had been quiet for the rest of the walk over, but as soon as we stepped into the shop and she caught sight of the little boy sandwiched between Joe and the glass counter in front of the frozen custard pies, she lit up.

The kid turned before any of us could say something, like he'd sensed her. He let go of his father's hand and Ivy barely had time to drop into a crouch before he had hurled himself into her arms, grinning like mad.

"Hey, kiddo," Ivy said. She put a hand on the back of his neck and shook him, like a mother cat wrestling with a kitten. His hair was slightly lighter than hers, dark brown instead of black, but they had the exact same eyes.

"Jamie, I'm guessing?" I said to Mom lightly, trying to hide my surprise. He was younger than I'd pictured—couldn't be older than eight. This kid was the reason Ivy couldn't stay in her own house and had to stay with us? Neither my mother nor Ivy had mentioned his age to me, but I'd kind of expected a surly teenager, six feet tall and burning with hatred. Someone like that boy we had run into outside of the school—someone who would push Ivy away, not cling to her like this.

Joe sidled over and pecked my mother on the lips. We meandered as a group over to the counter, where pieces of melting pie were lined up on paper plates. The woman behind the counter recognized my mother as well, and they chatted for a moment while I tried to decide who I should be eavesdropping on. Ivy's face was all weirdly indulgent and loose as Jamie talked a mile a minute, but my mother's lips pinched in at the corner in a way that meant she was chewing the inside of her cheek, anxious. Both conversations were distracting.

I accidentally made eye contact with Joe, and he smiled at me, awkwardly.

"This is your daughter?" The woman behind the counter looked from Mom to me, and I nodded. She seemed to be around the same age as my mother. Her eyes were shrewd under a pair of hyper-plucked eyebrows.

"Looks like you did all right then, Annie," she said. "Some had their doubts but not me."

My mother flashed her teeth. It wasn't a smile.

We sat out on the patio with our slices of pie, Jamie sandwiched between Joe and Ivy. Jamie stared me down over top of his brownie, suspicious (he didn't like pie, apparently). He'd clammed up now that he was across the table from two strangers.

"This is Adele," Joe said. "She's Anne's daughter, and she's almost the same age as your sister."

"Dell," I said. "Only one year younger."

Jamie nodded and whispered something to Ivy, which made her laugh.

"He says you look a lot younger than that," she said.

"That means I'll look younger than you by a lot when we're both, like, fifty," I said. "So I don't think that's a bad thing."

When Jamie laughed, he revealed a missing front tooth. Ivy looked at him like Paul looked at his kid sisters—like he was so cute she wanted to squeeze him until he popped.

Joe was coaching a kids' baseball team this summer that Jamie was playing for, and he talked at great length about how good Jamie was getting "after only two practices!" When my mother or Ivy asked Jamie a question, he would cup his hand to his sister's ear to whisper his answers, which she'd repeat to the table at large. I kept expecting Ivy to roll her eyes or get tired of it. She never did.

The apple pie was cloyingly sweet, sticking jealously to my teeth.

I ate more slowly than the other two kids. Joe and Mom had

started talking about some book he was reading when Jamie sprang off the bench and darted around the patio in between the picnic tables, Ivy hot on his heels. She would pretend to get just close enough to catch him, and then exaggeratedly fall or snatch at the air behind his back. Finally, she grabbed him in a bear hug, snapping her teeth by his face as if she was going to bite him. He laughed and protested, struggling half-heartedly against her grip. They spun around and around.

I kept catching my mother sneaking glances at them and wondered if she was thinking of her own sister. A terrible loneliness seized me.

"I need the bathroom," I announced. Joe had been mid-sentence, and he stumbled to a halt to give me directions.

Julie met me in the reflection above the sink, and I didn't shy away.

"I'm not hiding from them," I told her. My voice sounded like it came from underwater, which felt appropriate.

When I came out of the bathroom, I drew to a halt at the sight of Ivy kneeling by her brother only a few feet from me. I hid behind a display of loose clothing.

"Dad said I should probably not tell my mom I saw you today," Jamie said quietly. His voice was as little as he was.

"Did he?" A hint of familiar sourness leaked into Ivy's tone. It vanished shockingly quickly when she spoke again. "He's just being smart. Think of it like we're secret agents, having clandestine meetings."

"What's *clan-des-tin* mean?"

"No idea."

Their laughter was soft and faded quickly.

"Why doesn't she like you anymore?" Jamie said.

"We have a different opinion on something."

"I bet you're right about it."

"Are you kidding? Of course I am. But she's your mom. She's trying to protect you or something."

"You're not scary."

"Sure about that?"

He burst into high-pitched giggles. Through the thin threads of the cotton shirt hanging in front of me, I could see that she was tickling him, driving his shoulders up high by his ears. He fought her off and hugged her again.

"You're way not scary," he said.

"Okay, you caught me. I'm not scary at all."

"Does she know that?"

"Your mom?"

"No, the—" Jamie gestured toward the doors to the patio. Me, I realized. He was talking about me.

"'Course not," Ivy said. "That's our secret. I have a reputation to uphold."

"She's nice."

Ivy shoved his shoulder, making him rock back on his heels. "Okay, kid, you can shut up about that right now. You think you know everything—you're not even in double digits yet."

I never found out what it was Jamie thought he knew, because Joe came into the shop looking for them, and I had to slip back into the bathroom to make sure I wasn't discovered.

Seeing Ivy with her brother was like seeing a different person entirely. The sharpness was whittled down. It left me feeling like I'd missed a step and had stumbled into a different world, one where I wasn't sure I was welcome.

✳

Later, when we were back at the cottage, Ivy suggested to my mother that they sit out on the porch again.

"We could try painting the sunset this time," she said.

"Drawing was pretty relaxing the other day," my mother replied, smiling a little sheepishly.

It was clear I wasn't meant to be a part of this, but Mom insisted I come out all the same. Ivy got out her watercolor sketch pad and ripped out pages for us. She set a cracked, well-used palette of colored disks on a stool, three glasses for rinsing crowding together behind them. As her and my mother's paintbrushes dipped in and out of them, wisps of color spread out into the water.

I stared at my paper. A drop of watery red made its way slowly to the end of my paintbrush's bristles and dropped into the center, ruining it as surely as blood on underwear.

"I think I'm going to call Paul instead," I said.

"Are you sure, honey?" Mom said. "You haven't even tried."

"Sorry."

I left my paintbrush in one of the water glasses and skulked back inside.

Paul could only talk for around fifteen minutes before he was called to supper, and he spent most of that time venting about Steven.

"He keeps pacing around upstairs and having whispered conversations with my mom," Paul said. "He was supposed to just be home for a visit, so I don't know why he's still here."

"Have you tried asking what's bothering him?"

Paul mumbled an excuse then rushed on, asking how things were going with Ivy—a question I wasn't really sure how to answer.

"We've had a couple more swimming lessons and stuff," I said. "I don't know . . . Before, she was obviously just pretending to care about stuff I said in front of Mom so that Mom would like her. But now, it seems like sometimes she does want to know me just—just because."

"Maybe she actually wants to be friends," Paul said.

"Maybe," I said. "I miss you."

"I'll come visit once you've learned to swim. There. Incentive to keep going."

He sounded distant. He'd sounded distant the last couple times we'd spoken, getting harder and harder to reach through the digital waves between us. What if he really was gay, like Natasha had guessed, and he was starting to realize it? I wasn't there to support him. Did he think I'd be an asshole if he told me? Did I give off homophobic vibes?

"You suck," I said. "You're not just using me as an excuse to escape your brother, are you?"

"You caught me. You're one hundred percent right. My summer sanity relies on your swimming skills. You gotta save me, man!" Big voice, big jokes—Paul was probably fine. He was just far away, and that was throwing me off.

When I got off the phone, I looked out the window, craning to see the porch. Ivy and my mother still sat side by side, hands moving like witches casting spells. Ivy smiled up at Anne, open and easy, as my mother gestured with a paintbrush, clearly in the middle of some story. They looked happy.

The window was too low for me to see the sky properly, just the edge of the trees, so I didn't know what it was about it that was so special for them to paint. It was probably beautiful, but I stayed inside—went back upstairs and worked out an itch on my kitten sheets, straining with my hand between my legs until I was finally, gloriously, thinking of nothing at all.

The next day, a watercolor was taped up on the wall next to my mother's first drawing from the porch. It was a rough sketch of purple and orange sky over trees, sun blazing in thin strips of color. I recognized my mother's work. But there was no picture by Ivy to accompany it.

As a kid, whenever I felt like I didn't understand my mother, I'd look closely at her drawings—search for frustration in a heavy line or calm in a sweep of the flat of the lead. I wanted to understand Ivy like that. But if she had put anything of herself into whatever she had painted with my mother, I had no way to pick that out. The wall was empty, and I was no closer to understanding her.

Chapter 11

The summer advanced on us, and we advanced through the trash.

We hauled bulging bags of sweating plastics and moldy paper though the forest to rest them against the side of the cottage. We combed through the trees to find wrappers and cigarette butts. We pulled slimy clothes and indistinguishable objects from the shallows. Slowly, the land began to emerge from underneath Roger's hands. And still the island sat in the middle of the lake, a distant symbol of how much we still had to do.

Every day we spent at least a couple hours cleaning up and at least an hour swimming in the water hole. I learned how to tread water. I learned how to doggy paddle. I learned that my mother got freaked out by seeing either of us practice a dead man's float, so Ivy and I only tried it once.

Despite stuff like that, Mom got more comfortable leaving us alone at the house, seemingly confident that I wasn't going to immediately sink if I fell in the lake and that superhero Ivy could swoop in and grab me if anything went wrong. Sometimes, my mother would bring snacks to Jamie and Joe's baseball practice. Every time she left, she would make some sort of probing joke about what Ivy and I talked about when we were alone.

"Is it that Twilight trilogy?" she said once. "Dell loves those books; she used to talk about them so much. Are you batting for Edward's team or—who was the other boy? James?"

"That's not how you say it," I groaned. Ivy looked between the two of us, clearly trying not to laugh.

"I don't bat for either of their teams, Anne," Ivy replied.

"Let me guess, you're one of those pretentious people who didn't even read them but think they suck?" I said.

"Doesn't her vampire boyfriend watch her when she sleeps? Seems a little creepy." She stuck out her tongue at me. I whacked her on the arm, smiling despite myself. My mother looked absolutely delighted.

Ivy's good humor usually didn't last once Mom left for the practice, though. Apart from that one afternoon, she hadn't had a chance to see her brother again. She would nod understandingly at her father when he explained why Jamie couldn't join us, or where Jamie was going to be spending the day, and would seem completely fine with it until she turned away, scowling. I wanted to ask about it, ask whether this friction with her dad was related to her issue with Jamie's mom, but I didn't know whether Ivy and I had progressed to the point where I could poke at sore spots.

Another addition to our routine was Ivy and Mom drawing or painting together after dinner. Every night, my mother would invite me, looking hopeful and foolish with her arms full of art supplies.

"No thanks," I'd say.

"This is the best time to call Paul anyway."

"Do you really need to phone him so often?" Mom said. "You can always chat to me and Ivy. I mean, Ivy's another girl, so I'm sure she'll understand things that Paul won't."

"He's not an alien, Mother."

Mom continued to hang her daily drawings in the living room, but Ivy kept hers hidden in a folder on her side of our room. I had no idea what was so horrible about them that I wasn't allowed to see. I didn't want to ask her and break the truce we'd settled into since the swimming lessons started. I liked our truce.

"She was a drug runner," Ivy said.

"No," I said.

"She grew weed in the forest. Like, pot weed."

"No! Don't you need special lights for, like, weed plants or something?"

"What?"

"In documentaries they're always grown in basements with all this weird lighting, I don't know."

Ivy was sprawled on the floor in between our beds, facing a portable fan. It was too hot to be working outside, according to Mom, so we were stalled on the cleanup. I was sitting at the foot of my bed, Julie's photo album out again. With no computer, what else was I supposed to obsess about?

"What documentaries are you watching?" Ivy arched an eyebrow. "Okay, fine. She . . . smoked weed outside the church and accidentally lit a priest on fire."

"Why are all of your guesses drug related?" I said. "Also, I thought only Catholics had priests."

"You were the one who told me you think there's some sort of mystery around your aunt," Ivy said. "I'm just trying to help."

"My grandparents hated her," I said. "And never talked about her. My mother says she loved her, but she also never talked about her. So, like, what great shame did she bring to the family?"

"Shoplifter."

"That doesn't seem like enough."

"Depends on what you steal."

"I wish I could just ask my mom. Just be super straightforward about it."

"Why don't you?"

"You saw what happened last time she had to think about Julie before she was, I don't know, ready to face it."

What I didn't say was that the Nancy Drew of it all was kind of keeping me going. As the days passed, the closer the end of summer felt—when I'd have to return to school and settle into my new role as class laughingstock. Whenever my brain swerved anywhere near that thought, it felt like I was about to skid off the road into an ocean. Ivy, of course, didn't have to worry about stuff like that. She'd be away at her cool art university.

I'd already turned over all the photos in your album by now, looking for more secret messages from you, but there was nothing on the backs of any of them. So I just shuffled through the pages again and again, trying to glean extra information from the logos of the baseball shorts clinging to your legs, the blurred churn of your arms in action shots. I had hints about what had been wrong with you—whatever made you a mismatched part of the family in your parents' eyes, the way I was in mine. Maybe you were just too loud, too much, not respectful enough at church or something. But none of my theories were definitive enough to bring to my mother for confirmation.

"Maybe your aunt was a mean person and our parents just don't want to tell us," Ivy said. "Maybe she was a bully or something."

"No way," I said. "If she was anything like me, she got picked on, not the other way around."

"You know, I want to say I'm surprised, but I'm really not."

I threw a Polaroid I'd taken of some dandelions at her, and it wibbled its way through the air to rest harmlessly on her arm. "Shut up."

I looked back down at Julie's album then at the stack of photos I had taken, which I had laid out next to the album. I was just thinking of changing the topic, maybe bringing out my second-hand mp3 player to trade musical tastes with Ivy now that we were something approximating allies, when she spoke again.

"Did you ever have any trouble with boys?"

I froze.

Hunched over the photos as I was, with Ivy lying down somewhere behind my right shoulder, I couldn't see her face. The black hole threatened, and for the millionth time, I saw those pictures in my head, hemmed in by a computer screen, pale arms and legs and disgustingness. I thought of the hours the pictures had been up and the reach of the Internet to anyone who typed in the right keywords. The corners of my vision started to turn gray.

"What do you mean?" I heard myself ask.

"If you had trouble with bullies when you were a kid, I wondered if you ever had any guys bug you. In my experience, they're much worse than girls for that stuff."

Bullying. She meant regular old bullying. I stared down at the grain of the wood and breathed.

"Nah, it was mostly girls for me," I said tightly. "My elementary school friends abandoned me in high school because I wasn't cool enough for them suddenly, you know, it was a whole thing."

"That sucks."

I shrugged. The fan coughed. There was a thwack—Ivy hitting it, probably—and it sputtered back into its regular churn. I took a deep breath and turned to Ivy, who was sitting up now.

"What happened to you?" I asked.

"Nobody looks like me at my school, and I'm the principal's kid, so." She flopped back down. "It's not important. I just thought you should know you can tell me stuff if you want to."

"You don't even really like me," I said.

Ivy didn't deny it. "Makes me even safer, doesn't it?"

I could tell her about Christopher, I thought. Ivy wasn't like my mother—she wouldn't shrink me under a laser of disappointment and ask me "How could you be so stupid?" Ivy had to wash her sheets for the same reasons I did.

It surged up my throat like nausea. I was just opening my mouth when my mother's voice echoed up the stairs. Ivy's head whipped away from me to the door.

"Yeah?" she called back.

"Does anybody want to be my absolute favorite girl and help out with food?" Mom yelled.

"Coming!" Ivy hopped to her feet, pausing only to turn the fan toward me before she left. I was glad for it—my face was suddenly unbearably hot.

*

After supper, Ivy and my mother vanished to paint on the porch again, and I went back upstairs, fighting a weird, formless wave of despair. It snuck up on me sometimes, this sucking sensation of loss, like I'd been walking along fine and then stepped onto a pile of leaves hiding a huge pit in the ground, plummeting like Team Rocket in all those *Pokémon* episodes I devoured as a kid. And there at the bottom were all the things I'd been avoiding.

I hadn't told Ivy, but I did have "trouble with boys" before Christopher. Growing up, I was the kind of awkward that made me social poison for boys. If it got out that I had a crush on someone, that boy would be a joke for days. "Ew, Dell likes you? Are you going to be her boyfriend? Are you going to go on dates?" So even if that boy had acted totally okay with me before, the only way for him to distance himself was to loudly declare how gross I was, how he would never, not in a million years, want to kiss me. I couldn't be mad at them. I understood I was on the lowest rung, that they just didn't want to be dragged down there with me.

It was why I'd been so relieved when I got to high school and could—sort of—reinvent myself. It was why Christopher's attention felt like a gift from a god. Thinking about his smile now made my throat close up. I'd told him about my grandparents dying. He'd told me about his parents' divorce. I'd unfolded my body alongside his on a grassy hill and heard his heart beating under my ear as he held me. And then he'd ripped the world out from under me. Flattened my body into two dimensions and given it to other people.

I didn't want to be thinking about it again. If I did, I would have to think about how my mother hadn't talked to me about it at all outside of screaming at me. I would have to think about how she was downstairs with Ivy, chatting happily. I would have to remember how she didn't want to hear about Christopher, didn't care about me.

No. I wasn't going to spiral. I sat on the floor, shuffling through my Polaroids again. Surely, I thought, there was something that I'd missed, some clue of ghosts and the past to distract me; surely there was a photo I just hadn't looked close enough at—

And then, in a flash, I remembered that first set of photos I took the night Ivy and I fought on the hill above the island. I had brought them from home, but they were in a separate box stuffed under my bed with my luggage. I groped blindly under the bed, batting the box out, then dumped the photos on the floor.

There, on top of the stack—the photo I'd taken of the island in the darkness. The picture was almost totally black, but right in the middle, where the island was visible as a darker smudge of black: a tiny white glow. A sign, like a light seen from the top of a tree, a face in the water, words on the back of a photograph.

I was standing before I even realized I'd decided to, heading for the stairs. I had to show Ivy. I almost ran down the steps, heading through the living room into the kitchen, heading for that closed front door.

And then I heard my mother say my name.

*

When I was in Grade 10, the city tried to cut down an old tree growing in the traffic island across from my high school, and Paul and I had joined a group of environmentalist kids to chain ourselves to it and protest.

My mother had to leave work early to come and deal with me. She wasn't allowed near the site at first, but I could see her from afar, standing out clearly in a polka-dotted sweater while she argued with the principal and a man in a hard hat. Paul was practically vibrating with laughter beside me.

"She's going to murder us!" he'd said gleefully. "She's going to grind you into dust!"

Paul said his parents were too busy doing important, money-making things to pay attention to the little things he did, especially since he had so many other siblings. He complained about it a lot, but I don't think he knew how easy he had it.

My mother got permission to approach us finally, stomping past construction workers and machinery to stand in front of us, hands on her hips.

I remembered it as a face-off. Dead silence for a solid minute before I burst into nervous giggles and apologies.

Apparently, my mother remembered it differently.

"And we just burst out laughing!" she was telling Ivy now.

"No way."

"Angry workers all around us, and Dell and I were just laughing! It was ridiculous. I intended to give her a hard time, because really, what was she thinking? But she just looked so determined and small up against that tree, especially next to her friend Paul, who is so much taller."

I could hear them laughing, Ivy and my mother, sitting on the porch. I stood just inside the kitchen, watching them through a crack in the door, Polaroid still clutched in my hand.

Why was she telling Ivy this story? When I was chained to a tree and my mother was laughing, I had been a little afraid. I'd thought Mom was finally having some sort of breakdown over her irresponsible daughter. It was strange to hear the story from her side. I'd always assumed that moment was on a long list of times I'd disappointed her. It should've been nice to hear I was wrong, but instead it was just disorienting.

"The two of them aren't, like, a thing, right?" Ivy asked, and I had to check back in to realize that they were still talking about me and Paul.

"No," Mom said with another laugh. Then, a bit softer, "Did she say they were?"

"She says they're just friends."

"He's a lovely boy, of course."

"The only one she's mentioned so far."

Mom sighed, audible even through the door.

"But she's doing all right?" she asked. "It seems like you two have been getting closer."

"Yeah, she's cool."

"I kept trying to get her to invite some of her girlfriends over when she started making new friends in high school, but she's never felt close enough to any of them to do that. She hasn't had a girl her age to properly share things with since she was thirteen."

"Well, as soon as she starts getting in a sharing mood, you'll be the first to know."

"Ivy, I just want to make sure she's okay. There are things she won't talk to me about, and even if I pressed—some things aren't the easiest to bring up with your own child."

I leaned closer to the door. It didn't sound like she meant Julie and the cottage, but she couldn't have been talking about—she wouldn't have told Ivy about—

"I get it," Ivy said. "It doesn't sound easy, the stuff she's going through."

My mother hummed an affirmative. I felt sick.

When they didn't say anything further, I backed away from the door, scared of discovery. I went upstairs and threw the photo of the ghost on the island onto the pile of photos, kicked at them like a child until they scattered around and under my bed. The sun was bright through the windows, filling the room with hot white light, and the shadows of trees on the wall looked like arms. In my fit, I'd pushed Julie's photo album half under the bed; I crawled under to join it, where it was dark, and I could be sure Christopher couldn't find me. Maybe it was the dust, or maybe it was just me, but my throat was so dry I could barely breathe.

Julie, with her knee-high baseball socks and fast hands—she would have liked me, I thought. You would've been like me.

Chapter 12

I was following Ivy through the forest again, eyes fixed numbly on her back. It was late afternoon, and I'd spent the morning cleaning a section of the forest by myself so I didn't have to face my mother or Ivy. Mom had driven into town to visit the hardware store for more bags and gloves, and when Ivy came to find me, suggesting we go down to the water hole, I'd gone with her on autopilot. Ivy was babbling about something, acting all chummy with little glances over her shoulder. I was terrified in a strange, almost distant way of what would happen if I looked down at myself, certain with every other step that I'd see the body from Christopher's photos, not the shorts and shirt I'd put on this morning. It didn't really matter, of course, when my mother had already told Ivy everything about him.

We were a couple minutes away from the water hole when I turned off the path and started heading toward the lake.

"Hey!" Ivy said.

I kept going.

"It's not that way!"

Ivy stomped after me, and I picked up my pace, scrambling over fallen tree trunks and branches.

"I think I'm ready to go get that boat by myself. Pretty sure I don't need swimming lessons anymore," I called back. "Thanks."

Ivy laughed. "Trust me, you do."

"Not from you."

"What?"

"It's cool that you do whatever my mom tells you to, but I don't need you checking up on me or trying to pry things out of me, so you can go back and tell her that."

I caught sight of the lake through the trees and skidded down the embankment toward it, Ivy on my heels. I broke through the tree line onto a short, stony beach. I hadn't ever seen the island from this angle—it looked farther away, but the boat was clearer than ever before, propped up on the corner nearest to shore. I tugged off my shoes and socks.

"I don't know what you're talking about," Ivy said.

"Really? So when I get in a sharing mood, my mom won't be the first to know?"

Ivy didn't say anything.

"If you were hoping for the gory details about my fucking jackass boyfriend and me, the wonder slut, guess what, you're not getting them. My mom's not getting them."

Ivy tried to speak then, but I bulldozed over her, needing to get it out before it strangled me. "I don't need the pity friendship of some girl who has no friends of her own to hang out with for the summer. You are not better than me just because my mom likes you. Clearly, she has terrible taste."

"Clearly she does," Ivy said slowly. "Because she's wasting energy worrying about a piece of garbage like you."

I turned to look at her and had to take a step back. Her face was cold, closed.

"I don't know what kind of 'wonder slut' you are, and I don't care. Get over yourself. Your mom seems to be under the impression that you're not always such a goddamn wet blanket, though, because she told me she was concerned about you. She thinks you're depressed or something, thought you might want to talk to someone like me since your only real friend is a guy named Paul, who you think might be gay, but don't know for sure because you obviously talk about nothing important on those hour-long calls you have."

Depressed? My brain clutched at the word and it escaped, slippery and horrifying as an eel.

"Maybe asking sensitive questions that invade people's privacy isn't as easy for me as it is for you."

"You think it's easy for me to have to listen to you whine? You clearly never think about anything from your mom's side. The first time I met you, you were telling her you didn't even want her as a mom. Who does that?"

When I took another step back, my foot splashed into the water; I was right at the edge.

"'Cause you'd know so much about having a mother!" I said viciously. "Yours left you."

Ivy's hands jumped at her side, just slightly, like she was thinking of punching me. She looked wholly unfamiliar now—the girl who taught me how to breathe was nowhere to be found. My body kept flushing hot in angry, terrified waves, calm only where the water cupped the back of my heel.

"Better than dragging down my mom like you do to Anne," Ivy spat. "She likes her boyfriend's daughter better than you, trusts me more than you, actually talks to me! You're just a burden—I bet if she had to choose, she wouldn't even need a coin toss. She'd throw you over for me in a second. You're the junk she has to waste all this time trying to clean up, okay? You're seriously fucking garbage."

"Maybe I am!" I shouted. "If that's the case, maybe I should just go where I belong!"

I spun around and stormed into the water, ankles, calves, and knees swallowed up fast. It got deep here quickly. I kept going anyway, eyes fixed on the island.

"Fine!" Ivy yelled. "Sounds like a great idea to me!"

I held my middle finger up behind me. I needed to get my face into the water to hide why it was so wet.

Coldness crept up my body with every step. My clothes grew heavy, plastered to the skin that was above the surface and drifting away from what was below.

"You're such a baby, throwing a fit. You're being stupid!"

"Leave me the fuck alone!" I screamed back. I glanced over my shoulder, but my glimpse of Ivy went abruptly sideways as I took another step and found nothing there.

I flailed but then got my head back above the surface. The ground had dropped off, and I was using everything Ivy had showed me to stay up. I pushed out with my feet and hands, bobbing clumsily toward the island. I was getting closer. It wasn't that far.

"Dell, get back here!"

I couldn't respond—my chest was too tight, and I was focused on trying to breathe against the pressure of the water. I was still crying because I *was* a stupid baby. The water felt kind of nice, like showers used to before Christopher, like my mother's arms used to. My own arms were burning a little. I'd never tried to swim for this long without Ivy supporting me.

Ivy was still yelling, but she was so far away that I couldn't make out words anymore, just a pleasant sort of hum in the back of my head. The island pitched and swelled in my field of vision—I had to be halfway there, at least.

I faltered, dizzy. I kicked out into the emptiness and pain burst in my right leg, caught on something solid and sharp hiding in the water. I went under.

The world slurred into blue cement around me, peaceful. The sun left pockmarks on the surface above me, and there was no breathing anymore, just the water, its urgency like arms pulling me down. It wasn't scary, the way I'd always thought it would be. I sank, and the sun got disrupted. There was a face and then a hand reaching out. It looked like a photograph.

It looked like Julie, and I opened my hand.

Time slipped, or I did, and then my face was out of the water and the water was trying to get out of me. I coughed and coughed, the world swirling. A voice was swearing in my ear.

When I found myself, Ivy was holding me together, and we were standing on something flat and cold, still in the water. I gasped for air in the cup of Ivy's throat.

"I hate you," Ivy said thickly. "Can you move your leg?"

Ivy was warm, and I was tired. She shook me, and I looked

down. My blood unfolded fluidly in the water, like clouds of dark, sheer fabric. I tried to move my leg.

"No," I gasped. "No, no, I can't."

I looked around, certain the shore would be only a couple meters away, but I found we were still surrounded by water on all sides, the island even closer than before.

"What are we standing on?" I asked.

"A refrigerator, I think," Ivy said. "You were flailing around so much, you were gonna drown us both. Thank god this was close."

A refrigerator. I looked down again and a wet laugh bubbled up out of my mouth.

"Thanks, Roger," I said. "Convenient pit stop, right?"

"Just hold on to me, all right?"

"Okay."

Ivy towed me on her back, and the island receded into the distance again. As she pulled me onto the beach, my leg bumped against the ground, sending new jolts of pain through my body. I crumpled on to the rocks, eyes closed, and tried not to throw up.

"I don't think it's that deep," Ivy said, her voice close. When I opened my eyes, she was pulling off her own shirt, leaving her in just her bikini top. She wrapped the fabric around the wound on my leg, shushing loudly when I cried out.

"We'll get you to the house, and it'll be fine," she said. "Dell? Adele, look at me."

I am, I wanted to say, but I was having a hard time focusing properly on anything. It all seemed very vague, like I was still underwater.

"Did you see her?" I asked.

"What?"

"My aunt," I said. "You didn't see her?"

Snatches of Ivy's face were fading in and out before my eyes, but from what I could see, she looked upset. Soaked to the bone and strangely fragile with her hair tangled in wet lumps on her skull, she was beautiful. There was no other word for it, and it didn't bother me to see that now, the way it normally did.

"We're getting you to the house," Ivy said.

"Don't call me Adele," I said. "I want you to call me Dell."

I leaned heavily on Ivy as we stumbled through the forest. She carried me at one point. There was no room for anger between us now, not when I couldn't move without her support.

We had just spotted the cottage through the trees when we heard the sound of tires on gravel. Ivy swore and tried to pull me faster, but there was nothing for it—we had only cleared the trees when Mom's car came around the corner of the drive and jerked to a halt.

The door flew open, and Mom lurched out, staring at Ivy's red hands and me curled over against them.

"Dell?" she said.

I reached for her.

It was a bit of a blur from there. My brain kept stepping into a different room, going somewhere quiet for long moments at a time before reopening the door back into reality. I remember my mother's face, pale and stricken. I remember my mother's arms closing safe around me. I remember my mother's voice stretched high and thin to the point of breaking, and I remember my own panic cresting before I realized it wasn't me that my mother was yelling at.

It was Ivy.

She followed us into the bathroom, trying frantically to explain while Mom washed and bandaged me. "It was my fault," Ivy was saying, as my mother tested a washcloth against the edge of my cut. My leg twitched away with no input from my brain. "I just really wanted to go in the lake. I—I made her come with me."

"Put your feet in the tub," Mom said, and I sat down on the edge so my leg could go under the faucet.

My mother squeezed the washcloth out and blood swirled down the drain. Ivy was still talking. Lying, I realized. Telling Mom that we had tried to swim to the island together—not that we had fought before I tried it alone.

"Can I—should I get something, or—can I help?"

"No! You just stay out of the way."

My mother knelt in the tub, her knees going pink. My head rested on her shoulder, the only solid thing in the world, and my field of vision narrowed to those knees and the shiny white porcelain underneath.

"I—I just thought it would be fun to try swimming in the lake for practice. It just got out of hand. You know I didn't want this to happen."

"Do I know that? I assumed—I assumed a lot of things, apparently."

Mom's voice was getting louder, echoing weirdly in the bathtub, like there were more of her all around us, and all of them were ganging up on Ivy.

"I assumed you were mature enough not to intimidate a girl younger than you—who can barely swim and is afraid of water—into going into a lake filled with trash that I forbade both of you from entering!"

My mother fumbled with a tube of something sharp smelling. She dabbed it all over my cut, where it burned.

"I assumed you respected me enough to listen when I told you it was dangerous. I told you that, as the better swimmer, you'd be responsible for making sure Dell was safe when I wasn't around. I trusted you with that and this is what you do?"

"Anne—"

"No, I'm talking right now! You're not talking, you're not saying one little thing, you understand me?"

"But I—"

"Just—just go out into the hall, all right? I don't want to look at you right now."

I turned my head slowly, just enough for Ivy to cross back into view. She looked as shattered and shrunken as I felt, slumped in the corner of our tiny bathroom, my blood still red on her hands.

"Go!" Mom yelled, and Ivy, shocked into movement again, stumbled out of the room.

For a moment, as the door was closing, I felt scared, scared like I'd been when I was slipping farther and farther underwater. Distantly, I felt sorry for Ivy, because even now, tucked warm against my mother's side, I knew how she felt.

Somewhere, a coin had been tossed, and I was the winner. But I didn't quite feel that way.

*

I stayed in the bathroom all evening, even after my mother slipped away to give me some privacy. Ivy knocked once to ask if she could come in and brush her teeth. I stared down at the red smudges Ivy's fingers had left around my ankle and said no. Ivy stood outside for another moment before I heard her footsteps moving away.

I wasn't wet anymore, wasn't cold—Mom had wrapped me in a towel and rubbed me until my skin was pink and raw—but I still couldn't seem to stop shivering. My hands were cramping for a camera shutter. For some reason, the word "take" was stuck in my head on a loop, growing louder. Take, take, take it, take it back, take her . . .

I waited until I was certain Ivy had given up and gone to bed before I left the bathroom. The bandages on the back of my leg pulled at my skin when I walked, and I leaned heavily on the wall to move up the stairs. The cottage was quiet—it was past when I should've been asleep.

I'd only just pushed open the bedroom door, revealing Ivy asleep in a jumble of bedding, when there was a creak on the floor behind me.

"Dell," said Mom.

She was leaning against her own doorway in a nightgown, her legs startlingly white and vulnerable. She beckoned for me to come closer.

I hesitated. I could feel my face crumpling, my jaw going unsteady.

"Mom," I said. "I'm sorry."

Mom shook her head and beckoned again. I stepped in closer, and Mom took my hands. The darkness made everything tighter, like a blanket tucked around our shoulders, and for a second all I could think of was being a kid in our one-room apartment and huddling together to tell stories.

"If you need me to make Ivy go home, we can do that," Mom said quietly.

I stared. "What?"

"You had a rough end of the school year. I didn't mean for the summer to be the same."

"I thought the whole point was that she couldn't stay at her own house," I said.

"It worked out better for Jamie to visit if Ivy wasn't at home," Mom said. "But I can speak to Joe, and we can figure something out. It was Ivy's idea, but I was the one who pushed for her to stay with us, so if you want, she can leave."

"You don't want her to leave, do you?"

"Did she really force you to go into the lake?"

I hesitated—should I defend Ivy's actions or uphold her lies? I shook my head, but I'd waited too long, and my mother had drawn her own conclusions.

"You are my priority, not her." Mom sighed, gazing down at our hands. "I can't go through this worry with you again. If she's going to be another bad influence, we can finish cleaning up this place on our own. We don't really need an extra set of hands at this point. I can tell her I want her to go home."

"I don't know," I heard myself say. I pulled my hands away.

There was a sour taste in my cheeks, and I realized that despite how long I'd been in the bathroom, I hadn't actually brushed my teeth. "I want to go to sleep."

"We'll talk in the morning," my mother said. She opened her mouth like she was going to say something else but then simply turned and stepped back into her room, pulling her door carefully shut behind her.

My hands were cold where my mother's had touched them. I walked back over to my room and slipped inside.

I'd closed the door and was halfway to my bed when I noticed that the sheet curled over Ivy's shoulders was shaking.

I stared for a minute then took a step closer; the floorboard made a faint protesting sound under my foot and the lump on Ivy's bed went still.

"Ivy?" I whispered.

The blankets shuddered—there was a hitching, unsteady breath, like she'd tried to keep it in but failed.

"I thought you were asleep," I said helplessly. "Mom definitely thought you were asleep."

"Fuck off," Ivy said, low and muffled.

I crossed the room and sunk to my knees beside her bed.

"I can tell her I want you to stay."

"No need to lie." Her voice sounded thick, wet. "You're finally getting rid of me, both of you. I'm sure you're happy."

My eyes were adjusting—I could make out the back of Ivy's head, poking out of her blankets, her hair snarled up on the pillow, and I couldn't look away from it. It was going to get knotted together, tangled like that.

"Why did you say it was your fault?" I said. "You didn't force me to go in the lake."

"Didn't I?"

I put my hand on Ivy's shoulder, and she tensed.

"Get off."

"Mom's just angry right now. She wouldn't have said that stuff if she knew you could hear."

"Shut up."

I needed to see her face suddenly, desperately. I pulled at her shoulder, trying to get her to turn over, but Ivy was a rock beneath my hand, immovable.

"Get your hands off me," Ivy spat.

"It's not my fault you were wrong about who she'd choose," I said.

"Seriously, shut the fuck up."

"Ivy, I'm sorry, would you just—"

I tugged at her shoulder again, and all at once the sheets burst into the air—Ivy rolled over and lunged off the bed. I tried to stand, but her hands caught my shoulders and we crashed together, tumbling in a heap. For a split second I couldn't tell if I was up or down, couldn't register anything beyond Ivy's fingers at the base of my neck, and then my head was knocking into the floor and Ivy was on top of me. My leg screamed. Bright spots fizzed behind my eyes; Ivy's weight pressed me into the ground, pinning me at the hips and stomach.

And I knew all at once that this, this was what I'd been wanting. More than the shouted words at the edge of the lake, more than the open arms of the water, I'd been waiting for the full body relief of unleashing all the viciousness I'd been storing inside me since Christopher, or maybe even before—maybe since I'd looked in a mirror as a child and understood that I was a girl who would never want things or be wanted in a normal way.

I jammed my knee into Ivy's side, turned us over, and chased her down to the floor, slamming her back as hard as she'd done to me.

"What is your problem?" I ground out. We clutched at each other. I couldn't get close enough. My leg hurt. She grunted something I couldn't understand. I pressed my face into her hair behind her ear, imagined biting until she bled.

She was stronger than me. She flipped us again, and finally I could see her face properly above me, eclipsing the whole room. Her eyes were blown huge and dark, the skin underneath gone waxy from tears, and her mouth was twisted up in an ugly shape. It was the sight of that more than our tussle that took the air from my body—I was suddenly hollowed out under her, caught and staring.

"I told you to shut up," Ivy said.

She moved to stand. I grabbed at her arms, holding her still, holding her against me. I had no idea why.

I said her name.

She surged forward and kissed me.

The world shrunk in all at once; my body went soft and shocked under Ivy's, sluggishly stupid. My leg ached and my head ached and Ivy's mouth was moving over mine like she was trying to draw me into her, take me over. Ivy shifted, got a hand up to sink her fingers into my hair, palm folding over my ear, thumb bruising at my cheekbone. I could feel the pressure of her teeth behind her lips.

She sank down, kissed harder, opened her mouth and mine with it, and I bucked up and threw her off onto the floor next to me.

"What the fuck," I gasped. My arms were shaking, one hand fisted in Ivy's shirt. My eyes were open, but the world around me was deep space dark.

Ivy's hands were over her face. After a moment she started laughing.

"What the fuck?" I repeated, and Ivy laughed harder. Her mouth shone wet.

"Still want me to stay?" she said.

Chapter 13

I did not dream of the island or anything at all.

In the morning, I forgot about my leg and almost fell over when I tried to stand, reduced to clinging to my headboard and shaking.

On the other side of the room, Ivy was curled up in the center of her bed in a pool of morning light, covers thrown off. She looked small and hard, like the stone wedged in my throat.

My mother was sitting at the kitchen table when I crept into the living room, loosely sketching on a sheet of paper already cramped with faces. I had spent long enough with my aunt's photo album now that I recognized her even from a distance; Mom drew her looking a lot more worried than she did in photos.

I was about to move closer when my mother's face crumpled in all at once, like a planet struck by a sudden asteroid. She placed a hand over her sunken expression and closed her eyes.

"What am I supposed to do, Julie?" she whispered.

Was she crying? I stepped from the living room into the kitchen; my mother looked up and then stood immediately, putting her back to me as she shuffled papers from the table onto the counter.

"How does your leg feel?" she asked.

"It's not so bad."

"It's a good thing you got a tetanus shot last year. We should change your bandages."

"Can I eat first?"

"Dell, you know how much you worried me?"

She'd left one of the drawings on the table, but when I tried to look at it, Mom yanked it away and folded it up, tucking it into her back pocket. I was starting to get a headache.

"Remember when I was convinced I was going to be an artist when I was a kid?" I said. "And then I got last in that art contest I made you pay to enter me in?"

"Not last, Honorable Mention," my mother said.

"Okay, but they lined them all up, so it was clearly in order from best to worst Honorable Mentions."

"I think they just didn't know what to do with all the ideas you had," Mom said, a smile evident in her voice. "The winners were boring. No alien abductions anywhere."

"I was a creative kid," I said sarcastically.

"You were. I always knew you were going to do great things. You've got a spark that not everyone has."

I put my head down on the table and squeezed my eyes shut. The headache was reaching the corners of my eye sockets, crushing.

"You just think that because you're my mom."

There was a rustle, and then her hands were on my shoulders, moving soothingly across my back like I was thirteen again, throwing up my guts into a silver salad bowl on a sick day, crying and spitting. I wanted to cry now, wanted to tell my mother that I was sick again, that I was pretty sure I'd always been sick, sick, sick.

"Was Julie ever jealous of you?" I asked.

"Oh, Dell, I don't know." She smoothed her hand across my shoulder blades. "Sisters can be wonderful, but they can bring a whole world of hurt you don't expect. You don't need to have one pushed on you."

I meant to say that Ivy wasn't my sister, but when I opened my mouth, it came out as "I want her to stay."

"Okay." She didn't stop rubbing my back. "Okay."

I opened my eyes and stared past the edge of the table down at my bare feet, toes curling and uncurling against the floor. *What am I doing?* I thought. *What the hell am I doing?*

The first time I kissed Christopher, it had been a roller coaster kind of scary, the type where you knew you were strapped in and safe to enjoy soaring. I felt a bit like a superhuman for the next few days, sure that anyone who saw me would know that I'd taken control of new parts of myself.

This was nothing like that. My mouth felt swollen, like I'd taken a punch instead of a kiss. Again and again I replayed it: the pressure and slide of Ivy's lips on mine, muscle memory on overdrive. It felt like my mouth no longer belonged to me, and I kept touching it just to make sure it was still there.

When Ivy finally slouched down at noon, avoiding my

eyes, my mother told her that she'd been considering sending her home to her father.

"However, Dell has said she wants you to stay, and despite what happened yesterday, I'm glad to hear it."

"Oh," said Ivy. She looked shocked, even a little upset. When she glanced over at me, I realized quite suddenly that Ivy not only hadn't expected this result but had been banking on the opposite. I felt a strange sense of victory at having outwitted her in some way, even if it had been with a move of stupid self-sabotage.

"Now that you both know how dangerous the lake really is, I expect we won't have any more problems with trying to swim in it," Mom continued. "And there will be no more wandering off into the forest without supervision or working outside of the house while I am gone. Is that understood?"

Ivy and I nodded.

"I do not want to be disappointed like this by either of you again," my mother said.

Ivy was trying to meet my eyes—I could feel it. I just kept staring at my feet.

I lay on my bed, my phone open to a blank text message to Paul. I kept typing and then backspacing: "so last night"; "i think ivy is"; "something really weird happened and"; "paul i dont know what to do, i".

"Is there anything you want to say to me?" Ivy asked from the doorway.

My heart started going double-time. I shrugged and made a noncommittal noise.

"Anything you want to tell me, then?" Ivy said.

"My leg hurts," I offered.

"Are we going to have a problem?"

"I don't care if you're . . . Yeah. No."

"You don't care if I'm . . ."

Ivy's voice was even, like this conversation barely meant anything to her at all. I could hardly focus on my phone.

"Why didn't you tell her to kick me out?" she asked.

I rolled onto my stomach, and my leg shrieked at me. I groaned into my pillow, fixing my gaze on Ivy's side of the room instead of the girl in the doorway. Her sheets made a cliffside of red flowers down the side of the bed.

"Because you wanted to stay," I said quietly.

Behind me, Ivy laughed. It sounded sad.

"You have no clue what I want." And then, "Did you like it?"

I remembered it in Technicolor: Ivy on top of me, her hands digging into my hair, the wet heat of her breath on the corner of my mouth.

"You were the one who pulled me back in. It's okay if you liked it," Ivy said. "Doesn't make you gay."

"My leg hurts."

"I'm so sorry for you."

"Mom said I needed to rest."

"Oh, well, if your mom says so, obviously I should just get out of your hair."

There was an irreverence in her voice that had never been

there before when my mother came up. Ivy walked over to her bed and pulled her sheets back on top of it, tucking in the sides and back with military efficiency.

"Are you actually . . ." I started. Ivy stopped moving.

"What?"

I waved a hand.

"A dyke?" Ivy said.

"Do people really use that word anymore?"

"I don't know. You know how many out people are at my high school? Two. Both boys."

"You're not?"

"Gay or out?" Ivy asked. "Be specific, Dollface. Saying the words won't make it contagious."

"Don't call me that." I'd made the mistake of putting Paul on speakerphone one time when I thought Ivy wasn't around. Clearly, she'd heard more than I thought.

"Right," Ivy said. "That's his nickname for you, isn't it. The not-boyfriend." She paused then flapped out her blanket with a vicious snap. "Is that it then? You've decided I can stay so you can prove to yourself that you're not homophobic, that you and Paul can still be best buds even though you've got a raging crush on him?"

"You have no idea what you're talking about."

"That's what all the straight girls tell me."

It was as good as a yes to my earlier question and something squirmed uneasily in my stomach.

"Were you trying to threaten me?" I asked.

"What?"

"Still want me to stay?" I said, parroting her words from the night before. "What was that about?"

"That wasn't a threat," she said, and she actually sounded surprised. "What, did you think I meant that I'd—assault you or something if you told your mom I could stay?"

I shrugged.

"I wouldn't have done it if it hadn't seemed like you wanted me to."

I remembered pulling her back on top of me, how singularly important it had felt not to lose her weight in that moment.

"Done what?" I said.

Ivy said my name. Said it soft, like she knew me better than I did. Then, when I stayed silent: "I meant, 'Still want me to stay now that you know I'm gay?' Lots of people don't want to have me around them once they know that."

"That sucks," I said, but it came out so soft I wasn't sure if she heard me.

Ivy finished making her bed and looked at me.

"Are you going to tell her?" she asked.

"That we—?"

"No, that I'm—" She waved her hand, mocking me.

When I was fourteen, I'd told my mother about a play we were doing in drama class that involved a homophobic dad and a gay kid, and she'd gotten very uncomfortable and said some stuff about having "sympathy" for families in "those situations," especially when they "weren't told" and it was a "shock." Another time, she had changed the channel quite suddenly when they started discussing the upcoming Pride parade on the radio; the moment had inexplicably stuck in my head for years. I didn't think she would be shitty to Ivy about this, but I wasn't a hundred percent sure, and that uncertainty felt like a fist around my lungs.

"I won't," I said. "She really didn't tell you anything about me and someone named Christopher?"

"She didn't."

"Does—does your dad know? About you?"

Ivy nodded. "Since I was, like, thirteen. He's fine with it."

"You realize he's probably already told my mom then, right?"

"He hasn't!"

Ivy's voice peaked then dropped, a thrown stone. She swallowed visibly. "He wouldn't tell anyone without asking me. I've told him that. Specifically."

"I don't get you," I said.

I closed my eyes. After a long moment, I felt a hand on the back of my leg, curving gently over my bandages. I twitched, and the hand tightened, a dull pressure.

"Does this hurt?"

I exhaled slowly. It did hurt, but it felt good in equal measure, like the weight was pushing the skin back together. I had never had very rational responses to pain.

"Yes," I said.

Ivy took her hand away, and I felt immediately cold without it.

"Sorry," Ivy said.

"It's okay."

It was quiet in the room for long enough that I thought Ivy had left, and then there was a quick breath from the door.

"Next time," Ivy said, "I'll ask."

Her footsteps receded down the hallway and then the stairs. I lay still, my heart pounding; it felt like I'd been running flat-out for the whole conversation, like I was still running. I was numb with it, on the edge of the kind of exhaustion that fuzzes your brain.

I thought of Paul's tall body, his bulk. I thought of Christopher's crooked smile, the shadows of his eyes above me, that very first kiss. I thought of actors and boy bands and Joe in a suit, bending toward my mother.

The thrum in my body twisted into something familiar, and for once, it felt like relief instead of sickness. I was still who I had thought I was.

I didn't end up sending any of the texts, but, like he knew I was keeping something from him, Paul called a few days later.

My mother's usual overabundance of caution meant I had been confined to the house so I wouldn't get my cut infected somehow. She spent a lot of time inside with me, bringing me food and tea while I lay beached in bed, talking about everything except Julie or Christopher. But whenever she went outside to clean with Ivy, I would pull out my photos and keep searching for ghosts, futile as it was.

A few days after the lake incident, my insides cramped and flexed and squeezed blood out into the toilet below me. For once, my period was welcome—the familiar feeling of being full-body-disgusting seemed right. We were out of pads, so I stuffed a wad of toilet paper into my underwear and lay on my bed with my camera while my mother drove into town to buy more. I had this weird idea that maybe I'd take a picture of the blood-stained tissue, but I was derailed when my phone rang.

Paul sounded odd. Distracted. I told him about hurting my leg but not what came after. He updated me on his job and his siblings, with none of his usual flair.

"Are you good?" I asked.

"I'm fine. Why?"

"You just sound off."

"You're one to talk. You really went into the lake? You? I know you've been learning to swim, but I had no idea you'd defeated your fear enough for a lake." He dropped his voice. "Or did Demon Daughter have a resurgence from her nice disguise and try to drown you?"

"No! She—no, she's fine."

I shifted, sliding a hand into my shorts to cup the outside of my underwear briefly. Dry. The blood hadn't leaked through the toilet paper yet.

"I've been looking up your mom's boyfriend," Paul said abruptly. "You gotta make sure you look into the background of people who might become your family. Did you know Steven's girlfriend used to go to a Catholic school?"

"What do you mean, you've been looking up Joe?"

"Well, I didn't find much, just the website for his school. They have his phone number listed on the contact page. Work phone and cell phone. I could call him up right now and question him on his intentions toward your mother."

"Please don't do that."

"Scared his intentions aren't serious, or maybe that they are?"

"Both," I said.

"I hate that serious romantic feelings have to mean marriage and babies," Paul said. "Marriage isn't love. It's just people not wanting to be alone."

"My mother's not alone. She's got me."

"Both you and Ivy now. At least for another year until you move away for university and adult life. What's she supposed to do then? Die?"

"Are you for or against the idea of marriage?" I snapped. "'Cause you keep going back and forth."

"I don't know," he said quietly. "I don't want to be alone."

I didn't really know what to say. I didn't want that either—didn't know what I wanted, or what my mother did. If she married Joe, Ivy would be my stepsister, a doubly horrifying prospect now than it had been at the start of the summer. My mother wouldn't be lonely.

I realized suddenly that I hadn't seen Ivy paint or draw with Mom since the fight. Though, of course, I'd been trying to avoid Ivy ever since that night after the lake.

"You know, it's legal in Canada," I said absently. "Gay marriage."

"That was out of nowhere." Paul laughed. "You got something to tell me?"

"Do you?"

"What? Don't be dumb."

"Why don't you trust me?" I snapped. "I tell you everything."

Not true. "But all you do these days is talk about your brother's relationship with his girlfriend, never about what's actually bothering you. And you never talk about our other friends. Did they just die? Or do they think I'm such a slut they don't want to talk to you anymore because you're still friends with me?"

Paul was silent for a moment. I pictured him sprawled on his back in his big, fancy bed, in his big, fancy bedroom, in a house full of noise and laughter. Pain twinged in my gut.

"Whoa," he said finally. "That's a lot of shit to throw at me at once. What am I supposed to say to all that?"

"Nothing, apparently."

I rang off. Threw my phone against the side of Ivy's bed, where it bounced off and skittered across the floor. Shit shit shit. I hadn't meant to say any of that.

"Dell?"

My mother's voice from the hallway. I jackknifed into a sitting position, grabbing for Julie's photo album, open at the foot of my bed—but it was too late. My mother was already in the doorway.

"I got your pads," she said quietly, holding out a box. Her eyes flicked to the photo album. "You want to go freshen up, and then we can have a chat?"

After I'd slapped on the pad in the bathroom downstairs and flushed my wad of toilet paper, I rushed back upstairs to find the attic stairs had been unfolded, and my mother was walking carefully down them, holding a box.

"Come on," she said when she caught sight of me, as if her willingly going back up into the attic wasn't the weirdest thing I'd seen all day. I followed her into my room, where she sat down on my bed next to the album.

I hovered awkwardly in the doorway.

"I thought I could bring some things down for us to look at, since climbing up into the attic on that leg might not be the best idea," Mom said. "And maybe we can go through this together."

She put her hand on Julie's photo album, and it unstuck me from my frozen place in the doorway. I rushed forward.

"Sorry, I—"

"I knew you still had it," she said. "Did I really make you so afraid when we had that disagreement in the attic?"

I shrugged. Her body sank, and then she took a deep breath, patting the bed beside her. I sat.

"Are you and Ivy all right?" she asked, popping open the folded flaps of the box in her lap.

"What?"

"You two have been acting strange," Mom said. "Her especially. I just wanted to check in. I thought you'd made up after the whole swimming incident."

"Is she here? I thought she went into town with you."

"She's spending a few hours with her dad. She'll be back later."

"We're fine," I said. Would Ivy tell Joe what had happened between us? Were they close enough for that?

"I thought you two were becoming friends."

I felt a pang of loss, remembering Ivy's smile when we were swimming at the water hole. She'd been so good at seeming genuine. Even now, when I knew all she'd wanted was information to get on Mom's good side, I still felt taken in by the memory.

"We'll be fine," I said.

Mom started to dig through the box, passing me things as she unearthed them.

A recipe book Gram had frequently referenced—"She was a terrible cook, but god, she tried"—a few unbroken plates to match the teacups, a little "magazine" that Julie and Anne had made when they were kids.

"I may have been six, but I still was better at drawing than my sister, so I did the cover," my mother said. "The back illustration, though, that's all her."

The front had some careful lettering and a bizarrely competent pen sketch of some trees. The back had a messy pencil crayon drawing of a family with two girls and a mom and a dad, clearly drawn with more enthusiasm than skill. The paper was pocket-Bible thin, stapled together. I set it aside without flipping through the whole thing, wondering if you had ever felt inferior to your sister or whether you'd always been comfortable as this girl who couldn't draw and did anyway.

A small, faded blue box inside the bigger box held a stack of photos from some sort of church bake sale, with the burnt haze of a disposable camera lending the proceedings a dark, ominous aura. Gram held court in the middle of several photos, swaddled in a red sweater under an overall dress. Her arms were always out, either handing something off or waving someone over with a brisk, unbent arm.

"You never did tell me how religious you guys were," I said, holding up a photo of Grampa standing awkwardly but proudly in front of the church as if he had designed the building. "Was it, like, scary religious? Is that why you never mentioned it?"

"They were very strict about it," my mother said with a sigh. "Your grandmother was heavily involved in the church. It was her entire social life. I've mentioned before that they had a lot of conservative views on things—obviously, I've met many Christians who are both serious about their faith and lovely, progressive people, like your friend Paul, but my parents were the type of people who sometimes used their beliefs as a license to judge others."

I flipped through the photos. In one particularly dark frame, two teenagers in matching dresses stood hunched behind a long table of cups. I realized with a shock that it was my mother and Julie, my mother smiling in a forced way, and Julie looking transparently miserable.

"Were they 'You will burn in hellfire if you do a sin' type of people?" I asked.

Honesty did not come easily to my mother. I watched it battle it out on her face.

"I don't want you to think too poorly of them. They could be very caring people. And they loved you."

"Me? They never even told me anything about themselves. I feel like they barely talked to me when they visited."

"It wasn't their way," my mother explained. "Sometimes the love you want from a person is exactly the kind they're incapable of giving. They wanted me and my sister to be the best Christian young women we could be, and they disagreed with much of how I was raising you."

"Why?" I muttered. "You're super strict."

"I'm not that strict!" my mother laughed.

"You're not?"

"Did I inspect every single book or piece of music you liked to make sure I agreed with them first?"

I wanted to mention how nervous I used to get when picking books to take out at the library and how she got angry when I minimized the windows on the computer every time she walked by me ("What are you looking at that's so bad you have to hide it from me?"), but she probably had gone through worse with her parents if she thought she had been a lenient mother. Maybe if I ever had kids I would also hurt them while I thought I was doing my best.

"Julie was into Prince," Mom said. "Which did not go over well when my mother realized what some of the lyrics were about. They had a lot of fights over that. I had to play peacemaker so many times."

"So Gram and Grampa never talked about her after she died because, what, she liked music they thought was inappropriate?"

"No, no, of course not," my mother said, her voice becoming more clipped. "Look, we haven't even touched her album."

She grabbed it and flipped through the pages until she found a photo of Julie grinning, a huge cast on her right arm, and then launched into a story about Julie slipping on the iced-over lake one winter.

"She told everyone she'd gotten hurt wrestling a space alien," Mom said. "You got your creativity from her."

"Not you?"

"I don't have the ability to come up with things like you

two. You've seen my drawings—it's nothing more than what I can see with my own two eyes."

I looked down at our hands on the photo album. My mother's palm had shorter lines in the center, and her fingers were thicker than mine. There was no part of me that really matched with her.

"Sometimes, I can't quite remember what she looks like," Mom said. Her voice was distant, her eyes fixed on the pictures. "I can never get her right when I'm drawing. There's always something wrong, something I can't quite put my finger on."

Mom closed the album so abruptly it almost trapped my hand.

"My senior project had the best portrait of her I ever did. I should never have left it here."

"We might still find it," I said. "The portraits were in a red folder, right? We found that box of Gram's placemats down by the shore the other day, so maybe more of it is out there."

Mom looked at me sharply. "Is that why you and Ivy were trying to swim to the island?"

I was thrown for a moment before I remembered that my mother still didn't know that ending up in the lake hadn't exactly been my plan.

"No," I said.

Mom hummed but didn't pursue it. The room was sludgy with heat, sweat making a home between my thighs. I had the sudden thought that my mother had no idea that I had gotten off in this bed we were both sitting on, with Ivy listening.

I shook off the sticky feeling of that image. Ivy and I had both been absolutely silent in our separate beds since the day I almost drowned.

If I couldn't tell my mother about Christopher, I definitely couldn't ask her for advice on Ivy. The very thought of it sent a tidal wave of nausea crashing through my body, tossing me off balance.

"How did this get burned?" I asked, gesturing to the distorted cover of the album. Maybe this time she would give me an actual answer.

"Your grandmother threw it in a bonfire. I fished it out."

Mom turned her hands over and drew a finger down the white patch of skin on the fleshy part of her left palm.

"You told me you got that from cooking," I said, feeling distantly betrayed for the millionth time this summer.

"We were having a cookout at the time. I didn't want to be there, but Julie had—Julie couldn't be, and my parents insisted on my company. My father tried to bring out the album, and my mother, well. She was very angry, for many reasons."

"So she wanted to destroy all of the photos?"

"I don't know what she wanted. She wasn't exactly sober at the time."

The image of my mother as a young woman on her knees in the dirt, face lit up in horror and wrist deep in flames, flashed across my mind, unreal.

"I'm sorry," I said.

My mother pressed the burn on her hand down on the burn at the top of the photo album, lining up the marks.

"Children are not meant to see their parents weak," she said. "One thing I learned from mine."

She pushed the album back into my lap and stood up.

She was a tall woman, but from this angle she seemed completely unreachable. I didn't know what to say to her; my mother had always been the strongest person I knew, much stronger than me.

"I'm sorry I tried to keep you from looking at this," Mom said. "You have as much a right as I do. We can look through some more stuff from the attic soon, okay?"

She was almost out the door when I found my voice again.

"Would Julie have liked me?" I asked.

"Yes," my mother replied. "If she had been given the chance, she would have loved you."

Chapter 14

A couple days later, Mom gave the car keys to Ivy and told us to take a night for ourselves. There was still a pull at the back of my leg when I walked, but my mother had finally agreed that I was healed enough to leave the house. Joe came to pick her up for a date and Mom told Ivy and me to take her car to the drive-in and see a movie.

There was no way to say no without arousing my mother's suspicion over the extent of the friction between Ivy and me. I smiled and thanked her. Ivy took the keys. Ivy drove with one hand on the steering wheel and the other draped out the window. The car rattled over uneven pavement, the road unspooling between the slow rise of land on either side. It was mostly dark out, but the clinging light at the horizon lent a glow to everything. I felt Ivy in the car with me the way a hammock could feel the weight of a pebble—everything about me was bent toward her.

"Have you been to the drive-in a lot?" I asked awkwardly after five minutes of silence.

"I've been going to this drive-in since I was fourteen," Ivy said. "There aren't exactly many things to do around here."

She made a sharp turn onto a gravel road, and the car spat stones into the ditch.

"Joe let you drive when you were fourteen?"

"He doesn't let me do shit. I had older friends." She cracked a smile, darting a look at me. "Once, though, I went there in a tractor with someone my age. You can get a license to drive a tractor when you're fourteen."

I had never been to a drive-in, but books and movies had taught me that people only went to them when they wanted to have somewhere to park their car and fool around in the dark, though my mother, of course, would never have made that association. Could someone fool around in a tractor? I pictured Ivy and some faceless guy kissing in the back seat of a car and suddenly had to correct the image in my head—Ivy and a girl, Ivy pushing a girl's hair out of her face and going for her neck.

It was hot in the car. I wound down the window, and wind screamed by my head.

"Have you taken girls there?" I asked.

"Yes," said Ivy. "I do have friends, just so you know."

"I meant for, like, dates," I said. "You go on dates, right?"

"Yes, Adele, lesbians do go on dates."

"Yeah, but," I started, and didn't know how to continue. How do you know, I wanted to ask, who makes the first move? How do you know how much you have to pretend to protest before you give in if you're both girls? Do girls get called sluts if they sleep with each other right away, or does it not matter?

"If you're trying to use me to do research on the gay population, you can fuck right off," Ivy said casually. "If it's something different, just say so."

I gazed out the window at a cornfield rushing by, the rows stretching impossibly long, and felt like something was unraveling in me, going ripe in my head. I wondered what it was like to get lost in a cornfield and be found again.

Was this a date?

The drive-in screen became visible long before we reached it, a pale, angular shape rising out of the corn. I unbuckled my seatbelt and leaned out the open window to see it better. The giant white rectangle stood out against the dark sky like a sail straining against wooden struts, looking for all the world like it was ready to billow and rise into the air to reveal a ship that had been hiding under the earth. There was a sudden, otherworldly magic to it, and I breathed in deeply and watched it approach.

"How is that thing even standing up?" I yelled to Ivy. She laughed.

"We all figure the owner made a deal with the devil!"

My hair whipped in my face. The car went over a pothole and I shrieked. For a moment I felt the two of us were aligned against time, teenaged and never going to die.

Ivy paid for us both when we got to the drive-in, handing cash to the speccy kid at the booth before I could even get out my wallet. Mom had given me money for this, and when I pointed that out, Ivy just said, "She's not my mother. I can decide if it's my treat or not."

There weren't many cars there. Ivy parked in the second-last row, rolled up both windows, flicked on the AC, and cranked her seat back so she could recline slightly. I copied her.

Staticky color flashed up on the screen, and the previews started. There was no sound until Ivy reached over to fiddle with the radio—suddenly, there were voices coming out that synced up with the characters on the screen.

"That's so smart," I said. "If they used speakers, everyone would have to have their windows open, even if it got cold."

"Some people still do it like that, but this makes it more private," Ivy said. "So no one can hear what's going on in each car. Unless people get really loud."

"Oh."

"Pretty sure I heard a guy breaking up with his girlfriend two cars over once."

"Oh! Right."

Ivy glanced over. "You thought I meant something different."

"No."

"You're a lot more dirty-minded than you look."

It hit me in the chest, somewhere left of the memory of Ivy calling my mother a prude.

"Do you want popcorn?" Ivy asked after a moment. "I'll pay."

"No thank you."

We fell into an uneasy silence. A woman slapped a man in the preview onscreen, and he looked strangely thrilled.

"How's your leg doing?"

"It's fine."

"I'm sorry."

"I was the idiot who went in the water."

Another moment passed. A couple new cars came in,

headlights flashing across the screen and whiting out the picture in brief sweeps. It was very dark now, and Ivy was nothing but a black shape next to me.

She reached over suddenly and turned the volume down.

"Tell me something about your home. Like, right now, if we were parked on the road in the city by your place, what would it be like?"

I closed my eyes to picture it.

"It wouldn't be this dark," I said quietly. "The sky's always got this orange glow at night, because there are so many lights still on. We're not downtown—our area is kind of for people who aren't super poor but definitely aren't raking in the bucks."

"But you guys are, like, rich."

"No, we're not," I said, surprised. "I literally slept in the same bed as my Mom for years when I was a kid 'cause we couldn't afford a second bed, never mind a place with two rooms."

"Your family owns a lake," Ivy said. "If you guys were poor, it was because your mother needed to escape her parents."

I sat with that for a second.

"I think both my aunt and my mom hated my grandparents," I said. It was weird to actually say it out loud. "Based on everything my mom has said about Julie—and everything she hasn't. And I think my mom had some sort of huge argument with my grandparents, and that's why they didn't help us at all when we finally moved to the city. But there's so much I still don't know."

"You think you don't know your family?" Ivy said. "I don't even know who my real grandparents were. All I've got is foster grandparents."

"Your dad's adopted?"

"No. He aged out, I think." She was quiet for a moment. "I don't actually have foster grandparents; I was joking. The last couple who fostered him moved away from here while he was in university."

"What about your birth grandparents?"

"Don't know who they are. I guess social services, or whatever, thought they weren't taking care of my dad properly and took him away from them. Just up and stole him."

The car was still stationary, but we had moved somehow. Taken off the brakes and rolled into something deeper, some secret place where Ivy felt safe enough to tell me something so intimate.

"Sometimes people at school would make up shit about my dad and where we were 'from' or whatever, and assume my grandparents had been killed or just left him," Ivy said. "I know they didn't want to leave him. I'm sure of it."

The way she said all that, so matter-of-fact, kind of made me want to cry—but it would've been selfish to make it about me. This was a pain that I didn't have to think about normally the way she did.

"Those kids are assholes," I said. "They don't know anything about your family—they're just trying to make you feel worthless. And you're not."

"I know, but it still bugs me." Ivy sighed. "The whole missing family thing freaks me out sometimes—like, how do you decide that someone's such a shitty mom that their kid would be better off not having them around at all? I would kill for a functional family or even just a photo album with my grandparents in it."

I didn't know what to say to that. She was right—at least I had something.

"We learned about residential schools in history class, but I didn't know the government was still taking Native kids from their families that recently," I said. "That's way more important for us to learn about than, like, the War of 1812."

"Yeah, my history teacher got kind of awkward when I asked her about the Sixties Scoop," Ivy said.

"Wait, the sixties? But your dad went to high school with my mom."

"My dad was in the tail end of it, I guess," Ivy said. "I mean, it still happens today. They just haven't updated the name."

A shiver went through me, and it had nothing to do with the AC.

"That's so scary," I said. "It's bullshit how Canada loves to pretend this stuff is all in the distant past."

"This shit just morphs," Ivy said.

"Like a Hydra." I mimed swinging a sword. "Cut one head, two more come out."

Ivy laughed, which I hadn't expected. (I hadn't been joking.) I wanted to hear her laugh more, I realized, was yearning for it like a person waiting for their favorite song to be played at a concert.

"So you guys don't even know, like, what town or province your family is from?" I said.

"I mean, I'm definitely 'from' here," Ivy said, gesturing to her face in a wide circle. "Way more than you are. You go back far enough, you're from England or something, not Ontario. But my grandparents could've lived in Alberta for all I know. I think my dad is trying to find out."

We were quiet for a second. I wanted to keep talking but didn't want to pry.

"You didn't finish describing your house," Ivy prompted.

She was stepping back from the previous intimacy. I followed her lead.

"Apartment, actually," I said. "It's pretty good. I've even got my own room. But we live near a strip club."

"Bet Anne was not happy about that."

"Oh, she fully pretends it doesn't exist. I didn't even realize what it was until I was, like, fourteen because it's one of those 'tasteful' ones that don't have giant pictures of boobs posted outside." This time, Ivy's laugh was bigger, full enough to fill the car.

"It's the fanciest building near us," I continued, bolstered. "There'd still be loads of cars and people about right now, and the Coffee Time at the corner would be open late, and there's this falafel place that never closes, so there's always at least a couple people around."

"Never quite alone," Ivy said.

"Yeah."

"You can get so alone here. I once walked down the middle of a road for two hours at midnight and didn't see anybody. No cars, nothing."

"It sounds beautiful."

"It's not bad sometimes."

"Is it lonely?"

Ivy hummed. I could see she was actually thinking about it,

trying to give me as honest an answer as she could.

"In movies and stuff, they always talk about little towns like you can't be lonely there, 'cause everyone's in your business all the time," she said. "But that just means if there's stuff about you that doesn't fit, it stands out more. Like, my dad's been taking me to the Pride parade in the city every year since I came out, and coming home after something like that always kind of sucks."

The light of the movie screen reached only the very edge of Ivy's profile, a glowing outline. I knew I was staring, but I couldn't help it. It felt like something had gotten tangled around my lungs—the image of her trapped in this one-color town, maybe. Everything I could think of to say felt too big. The one time I'd gone to Pride with Paul and Daysha, I'd just felt this strange loneliness all day, like there was plexiglass between me and the celebration, keeping me from having fun. I had the sense that everyone around me knew who they were, and I was the odd one out.

So instead I just said, "I'm sorry, that's shitty," and wanted to kick myself.

After a moment Ivy sat back, blew out a noisy breath, and turned to me.

"Mind you, I bet you've never shit in a cornfield," she said.

"What?"

"Country kid privilege," she cackled. "There was a barn party on someone's farm last year after the semi-formal, and they wouldn't let people use the bathrooms in their house. So everyone just went into the cornfield if they had to go."

"That's disgusting," I said, unable to keep from grinning at the grossness.

"It was kind of freeing, actually. Like, I'd peed in weird places, but taking a shit is so much more private, you know? Out in the open, barely hidden by five layers of corn, with my dress hiked up, squeezing it out, and I could hear people laughing in the distance, and I could see all the way down the row on either side of me. Felt like I could see for miles."

She was leaning closer to me, clearly trying to gross me out, and I shoved her back, laughing.

"Do you have to go into that much detail?"

"You're telling me you've never done anything like that?"

"No! Maybe. I peed in a sewer grate once on the school playground because I was really scared of the teacher on duty and didn't want to ask permission to go back inside."

"How the hell did you pull that off?"

"I was wearing a long skirt. Shimmied my underwear down and literally just sat on the grate. No one even looked twice at me. Kids sit on the ground all the time."

The movie could have started, and I would've had no idea because I couldn't look away from Ivy. Legs sprawled wide, head tipped back so her neck was trembling up at the ceiling with laughter. I wondered if people in the other cars could hear us, if we were being that kind of loud now.

"Skirts are the best," Ivy said. "Easy access for all sorts of things." Her hand had landed near the gearshift. I watched the tendons move as she applied force, pushed herself up into a proper sitting position.

"Have you gone on lots of dates here?" I asked for some stupid reason.

"No," Ivy said softly. "Don't have many people around here to take."

"Have you ever . . ." I trailed off awkwardly. It was dark enough that I had to lean into the middle to see Ivy properly, and it felt a bit like I was falling toward her, no seatbelt around my chest to keep me safe.

"I'm not a virgin," Ivy said quickly. Her tone was defensive again, her guard up. "Just because there aren't many girls to date doesn't mean there aren't plenty who want to test things out."

"That sounds kind of sad."

"Trust me, it doesn't feel sad."

Ivy glanced down at her hand playing with the gearshift, and her eyelashes cast a dark, curved fringe against her cheeks. They looked like they would be soft to the touch.

"What about you?" Ivy asked.

"I've done stuff," I confessed. "Not all-the-way stuff. I don't know. What counts?"

"I think it's just whatever you think counts."

I didn't realize just how much we were tipping in toward each other until Ivy straightened up and turned back to look out the windshield. She turned the radio volume back up, and the sound swelled sharp and huge around me, breaking some sort of spell I hadn't been aware of.

"The movie's starting," Ivy said.

I had forgotten that was going to happen. I slowly sank back into my seat and fixed my eyes on the screen, trying to calm down. The windshield swam in front of my eyes, Matt Damon forming out of the blur.

I thought it would get better the longer the movie went on, but something kept mounting in my stomach, slow-cooling lava carving out new ground. We were watching a spy movie where the main character had amnesia, and I could see too much of myself in him—running from everyone and unable to recognize the person in the mirror. The inside of the car was hot and dark, and Ivy wasn't a pebble at all but a brick on my hammock, ripping the fabric open and leaving a gaping hole. We were so close.

My left hand was resting next to my leg on the seat. I remembered sitting in movie theaters with Christopher, his hand expectant on the arm rest. My stomach lurched so violently I thought I was going to throw up for a moment, shaking and sweaty with the threat of it.

Ivy said my name, touched my hand carefully with two fingers. I lurched into the car door, scrambling for the catch.

"I'm going to get popcorn," I said.

"I thought you didn't want it."

"I changed my mind."

Ivy said my name again, but I was already out of the car, cool air washing over my face. Above me, the sky was peppered with thousands of stars. The concession stand glowed with warm yellow light behind the rows of cars, and I set off toward it. My leg ached with every step.

The front of the stand was closed, with a "Knock for Service" sign on it. I knocked, and it slid open after a moment to reveal a boy who looked even younger than the one at the front gate. The smell of butter was thick in the air. As soon as he handed me the popcorn, he slid the front of the stand shut again.

When I turned, Ivy was coming up through the cars behind me. I ducked around the concession stand, but she had already seen me and easily caught me at the side where the overhang covered us in fat shadows.

"Hi," I said.

"You were gone awhile," Ivy said. "I was worried. Your leg."

She brushed the back of her hand against my thigh, catching on skin where my shorts ended. I dropped my popcorn on the grass. Neither of us looked down.

"It's fine," I whispered.

Matt Damon was hanging on to a building by his fingertips on the screen. Ivy swayed in toward me, and I stopped breathing. If I so much as shivered, I would knock against her; my skin was screaming for it.

Her nose pressed up against my jaw, still an innocent touch, still something deniable.

"Can I?" she asked softly.

I closed my eyes.

"Yes."

Ivy drew her mouth across mine, and we kissed, slow. Her hand slid up tentatively to my waist. My whole chest felt like it was squeezing in. My arms hung loose at my sides only until Ivy started to draw away, and then my body rocked forward, grabbing at her, begging her back. She crushed me slowly into the wall, pinning me safe and trapped. It was so different than Christopher and just the same all at once. I could almost pretend that Ivy was someone else, except I couldn't—I knew that mouth now, knew those hands and the sound of her breathing. I was a swollen hot-air balloon, tied to the ground only by the hook of her fingers, and I knew I'd drift away if she let go.

Somewhere, someone accidentally pressed their car horn, and a man yelled. An owl called, pricking holes in the silence. Snatches of time disappeared into the haze of Ivy's mouth; the hand at my waist was on the button at the top of my shorts, thumbing the metal.

"Can I?" Ivy asked against my cheek.

"Yes."

We were both underwater, and no one was pulling us to the surface anytime soon. I didn't need air, or anything other than the edge of Ivy's knuckles. I could smell dirt and popcorn butter and the clean hardness of Ivy's skin surrounding the two of us in the strange cradle of the darkness. My eyes were open again. Ivy asked, with explosions billowing out on the screen behind her head, soundless and huge, and I said, yes, yes, yes.

Chapter 15

Paul had texted me three times since we'd fought. The first was an apology, the second was asking how my leg was and complaining about his brother in a clear attempt to get things back on neutral ground. The third came in the morning after the drive-in, while I was sitting on my bed and staring at Ivy sprawled on the other one. It said only "dell?"

Paul had hated Christopher—thought he was a tool.

"I've taken gym with that guy," he'd said. "You don't want to know the kind of shit I've heard him say in the locker room."

When I pressed, Paul wouldn't give details, but I'd always assumed boys said lots of gross things about girls when they were in big groups together—it was a posturing thing.

Christopher had said that was the reason he didn't want us to be public at school until we'd been dating awhile. He said he didn't want other guys saying things about me, because they didn't know me like he did.

"A couple of the guys actually thought you were a lesbian, if you believe it," he'd said. "Just because you'd never really gone with any guy, not because you look it. Trust me, you don't look it."

I'd known he meant it as a compliment, but it still hit me like a threat.

I think that going to high school sometimes means just being constantly terrified. You see all the horrible parts of yourself in ways you never did when you were a little kid, now that you're half-grown, and monstrous for it, too young to handle all the things you're starting to realize you've been built for, but too old to be unaware of all the ways you're making a fool of yourself every day. You can't live comfortably in a body that is twisting and stretching and transforming on a regular basis, so you get kicked out, floating outside of yourself, seeing the mess that everyone else sees.

Yes, I wanted Christopher's attention and his hands and his jokes and his smile and everything about him, but sometimes I think I kept wanting him after the bad things about him started eclipsing the good because he made me less terrified. I made more sense in the world when I was with him.

*

"Do you want to go through the attic today, girls?" Mom asked at breakfast.

"I thought me and Dell might hike around to the back of the lake and give it another swipe through for garbage," Ivy said.

My mother looked surprised, glancing at me as if expecting me to insist on staying behind, going through the past. Under the table, Ivy curled her hand around my thigh, just above the knee.

"Yeah, just for a few hours," I said. "I promise I'll go easy on the leg."

As soon as we were inside the tree line, Ivy crowded up behind me, giggling. She pressed her mouth to the side of my neck.

"My mom could be looking out the window."

"So? We can do what we want."

She pulled back and we went a few meters deeper into the forest until the cottage was hidden from sight. I pulled Ivy behind a thick tree trunk. She gripped my chin and tilted it up, but I was the one who moved to put our mouths together. Ivy kissed like she was hungry—she wasn't as good at it as Christopher had been, and that somehow made it even better.

"Let's go down to the lake," Ivy whispered. "Let's just vanish into the forest and not come back. No one would notice."

"There's only three of us here." I laughed. "Pretty sure she would realize."

"I'll disappear first then and just come back to carry you off at night."

"You sound like a vampire."

Ivy clacked her teeth together and bit at my neck, gentle but firm. I sucked in a breath and clapped one hand over the spot as soon as Ivy pulled away.

"You can't leave any marks!" I screeched. "You're going to get us caught."

Ivy didn't seem all that bothered. If anything, she smiled wider.

"Live a little," she said.

We moved through the forest, garbage bags flapping out behind us, picking up the occasional flash of plastic or paper, and stopping every ten seconds to kiss. I wanted to ask, What are we doing? But I didn't want it to sound too serious. I wanted to ask her what she was thinking, but I also wanted to pretend we were on the same page, the way we had been when we both decided it was okay to jerk off in the same room and never talk about it.

When we were as far away from the cottage as we could get, we sprawled out in a clearing and kissed until I got too nervous and had to jump up, rooting through my camera bag in order to hide how flushed I'd gotten. I climbed a tree, ignoring the vague ache still in my leg, and took photos from the top of it, trying to crane the camera up so I got more than just the fluffy heads of trees.

"Have I freaked you out?" Ivy called from down below.

"No," I replied, which wasn't true but also kind of was. I was the one who had freaked myself out. My reactions. My inability to control them.

"What's this?"

I looked down and saw that Ivy had pulled a collection of paper from my camera bag—the childhood magazine my mother and Julie had made. I'd forgotten I'd put it in there.

Something about Ivy leafing through it made me anxious. I quickly climbed down through the branches. Just as I hopped to the ground, I saw a ribbon of gold slide out of the magazine and fall into Ivy's lap. She scooped it up, peering carefully at it.

"Did you know this was in here?" she said as I approached.

It was a shiny locket in the shape of half a heart. There had been a word etched on the golden front at one point, but the surface had been worn down so only a few letters were visible: an "F" and "IE."

"Here we are," Ivy said. "Friends."

She held the necklace up like it was a medal ceremony. I automatically bent my head, and Ivy slipped the locket around my neck.

"I didn't see it in there earlier," I said. "Weird. Was there a second one?"

Ivy turned the magazine upside down and shook it, the pages beating at the air like wings. She handed it to me with a shrug.

"Maybe there was only ever one and they took turns wearing it."

"You know I like guys, right?" I blurted.

Ivy stopped moving, looking down at her hands. I watched her right shoulder twitch. "So if I kissed you again, you wouldn't kiss me back?"

"You said before that it didn't make me gay. If I liked it."

Ivy snorted. She looked back up, snagged the necklace dangling around my neck, and tugged, lightly.

"I was joking," she said. "'Cause I thought I'd made a big mistake and read things wrong."

I stared down at the locket and at Julie's drawing on the back of the magazine, trying to imagine I was a girl with a different name, with baseball socks and ears like my mom's. I focused on the thought until the fog of panic receded slightly.

"Don't think about it so hard," Ivy said quietly. "Do you wanna tell her?" When I looked back at Ivy, she was gesturing to the necklace.

I picked up the heart and slipped it under the neck of my shirt so it rested cool against my skin.

"It's mine now," I said.

Ivy stood up and kissed me again. Her hand at the back of my neck cupped the chain, pressing it into my skin. I had a sudden moment of clarity: if I shoved Ivy away now and told her that I didn't want this, she would back off. It was a test. All I had to do was not kiss back, and I could be who I'd always been.

Ivy made a tiny sound against my mouth, a question, and the thought slipped away like steam under the heat of her—I kissed back until we were both swaying, unsteady and weak in the middle of the clearing.

The magazine in my hands was open to where a photo of two little girls had been carefully taped in: one in a dress and the other in pigtails and a tank top, both sporting gold necklaces. I pulled my hair up on either side of my head in bunches then looked up at Ivy again.

"Do you think I look like my aunt?" I asked.

"Just like her," Ivy said.

✳

So yeah, Ivy and I snuck around, stole moments, just like I had done with Christopher. I was just a person who did these things in secret, it seemed, because I had no self-control.

We'd be picking up garbage and Ivy would swoop in for a kiss as soon as my mother's back was turned. If we were helping to make supper and my mother went to the bathroom, I'd sidle in next to Ivy at the stove to press my body along hers. At the dinner table, Ivy would try to stroke the inside of my leg with her foot like a weirdo, and I'd miss half of whatever my mother was saying. I vacillated between giddy and nauseous every ten minutes.

The only way I could be fine was to not think about it. Or to think about it only in bursts of questions, all with no answers. People went through phases, right? Ramona from the Scott Pilgrim comics dated a girl once and said it was just a weird stage in her life. Boys think "bicurious" girls are hot, right? Maybe what was happening in my head and body right now was like those motivational posters that are like, "Do one thing a day that scares you." Maybe this was my character-building, terrifying experience. I wasn't leading Ivy on, was I?

I tried to remember if anyone in the Gay-Straight Alliance at school claimed they were into more than one gender and came up blank. It made sense, though—kids in the GSA had already accepted their low social standing at school, so why would they waste time pretending they were still half-straight? Especially when people who used to be on your side—Natasha flashed into my mind—would think less of you for only coming out halfway.

As for me, I knew I wasn't gay because I still liked boys for sure, and I couldn't be bi or whatever 'cause I knew that wasn't an actual thing.

I couldn't actually remember whether I'd known that from the first time I'd heard of it, or whether I'd just figured it out from what other people said. It's hard to track the genesis of an idea once it's in your head. I remember thinking at first that "bisexual" was just a fancy word for slut after overhearing a conversation at school, boys in math class speculating on how many people they thought some MySpace-turned-reality-TV star had slept with. It seemed almost offensive to me that actual gay people were being lumped together with someone who just boned everyone. After all, everyone knew that you weren't supposed to be a slut, so how could it also be a sexuality that you were supposed to be proud of? I didn't like thinking like that—it felt mean. Bisexual was an incompatible, incomprehensible scab of a word, jarring against my understanding of the world, my desire to be a good ally to gay people, a good person who accepted others.

When Natasha explained that bi just meant gay people in the closet, everything made way more sense. Her explanation was more charitable, more convincing than the gossiping of some jerks in math class. And she said it so confidently that I figured she must have known people who came out as gay after saying they were bi.

I knew that wasn't me. So what it had to boil down to was that I was just so gross, so hamster-brained and sex-obsessed compared to other girls, that anything got me going. Even another girl—a girl whose dad was my mother's boyfriend.

I knew I was messing everything up, distorting this fake family unit my mother was trying to build with Joe and Ivy. But somehow I found myself unable to stop it. I was a kite, and Ivy had the string, and no matter where the wind dragged me, if Ivy pulled, I couldn't stop from going.

I didn't know what that meant and how it fit with who I thought I was. At least before, I'd understood my mutations. Now, I was morphing into something else entirely.

*

I created a house in my head that looked an awful lot like the cottage and kept everything locked in different rooms: my issues with my mother in hers, my obsession with my aunt in the attic, and whatever was developing between me and Ivy kept safe and secret in our bedroom.

I hadn't answered Paul's texts in a week.

I kept thinking up Google searches, questions popping into my head without clauses or endings, like lines in a shitty, extended poem.

(how do I know if I'm

how to stop wanting

am I a

if it's just one girl, does it mean I'm

can you be gay for one person)

Having no access to the Internet had been a weird godsend this summer because I couldn't torture myself by stalking my classmates on social media to find out what they were saying about me. But now, I just felt stranded, with no one to ask all the questions boiling in my head.

I felt like I was going insane.

So when Mom mentioned running into town to get some groceries, I jumped on it.

"Could I pop into the library?" I asked. "I thought it might be nice to say hi to Lucy and maybe grab some books."

My mother beamed at me, and I tried not to feel bad for deceiving her in another tiny way. Ever since the lake, she kept trying to hang out with me more, but I mostly felt too guilty to even look at her.

"Is Ivy doing all right?" Mom asked in the car.

"Why do you ask?" Ivy had stayed behind at the cottage, sulking because she'd carefully pitched a plan to babysit Jamie by encouraging our parents to go on a date, and Joe had shot her down. She'd pretended to seem understanding on the phone with him, but the act dropped as soon as she hung up. I didn't know how much of this my mother had picked up on.

She shrugged.

"I haven't really cleared the air with her about getting so mad after that whole business with the lake," she said. "I'd thought things were fine, because you two made up pretty quickly, but she's been acting strange around me."

"You're probably imagining it."

"Maybe you could help me corner her into doing some painting again, make it an activity for the three of us this time, huh?"

"Sure. Whatever."

Lucy met us at the door of the library, the woman who had taken care of me all those years ago during Gram's and Grampa's funerals. She and my mother hugged for a very long time. Lucy looked the same as I remembered—straw-blonde hair and tired eyes.

"It's good to see you," she said, after my mother had left us to go to the grocery store. After tying the loose end of her one sleeve into a knot where her arm ended at the elbow, she balanced stacks of books so competently that I felt stupid and rude immediately offering to help her reshelve things.

She thanked me and passed me some books nonetheless.

"Do you still like adventure books?" she asked. "I remember

you reading all sorts of books about kids discovering caves and secret tunnels and things when you were little."

"I don't know," I said. "I feel a little maxed-out on adventure this summer, to be honest."

Lucy laughed.

"You were my aunt's friend more than my mom's, right?" I asked. Apart from Joe, Lucy was in the most photos in Julie's album, even more so than that red-haired boy.

She hesitated then continued bending so she could adjust some more books on the bottom shelf.

"Yes," she said. She had a wispy voice, like morning fog. "It's good to hear your mother is ready to talk to you about her."

"Did she tell you not to talk about Julie to me during the funerals?" I asked.

"Not exactly. She just acted so spooked when I tried to bring up the topic between the two of us that I figured she hadn't gotten over it enough to really open up to you."

"Was it really bad for her when Julie died?"

"It wasn't bad," Lucy said slowly. "It was the end of the world. For everyone who loved her. But especially—your mother, yes. We were only kids. And it changed her entire life."

She held out a stack of books to me, gesturing to show me their section. The library was even smaller on the inside than the outside would suggest, and I could cross to the self-help shelves on the other side of the room in barely three steps.

"I never agreed with her decision to ignore it though," Lucy continued. "Your mother, like her parents, never wanted to talk about Julie after it happened. When someone you see every day, someone you love with every part of your heart—when someone like that disappears from your life, it can leave a hole so huge that for some people the only thing they can think of is to hide it. Cover it up with a tarp and put up signs so no one wanders over and falls in by accident. It doesn't make it go away. It doesn't help. But it protects you from the pain."

I nodded, distracted. There were books flashing words like "sexuality" and "queer" across their spines only a foot away from the ones I was currently shelving.

"I'd hope that the one thing you'd learn from your mother not talking to you about her sister is that it's always better to reach out than not to," Lucy said.

She was at my side suddenly, her hand on my shoulder. I jumped and clapped shut the book I had grabbed that began with "So you think you're—"

"And I'm sure you understand where she was coming from," Lucy said. "There are probably things you have trouble bringing up."

"Okay," I said. "Thanks. Can I use one of the computers without a library card?" I gestured to the two gray cubes in the corner.

She raised her eyebrows but didn't call me on my avoidance of her careful words.

"Just let me give you our guest log-in," she simply said.

I booted up the computer, struggling not to keep looking over my shoulder every ten seconds to make sure Lucy wasn't watching. It was old enough that it had to use dial-up to connect to the Internet. When Google finally loaded, I put my hands to the keys and held them there, motionless. I felt like I was going to sweat my brains out of my ear. All my planned search questions about being gay were gone.

My fingers finally moved, typing "Facebook."

If Paul were here, he'd smack my hands away from the keyboard. I hadn't opened Facebook since the day the pictures dropped. But for some reason, here I was, filling in my password, pressing Enter.

The homepage looked normal. Apart from the little bubble telling me I had sixty-seven new notifications.

The top post was a status update from Natasha, a photo of her and June and Kelsi laughing with ice cream cones. "living that summer dream with the giiiirrrls," the caption said. A lump rose in my throat.

"If you're trying to research something, I could always help you find the right book," Lucy called from across the room.

When I looked back at her, I could swear her eyes tracked past me to all the rainbow-colored spines I had been very deliberately not looking at before.

"No," I said. "I'm good."

I took a deep breath and went to my settings. Deactivated my account without ever once loading my wall and seeing the posts meant for me.

That afternoon, I told myself I was going to have a conversation with Ivy, explain that this had been some sort of weird blip and that we needed to go back to being just friends (instead of whatever the hell we were now). Two hours after I made this decision, Ivy touched my thigh under the kitchen table, and two minutes after that I dragged her into the bathroom and let her jam her tongue down my throat.

*

We loaded all the full garbage bags we'd been stacking beside the house into Joe's truck a few days after I visited the library and headed to the dump an hour outside of town. Jamie sat sandwiched between me and Ivy on the truck's claustrophobic back bench—Ivy kept her arm around him because there technically wasn't a seatbelt for the middle. Joe and Mom held hands over the gearshift. Jamie looked at me like he knew every horrible thing I had ever thought about his sister.

I had never been to a dump before. It was like a strange, miniature mountain range of trash, the island duplicated and swollen ten times over. Part of it was just garbage-garbage, but when we drove five minutes farther into the property, we came upon the salvage heap area. Joe and Mom paused to talk to the grizzled man who ran the place, and us kids tried to head off to climb and go treasure hunting.

Or at least we tried to.

"Jamie stays down here with me," Joe called.

Ivy tightened her hand around Jamie's.

"Dad, come on, I'm not going to let him get hurt."

"I know you wouldn't. But he's too little for that kind of horseplay."

"He is not! I was doing way worse shit when I was his age. So were you, Jumps."

"Doesn't change my mind." He beckoned. Jamie looked from his sister to his dad.

"You wouldn't be like this if you weren't so worried about what Elizabeth would say," Ivy said.

It was the first time I'd seen Ivy let slip a hint of real anger in front of Joe over Jamie. He looked taken aback.

"Do you want to go sit in the truck with Jamie, or do you want to go look around with Dell? Your choice."

"Whatever."

Ivy let go, smiled at Jamie, ushered him back toward Joe. Then she and I took off together.

We weren't necessarily supposed to scamper all over the scrap yard, but the man watching the dump didn't try to stop us. The sun was high; heat sizzled off metal platings and seared up through the soles of our shoes and the palms of our hands. We scrambled up piles of trash like we were scaling cliffs. Ivy sweated through the back of her shirt, dark, damp patches that I wanted to put my face to.

On a hill of mattresses and clothing, we raced to the top. I made it there first, swaying triumphant and dizzy with the dump unfolded around me like my own disgusting kingdom.

"Booyah!" I screamed, just because I could, and Ivy collapsed with laughter halfway to the top. I could see our parents' heads dipped close together way down at the bottom of the hill—my mother looked up at the sound of my voice.

"Girls, be careful!" she called.

Down below, Jamie strained against his father's hand, pulling like a puppy tied to a telephone pole. When he gave up, he glanced in our direction, and Ivy waved, the arc of her arm huge and exaggerated. He waved back, his face splitting into a smile big enough that it was visible even with the distance between us.

"Sometimes I wanna kidnap him," Ivy said, in a brief flash of melancholy. "Just grab him and take off and leave both of our parents behind."

"Cool," I said. "Just let me know if you need any backup."

She laughed. "Backup? I'd be worrying about you the whole time!"

"Hey, I think I'd be good at being on the run!"

"You're soft. You'd need someone to protect you."

She smiled and thumbed at my cheek, a quick brush. A memory sparked.

"Is that why you told me to hide in the closet when we first met?"

Ivy groaned. "That was so embarrassing. But yeah, I do dumb things to impress cute girls."

"You thought I was cute from the start?"

"Obviously. You had this whole angsty thing going for you, but then you'd get all big-eyed excited about, like, looking at trees. I mean, you were also annoying as hell."

"As if you can talk! You acted like it was your job to defend my mother at all times."

I regretted bringing it up as soon as I said it. Ivy's shoulders stiffened. She ripped a strip off a rotted mattress and flung it down the side of the trash heap.

"I don't know," she said. "The reason my dad is even letting me go to school for art on the other side of the country is because your mom convinced him. She stuck up for me. I thought she saw something in me."

"Right," I said. The horizon had gone squiggly with heat. "You're leaving in, like, a month, aren't you?"

Ivy nodded. I'd forgotten somehow, probably because the last time her fancy B.C. university came up, it still felt like we were rivals. Suddenly it seemed like an ending rushing up, a deadline.

"We better make it out to the island first," I said.

"Yeah?" Ivy teased. "You want me to finish teaching you to swim?"

She waggled her eyebrows. I wondered if there was a way to trace when the rewiring had happened inside me—at what point my brain had started reclassifying things about Ivy that made me jealous into things about Ivy that made me want her.

"Don't look at me like that," she said, the joke dropping from her face. "That's not fair."

"Why were you so mean to me if you liked me?"

"Liked you? Don't get ahead of yourself," Ivy scoffed. "But you know. I couldn't hit on you, you were pseudo-related to me."

She moved away across the mountain before I could ask her what exactly had changed between then and now. When had she decided being "pseudo-related' wasn't a problem for her?

When we came back down, Ivy dashed off for one last scan of the dump to see if there was anything she wanted to claim for her own. Joe had headed over to the truck to start it up, Jamie still at his side, and my mother stood alone, watching me approach. She was smiling strangely, and her eyes looked shiny.

"Sorry," she said when I got close, swiping at her eyes. "The two of you looked like you were having fun, running around."

"We were," I admitted.

"This is the kind of thing I want for you," Mom said. "You know that, right? I just want you to be happy. To be able to be just a kid again. I was so afraid that you'd lost that."

"Lost that," I repeated dully.

My mother fluttered a hand in the air. She wasn't looking directly at me anymore. "I shouldn't have avoided the topic of that boy and that whole mess for so long. I was waiting for you to come to me, but that was unfair to you."

You weren't waiting for me to come to you though, I thought. You were banking on me going to Ivy and then her telling you.

"I should've been more clear with you when it all happened," Mom said, "that it wasn't your fault, and that I don't blame you."

The sun had shifted off my face; I felt suddenly cold, my mother's words dropping into my stomach like coins into the bottom of a well. She was still talking, something muffled about being uncomfortable with certain topics.

"You told me I was stupid," I cut in. "You said I should've known better than to be a slut, and you said you thought I wasn't that stupid."

"Dell, I was scared," Mom said. "It's no excuse, but I was just scared for you. We all make mistakes."

Her hands were on my shoulders now, and when she folded me into a hug, I didn't push her away. The camera that used to belong to Christopher dug in between us, a huge lump in the front pocket of my cargo shorts.

Mom had been scared, but she hadn't taken it back.

I was angry, I realized. And I was pretty sure I had been angry at my mother for a long time. Since way before she screamed at me over Christopher. It was almost more a sense of betrayal than pure anger itself. She was my mother; she was supposed to equip me to be able to handle the world, handle myself as I grew into it. But there was so much she'd never talked about—the past, and bodies, and emotions, and the train wreck of being a teenager.

For a split second I imagined kissing Ivy right in front of her, watching her understand that the happiness she thought she was seeing was still tied up in my stupidity.

Somewhere in the dump, Ivy found a silver picture frame and a box of soft chalk pastels, most of them worn down to nubs. She showed me and Jamie but not my mother. The man who ran the dump gave us lumps of maple sugar candies, and I held mine against my tongue while Joe talked tree tapping and maple syrup with him. I took a picture of Ivy and Jamie in front of the biggest pile of garbage, arms spread wide in the air, and when Joe saw my camera, he held his hands out. I handed it to him automatically, assuming he wanted to curate some pictures of his children.

But then he suggested we get a picture of the five of us, together.

"It is such a scenic area, after all," he joked, and Mom laughed too loudly.

My lungs shrunk down so small it felt like they'd gotten lost in my chest.

"I don't want to be in the picture," I said, but no one seemed to hear.

My mother slung her arm around my shoulder, pulled me into

her side. Ivy shuffled in next to me, rolling her eyes, and suddenly I was pinned, caught between the two biggest problems in my life. Jamie was tucked into Ivy's other side, Joe on the end.

The dump guy was holding my camera now. As he raised it, I could see, superimposed on top of him, blond hair and red-patched pale skin, the soft, thick jaw of a teenage boy who hadn't yet grown into his skull.

"Hey," Ivy whispered. "You okay? Look at me."

I twisted my face into Ivy's shoulder, wrenching my left arm where it had gotten caught behind my mother's back. If the shutter clapped, I didn't hear or see it—my world was only Ivy.

In the truck on the ride home, Ivy put her arm across the back of the bench to knock against my shoulder above Jamie's head and held the picture up in the wind coming from the open windows until our five figures became visible.

The person in between my mother and Ivy was all but completely hidden by a curtain of hair in the picture. Ivy had put bunny ears up behind my head. It was a relief I had no way of expressing.

"Can Jamie stay at the cottage tonight?" Ivy asked. "Like a sleepover. Just for one night."

"No," said Joe.

"I'm not saying you go home by yourself; you could stay, too."

"Ivy, you know that doesn't change things."

"What, so you don't want to get laid?"

"Ivy!"

When Joe pulled up to the cottage to drop us off, Jamie hugged Ivy like she was going off to war.

"Why don't we draw something together this evening, Ivy?" my mother said. "We haven't done that in a while."

"No thank you."

I watched a cloud move across my mother's face and then watched her dismiss it, tacking on a smile. Maybe I should've felt a little bad for her. I didn't.

Christopher had started hinting at it long before he pulled out the camera and convinced me to pose. Dropping little things about missing me when I wasn't around and praising the concept of nude modeling and how artistic and empowering it was. Then, more obvious probes:

"I've never waited for a girl for this long. I'm cool to wait, obviously, but I might need a sneak preview if you're going to keep holding out on me."

"You love it when I take pictures of you normally. How would this be any different?"

"You'd look so good. And they'd just be for me, not anybody else. You told me you liked me."

I did like him. I liked him so much I thought I would explode with it. I liked his attention to detail, the little things he noticed in a photograph, when we went to a park and he made me a daisy crown. I liked it when he kissed me and my body felt like a champagne cork getting popped. I liked it when he took his shirt off and then took my shirt off in his room when his parents were out of town. I liked him so much I was the one who unzipped his pants first, who asked if I could touch there. Because I'd read about it and watched it, but this was the first time I'd been the girl who someone wanted to ask out on a date, a girl who had the chance to do this for herself. And all of that felt safe. And good.

And then I got these waves of hypocritical, cowardly terror the second it seemed like things were going further.

Everybody said it hurt the first time. Everybody said it was supposed to, said you would bleed. And what if I looked gross down there? And what if I cried and it was humiliating? I didn't know how to say any of it, didn't have anyone I could ask for advice. I remember staring up at the stained, bulbous off-white light fixture on Christopher's ceiling, wondering distantly where all the good feelings had gone and where the panic had come from. The light fixture had a hard golden knob in the center, like a nipple on a boob. I couldn't feel my body.

"What do you mean you don't want to?" he said. "You clearly do. You're wet."

He started asking for pictures after that. And he had a point, didn't he? I liked him and had liked doing other stuff with him, and after all, I was obsessed with sex, so I should've wanted to that time. It was mean to hold back this one thing, right?

With Ivy, it was different.

She stretched out on my bed one night when my mother had gone out to dinner with Joe, and she made the sweetest sound when I pressed my face to her stomach, sweeter than maple sugar on the tongue, or the triumph of standing at the tallest point of a mountain of trash. We'd been messing around for a million years now or maybe just a couple of weeks, and while everything was new, this was the newest of all. It was like learning to swim all over again; I didn't know how to move, or breathe, but Ivy was holding me and saying, "Look at me, Dell, just look at me," and I was safe in the bottomless feeling of it.

And when I froze again, with that same inexplicable fear, she didn't get mad at me.

"Are you good?"

"No. Yes. I don't know."

She drew away from me, propping herself up.

"Here, I'm not touching you anymore. Do you want me to go back to my bed?"

"No."

"Okay. Is it too weird that I'm a girl, or does this have to do with how much you hate mirrors?"

"You noticed that?"

"You kept turning around my mirror when I wasn't in the room. Yeah, I noticed."

I breathed for a long moment, staring at the ceiling. Ivy sounded so calm. Her voice grew closer as she moved up the bed.

"We don't have to do anything else," Ivy said.

"I still want to. I just feel kind of . . . scared, I don't know," I said. "I know that's stupid."

"It's not stupid."

Ivy kissed me on the forehead, nothing but a dim shape above me in the dusk half-light.

"Sorry," I whispered. "I know you've got loads of experience with other girls and I'm being weird."

"One other girl."

"What?"

I finally looked at her, my eyes struggling to take in her face. She seemed almost rueful.

"I've only actually—had sex with one girl before." Her words rushed out. "We had an on-and-off hookup thing before she moved away. I've made out and gotten to second base with a couple others, but I'm not—I don't know everything. You're not weird."

"But you talk like—"

"You didn't know me from school," she said. "I could act as confident as I wanted around you. Talk big."

She wasn't leagues ahead of me in life, thinking I was a loser. She wasn't making fun of me. Her armor was stripped bare, same as mine.

When she bent close a second time, I reached up and hooked my arms around her, dragging her back down on top of me, the way I had done after tasting the bottom of the lake.

"I only want to do whatever you want to do," she said. "So it's all you, Dollface."

"My name is Dell," I said, but I was smiling again.

She asked before she did anything and let me take the lead. She didn't laugh at me when I didn't know what to do, but she did laugh with me, just the two of us and the giddy absurdity of flesh. In that room it didn't feel like something wrong was happening—it didn't feel like something that couldn't be called innocent. Her mouth made me honest, whether it was on my lips, or my chest, or pressing in between my legs, and that couldn't be bad.

The strange thing, too, was that I didn't stop being scared. I just realized I wasn't scared of her.

And if I can share something with you, Julie—'cause sure, it's probably weird, but I feel like you wouldn't think I was weird for thinking it the way Mom definitely would—I had the strangest thought when I was all tangled up in Ivy. See, I realized it was the first time I'd gone out of my way to see what was under another girl's underwear since Grade 1, and while I was down there I had the distinct thought that I was finally fulfilling the quest that tiny six-year-old me had set in motion that day. I'd found the answer I'd wanted: she didn't have a wound between her legs. She looked and tasted kind of like me and kind of not. Enough like her that it felt special to be allowed to see her like this, and enough like me that I realized if I thought her body looked exciting and cool and kind of pretty between her legs, I couldn't think of that part of my own body as gross.

I dozed, after, and woke to the sound of Ivy humming under her breath—the room had gone silver around us, hazy like a wet hand swiped across paint, and Ivy was sitting up, her back glowing in the faint light. The kittens on my sheets were playing in crumpled piles around her waist. She had Julie's photo album open on her lap.

I sat up beside her, pressing close. Ivy had her fingers on a picture of my grandparents standing with my mother and Julie smiling between them, an eerie parallel to the photo taken at the dump a few days ago. Ivy was tracing Julie's face.

"She really does look just like you," she said quietly. "It would be freaky to actually catch her on film if she is haunting this place."

I still hadn't shown her, I realized. In all the stress and upheaval between us, I had somehow forgotten about my revelation, the glow on the island. I hesitated, remembering how I'd felt overhearing Ivy laughing with my mother on the porch. But if I could sit like this with her, bare skin nudged together, I could trust her.

"I have caught her on film," I said.

"Really?"

I reached over Ivy and turned the album to the empty pages at the back, where I had slid in some photos I took of the forest to keep them safe. I pointed at the one of the island at night, with the white streak shining ominously in the center.

"Holy shit," Ivy blurted, bringing the album closer to her face.

"It really looks like it could be something, right?" I said, feeling vindicated and slightly relieved by her reaction.

"Yeah, that's definitely not natural. I guess your camera could've glitched, but it was dark out, so it all should have been pitch black."

"That's what I thought!"

"Is this the only time you think you've actually gotten a picture of her?" she asked.

I nodded. "If it really is, I don't know, an imprint of a ghost, I doubt we'll see any more of it until we get out there for real. The island is the key."

"We haven't gone swimming since you hurt your leg though; do you still think you could make it to the island to get the boat?"

"Well, I mean, I have to, right? I can't let you swim it alone. You need someone to watch out for you."

Ivy huffed out a tiny laugh and flipped a page in the photo album.

"It would be cool to see a ghost," she said.

"I kind of already have, I guess," I admitted. "It's part of why I don't like to look in mirrors."

"What do you mean?"

"It's how she haunts me. Ever since I got here, every time I see my reflection, it's her instead of me."

"Well, she looks a lot like you, right?" Ivy said. "Maybe you just don't recognize yourself right now."

I didn't know what to say to that.

"How was hanging out with your dad one-on-one the other day?" I asked instead. Jamie had gone to a friend's house after baseball practice a few afternoons ago, and Joe showed up unexpectedly to pick up Ivy.

"It was kind of weird," Ivy confessed. "My dad thinks he found out where he was taken from as a baby. He keeps talking about bringing me on a trip down to this reserve on, like, Lake Huron? He thinks maybe we've still got family there."

"That's awesome! When are you guys going?"

"I don't know that I want to go."

"Why not?"

She shrugged. "I don't fit in with anyone around here, and I've got half of that in me, right? Why would I fit in there?"

I thought of Ivy's mother—the blonde hair in the photo, the pale face. I wanted to argue with her. Console her somehow. But I was out of my depth.

"Have you told your dad how you feel?"

"Him?" she scoffed. "Like he would get it. He'd just say I was being dramatic."

"Maybe he would get it, though," I said. "I mean, isn't he the one person in this town who actually could understand?"

Ivy shrugged again, clearly eager to change the topic. She flipped through the few album pages that held my photographs, assessing them, and brushed a hand down the outline of a tree. I felt the atmosphere shift into something lighter. "You take good pictures."

"Polaroids make everything look cool."

"I'm an artist—I know good shit when I see it."

"Why don't you draw with my mom anymore?"

Ivy gave a short, sharp laugh. "She doesn't really want me to. If she did, she wouldn't have given up so easily on the whole idea."

Mom still had the pictures she'd done during those sessions taped to the living room wall, so I didn't think that was it. But I didn't want to risk saying the wrong thing, not when Ivy was letting me curl into her side like this. On Ivy's dresser, I could see the silver picture frame from the dump on top of the box that contained her mother's picture.

"I've never seen any of your art," I said.

"I know," Ivy said. "And you can't, because I threw it all away."

"What? Why would you do that?"

Ivy closed the photo album with a snap.

"Because they didn't work out."

"You couldn't have kept them to learn from whatever you did wrong?"

"That's not—" Ivy said. "Listen, if I throw it away first, then no one can find it and use the fact that I once liked it and thought it was good against me, okay? You ruin it first, and then you're in control. It doesn't control you."

"I thought you liked art."

Ivy's expression changed. She set the album down on the ground beside the bed.

"I like lots of things that don't work out," she said. "Do you really want to talk about art or my weird family issues with me in your bed?"

I did. I was slowly realizing I wanted all the little bits and pieces of Ivy that I'd only glimpsed before, all the sticks and stones and buried treasure waiting to be unearthed. I wanted to put my teeth into all the places where Ivy's seams had gone loose and pull until the stuffing came out. I didn't know how that fit with how I'd been acting day by day, moment to moment, pretending that none of this meant anything about me, that everything we did was like shadow puppets on the wall—created by my choices, my hands, but so disconnected from reality that only a child would mistake the events unfolding for real life.

I couldn't trust anything I felt, not anymore.

I opened my mouth for Ivy's kiss and fell back against the bed. I tried not to feel like I was drowning.

*

Ivy was supposed to leave my bed before my mother got back—she didn't. I woke up to the sound of our bedroom door creaking slowly open, and I froze, Ivy draped along my back, her arm around my waist pinning me down. The blankets were high enough that our nakedness was covered, but we were still in the same bed. On the other side of the room, Ivy's mirror was tipped against the wall at such an angle that I could see the reflection of my mother in the doorway. I squinted my eyes almost shut and didn't move, paralyzed in fear.

My mother's face was in shadow, but I could still make out her smile.

Was friendship all she saw in this bed? Sisterhood? Or was she even seeing us at all—was she remembering instead nightmares or sad nights when she'd curled up with her sister? She couldn't see the truth of it, not if she was smiling like that. A distortion was happening somewhere between Ivy's breath on my shoulder and where my mother stood in the doorway. Maybe it was happening in my head.

Mom closed the door after a moment and left us alone in the black again. Ivy shifted against me, her face nudging into my neck. I still didn't move.

My mother's misinterpretation should've been a good thing—it meant we weren't caught. But instead, I felt like I was going to be sick. It was clear to me suddenly that there were no facts in the world anymore. I didn't want boys or girls or anyone. I couldn't be sure my limbs were even all there. If my mother couldn't see it, maybe none of it existed at all; maybe I didn't exist, and none of it had happened, not Christopher, not Ivy.

Maybe my mother had just never seen me as I was—not once in my life.

I was paper thin. The darkness pressed heavy hands to my skull and compressed me down into nothing. I didn't move. I couldn't.

Chapter 16

I didn't want to get up the next day.

Well, it's more like I woke up with a complete inability to want to do anything. Move a leg, roll over, say words. I stared up at the ceiling past Ivy's shoulder and tried to muster up some sort of emotion, then tried to feel alarmed over failing to muster up some sort of emotion. But the world felt completely gray.

Ivy sat up, jostling my body. I didn't look away from the patch of ceiling I had claimed as my own.

"Do you want some tea or something?" she asked.

"I don't know," I said.

"You good?"

"I don't know."

Her face crossed into my ceiling view, and she looked kind of upset. It pulled something out of me, relief coming with the whisper of feeling.

"You're good," I said. "I just feel off right now. You didn't do anything."

"I think your mom's up and making breakfast," Ivy said. "I'll see if I can bring you some in bed maybe."

She disappeared from the room. I stared up at the ceiling some more and wondered whether I could just become a ghost if I lay here long enough, join you and stop worrying about all this shit.

After a while, I became aware of voices at the bottom of the stairs. Growing louder, as if one person was following the other through the house.

"Why don't you calm down," my mother suggested distantly.

"I'm not fucking calming down if you're not going to tell me what's happening with my dad and my brother," Ivy's voice came in reply.

"You will not be so rude in my house!"

"You're not my mother!" A clatter on the stairs, a person going up a few steps then changing their mind and moving back down. "I want to talk to my dad. Give me the damn phone!"

A second of silence, and then someone was rattling up the steps and crossing the hallway into my mother's room. But it was Ivy's voice that I heard, muffled, clearly speaking on the phone. Her voice drifted out occasionally, in loud, sharp bursts, cutting around shards of sentences: "my brother" and "why can't I just come" and "she says?" I tried not to listen, tried to close my eyes and fall back asleep.

It must have worked, because the next time I opened my eyes, it was to the sound of tires in the driveway pulling away, and Ivy was shouldering her way back into the room.

"What's going on?" I said thickly, struggling to sit up.

"Your mom is helping my dad out today," Ivy said sharply. "At a stupid baseball game. My dad asked your mom to come spend the day with them, but I'm not allowed to go to my own brother's baseball game for some stupid reason my dad wouldn't explain."

"That's weird," I admitted. "But do you even want to go? You haven't pushed to go to any of his other games."

"This is the finals—it's more important," she snapped. "And he told your mom not to even tell me she was going to help him slice oranges or hand out water bottles or do whatever parents do at these things, and I had to practically force it out of her. It's all just bullshit."

"Sorry," I said. "She just left?"

"I told her you were still asleep. She left pancakes downstairs."

Ivy was bustling around the room, rifling in her plastic drawers. I felt like I was emerging slowly from a swamp.

"Are you going somewhere?" I asked.

"Just for a walk. You stay here. Eat pancakes or something, I don't know."

She kissed me on the forehead, quick, like we were a proper thing, had been a thing for years, and this was part of our schedule, a kiss on the forehead before she went to work. It left me feeling even more disoriented than before.

After Ivy left, I somehow managed to peel myself out of bed. I pulled on shorts and a T-shirt and wandered downstairs to eat a pancake, cold, syrup-less, holding it in two hands and tearing into it like a feral child. When I climbed back upstairs, my eyes caught on the unfolded attic steps.

Through my gray fog, one thought penetrated: my mother didn't see me when she looked at me, but maybe Julie would've. Maybe you could help.

The attic was emptier than the last time I had been in there, what felt like months ago now. My mother had swept, tipped the filing cabinets back on their feet, gotten rid of the excess papers and broken china. The intact teacups were lined up on the desk. When I got closer, I could see that they didn't just have designs etched on them but names, Susan and Anthony, intertwined around the rim. I sat down next to the desk, my back facing the side of it. I thought of my mother looking at me and Ivy in bed last night, of Ivy yelling at my mother on the stairs. Everything was unraveling so much faster than I had thought possible.

"Julie, I'm so screwed," I said. I slumped back against the desk, my head hitting the wood with a thunk.

The desk skidded under my weight, pulling away from the wall. I lurched into the new space, falling back on my elbows. Something clattered to the ground to my left.

I pushed myself back up to a sitting position, and when I looked over, there was a small box lying on the floor just behind the desk.

It was small and black, about the size of a pocketbook. There was a tiny lock on it, but the impact of the fall had popped the lock open. It seemed to have fallen out of a hole carved into the back of the desk, just big enough for the box to nestle in.

The box contained a few folded sheaves of lined paper, ripped from a notebook. I unfolded one to a spray of cramped cursive writing. There was no name at the top, no greeting, just *I wish I could tell you how I feel.*

You looked so beautiful today. I'm writing this the day of the maple sugar festival, for future reference. You wore that dress that's basically see-through and before we left my house you asked me if

I thought you needed to wear shorts underneath, and I could see your polka-dotted underwear, and I was almost going to tell you to forget shorts and forget leaving this room, when Anne came in and you rushed to put on the shorts, like you'd only wanted me to see you all see-through, but maybe I'm projecting. Mom says I'm always projecting, but I think she has forgotten how to imagine anything. She doesn't know about this, obviously. I'm sure about it now. I just feel so crazy when I look at you, like I'm one of those cream sodas you love, all shaken up by the time you open the bottle 'cause they don't sell 'em in the store closest to school so you drag me ages away at lunch and run back with me with it sweating and fizzing in your bag and I've totally lost control of this sentence because you don't really inspire control in me, you know? God, what I'd give to actually be one of those glass bottles so you'd put your mouth on me. I'm sorry I'm gross. But that's how I got sure what way I wanted you. 'cause friends want to be closer and laugh together and maybe even hold hands but friends don't want to know what you'd taste like between your legs, if it would be weird-tasting like I am, or if I'd like it.

Ahhh I would never say that to you in real life. I could never. (If anyone is reading this and it's not you or future me, GO AWAY, you never SAW THIS)

But it's nice to pretend I could send you a "romantic missive" like the ones in all those flowery books you read. Giant nerd. I'd sign it like this:

love, Verne

(maybe one day I'll say it for real. Please please please one day)

My ears were ringing when I finished reading. I flipped to another one. It was similar—the same guy, this Verne, singing praises of "you."

These had to be letters for Julie. Some boy had written Julie these weird, intense, dirty letters and finally worked up the courage to give them to her, and she'd kept them in a little box, treasured. I thought of the photos with Lucy and that redheaded boy. The cursive scrawl was weirdly familiar, and I pictured Julie and this boy writing in nearly identical hands, like lovers who start to resemble each other after long enough together.

Today is the day you told me you loved me too. We kissed by the water hole, and I was so scared Anne would walk in on us, but you said you weren't scared at all. I'm so stupid happy I don't even know how to write right now. I just want to remember how I feel in this moment, like I could fly. Fuck my parents, or your parents or the whole world, we'll go somewhere where no one knows us and we'll be together forever. 'Cause I can't see me ever not wanting you.

No wonder I had felt this kinship with my aunt from the moment I learned of her existence. She really had been like me, hiding a relationship from her parents.

The nothingness of the morning was gone. I was going nuclear on the inside. I wanted to call my mother immediately to come home, shove the letters under her nose—scream that her sister had also been drawn to a boy who talked love and want in equal measure like Christopher had.

Maybe she had never known that her sister had probably done

stupid, sexual things with a teenage boy the same way her dumb daughter had. Maybe my grandparents found out and that's why they hated Julie, this slut who broke their idea of what a good conservative daughter should be like.

Did you know I needed to see something from you right now? Was this another example of you haunting me? Showing up in lakes and mirrors, sending me lights and now letters—

"Dell?"

I shoved the box back into its hole behind the desk and stood up. Ivy's head appeared in the trapdoor hole, smiling and sweaty.

"I have something to show you," she said.

"What, now?"

"Yes, now! Come on."

*

We took off into the forest, Ivy leading the way, me with my camera bag slung over my shoulder. She was already damp, the tie of her bikini top visible where it stuck out of her T-shirt at the back of her neck, so I expected us to be heading for the water hole, but halfway there, Ivy swerved off the path, heading toward the lake.

I saw it through the trees before we had made it out of the forest, and I gave a shout, picking up my pace to speed past her. Her laugh trailed after me as I ran out onto the beach and up to the tiny wooden boat tied there.

"Is this the one from the island?" I asked. It felt solid to the touch, reliable. "Did it wash back to shore?"

"Nope," Ivy said. "Banking on doing more swimming lessons before the end of the summer seemed dumb, so I just decided to give it a try by myself. Cool, right? Now we can both go see the island, like we planned."

I looked out at the island, seeming tiny in the distance. "You swam out and got it by yourself? I thought you wanted someone to watch your back in case you couldn't make it or got hurt or something."

Ivy shrugged.

"Well, turns out I was fine. Do you want to go out now? Come on, I barely got to see the island, I just pulled at the edge of the boat to get it to slide off."

"I'm just saying, if you'd told me, I could've at least spotted you from the shore."

"You were feeling off this morning. Besides, last time you tried to swim in the lake it didn't go so well."

I opened my mouth to respond but found I had nothing to say. I'd never thought about how it must have felt for her, being on the shore while I was trying and failing to swim after our fight. At what point had Ivy decided to go after me? It had to have been before I went under, or she wouldn't have reached me in time. I wondered if Ivy had thought about what would've happened if she hadn't gotten to me in time.

"Do you want to go out there or not?" Ivy asked. She was jittery, and I wondered how much her fight with her dad had driven this move. But the boat was here now, and despite the risk, she was okay. And she was asking me.

I looked out at the island, standing out against the water like a dark stain. I thought of hands in the lake, of lights seen from treetops.

"Yes, I want to go out there."

✳

There was only one set of oars, so Ivy decided she would row. I didn't argue—just sat on the opposite bench and watched her, trying to reconcile the girl I'd met with the girl in front of me now.

"What are you staring at?" Ivy said eventually.

"Sorry," I said. "You didn't have to go and get the boat yourself."

"I'm not doing this for you," Ivy said, prickly as ever. "Maybe I'm just bringing you along so someone can take pictures if it looks cool."

The sun had only just made it over the trees, and the lake was streaked with long dark shadows on one side. My face was warm and Ivy's looked the same, pieces of hair leaking out of her ponytail. In that moment, I wanted to kiss her, and it felt like a soft glow in my stomach instead of acid.

"You like me," I said.

Ivy pulled harder on the oars. She smiled down at her lap, a brief flicker. "Shut up."

I took my camera out, snapping pictures of the cottage in the distance, and the trees, and the water. Out in the center of the lake, we couldn't hear the birds anymore, and it was strangely silent apart from the swish of water. I closed my eyes, imagining ghostly hands on the bottom of the boat ushering us toward the island.

"You okay after this morning?" I asked.

"I don't know," Ivy confessed. "When your mom wouldn't tell me what she was talking about with my dad on the phone, I thought maybe Jamie had gone and run off again. Made me flip out a little more at Anne than I probably should've."

"Again?"

"He's a jumpy kid. Like me."

"And your dad," I pointed out. Ivy rolled her eyes.

"Sometimes he needs to take off for a while," she continued. "When he started doing it the last summer we spent together, I'd always be the one who could find him, hidden in a cornfield or exploring some corner of the neighborhood or something. Sometimes during the school year he'd run away from his mom's for a few hours and I'd get called in to find him. But it's been months since he did something like that."

I lowered my camera.

"Did you and your brother and dad used to be closer? You and your dad have been kind of weird with each other all summer."

"I don't think my dad cares about me in the same way your mom cares about you, okay?"

It was a sudden shift, a cloud over her face.

"Why would you say that?" I asked. "He's always trying to talk with you; you're the one who has been, like, rejecting his friendliness."

Ivy stayed quiet. I had the feeling she regretted the strictness of her phrasing, but she was sticking to it now, stubborn.

"He seems like he cares a lot," I continued. "I don't know, but

I feel like our parents probably do a lot for us that we take for granted."

"The only thing my dad's done for me is put a target on my face for all the assholes at school," Ivy snapped. There wasn't much I could say to that.

We paused for a break over the white square top of the refrigerator. I left my bag and camera in the boat and we slipped into the water, me clinging to the side of the boat to make sure it didn't squirm away like a fish. Ivy swam circles around me, and I watched the tension flow off her back into the lake in tiny, shining droplets.

"You know what my dad really cares about?" she said. We were standing on the refrigerator side by side, arms folded over the edge of the boat. Our legs were cool and alien where they touched under the surface—Ivy had taken off her sweatpants, and I had taken off my shorts so they stayed dry. "That stupid high school."

"It's your high school."

"You about to tell me you actually like your high school? His favorite disguise to wear is the principal coat. You know how adults are never, like, real? They're always slipping into different personalities. He's got the 'Ivy's dad' coat and the 'Jamie's dad' coat—trust me, there's a difference—and the 'cool, friendly principal' coat. He walks down the halls at school, like, high-fiving kids. He's always going on about parent-teacher meetings and assemblies he wants to have, and asking me what 'the student body' thinks. As if I'm just a representative of them."

She shook her head, fingers tapping out a beat on the wood.

"And if I step out of line even a little bit, he just thinks about how it reflects on him as principal. Like, he literally told me I wasn't allowed to hang out with my friend Mackenzie anymore just because her parents caught her smoking weed once. He sat me down and tried to be all 'I understand the cool kids want to do this stuff and might peer pressure you, but you have to think about your future' or whatever."

"Did you actually stop hanging out with her?"

"No. Obviously. I just have to not mention her. I was all 'Oh, I've never tried weed, no sir,' which—" She waved her hand dismissively, making a face that made it clear what she thought of that lie. "This county is literally, like, the highest in Ontario for weed use, so, he knows, probably." She laughed.

The boat bobbed a little farther away, tugging me enough that I slid forward on the refrigerator. I found my feet and pulled the boat back. The sun was golden where it outlined Ivy's forehead, like a halo.

"Sometimes I get this crazy urge to just—just burn it all down. The whole school. But it's his pride and joy, so."

"Do you think maybe that's why you want to burn it down?" I asked. "Because it's his pride and joy, and you feel like you aren't?"

Ivy fell quiet. After a moment, she said, "Should we keep going?"

Once we got back in the boat, the island seemed to approach fast, its shadow creeping closer with every stroke of Ivy's arms at the oars. It was wider than I'd thought it was from the shore, spreading out into the water in such a thin layer that it was like it had its own beach of garbage fanning out around it. The edge closest to us seemed to be a pile of white siding and spikes of green gutters, water churning at the openings. There was a broken table sloping up toward the middle of it, wedged against the end of the truck cab.

I'd put my shorts back on after our swim, but Ivy had left her sweatpants off. We used them to tie the boat to a metal pole sticking out of the side of the island. I slung my camera bag around to rest on my back and held on to the pole, bracing myself against Ivy's shoulder as I reached out with a leg for a plank of wood that seemed sturdy. When it didn't sink, I took a deep breath and pushed off the boat, stepping fully onto the island.

The board slid and I shrieked, scrambling farther up the slope until nothing under my feet was moving. I blinked down at Ivy, who was still in the boat, and then at the garbage around me, which was impossibly sticking out of the water and yet solid underneath me.

"Shit," I laughed. "Jesus, oh my god."

"Don't think your mom would be too happy about that language," Ivy said.

"My mom hasn't been happy about anything I've done in a year," I shot back. "Get up here."

Ivy wobbled her way onto the island, practically falling into my arms when I reached out to steady her. We climbed carefully up the landslide of wooden planks toward the kitchen table at the top of the peak.

"I can't believe it's so solid," I remarked. "It really is a mountain, not an island."

"It's almost as big as our room," Ivy said.

I pulled myself up onto the plateau at the top, and the roof of the cottage was suddenly visible across the lake. For the first time it really struck me—the distance between me and the land, the water cupped all around us, the island held precarious in its palm. But I couldn't be scared. Ivy was with me.

We split apart slightly to move carefully around the island, picking our way between the planks and siding sticking up from the surface like spines on the back of an enormous, slumbering trash hedgehog. At first, I was excited. Any second now, I'd spot it, I was sure: a box clearly marked "JULIE" or "FAMILY THINGS" or "HERE'S ALL YOUR ANSWERS." But as cool as the island was, it seemed just like the scrap heap at the dump, full of furniture and metal and no human things.

Whatever had shone a light for me to follow before had dimmed now.

"It's not what I expected," I said after a while. I was sitting on the edge of the tilted truck, with my camera bag resting beside me. It was only the frame of the truck, dusty red, curls of cotton candy insulation stuffed in the empty space where the wheels would've gone. There was a crumpled blue tarp spread out where the seats would've been, but I couldn't do much more than brush it with my fingertips before it started feeling precarious to lean into the vehicle that far.

"What did you think it would be like?"

"I don't know," I admitted. "I kind of I thought I'd figure something out up here."

"We might still find some of Julie's things," Ivy said, somehow knowing exactly what I was missing. "He can't have gotten rid of your whole family history."

"Would it matter anyway? History is weird—people make the same mistakes over and over again, even when they know it'll lead to a war, or famine, or whatever. It's probably not any different on a personal level."

I grabbed my camera from the bag and took a picture of the cottage across the stretch of water. I wondered how angry my mother would be if she knew where we were right now, her two girls.

"Dell?"

I hummed.

"Are you actually depressed? Like your mom thinks?"

I kept my eyes on the water.

"No," I said. I had to squeeze it out; my throat had gone thick and tight. "I don't know. I don't think so. Isn't everybody?"

"You knew you wouldn't be able to make it to the island when you tried to swim here alone."

"You made it."

"Adele."

I flapped the photo in the air, stinging the edge of it across my left palm. Christopher had told me once that you actually weren't supposed to shake Polaroid pictures—that it could ruin the photo, not help it develop.

"I've told you not to call me that."

My phone went off in my shorts pocket. The screen showed my mother's name, and I handed the phone to Ivy without answering it—I knew I couldn't lie to her right now, even by omission. I was tired of lying to my mother.

I was close enough that I could hear her through the phone.

She asked if things were okay with them after the conversation that morning. Ivy listened with a stony face, providing the appropriate agreements and apologies; it was not a long conversation.

"No, Dell's up and about now," Ivy said. "She's just in the bathroom. Yeah, we ate the pancakes. I'll tell her what you said."

My mother would be staying over at Joe's that night, apparently. There was leftover fried rice in the fridge for us to eat.

When Mom rang off, sounding distracted, she said, "See you later. Love you!" the way she did every time she talked on the phone to me, and Ivy recoiled like she'd been struck. She shoved the phone back at me, and we sat there in silence for a long moment.

"At least she didn't sound suspicious about what we're up to," I offered.

"The last woman my dad properly dated was when I was nine," Ivy said abruptly. "It was this white lady named Elizabeth. She didn't like me very much, but I guess I thought she did, 'cause I started calling her Mommy. She broke up with my dad because of me, and I know it was because of me 'cause I overheard them."

She kicked her feet against the front of the truck, her bare leg shifting against my shorts.

"Didn't stop her from letting my dad knock her up though."

"And that was Jamie," I said. I knew some of this already, but it was different hearing the full story from Ivy.

"Yeah."

"She didn't like you calling her Mommy, but she had a kid with your dad?"

"Guess she prefers boys. I'll never understand that. Which she found out a couple years ago."

She was quiet so long I thought she wasn't going to finish the story. But I knew I couldn't ask. She would tell me or not, here on this island of unwanted things where no one else would hear us.

"Elizabeth came to pick up Jamie after his weekend with us—'cause he used to be able to spend every summer with us and every other weekend, too, during the school year—and she caught me coming home with Mackenzie. And we weren't even— we were just holding hands. Mackenzie never wanted to do more than that, except when we were really high. But Elizabeth flipped out so bad I ended up saying, 'Yeah, you know what, I am gay, so what about it?' Next thing me and my dad knew, she was talking about fighting for sole custody of Jamie because she didn't want him around me if I was going to have a 'lifestyle' like that. Be a bad influence."

I flashed back to my mother's words in the hall the night Ivy first kissed me—calling Ivy that same thing.

"And my dad was so scared that she'd win and he'd never get to see Jamie again, so now he lets Elizabeth set all the rules. That's why Jamie could only come for the summer if my dad agreed to keep me out of the house."

"My mom said you were the one who suggested that."

"I did, yeah."

"So you're mad at him for agreeing to your plan?"

"I don't know. He wasn't supposed to agree so easily!"

"He can tell you're angry with him," I said. "But he thinks it's about some sort of art school argument you guys had months ago. He thought it was a petty thing; he doesn't know it's a legitimate thing you're pissed about."

"Really?" She laughed. "Well, after I yelled at him on the phone this morning, he probably doesn't think that anymore."

"Why don't you just tell him you're upset about it?"

"What would that do?"

A lot, I thought. Joe had probably been grateful that Ivy had given him this way out, this way to not have to choose between his daughter and his son. But he'd take her side against Elizabeth if Ivy asked. I knew it.

"And my mom knows all this?"

"Clearly, she does. I bet you're right, and my dad did tell her about me being gay. So screw him."

I thought for the hundredth time of my mother looking down at us in bed, clueless.

"I'm pretty sure she doesn't know about you being gay," I said.

Ivy said nothing, just looked down at her hands in her lap, picking at a tag of loose skin around her thumbnail. I watched her face, feeling vaguely lost. I wondered what happened in Ivy's head when she looked at me and decided to trust me with something. Was it really trust, like I had felt at the water hole or in the boat, or was it what she'd said weeks ago, that I was safe only because she didn't care what I thought?

"Why do you tell me this stuff?" I asked.

Ivy didn't look up. "I wouldn't actually tell your mom about it," she said. "If you wanted to talk to me."

"About what?"

"I don't know. Whatever makes you a 'wonder slut.' That was what you called yourself when you were accusing me of being a spy, right?"

I cringed a little at the sound of it, fiddling with my camera.

"Does it have to do with being a lesbian?" she asked.

"Do you have to say the word all the time?"

"Words have power," Ivy countered. "That's why people are so scared of actually saying it. You don't need to be scared of saying it."

"I'm not."

"Scared?"

"A lesbian."

The water sucked at the edges of the island, soft. Ivy slid off the truck and aimed a vicious kick at an empty soup can; it flew through the air, hitting the water with a hollow smack, and Ivy's hands curled at her sides as if she was holding herself back from following it under the surface.

The island smelled slightly, deep underneath the clean edges of wood under my feet. My eyes hurt from looking into the sun where Ivy stood.

"My boyfriend," I said, and stopped. Ivy didn't move. "My boyfriend took pictures of me naked and put them on the Internet."

Ivy turned then, but I was staring at the newspaper mulch under my feet, which seemed very far away from my knees. Half of a headline was visible under a sheet of rusted metal—it was just the word "END". I wondered whether Ivy would laugh first or ask me why I was stupid enough to let him.

A pair of feet appeared in front of me, covering the headline.

"That's shit," Ivy said. "I'm sorry."

I looked up; the sun was behind Ivy's head, blazing out in a white corona. She looked sincere, and I didn't know what to do with that.

"What is that supposed to mean?" I asked.

Ivy made a small, disbelieving sound. "It means he's a piece of shit, and I'm sorry. Anne made sure he's going down for it, right?"

"Yeah," I replied.

"Good. That's fucking good. Jesus."

"His name was Christopher." I hadn't spoken his name in almost a month—it tasted like hard, sour candy. "Paul calls him King Trashbag. He said he needed pictures because I hadn't put out yet, and he needed something to tide him over. And I posed and everything. And then we had this fight because I just wanted him to call me his girlfriend in public, and he said all his friends already knew he was trying to get with me, but it had been so long and I was making him look stupid in front of them by not giving it up, so he'd decided to get the photos to prove he did fuck me. And I called him an asshole, and he threatened to post the pictures. I didn't believe he would, and then he did and everyone, everyone at my whole school knows I'm a stupid slut."

"You're not."

"I am. He said so, everyone said so. If they believe it, that's what it is, that's who I am."

"Don't think about him now," Ivy said.

She kissed me then, on the cheek, a soft, abrupt pat, like she couldn't hold herself back from it. I closed my eyes and reached out blindly to find the solidity of her waist, sun-warm fabric giving way to skin. Ivy tagged kisses all over my face—my chin, my forehead, the bridge of my nose, my jaw, and with each one my chest sweetly compressed a little more. I wondered if this was how evangelicals felt in church, on their knees with the touch of a holy hand on their face.

"I first had sex when I was fifteen," Ivy said. "Do you think any worse of me?"

"No."

"Then you can't call yourself a slut like it's some gross thing just because other people would. They're assholes, and they hate girls, and it's not fucking fair."

"Other girls were saying it about me, too."

"But they weren't the ones who came up with it. This shitty world made them hate themselves—you don't have to. That asshole should never have posted those pictures, and no one should have been spreading rumors about you, but that word doesn't make you less. If guys get to be happy and proud about sex, so do we."

She made it sound simple, like it was less than the iron weight hanging around my neck. I didn't know how to explain that it was different, that I was different.

"Then I'm stupid."

"You're not stupid."

"Mom doesn't think that."

Ivy pulled away slightly, and I dug my fingers into her waist to hold her there, suddenly terrified that she would leave me all alone, here among the junk.

"Your mom doesn't know her daughters all that well," Ivy countered.

The weight of the camera suddenly disappeared from my lap. When I opened my eyes, Ivy was holding it, her lip curled.

"You're always carrying this around," she said. "Does that have anything to do with him?"

"He gave it to me," I admitted.

"You don't need to torture yourself with a reminder of him."

My hands had gone loose; Ivy backed out of my grip, looking toward the water. I shot to my feet fast enough that something shifted deep underfoot. Everything was sliding.

"Don't," I warned.

"The lake's already got junk in it—what's one more piece?" Ivy said, waving the camera. "Christopher's little toy belongs down there way more than your aunt's stuff does."

"It's not Christopher's, it's mine," I said. "It's mine now, and as long as I'm behind the camera, I know I'm not in front of it."

"Have I—" Ivy began. "I haven't ever made you uncomfortable, have I?"

I remembered tangling in my bed, Ivy's hands urgent at the edge of my shorts, yanking them down. I hadn't really seen my own body, not when Ivy was a sweaty confusion of limbs above me.

"That was fine," I said. "I was looking at you, not me."

"You like looking at me?"

She was smiling suddenly, looking soft. I had to be honest—I nodded, my ears hot.

"Okay," Ivy said, and handed the camera back to me.

She stepped back, pushed her bikini bottoms down her thighs, and stepped out of them. She pulled her shirt over her head, undid her bikini top, and dropped them both at her feet.

"Take a picture," she said.

"What?"

She stood there, watching me with her eyes dark. My mouth had gone dry. The camera in my hands weighed as much as the boat we rode in. It was different to see her bare in the sunlight, more exposed than ever.

I'd come here hoping to find you, Julie. This was something else.

Ivy spread her arms casually, as if she wasn't completely naked on a pile of trash. "Do you need me to do a pose?"

If she was worried about how she looked, she didn't show it. She was unashamed and more beautiful for it: hair curling wild between her thighs, a few spots of acne following the top swell of her breasts. She didn't have a flat stomach, and her nipples were puffier than they were supposed to be, according to what I had seen in porn. I wanted to measure myself against her, to touch, to consume the way Christopher had with his gaze. Guilt made me look away—desire made me look back. For me, desire had always been the stronger force.

"I didn't say I wanted to be him," I said.

"I promise you aren't," Ivy said. "I'm asking you to take a picture. I want you to. Did you want him to?"

I had been smiling by the last photo because he kept joking throughout, like it wasn't serious, like it all meant nothing. I hadn't been smiling at the beginning.

I raised the camera and took a picture.

Ivy appeared smaller when I looked through the camera,

distant and trapped in the frame, but not unhappy about it. She didn't pose, instead moving around the island, occasionally looking back at the lens. My finger was greedy on the shutter. The camera pressed to my face felt like control.

I took sixteen photographs before the camera clicked empty in my hand—out of film. I'd taken them so fast that they were all still gray in my hands, except for the very first, where Ivy's form was unfolding aggressively out of the fog. I put the camera back in the bag while Ivy put her swimsuit and T-shirt back on.

"I look good," Ivy said, gazing over my shoulder. "You take good pictures." She glanced at the mess at our feet and bent down. When she straightened back up, there was a lighter in her hand. "And you and I already know how good I look, so no one else gets to."

We burned the pictures one by one, standing as close to the edge of the island as we could. I held each one up over the water with two fingers pinched around the top corner, and Ivy set the flame of the lighter to the bottom corner. Fire ate them up right to my fingertips, and I dropped them into the water. I kept thinking I was going to let the fire reach my fingers and keep holding on anyway, but I got spooked every time the heat got too close and let go before I meant to.

"Just pretend you're setting him on fire," Ivy said. "Him and all the pictures he took."

"Fuck you, Christopher Smith," I said, and flicked the lighter again.

He was disappearing into the sky along with Ivy's photos, becoming nothing. It was exactly what he should've been in the first place.

It was strange, watching Ivy's body curdle and coil into smoke and orange—it felt like relief in a way I hadn't anticipated. I leaned back into the shelter of the girl beside me and embraced the fear of the flame.

"It looks cool," Ivy said distantly. "Like I'm moving, like I'm melting into something. It's funny, 'cause people think of burning as destroying something, right, but it's not really. It's just making it into something else."

"Ash," I said. "Smoke. Conservation of matter or something like that."

"It's creation if you look at it the right way."

"The whole phoenix rising from the flames thing."

"I think I'd like to go by fire, if I had to choose," she ventured. "It would be dramatic and badass."

"How would you even go about setting yourself on fire?"

I flicked ash from my fingers and held up a new picture, this one of Ivy looking out toward the water. Ivy was silent as she lit the corner.

"I was picturing a forest fire, or me saving a child from a burning building. I didn't say I'd kill myself," Ivy said softly.

I didn't know why I'd assumed that. The picture was hot in my hand, and I felt a bright spark of pain before I dropped it.

"Maybe you'd become a phoenix and get to fly away from all this shit," I said.

"Maybe it'll happen right now. We're in a drought—maybe we'll just light the whole place on fire."

We were on the last picture. I let it go while it was still burning, and it landed on a sheet of metal that sloped down into the water. When it slid, and the edge of the flame touched the lake, I almost expected fire to race out across the surface like oil, but it only flickered a few more times before it sank.

"It's not fair that you felt you had to do stuff with him," Ivy said. "Just because society expects all girls to like boys. You shouldn't have to hide who you actually are."

"I did like him," I said.

"Yeah, but you didn't want to fuck him. You know what I mean."

"I did."

Ivy shifted beside me, and I held still, staring down at the picture in the water.

"We've been through this," Ivy said. "Why do you think you need to lie to me? You see anyone else around in the same boat as you? You know any other lesbians?"

"I'm not a lesbian," I said, my voice squeezed thin and fast. "If I was, I would tell you; it would be great, and everything would make sense. But I wanted to fuck him. I've always liked boys, okay, since I was in kindergarten. I used to steal romance novels from thrift stores when I was twelve because I wanted to read about sex—between men and women—so bad, so yes, I wanted to fuck him."

"Did you then?" Ivy asked. "Was it before or after he took the pictures?"

"I didn't," I said. "We did some stuff, but not that, 'cause I was scared of it. Of him. And I wanted to ask my mom what I should do, but I couldn't talk to her about any of it at all, so I messed everything up."

"So all of this is just, what, a little distraction?" Ivy said. "You'll let me get your rocks off and then you'll just head off because you miss cock too much? Are you one of those girls?"

"I don't care about—it's not body parts that I like," I said. "That's not what makes the person. I just like . . . boys."

"You didn't seem to like them all that much when you were kissing me ten minutes ago."

My face crumpled; it felt like the island was pitching underneath me, getting ready to throw me off. I was something too disgusting even for a heap of trash.

"Aren't there, you know, people who date more than one gender?" I tried desperately to scrounge up one example, one celebrity or actor or character in a TV show.

"You can't just go around messing with people's feelings," Ivy said.

What feelings are you talking about? What do you feel about me? I wanted to ask, but she was barreling forward.

"Which is more real to you—wanting an asshole like Christopher, who you said you were scared of, or wanting me? One of them is a lie, and I think you know which one. Straight boys are terrifying dicks, that's who they are. You don't want that."

"I'm not scared of all boys. I'm not scared of Paul," I said, my voice tiny.

"And he's gay!" Ivy shouted. "So what does that prove?"

I'd known other boys and wanted them, and I hadn't been afraid of anything more than the strength of my own desires, but I couldn't find my voice to say that. Ivy was wrong—I had no idea which was the lie. I knew only that I was one myself. I was tired suddenly, dizzy on my feet, and my dreams flashed horribly in my head, overlaying onto the island.

"I want to go back now," I said. "Please."

✳

We did not speak in the boat ride back or on the walk to the house. When we reached the porch, Ivy turned away from the stairs and started marching down the driveway instead.

"Where are you going?" I asked.

"It's a twenty-minute walk to town, and I'm going to go watch a baseball game, no matter what my dad says," Ivy said, throwing her arms out. "Wanna come with?"

"You don't even know when the game is. Maybe they've already played. Or it's in hours."

"Cool, got it. You're staying here. Have fun."

"Ivy!"

She walked on, ignoring me. Déjà vu struck—we'd flipped, and I was the one yelling her name as she moved closer and closer to drowning.

I went back inside.

I crawled into bed and took Julie's photo album out and laid it on my chest, the weight enough to almost be another person. I missed being seven and sleeping with my mother beside me in bed, back when everything made sense. I missed being a person and having a mother who knew me at all.

I fell asleep.

Chapter 17

The house was full of shadows when I woke from my nap, and I could hear people laughing somewhere. There was the skid of gravel under fast feet; I sat up, remaining still for a moment for my eyes to adjust before I crossed to the window to look down at the driveway.

Two figures in board shorts and muscle shirts were snatching at each other's arms and running in circles in front of the porch in the dying sunlight, each with a bottle in hand. Boys, around my age. One had blond hair, and he seemed heart-stoppingly familiar until he reared back and laughed soundlessly with too large a mouth. I stopped breathing for a moment, trying to figure out a course of action—but then a third, smaller figure ran down the porch steps and thumped one of them on the back. Ivy said something I couldn't hear, and pointed to the left, toward the forest. The fear drained out of me, replaced with thick anger.

When I got downstairs, Ivy was bursting through the front door, carrying what looked like a mickey of vodka.

"What the hell?" I said.

Ivy blew past me to pull open the drawers next to the fridge.

"Do you remember where your mother keeps the flashlights?"

"What do you need them for?"

Ivy yanked open another drawer and made a sound of triumph. She pulled out a couple of fat flashlights.

"Just having a little gathering by the water hole," she said. "I know the sun's still up, but we might need them later. You're free to come if you want."

She shot me one of her manic smiles and left the front door swinging in her wake. I hesitated only a moment before I grabbed a mini flashlight and my phone and took after her.

It couldn't have been later than 7 p.m., but clouds were starting to drift in across a bruising purple and orange sky. The boys had gone ahead. Ivy strode confidently through the trees, and I stumbled after her.

"What happened at the baseball game?" I asked.

"Nothing. Jamie's team won. I ran into some people who had nothing to do for the evening, and I realized I had access to some free real estate."

"Mom definitely didn't say we could invite people over," I pointed out.

"She also didn't say we couldn't," Ivy shot back.

"I know my mom—she'd pitch a fit, especially if people are drinking. Where'd you even get that?"

Ivy waved the vodka.

"It's not for me; I'm not really into getting wasted. But I told you I had older friends. Let me guess—you've never been to a party?"

"I have."

I hadn't, unless getting drunk at Paul's house with him and

Natasha after he failed Grade 10 math counted. Paul's parents were away a lot and thought he didn't know where they kept the alcohol.

"Mom's going to kill you," I said.

"Your mom isn't going to find out," Ivy countered. "She'll be too busy fucking my dad tonight and won't be coming home till morning—everyone'll be gone then, and you think she'd notice a couple extra beer cans in among the shit that's everywhere on this land?"

"She'll notice if someone falls in the water and drowns 'cause they're too hammered," I replied.

We passed a couple of girls messing with the filing cabinet beside the path, and Ivy yelled at them to get over where everybody else was. I paused, remembering how desperate I had been to find this cabinet earlier in the summer, but Ivy was surging forward, and I had to catch up.

The closer we got to the water hole, the louder the voices got. When we reached the cliff and looked down at the water, there were maybe fifteen people milling about the edge with bottles or cans in hand. Cases of beer sat against a cooler on the ground. The light was weaker here, struggling to filter through the trees, and a couple portable lanterns scattered around the rocks gave everything a sticky yellow glow.

"There's someone in the water," I said, pointing. A girl with red hair was floating below us on her back, kicking slightly, her T-shirt billowing out around her.

"Jess!" Ivy called, and the girl started, smoothly bringing her legs underneath her to tread water. "You haven't had anything yet, have you?"

"I could drive a semi through a police blockade, girl, I'm fine," Jess shouted back. One of the boys on the shore muttered something barely audible about what he could drive a semi through, and Jess spun to face him, splashing indignantly.

Ivy turned to head down the stairs, and I scrambled after her. I could see glances being flicked my way under the shadow-heavy brows of the boys—I tried not to let my own gaze linger, terrified of making eye contact.

"Who is this?" asked a boy in a red T-shirt, gesturing toward me with his beer. I realized, with a shock, that I recognized him: he was the asshole from the day we went into town. Parker.

"My sister," Ivy said casually, slinging an arm around my shoulder. A sick thrill clutched my insides. "So you better be nice."

"No way that's your sister," Parker said. "She's missing your permanent sunburn."

Ivy smiled at him. "Maybe try shutting the fuck up if you want to stay."

She pulled me past them toward the flat rocks we used to lie on after swimming lessons and set her vodka down carefully.

"Why is he here?" I protested. "Thought you wanted to stay away from the racists at school."

"I ran into him while I was inviting my actual friends at the baseball game, okay," Ivy answered. "He said if there was a party, he'd bring free beer. And it looks like he kept his promise. Why don't you take a can and make him regret bringing it?"

Her hand was warm on my side, curving sweet just over my

hip bone, her thumb stroking a slow, distracting path. There was a cluster of boys a few meters away who were still looking in our direction, and I felt sure that Ivy's hand was as obvious as a screen at a drive-in theater. I wrenched free of her grip.

"We're not sisters," I said. "Don't be gross."

Ivy took a tiny sip of the vodka, eyes darting around. "Yet," she said.

"Give me that."

Ivy considered the bottle then me. She handed it over, and I tipped it back for a swig. I got more than I was planning on, the alcohol burning down my throat and making my nostrils sting. It was like gasoline in taste and smell, but I kept it all in my mouth and didn't choke.

I coughed a little when I handed it back to Ivy, trying to be nonchalant. Someone called her name, but she didn't look away from me.

"What are you going to do if Mom comes back early?" I asked.

"*Your* mom is busy. Like I said."

"Don't be gross. My mom probably hasn't even had sex with him yet. She's old-fashioned. You don't know her—she doesn't even let me watch PG-13 movies. She fast-forwarded through a super-tame sex scene in *Troy*, that movie with Brad Pitt."

"Then clearly your mom staying with my dad tonight is a sign that things are getting . . . Real. Official."

Ivy punctuated each word with a little grind of her hips in toward me. I could hear the boys' laughter floating around me, in the air like sweat and sweetness. Ivy looked strange, as if her skin was a different texture than what I had learned under my mouth, and I was pretty sure it wasn't just the booze messing with me.

"Are you wearing makeup?" I asked.

"Yeah. It's a party."

It wasn't the texture, I realized; Ivy's arms were an entirely different color than her face. She'd used a foundation several shades too light, and she didn't look like herself anymore. None of this felt like her—she was trying very hard at something, and I didn't know what it was.

"If you don't get them to leave, I will," I warned.

Ivy's name was called again, louder this time, and her gaze snapped away from me, distracted.

"Good luck with that," she replied. "If you're gonna stay, don't be embarrassing. And ignore anything Parker says."

She was off before I could find the words in my gummed-up mouth to ask her to wait. She'd called my bluff. I was alone beside the case of beer, watching Ivy jog over and throw her arms around the redheaded girl stepping out of the water. I quickly grabbed a beer to give the illusion that I had some sort of purpose here and moved off to the edge of the clearing, where I sat down on the rocks.

I pulled out my phone and flicked automatically to the last thing Paul had sent. He'd stopped sending me messages asking about my silence after a while, but this morning my phone had buzzed for the first time in days, and there was a huge chunk of words across several texts waiting for me.

"maybe youve lost your phone," it said. "or maybe Demon Daughter killed you and they haven't found ur body yet. Maybe ur just being a dick and really hate gay people?? Which im not anyway?? I miss you tho. Steven's getting married. He proposed to his girlfriend yesterday and the whole family is going apeshit over it and i know im supposed to be happy for him and i am, but my parents are already making jokes about how it'll be my turn next because im the second oldest, and i hate it. I told Tool Coworker i wasn't interested in her the other day cuz she was getting too obvious and she just told me she was sure she could figure out how to 'rev my motor' eventually. Everybody's always pushing stuff on me like 'this is how you have to be' and i don't even have you around to complain to. I want them to shut up and i want you to come back from trash land and stop ignoring me."

I took a swig of my beer. It tasted like sour piss and did nothing to help the lump in my throat. I'd been so caught up in myself—in Christopher, my mother, Julie, Ivy—that I hadn't been there for Paul when he needed me. I suddenly missed him bitterly, but I couldn't imagine trying to type out any of what I was feeling.

I put the phone down on the rock beside me. *I'm sorry*, I thought futilely at it. *I don't think I'm a very good person, or friend.*

"Hey."

A boy with curly brown hair was in front of me, holding out a bottle with something orange inside. I'd seen him over with Ivy's circle of friends earlier, talking to Jess.

"Thought you might want something better than that shit," he said easily. When I hesitated, he shook it a little bit. "Seal's still on—it's okay, you can check."

"I'm fine," I replied.

"It tastes like a Creamsicle and it's got rum in it," he said.

I took it from him—still sealed, he hadn't lied—and twisted

it open to take a sip. It did taste good, and I was as thirsty as if I hadn't had anything yet.

"There's a whole bottle; you don't need to drink it all at once," the boy laughed.

I pulled it away from my mouth so fast I spilled a little down my chin. I passed it back to him.

"Ivy hasn't talked about you much."

"Oh," I said.

"No, that's a good thing! Or at least, it makes me think there's something more about you. She talks about everything, even when no one cares. You, she's keeping secret."

I could see Ivy past the boy's shoulder, lit up in the greenish glow of an electric camping lantern. She was smiling at Jess, tipping in toward her. She hadn't told me about any of these friends, so maybe they were the most important thing in her life—at least by this boy's logic. Was Mackenzie here, ready to hold Ivy's hand and steal her from me?

"Maybe I'm just not very interesting," I suggested.

"You could tell me a little about yourself if you want," the boy said. "And let me be the judge of that."

I was almost positive he was flirting with me. This would make him only the second boy ever to think I was worth that. I was warm all over with the rum and the look of his hands curled around the neck of the bottle. It made me think of other things that boys' hands wrapped around . . . What was wrong with me that my brain always went to places like that?

Across the clearing, Jess was smiling back at Ivy, and I pictured myself standing up and crossing over to them, hooking my fingers under Jess's sweet, upturned chin, and ripping her face off.

I reached out for the bottle, and the boy gave it to me easily.

"I'm Alex," he said.

"Adele," I said. "And I don't think you would like me very much if you knew anything about me. Anyway, I'm with someone."

Why had I said that? My brain buzzed. I very purposefully did not look at Ivy.

"That's cool," he continued. "Not going to lie, I think you're pretty cute, but I mostly came over because you looked lonely."

"Oh, thanks."

"No!" He was laughing now, sweet and unbothered by my awkwardness. "I didn't mean it like a bad thing. Just come on over and sit with the rest of us—I promise I won't hit on you."

The problem was, I wanted him to—he was cute, and I wanted him to want me, and I wanted that want to be enough to supersede Ivy's weird hold over me, to prove it false. But even now, I knew I would've traded in this whole conversation for one second of Ivy looking at me.

I took another swig. How much had I had already? I liked it. A lot. As my head tipped back, the stars slid into my vision like a mask shifting down over my face.

Someone laughed, loud and raucous. I came back down to earth to see two boys walking past my shoulder. It was the asshole and someone else.

"Hey," I said, then louder, "hey, Parker!"

The boy came to a halt and looked over at me. He had lips as thin as a paper cut.

"You shouldn't talk to Ivy like that," I said.

"Do I know you?" he asked, half smiling.

Alex started to say something, but I cut across it.

"That was some racist bullshit earlier," I said. "You should never treat people like that, but it's an even extra layer of asshole when they're the one who fucking invited you. You don't know her."

"No, you know what? I think I do," Parker said. "And I think I know you, too."

He was moving toward me now, with the slow, rolling gait of someone who was trying to disguise how drunk he was. He pointed at me.

"I've seen you somewhere."

"I saw you heading into summer school," I said.

"No." His voice had changed. "That's not it."

My entire body went cold.

"Go away, Parker," Alex said. "She doesn't go to our school; you don't know her."

Parker's smile had gotten big and certain.

"No, I definitely do," he said, slurring his words. "I've seen your fucking tits."

I tried to push past him, but he caught my arm, fingers sticky against my skin. He looked me up and down.

"You're the slut whose pictures were going around," he said.

"Get off me," I said shakily. I pulled, and nothing happened— he was so much stronger than me. "Get the fuck off me."

I heard Alex say something distantly, maybe "leave her alone," but everything had tunneled down to my insides folding sickly in on themselves and Parker's sneering face looking down at me.

I yanked again, with all my strength, and shifted us both a few steps closer to the edge of the water hole.

"You looked good like that," Parker said. "Give us a smile— you were smiling nice and easy then."

I hit him in the face—hard. He shouted, "shit!" and let me go, and I stumbled back into the shallows of the pond, water racing soothing and cold up over the tops of my feet. My ears were ringing and my hand on fire. It was very quiet in the clearing all of a sudden.

Parker's face was red. When he stepped toward me again, Alex tried to push him away, but Parker was bigger, and he shoved him to the ground. With the water behind me and a boy's furious face in front, I had nowhere left to go.

"Bitch," Parker snarled and lunged for me.

His hands hit my shoulders and my feet went out from under me. The water closed over my head with a muted snap. Two thick thumbs found the center of my neck and pressed down— my eyes were open, but his face was split into a kaleidoscope of blue through the water, and I didn't know if I was choking or drowning, whether it was the water or him that was doing it. The water shimmered and Christopher's face was above me, Julie's, my mother's.

I thought, very clearly, *You are not my family*, and kicked out. His hands disappeared and another set plunged down, snarling in the front of my shirt and yanking me up.

I broke the surface with shredded lungs. Parker was on his back in the water beside me, and a fist was flashing down again and again into his face. I coughed until it felt like blood was in the back of my throat and watched with a strange detachment as Ivy brought red lines up between Parker's teeth.

"You think you can touch her, think again," Ivy spat, and Parker's head shook like a rag doll's. "I'll split you open like a peach. I'll fucking eat you alive."

She was braced on her knees in the water beside me, holding Parker's collar to keep him in striking range. He pushed his hand up against Ivy's chin, trying to force her off. A fierce swell of hate seared up through my chest, and I surged over and sank my teeth into his wrist, biting as hard as I could. He made an ugly, animal noise, and I ground down, biting until my jaw was shuddering hot.

"Jesus," someone said distantly. I let go and swayed sideways—my temple hit Ivy's thigh, and I stared past it to where Parker's basketball shorts were ballooning in the shallows of the water. I felt very empty.

"I'm not a slut," I said.

"I'm going to kill you," Parker rasped. "Both of you."

Ivy's leg jerked under my head as she got up to stomp hard on Parker's stomach. The air left him like a popped balloon.

"What you're going to do is leave my property," Ivy said. "Before me and my permanent sunburn make sure you're leaving this earth. You don't get to talk to me or her like that."

She pulled me to my feet and held me steady, hands on my arms. There was a spot of blood high on her cheek that the water hadn't washed off—I imagined leaning forward and licking it off.

"Thanks," I breathed.

"No one hurts you on my watch," she replied.

She touched my cheek and leaned forward. I flinched backward violently. There were still people all around us, watching. Ivy followed my eyes and stared them down.

"What?" she said flatly.

"Your hand is bleeding," Alex said.

Ivy looked down and laughed.

"Whoops. Anyone who wants more beer, you better go grab it now, because it's probably gonna be gone soon."

I pulled away and staggered out of the water, shoes sloshing and skin trying to vibrate off my flesh. The crowd parted to let me through as if I was carrying an infectious disease, and I made a beeline for my phone still lying on the rock.

"Adele." Alex was at my side, bending down to catch my eye. "Hey, are you all right?"

"I said you wouldn't like me," I said. I grabbed his rum drink first then reached for my phone. Another hand beat me to it.

"Here," Ivy said.

I snatched it from her and headed blindly into the trees. Behind me, there was more yelling—probably Parker's friends coming to his defense. But it sounded like most people were yelling at them, not me, so I kept going.

I was only a few steps into the forest when Ivy caught up with me. "Everyone else will make him and his friends leave," Ivy said. "You don't have to go."

"You tried to kiss me in front of everyone."

Ivy faltered then seemed to rally.

"So?"

I stopped. We were far enough away now, and I needed to get Ivy to stop following me.

"You introduced me as your sister to these people!" I hissed. "It doesn't matter that it was obviously a joke, you've been doing this for weeks—just going for it no matter who's around, no matter if my mom is, like you don't care if we get caught. And throwing a party while Mom is gone? It's like you're trying to ruin your own life."

Ivy's face was in shadow, but I could still see that her intake of breath drew her taller, then made her sink back down again. Something cold trickled into the back of my skull.

"You are, aren't you? You're using me to do it."

"I'm not doing anything," Ivy exploded. "I'm just sick of playing house with your mom as if it's going to come to anything or mean anything. You really want to be my sister? Wanna take my last name and wake up to me every morning and pretend you haven't fucked me? You think she would actually want me around if she knew anything about that? You think she actually wants me around anyway? She made a good show of it at the start of the summer, but she doesn't want a second daughter—she doesn't really want me! That's just how this shit goes."

She spun on the spot, like she was about to run off, then she surged back in close to me.

"You want to know what happened at that baseball game? I come around the bleachers, all sneaky, like I'm going to surprise Jamie and make his day, and then I see he's already with someone. He's being hugged by this tall red-haired bitch in a pink dress like Ariel from *The Little Mermaid*, over by the bench, with my dad standing nearby, watching. I didn't get an invite, but Elizabeth did. My dad invited her to come watch her baby play baseball, and that's why I couldn't come, and that's why he couldn't tell me I couldn't come, because he will always pick someone or something else over me, just like everyone will."

"So you want to drag me down with you," I said. "You're trying to make me go off the rails, too, so you won't be alone."

"Oh, is that what I'm doing? Listen, I don't care what happens with you, I'm just bored."

She got right up into my space. There was still a streak of Parker's blood on her cheek, and the heat of her was Pavlovian now; my body was on the edge, preparing for fight or fuck.

"Other than you, what else is there to do around here?" Ivy asked.

I wanted to burn a thousand photos of her all over again, set fire to the whole forest and reset. No lost family heirlooms, no garbage, no proof that I was ever standing here. Ivy didn't stop me when I started backing up, just stood still with her hands at her side.

"Okay," I breathed. "I'm done then. I'm done."

I started running around the time I started crying properly. The trees pitched around me in a purple and green haze, and the light sunk dark and sleepy. I kept tripping; the ground was trying to move away from my feet. My breathing came out in huge, shuddering gasps.

Every time I looked at Ivy, I felt like I was sinking into something deep, a pit I wouldn't be able to climb out of, and Ivy—Ivy was just bored.

Chapter 18

I found myself on the shore of the lake, the boat a few feet away and the island looming in the distance. I toppled onto my back and stared up at the spinning sky for a moment, panting. The sun had set, and the last bits of daylight were fading. My crotch was itching where some pubic hair had gotten caught in my underwear; I jammed my hand down between my legs and scratched. It felt good. I scratched harder, pressed and dug in against the seam, searching for a way out of the panic. It only made things worse—I could feel the hysteria climbing back up my spine, so I fumbled my phone out of my pocket and dialed.

He picked up on the third ring.

"Dell?"

"Paul," I said but couldn't manage any more. My whole head was swollen with tears, snot dripping down the back of my throat. I flattened a hand against my eyes and pressed down.

"Hey," Paul said. "Dell, it's okay, you're all right, tell me what's up. I'm here."

"I'm sorry I've been ignoring you," I said. "I had sex with Ivy."

Paul didn't say anything for a long moment, and I curled onto my side, staring at the boat.

"Okay," he said. "I wasn't expecting that, honestly, but okay."

"I think there's something really wrong with me."

"Dell, there's nothing wrong if you like girls."

"I think I'm a nymphomaniac," I said wetly. "'Cause I still think of guys, but I want her to do all this stuff to me. Can you be a nymphomaniac if you've only had sex, like, three times?"

"Are you drunk?"

"No," I replied, but that was a lie, and I was done lying to Paul. "Yes, but it doesn't matter."

"Where are you? Where's your mom?"

"I'm at the stupid cottage—well, I'm down by the lake. Ivy is throwing a thing. Mom is staying over at her boyfriend's place and is probably going to marry him and then I'll have a sister who I've had sex with because I'm disgusting."

"You're by the lake? You're not in the water, are you?"

"Mom got to have a real sister, and I didn't even get to meet her. All I ever wanted was to be like my mom and I'm nothing like her."

"Dell."

"I'm not in the water. Is Steven happy he's getting married? Tell me about Steven. I'm sorry I haven't been answering."

"Dell, listen to me. You're not a nymphomaniac. You hadn't even done anything before Christopher, and he was a piece of shit who messed you up."

"But everything makes me think about sex."

"From what I hear, most teenagers are like that."

I hated it when Paul did that—pulled himself back from it and said "teenagers" like he wasn't one.

"Boys are like that," I said. "Girls aren't. You guys are different."

"Not all of us are," he objected.

"I don't fit in with Ivy, and I didn't fit in with Christopher—I don't have a place with gay people or straight people, or girls or boys—no one wants me. I don't fit anywhere."

I could hear the water pulling at the edge of the sand, sucking soft behind my head. It had been so different being underwater when my own hands had brought me there, not like when Parker's were pushing me down.

"My mom knows it," I continued. "That's why she wants a new family. She knows I'm all wrong and I don't fit with her anymore."

"Your mother loves you," Paul said softly. "And yeah, it's weird that you're hooking up with her potential stepdaughter, but she won't stop loving you if you tell her you like girls."

"But I don't just like them," I said. "Are you not listening, I'm not just gay like you, it's something grosser."

Paul went quiet on the other end of the phone.

"Dell, I told you I wasn't gay."

"I've been truthful with you," I said. "And you think you can't trust me? Why else would you be so against hooking up with your coworker? I've seen her—she's hot!"

"So not wanting to sleep with an invasive asshole makes me gay?"

"No," I croaked. "I didn't mean it like that. I know she sucks, I just—you're so confident in every other aspect of life, and yet somehow I never see you flirting with girls? I just want to understand."

Paul paused. I was alone again on the shore, stuck in free fall until he spoke.

"Look, all that stuff that we've been told—that guys always want sex and girls never want it, that there's all these rules to how we're supposed to behave, or we're, like, not the 'right' versions of our genders or whatever—what if that's just a lie?"

His voice had gone higher, intent and nervous. I had been halfway through reaching for the orange rum a few feet away. Now I went still, fingers just touching the plastic, waiting.

"I've been looking things up," he said, "trying to find something that fits. I figured it would change as I got older, that I would meet someone who made me feel different, but it hasn't happened, and I'm tired of feeling like I'm broken."

"Broken?"

"I do like girls but not the way I'm supposed to."

"Because you're gay?" I said, feeling like I was missing something.

"No. I think I'm asexual."

I blinked up at the sky.

"The idea of holding hands with girls and kissing them is, like, really nice," Paul said, "but I don't look at them, at anyone, and want to have sex with them. So when everyone else started to get so openly . . . I don't know, sexual, it felt scary to actually tell girls I liked them, in case they told everyone I was weird for not trying to mack on them constantly."

I rolled it over in my head. "That's a thing?" I asked.

"Yes," Paul said firmly. "For me, it means I don't experience sexual attraction to people. And I tried. I even assumed I was gay for a while, too, but when I tried to get myself to be attracted to other boys, I got nothing. I want to date girls, but I don't want to bone anyone."

"But you told me that one time that you got, like, fear boners when you were thirteen."

"Of all the dumb shit I've told you, you have to remember that?" Paul groaned. "My junk isn't, like, dead. Blood still flows, dumbass. I just am totally 'could take it or leave it' about the whole idea of having sex with people, and from everything I've read, every other teenager I know actually, like . . . wants it. And thinks about it and stuff. Sounds exhausting."

"It is," I said. "You can turn it off? Can you lend me some of that?"

"Oh, Dollface, it does not work like that."

"But maybe you just haven't met the right person." I tried to imagine existing without the heat in my veins at the sight of girls like Ivy—or boys like Christopher or Alex. For all that I'd wanted it gone, I didn't know who I'd be without it.

"Well, maybe. I can't tell the future, Dell, but I'm also tired of people saying that. Asking me to live for a potential person who might never come around instead of trusting what I know about myself right now."

I could hear the strain in his voice. I was messing this up.

"Thanks for telling me," I said. "I'm sorry. I didn't mean to force anything out of you that you weren't ready for."

"You were right when you said I'd been hiding something from you. I've been thinking about this for a while."

"How long?"

"Back when you had a crush on Steven, you looked at him all the time like you wanted him to, like, destroy you. I'd thought I was just more into relationships the way everyone says girls are, but you were a girl and you still wanted sex stuff, so I had to start wondering if there was something else."

"I made you think there was something wrong with you?"

I sat up with great difficulty, suddenly horrified. My phone gave a strained beep—it was running low on battery, and I clutched it harder to my face.

"But that's what I'm saying," Paul said. "There's nothing wrong with either of us. We're just different. And maybe it'll change later, I don't know, but—if it's real now, it's real, you know? I found this word, and it suddenly made all this stuff about me make sense. It was this huge relief."

"I wish I was gay," I said. "I wish I could choose. Ivy told me that I'm lying about liking her and liking boys, but I don't know which one's the lie."

"Fuck Ivy. You can like both."

I laughed, and it sounded sticky. There were thick clouds gathering overhead, turning the remaining sunlight into a flat, blocky gray. They looked close enough to touch.

"No, you can't," I said.

"Dell, you're probably just bisexual."

And there it was—the impossible word that had been crouching at the back of my skull for what felt like weeks now, jabbing me in the brain whenever I thought too hard about anything.

"But everyone knows that's not a real thing," I said, trying to conjure some of Natasha's certainty, her worldly aura, so I wouldn't look like an idiot for wishing, for imagining that I could stand somewhere without the rug being pulled out from under me.

"It means people who are attracted to their gender and other ones. So you can like girls and boys and other people, too. It's a thing."

"I know what the word means," I said. "But it's just a thing people say when they're scared to admit that they're gay. It's a"—a memory popped into my head, watching old *Sex and the City* episodes at Natasha's house—"a layover on the way to Gaytown."

"Why?" Paul asked.

"What do you mean, why?"

"Why can't it be a real thing that people can fall in love with more than one gender? Isn't your thing with Ivy as real as your thing with Christopher?"

I had no answer for that. Paul sounded serious. He hadn't told me yet that I must have imagined ever liking Christopher or that this thing with Ivy didn't matter.

"Bisexuality is a real thing," Paul said. "I promise you. It's just that no one ever properly told us it was an actual option."

"Okay, but nobody believes people when they say they're bi."

"One second ago, you were the person saying it wasn't real."

"Because if I say it first, no one can call me a liar!" I blurted. "I'm tired of feeling like a liar, of having people look at me like I'm disgusting. Nobody trusts people who call themselves bisexual; nobody wants to date someone who is always going to be hitting on everyone in the room and cheating on them. Nobody wants somebody easy!"

My mouth felt like it was full of chalk. Paul was quiet on the other end of the phone, and I knew we were seeing the same thing, even if he didn't want to be picturing it—my stupid smile, my bare skin, that awful caption Christopher wrote.

"All I'm getting from you is contradictions," Paul said softly. "Is it that you don't think it's a real identity or that other people won't believe you? Is it that no one is bi and they're pretending or that anyone who is bi is just, like, a cheating ho? 'Cause it sounds like you're throwing anything you can at the wall just to see if it sticks. To find an excuse."

"I don't know. I . . ."

I trailed off. The problem was that I had all these things I did know for sure—things learned from other kids, from the things my mother didn't say, from TV shows, celebrities, Britney and Madonna kissing at the VMAs just to make people talk about the performance. All these things that said bisexuality was fake.

I knew that, and I knew that meant it couldn't fit me—except there was so much stuff I'd "known" earlier that had turned out to be wrong.

And Paul I knew more than I knew myself. Paul I trusted, and he was saying he believed this was a real thing a person could be.

"Are you sure it's not just another word for selfish sluts who can't pick a side?" I asked.

"There's no sides," Paul replied. "Only people you want to be with or not. It's not perverted that you could be drawn to people of more than one gender. And I mean, you don't just want to bone Ivy, do you? You're obsessed with her;

you have romantic feelings for her. Same way you did with Christopher, or Trevor in grade nine."

"I'm not, like, in love with her. That's ridiculous!"

"Is it?"

I remembered the feeling in my chest that I'd tried to describe to Paul one afternoon in a park—how similar it seemed now to the feeling of meeting Ivy's eyes in the middle of the lake, standing on a refrigerator calm and unguarded.

"Do you believe me when I say who I am?" Paul asked, sounding uncharacteristically nervous. "Are you going to tell me it's not real?"

"No," I answered, because even if I hadn't heard of it, how could I not believe him? "I'm sorry if I said anything stupid before. You know I love you, and of course I believe you."

"Then if I believe you are who you say you are, maybe we can forget about everybody who thinks it's fake. Who made you think you couldn't be this."

There was more room in my chest for my heart now—my rib cage was expanding. I felt more than a little dizzy, and I kept looking down at my hand in my lap, curling and uncurling my fingers. I took the phone away from my ear just to see both hands at once, turning them over and over like they belonged to someone else.

Then Paul yelled something, and I fumbled the phone back up to my ear.

"Sorry," I said.

"I thought you'd passed out," Paul said. "How much have you had?"

I waggled my hand before I remembered he couldn't see me. "I don't know. Not that much."

"You should get away from the water and find Ivy."

"I can't," I said. "She wouldn't get it. She doesn't care about me. I've never met someone who said they were bi. My mom never told me about them. Are you sure you believe me?"

"I'll print out pages of stuff and come and visit you and show you that there are tons of other people who believe you, too. Are you going back to the party? I don't want you to be alone right now. Do you want me to call your mom? I don't know her number. Or I could call her boyfriend. I found his number online, remember? I'm looking out for you. Dell? You still there?"

My hands looked like a different color than normal.

"My hands are blue," I said. "When I was a kid I used to think naming things changed them. Am I gonna change now?"

Paul said my name again.

Julie's hands had looked blue in that picture of her and the redheaded boy and Lucy. If I went back to the party, I'd be alone still anyway because no one there had purple and blue hands, not even Ivy. My phone beeped again—like me, endurance was not its strong point. I'd lose Paul soon; he may not have been broken into the same shape as me, but he was the only one who knew who I was and didn't care.

If I can be this way, I thought, speaking to the dark trees and the sand and stone under my legs and the cup of the sky, *if I can be this way, give me a sign.*

"My phone is dying," I told Paul. "I'm sorry I haven't been there for you this summer. You're the best person I know. We can get married if no one wants to marry either of us, and then your parents will leave you alone."

"We'll have yellow roses at our wedding."

"Steven will be so jealous."

A noise erupted from somewhere behind me back at the party, so unearthly that I almost didn't recognize it as a human voice. A laugh or a scream—my ears had gone heavy, and everything sounded the same.

Something flashed on the island. The tiniest, briefest light.

"Julie?"

"Did you say something?" Paul's voice sounded like it was coming from underwater. "Dell?"

"I've got to go, Paul," I said.

"Back to the party?"

I stood and wobbled toward the boat but lacked the energy to push it out into the lake. In the struggle, one foot splashed loudly in the shallows.

"Was that water?" Paul asked.

"Ivy taught me to swim," I said. "I'm not afraid of it anymore."

He started to speak, and the phone snapped cold and silent against my head, voice and comfort shut off in a split second. Someone screamed again from the party—this time, it sounded almost like a name.

This is where it gets hazy, Julie.

I wanted to go to you right away, see. I saw your light. I saw the sign. And I get it—you couldn't talk to me earlier on the island, when Ivy was there. You needed me to come alone. But from that point on the lakeshore, the path to the island was longer than any other, and I wasn't sure if I could make it even to the refrigerator if I tried to swim. So I didn't go toward the light. I followed where it pointed.

It was weak at first, but night was claiming the sky, and the full moon was starting to shine. Every time it slipped out of the purple clouds above, a glowing point of light would appear on the island, and that same light extended into the forest just past my shoulder—something on the island was reflecting the moonlight, directing me to somewhere deep in the trees. If I stepped in front of the light, it would disappear. I had to keep low, creeping through the underbrush, and eventually the tiny circle of blazing light got bigger and clearer and closer, until I was there.

The light had found its home on the handle of the filing cabinet—the missing one from the attic. The girls who had been clustered around it before had disappeared, but in their wake, the top drawer was cracked open, a crowbar still dangling from its jaws.

I planted my foot against the side of the cabinet, grabbed the crowbar, and heaved.

And it was like you weren't the only one there, haunting me and this forest. I could feel Grampa's arthritic hands, Gram's hunched shoulder pressed against mine—even my mother's breath on my neck. We all pulled together.

The last, rusted resistance of the drawer gave way all at once, and it wheezed open.

There were only a few things inside. A copy of Jules Verne's *Twenty Thousand Leagues Under the Sea*, which looked battered as hell, more loose pages tied up with blue string, a collection of baby shoes, and a thin red folder, one corner bent toward me like it had been shoved into the drawer haphazardly.

I picked up the folder. My flashlight was still in my pocket, so I sat down on the spongy ground and wrestled it out. The trees rustled around me: the wind was picking up.

The paper inside the folder had been bent along with the cover, and it separated uneasily from the front flap when I opened it. They were thick cream pages, drawings done in dark, vicious charcoal. The lines had gotten smudged, but I could still see that the top drawing was of Gram. Instantly, I knew what it was I'd found—the portraits that my mother had drawn in Grade 12, all the people she said she'd loved then. The senior art project whose loss had sent her running into the lake earlier this summer.

I didn't need to be able to draw to see how good it was—Gram had flowers curling up around the sides of her head and branching out, and she was in profile, her jaw set in the inscrutable expression I remembered seeing as a child. I flipped to the next drawing, and there was Grampa, his eyes sunk deep and yet still bright under his heavy eyebrows. There were branches around him, extending out almost like a crown. The next picture was a woman I didn't know, with "Ms. Sharpe" written in the corner, and after that, a teenage boy, his face scribbled over in rough red pen.

Scott, my mother's childhood sweetheart. Dad. I paused for

a moment on him—I knew who he was to me but found I didn't care. The pen covered too much to tell if any of his features had transferred to me.

I flipped the page, and there you were.

Your eyes grabbed me at once, and we looked at each other in solemn silence for a minute, the flashlight's beam almost whiting you out. The flowers around you were prickly ones with wide petals and twisting, climbing ivy. Your hair blended into it, so you seemed to spring fully formed from the background. My hand shook when I went to touch the paper, and I left a wet, crinkled streak at the corner—there was still some of the lake on my fingers.

"What do I do?" I asked, but your mouth was drawn shut, an intense look that was not a smile or a frown, and I couldn't find an answer in the lines of your face.

It wasn't what was supposed to happen. I'd assumed that if I opened the right box, my aunt would reach out, her hands open, and she would rise up and sweep me into her arms and let me be honest the way I could never be with my mother. Julie would know if being bisexual was okay. She'd know if I existed.

I pulled at the drawing of Julie to get it out of the folder—and found there was one more drawing behind her.

It was a baby, a toddler, eyes open and mouth pursed, with fat cheeks and hands drawn up into little fists. The baby had a halo of pine needles ringing her head, and in the corner was a name in curly lettering:

Adele.

The look on Julie's face had resolved into a frown now. My

stomach began to climb up my throat, and I swallowed it down. I felt like my whole body was spinning.

My name came ghostlike across the lake, and this time I recognized the voice. Ivy's.

"I'm fine!" I tried to yell. It didn't come out. "I'm fine. I'm fine."

*

Back on the shore next to the beached boat, then.

My feet in the water, holding the two drawings over my face. It had to be past nine; the world was a cobalt blue and the moon had been hidden by the growing clouds.

There was a crash in the underbrush behind me, a sound that couldn't be made by wind alone. I looked over my shoulder to see a person struggling through the forest, a flashlight beam flickering at their feet. For a heart-stopping second, I thought it was Julie, and then I recognized the knees in the beam of light.

"Dell!" Ivy yelled.

"I'm here."

She staggered out of the tree line and stared at me. Her hair was wet. Had she been looking for me in the lake?

"What the hell were you thinking?" Ivy said. "You weren't about to get in the boat, were you?"

"Go back to your party," I snapped.

"Don't be stupid. The party's over; they're all heading home. I had to find you."

I didn't say anything.

"Lecturing me about being reckless in front of your mom, and yet you think it's a good idea to try to take a boat out to a mountain of trash when you're drunk and it's dark out and a storm is brewing?"

"She's not my mom," I said.

Ivy stomped down the incline of the beach, her mouth twisting.

"Fuck you," she said.

"She's not," I said. The hysteria that had disappeared under the sound of Paul's voice was rising again. Saying it out loud made it all real. "I found the drawings Anne did in grade twelve, the ones that we couldn't find in the attic. There's a picture of me among them."

"So?"

"She would've been seventeen when she drew those. But she always said I was born when she was twenty, so how could she have a drawing of me as a baby that she'd made in high school?"

"Anne told you she was twenty when you were born? Seriously?"

Why was that the part she was focusing on? "Yes! My whole life!"

"That's fucked up. My dad was always honest with me about the whole 'teen parent' thing, 'cause he was nineteen when I was born. Still older than your mom, but—"

"What?" I said. It was like we were talking about two different universes. "You're not listening. I'm saying she's not my mom. She can't be. The drawing of me wasn't even of a newborn, so Anne had to have been, like, sixteen when I was born to draw that at seventeen."

"I know."

I stared at her. What was she talking about?

"I did the math as soon as she mentioned you," she said. She'd moved into the water to stand between me and the island. "You're sixteen now, and I'm seventeen. My dad is four years older than your mother. If he had me when he was nineteen, she had you at sixteen. I thought you knew."

She paused, fixing me with her steady gaze like I was a particularly slow child she felt sorry for. "I'm sorry she lied to you about that, but it doesn't mean she's not your mom. What, do you think she stole someone else's baby when she was sixteen?"

"No, I—"

I wanted to scream. My entire worldview was crumbling. My mother couldn't have gotten knocked up at sixteen. My mother would never have been as stupid a teenager as me—would never have let a boy touch her unless she was wearing ten layers of clothes. That's what she'd called me when I told her about Christopher. Stupid. Surely, she wouldn't have said that if she'd had sex with a guy when she was my age. She would've understood; she would've actually taught me stuff about sex, wouldn't have stood by and affirmed the whole world making me think I was a weirdo for ever having sexual thoughts.

I kept hearing her voice in my head, telling teachers and other parents that she had been twenty when I was born. Twenty. I cast my eyes down at the drawings sitting in my lap again, my own baby face overlapping Julie's.

Julie, who was four years older than my mother.

And I remembered Julie's photo album. Remembered a box of love letters she'd been given, detailing a secret relationship. Remembered that she had done something to make her conservative parents hate her, shun her, right before she died.

I knew that Julie liked being outside the way that I did, that she loved being in photos the way I used to. I knew that Julie looked almost exactly like me, way more than my mother ever had.

Anne had refused to talk about Julie for years, and even now she would barely talk about how Julie had died. Anne was pure in a way that I had never been—it had never made sense that I was her daughter in the first place. She might've been sixteen when I entered the world, but maybe she hadn't lied about my mother's age.

I held up the drawing of Julie. "She would've been about twenty when I was born."

Ivy stared at the picture, uncomprehending, the water slick and dark as oil behind her. It spread out around us, black all the way to the distant, shadowed shores of the island. We were alone, Ivy and me, and my mother.

*

I headed for the house, unsteady. Things had become very clear and cold in my head; I was twelve and being given pads and little instruction; I was fourteen and frantically erasing the computer's search history so Mom wouldn't know the gross stuff I'd been watching; I was sixteen and standing in front of my mother's bedroom door, too afraid to ask for advice about a boy I wasn't supposed to see; I was sixteen and feeling sick with Ivy's eyes on me. I was every age at once, desperate to be the person I thought my mom was. Memories were unraveling—childhood under the hands of a liar. Maybe that was the only thing I'd actually inherited from her, the only way we were similar.

The trees seemed to unfold around me, letting me pass with no struggle. Ivy was crashing through them; I was the one who fit in the landscape now.

"Slow down," Ivy said.

I didn't respond.

"Anne would've told you if your aunt was your real mother."

"Would she?" I asked. "Has she told me anything about this place or Julie or myself in sixteen fucking years? Julie got pregnant from her secret boyfriend and that's why my grandparents hated her. That's why she's been haunting me all summer!"

"You're drunk."

She made a swipe for my arm, and I wrenched away, picking up the pace. I remembered my mother's eyes on me and Ivy lying together in bed and the disconnect between what my mother saw and what the truth was; it finally made sense now. My mother had never seen what I actually was because there was nothing of her in me.

"Looks like we won't be sisters in any way," I threw back. "You want a mom so bad, you can have her."

"You don't know what you're talking about."

"I do when it comes to you."

I could see the cottage through the trees, strips of shadowy blue-white like ribs. This time when Ivy made a grab for me, her hand connected; she spun me around and we both swayed, off-balance. My entire world was swinging around the axis of Ivy's face.

"Hey," Ivy said, soft. I didn't know I'd been crying until her hands came up to my cheeks, holding me in place. The touch felt wet. "Stop it. Just stop for a minute."

"I don't know what to do," I said. Somewhere along the way, I'd tightened my fingers too much on the portrait of Julie, and I could feel that I'd ruined it, smudged and crinkled and crushed the drawing under hands that always touched things they weren't supposed to.

"Only one of us should be ruining their life," Ivy said. "I don't want it to be you."

"It was ruined when I was born." I could hear how petulant I sounded, how childish—I'd done too much to still sound like a child. I screwed my face up, trying to stop crying, and Ivy shushed me and leaned in.

She kissed me like she was offering me a lifeline, and I grabbed on as hard as I could. Ivy was the only solid thing in the world. The kiss was gentle, undemanding, and yet it felt somehow like more than any other kiss between us. I was stuck on the miracle of Ivy's shoulder blades under my hands, our shared breath. *I can do this*, I thought, *I can be this*.

Something cracked behind me, a sound like a door shut very abruptly. Ivy was gone, one or both of us pulling away, and when

I opened my eyes, my mother—the woman I'd thought was my mother—was standing at the edge of the tree line, staring at us.

At first, her face was completely, frighteningly empty, eyes gone wide and white. But then her expression morphed into a familiar horror.

It didn't matter in that instant if she had lied to me. She'd still been the most important person in my life for sixteen years. Everything pitched and flipped over inside of me like a house caught in a tidal wave—I turned. Ran.

My mother yelled my name. I'd lost my grip on Julie's picture and now I was alone, just me and the shaking, shattering image of my mother looking at me like she didn't recognize me. Looking at me the exact same way she had when she saw Christopher's photos—before she'd mastered her shock enough to hide it. It was a look that said one thing.

Monster.

✱

When I came out of the trees, I splashed straight into the water, the lake rising to claim me with each step until there was no more ground beneath my feet. I hadn't made it last time, but now I had more to escape. My legs didn't find anything sharp. I'd dreamed of being stranded on the island over and over; now, I figured I might as well do it to myself before my mother had the chance. The brewing storm above had turned the lake into a churning mess of waves, but I didn't need to battle against them. They sucked me forward, chaos greeting chaos.

My arms were shaking when I pulled myself out of the water and onto a broken doorframe at the edge of the island. I couldn't hear any more yelling.

I inched up weakly until I could sit on the slope of shingles next to the truck, my feet stretched down to the spot where Ivy and I had stood to burn pictures. It felt like days ago, not hours. I peeled off my shoes and socks and stared at my feet, pale and shrunken like a corpse.

Like the island around me, I was falling apart, piece by piece. It felt like a physical transformation, like I was becoming the monster my mother had seen. My whole face was being pulled downward; jaw sagging and heavy and sore and hot at the join by my ears; saliva collecting in my mouth; tears forcing themselves down my cheeks; and everything sinking, pressure at my ears like someone was pushing their knuckles very firmly against the sides of my head and squeezing me into a new shape.

Everything that was supposed to stay inside was overflowing. Wrecking balls and demolition teams were swinging wildly; the rooms in my head crashed together, sawdust choking me. Ashes to ashes, I thought nonsensically. That was it then. Here I was. The island was a black hole, and I'd passed the event horizon the second I met Ivy. I was always going to end up here.

"Oh, sweetheart," someone said. "How have you gotten like this?"

And I opened my eyes, and you were there, perched on the edge of the car frame, chin in hands, in pigtails and baseball socks, glowing faintly.

"Tell me what's happened," you said, and so I did.

That's it. That's everything. I've told you now. And we're here.

Chapter 19

The island is smaller when I'm done talking. Julie has had to move as I've told my story—everything is fragmenting, bits of trash breaking off the edges and floating away on choppy waves, and the truck is starting to sink very slowly into the water. It's still solid where I am but only just. I've timed my breakdown well— the hot shell of summer is finally cracking open, and it looks like the storm is poised to take all the trash with it, human-made and human being alike.

"That's a lot, kid," Julie says.

She doesn't look cold. Her hair floats serenely in two clouds around that eerily familiar face, ignoring the patterns of the wind whipping around us.

"I'm not a kid," I say. "I'm not that much younger than you were when you had me, aren't I?"

Julie sighs. "Is that really what you want to ask me?"

Pieces of debris are floating like cornflakes around the island. It's like the island is shedding its skin—shingles, small pieces of wood, a box of packing pellets, all drifting free. It's too dark to see just how angry the sky has gotten, but I can feel it in the air. I wonder whether dying by lightning would be worse than drowning. Maybe I'll just get crushed by the island as it crumbles. It would be fitting.

"Does it hurt?" I ask.

"Dying?"

I nod.

"Anne would want me to say no," Julie says. "She was always the kind of person to protect people by leaving things out. Yes, it hurts. Even if your body doesn't register any actual pain. Because when you realize it's happening, you want to stay. You think of the things you'll miss."

She sits next to me. Takes my hand. Her skin feels like warm static.

"I missed out on you. And I couldn't help my sister when she needed it."

"I've wanted to talk to you all summer," I confess in a rush.

"You don't have to be guarded here," Julie says. "You know it's not me you've really been wanting to talk to."

I stare at her, at that face that had replaced mine in every reflection this whole cursed, metamorphic summer.

"What do you mean? Is there going to be someone else when you take me with you? It's not the gay-hating God your parents believed in, right?"

Julie laughs and lets go of my hand.

"My parents were definitely not right about God, but I don't think you're ready for that kind of conversation. You've got too much unfinished business here."

"It's going to be better for everyone in the long run, I swear. I know what I'm doing."

I can see mine and Ivy's boat drifting through the water off to my left, pulled from the shore by the waves. It looks lost. I wish I had my phone—or my camera. My phone so I can call Paul and apologize again and tell him a list of people he needs to deliver my apologies to. My camera because the sky looks like a mouth, and I want to record it before it closes on me. The despair had numbed while I told the story, leaving me flat. I am an envelope ready to be posted.

"I'm freeing all of them," I say. "You were listening, right? Anne doesn't want something like me around; she doesn't need me." I feel a little pang about Ivy, but she said I was just a distraction anyway, right?

Julie nods. Thunder coughs thickly in the distance.

"Well, sounds like there's no point in showing you what Roger left here then."

"What?"

She flits, like a shaft of moonlight, to the side of the truck. "You missed it earlier: Roger did put some things from the attic here. It just wasn't obvious." Julie reaches fearlessly into the back and untucks the blue tarp that I had thought was simply crumpled up, revealing a stack of boxes underneath. I can see clothes and picture frames and knickknacks poking out, and horror clutches at me.

"It's all going to go in the lake," I cry. "It's too late now to get any of it to shore. Why didn't you show me this when I was here the first time?"

I scramble to my feet, almost falling toward her. My out-stretched hand passes through Julie's pale side, with a fizz of false contact, and slaps against the truck's bulbous face. A flash of lightning cracks above me.

I can see a thick green leather photo album—Anne's?—and books stacked high, and an open box with more sheaves of paper that look like the letters Verne sent. I grope for the photo album uselessly, too far away.

"Yes," Julie says, like she can read my mind. "That's my sister's. Should be some pictures of you in there, too."

Still closer to the trove of objects than I am, she nimbly plucks things out of the back—frames and small boxes and paperbacks. I reach out, but instead of passing them to me, she winds up and throws them over the car, into the cresting, dark water.

"What are you doing?" I yell.

"If your mom doesn't need you, surely she doesn't need any of this."

Julie hefts the photo album in her hand.

"Please, not that," I say. "Just let me see it first, just let me—"

I cut off as Julie throws the album. It arcs through the air, just above the stretch of my fingers, and lands in the water with a splash large enough to be heard even over the sound of the storm. I gape at the spot where the album disappeared then at Julie, who seems completely unaffected.

"Why would you do that?" I say. "That was my last chance!"

"For what?"

"To see if she was anything like me ever!" It screams out of me. "To find out if she ever looked like me or felt as stupid or gross as me when she was my age!" My insides contract. "Not that it matters, since she's not even who she said she was all this time!"

"Why would a picture of your mother as a teenager change anything?" Julie asks. "I thought when you came out here you were planning on going down with the ship."

"Don't call her that. Don't look at me like that," I say, because she's fixing me with a remarkably familiar Anne look. "You didn't want to die when you did, but it's different for me. I don't want to keep going like this. I'm tired. I'm tired all the time. I'm tired of being lied to and I'm tired of existing and I'm tired of having a body—of having a body other people expect things of—'cause no matter what I want, it keeps doing and feeling things that I didn't ask it to."

The island shudders underneath me, and I cling to the axle of the truck and stop trying to move.

My throat feels so thin I can barely get the words out.

"My whole life, I've been sinking in quicksand and struggling out again only to get sucked down deeper than before. There has to be some point when you realize that's just what's supposed to happen to you."

"See, I don't buy that," Julie counters. "And I don't think you do either. I think I'm here right now because you don't want to give up. And my sister's not going to either."

She points behind me, and I turn to see a small red rowboat crest the hill behind the cottage. A second later, I realize it is being carried to the water by a group of four indistinct people. One of them climbs inside and starts rowing with difficulty through the waves toward us. I don't need to see the face to know who it is.

"But that's just stupid," I say. "She could fall out or get hurt or—"

"And yet she does it anyway. Maybe she sees something out here worth getting back. And I don't mean a photo album, or anything of the past."

Julie doesn't sound like I'd thought she would, those hours I'd stayed up late in my room, looking through her photo album, finding kinship in every ugly expression or unphotogenic moment of blurred movement. Her voice is snappier, faster. I don't really know what I'd expected.

"You thought I'd have answers?" Julie says. "I don't know anything. Death doesn't give you wisdom. I'm just selfishly glad I got to meet you. Anne was right: I would've loved you so much if I'd gotten to know you in real life." She laughs. "God, I could've finally had someone to give advice to about girls."

"Girls?"

There is a vicious, grinding squeal as a huge sheet of metal siding suddenly tips, pointing directly into the air like the *Titanic* before disappearing under a wave at least three feet high. Julie flickers, and for the first time, as she fuzzes in and out of existence, I see it: a golden half-heart necklace hanging around her neck. When she tips in the right direction, it catches some nonexistent light, blindingly bright. Like a sign.

"I think we're running out of time," Julie says. "Dell, listen to me." She takes my face in her hands. "You wanted to know if you, and all the things you feel, exist: of course you do. We can want whatever and whoever we want. But you need to let go of this obsession with the past. You don't need to be like Anne or like me to be worth something."

When she lets go, I sway, desperate to be held just a second longer. But she's ducking her head and slipping the necklace off.

"Will you keep this safe for me for now?"

I nod instinctively. She moves the chain over my own head, tucking the heart into the front of my shirt, where it rests against its twin. One ghostly hand stays on the back of my neck for a lifetime more, pressing the chain links deep into my skin.

"Still, though, you do remind me so much of Anne," Julie says. Her eyes are brighter now, like she's either crying or about to go supernova.

"That's weird. Everyone always says I look so much like you."

"Oh, it's the other way around, sweetheart," she says. "You're alive, you're present. I'm the memory. I'm the one who looks like you."

Someone calls my name behind me, the voice so distant it almost gets lost in the howl of the wind. Julie is fading. I clutch at her.

"Mom," I say. "Mom, don't leave me, I don't want to be alone."

"You're not," Julie says. "See? She's coming to get you."

When I look over my shoulder, the little rowboat has almost reached me. The cold hand on my neck vanishes all at once, and I stagger, lost without its weight.

"No!" I'm whirling around, searching for a glowing figure, a door, an exit, an escape. I'm crying again, uselessly. "You were supposed to bring me with you! You were supposed to—" My body, contrary as always, is done with being upright. I sink to my knees.

Julie is gone. I'm alone on the island.

In the lake, the boat is still battling forward, bearing its sole occupant ever nearer.

Anne is not good with oars. It's hard to understand why she's bothering to row out to me, other than out of a sense of duty. To her sister, maybe. She knows what I've done to ruin her found family now—the fact that she's still pushing her way through the wind and waves doesn't add up.

"Go away!" I scream. The wind snatches it away, and Anne doesn't look up from the water in front of her. Her hair has escaped from her ponytail and is lashing around her face.

"I mean it!"

She looks up then, her face drawn tight and waxy in the gray light. Strangely, it's more familiar than ever. As soon as she gets close enough to be heard over the storm, she calls out to me.

"Adele, you are getting in this boat!"

"You're not even my mother!" I shout. "I don't need to listen to you!"

The woman in the boat stares. She has never looked so old.

"That's why you never told me anything about Aunt Julie, right? Because she's my mom and she died after having me, and you were forced to take care of me, and you've just been pretending this whole time."

"That's not true."

"Bet you regret it now, having to call something like me your daughter."

A wave of cold water splashes up my legs, and when I shove backward instinctively, the island creaks ominously. It's coming apart somewhere below the surface, but I have nowhere left to go.

The boat bumps up against the side of the island, and Anne holds out her hand. It's shaking.

"Dell, I need you safe. Please, get in the boat."

"No," I say, strangled. "You don't even know me. Just leave me alone."

"I don't know you?" The boat is trying to move away again, and Anne lunges forward and scrabbles at the edge of the island, dragging herself closer again. Her fingers are white on the wood, inches from my feet, almost white enough to be a second ghost.

"I have been with you every step of your life," Anne says. "I have given up everything for you."

"I didn't ask you for that! Julie didn't ask you for that!"

Her face distorts wildly, a mirror of the storm around us.

"She didn't need to!" she yells. "Because she wasn't there!"

Wind screams in my ear; behind me, the tarp is making a noise as sharp as lightning, flapping nonstop. Either the boat is growing closer or the island is sliding down toward it, because I can see myself in Anne's eyes, tiny and distorted.

"I was in labor with you for twelve hours," Anne says. "I was sixteen years old, and I was so scared, and I did not go through that for you to give up on me here. You are mine. Not my sister's child, not anyone else's."

I can remember her face screwed up in fury over Christopher—it had looked strangely like the fear on her face now. I realize suddenly that I can see what Julie meant—like this, I can see the resemblance between me and Anne.

"I should have told you," my mother continues. "But I didn't want you to think badly of me. I didn't want to be a bad example of how to be a teenager, how to be a woman, I—I was terrified you would turn out like me, and I didn't want that for you."

"Mom," I say. The storm takes the word away, but I am heard anyway.

"I don't care if you're a lesbian; I will support you no matter what. I just need you to get in this boat."

"Bisexual. I'm bisexual."

"Bisexual!" my mother breathes. She gives an exhausted, tremulous smile. "That's great, that's—that's beautiful. Please get in the boat. I've already lost a sister to this lake, Dell, please."

I look down, and the necklaces are still there against my chest, one hanging too short to match up with its other half. I think of Julie's portrait, crumpled up somewhere in the forest by my careless hands. Think of the glowing face that had appeared to me here.

"I tried to save the stuff Roger put on the island, but it all fell into the water," I explain. "I'm sorry, I messed up. I lost your things."

"I couldn't care less. I just need you to get in this boat."

"Promise you want me to?"

There is salt at the corners of my mouth. I can't see through the sting of wind and tears, and I'm being turned inside out again, all the soft bits coming out to make me ache. Why am I sitting here again? It hurts, in my joints and teeth and chest.

"I want you to more than anything," my mother says.

"Promise?"

"I promise."

"Ivy?"

"Yes, she does. It's all right."

"Everyone?"

"They would love for you to get in the boat. I promise."

In my dreams, I was stranded on the island. Choice wasn't an option. But I'd carried myself here, and that matters more than any of the hands at my back that pushed me on, more even than any left open to pull me in.

"I want to get in the boat," I say.

*

As we approach the shore, Ivy and her father and brother emerge out of the dark, huddled together on the shore. Ivy breaks out of Joe's arms and wades in to meet us, splashing up to guide the boat home. She pulls me out and holds me so tightly it feels like we will fuse together. I hold her right back—bury my face in her shoulder so I won't have to see my mother's expression. No one comes to tear us apart.

We get the boat up on the beach and watch the island crumble at the edges, pulled down piece by piece into the water. All of it gone—Roger's junk and Julie's baby clothes, my mother's photos and the shoes that I had forgotten to put back on. The five of us stay outside even when it starts raining, me and Ivy, and her brother and our parents, with our feet stuck deep in the mud.

The island disappears, and I start to breathe.

Chapter 20

"I was in the lake when my water broke," my mother says.

We are on the porch, Julie's photo album between us. Ivy and Joe and Jamie are inside—I can hear them laughing even from out here.

"I couldn't swim anymore while I was fully pregnant, but I was wading out in the water, about waist deep. I'd avoided the lake ever since Julie died the year before, but that day, I don't know." She shrugs. "It's like I could feel her out there."

"I was born in the lake?"

My mother laughs.

"Oh, you took hours, trust me. I made it back to the shore and when my parents came home from town, they took me to the hospital. You just decided you were ready to come out when I took you down to the lake for the first time. I always figured it was a toss-up whether you'd be a natural swimmer or terrified of water."

"So Julie really did . . ." I trail off. "Drown" is too big of a word after what I almost did.

"There was a storm," my mother says. "And Julie had gone swimming. I was at a friend's house. When I got back, my parents were frantic. The whole town came and spread out through the forest, looking for her. Boats all over the lake. Joe and I found her. She'd washed up right near the little river that leads to the water hole."

We take a deep breath together. It comes to my mind unbidden—a floating body, facedown. A tiny teenage version of my mother spotting it through the trees, mouth opening for a scream. The scramble to touch, to turn her over, hold her. My throat hurts.

"I was fifteen. The week before, we had gone strawberry picking with Joe, and she'd teased me for having a crush on him despite the fact that his girlfriend was about to have a baby."

"I'm sorry," I say.

"You do get a lot from Julie. She had the strong genes in the family. I told her everything. Asked her for advice with everything, not my mother. Parents seemed like another species." She laughs, a little bitter. "I didn't expect to be morphing into that species so soon, but I was very fragile once she was gone. When a boy named Scott started paying attention to me and asking things of me I wasn't ready for yet, I didn't have a sister to go to for advice anymore."

I remember my mother pushing me toward Ivy at the beginning of the summer, smiling wistfully whenever she thought we weren't looking. Trying to solve things the only way she knew how.

"So the stuff about Julie dying the year before I was born, and my dad being a childhood sweetheart you met in high school—that was all true," I say. "You just changed the year this all happened. Scott never followed you to college; you just had to say that so the time line matched up."

My mother nods.

"Is he dead?" I ask. "My dad." It's weird to call Scott that, since we've still barely talked about him since our fight in the attic.

"No. He promised to help and stuck with that for about a year. He took off after high school without telling anyone where he was heading, not me, not his family. They blamed me, especially his younger brother. It's why I was so surprised when that same little brother showed up at your gram's funeral and said he wanted to make amends, offering to rent our property so I didn't have to think about it all."

"Roger?" It felt almost like a punchline. The person who had brought us all here.

"Maybe he did blame me. Maybe he was looking for something, looking for answers like you were. Or maybe he just had a lot of friends with garbage lying around. I don't think we'll ever know if this was malicious or not."

My mother looks like she's lived a thousand years. It's been a day since I went to the island, and I still haven't been yelled at. I'm starting to think it's not going to happen, that maybe we can just sit here and finally talk. The air is lighter after the storm, the trees greener.

"Why didn't you just—" I stop, unsure how to say it. "Decide not to have me? Did your parents not let you make that decision yourself?"

"No, they thought that would be for the best, actually," my mother says. "Which was pretty hypocritical considering how they'd spoken about other teenagers who'd been rumored to have had abortions. I think they were more concerned with our image as a family and thought it should be taken care of secretly. And I considered it. But I'd just lost my sister, and my parents could barely speak to me, so I—" She shrugs. "In a way, it was selfish. Because I just needed something."

Her voice goes small. "I needed you."

I want very badly to hug her. I don't know if it's allowed.

"Did you pick twenty as the fake age you had me on purpose?" I ask. "Because it's close to how old Julie was when she died, but it's not in the teens anymore?"

She shakes her head. "There was no actual thought process. I never planned to lie to you. But I felt so out of place among other mothers when we moved to the city, so that's what I started defensively telling other women: I had you when I was twenty. It seemed believable. And then one day"—she laughs a little—"I heard you repeating it to your classmates. That I was twenty. That I'd been in university. The whole story. I didn't realize other kids were ragging on you about your visibly young mother, too. And I just got caught up in that fiction. And it made it easier to never talk about Julie because she was tied up in that whole situation, and I wanted the lie to be true."

"Even if it meant lying to me?"

"I justified a lot of things. That shouldn't have been one of them."

"I found your grade-twelve drawings," I say. "They were really good."

"Were they on the island?"

"No, but a lot of stuff was. And I think it's all gone now. I know I ruined the drawings of me and Julie, but if the rain didn't destroy them, the other ones might be still in the forest where I found them."

My mother sighs, turning a page in Julie's album. She traces a finger over the side of Julie's face. "You've changed a lot since you were a baby. I ought to draw a new picture of you anyway."

"I'm sorry."

"Don't be."

"I thought you wouldn't understand if I told you about Christopher," I confess. "You were always so strict about dating and swearing and you looked so horrified anytime any suggestion of sex came up. I thought you'd just hate me."

Anne puts her hand over her mouth, very carefully. After a long moment, she says, "That wasn't the first time he'd asked you for photos, was it?"

"No."

"And if I'd just let you know you could trust me, you would've told me he was pressuring you?"

"Maybe. I don't know. I wanted to."

"Oh, Dell."

"I wanted to ask you about so many things," I say. "Like, all I do is jerk off all the time, and I wanted to ask you if that was normal or if you had done that, but it's terrifying."

A fun cocktail of terror and humiliation rises instantly. I hide my face in my hands again. After a second, I become aware that my mother is either choking or laughing, and I peek through my fingers.

Her face is bright red. I rush to apologize, and she waves me off.

"Once, my sister came home early from baseball practice to find fourteen-year-old me occupied," Mom says after a long moment. "And by that, I mean that I was using the rare peace and quiet to engage in a private activity, and I'll leave it at that."

I'm laughing, too, half just out of relief.

"Of course I did that when I was your age," my mother continues. "Many, many times. And, you know, as an adult. I'm guessing this reassurance is coming a little late from me, but it is normal."

I close my fingers over my eyes again, trying not to drown in the stupidly large tidal wave of warmth. This, no matter how awkward it is, is what I'd been wanting from her for years.

"Thanks. Got it."

"There are a lot of things that I find difficult to speak about," Mom says at length. "Sex being one of them. Not because it's actually inappropriate for someone your age to think about, or for us to discuss, as I've claimed before, but because I don't have a good relationship with the topic myself. But from here on out, we're going to talk. And I'm going to find someone—a counselor, something—for you to talk to as well. No arguing on that one."

"Okay," I concede. "With one condition."

"Anything."

"You talk to someone, too. About Julie."

After a moment of quiet, she nods. "That's fair."

From inside the house, I can hear the low roll of Joe's voice mixing with Ivy's higher one, like the sound of a bird over distant rain. Ivy sounds happy in a way I've never quite heard. She and her father had a long conversation last night after I was put to bed. This morning, a red-haired woman had pulled up in a shiny car and yelled at Joe outside the house for half an hour while he held Jamie close to him, his other arm around his daughter's shoulders. Joe let go of Jamie to step forward and yell back. When Elizabeth reached for Jamie, he shrank back into his sister's arms. Elizabeth drove away.

My mother takes a deep breath. "Also, I'm sorry if I ever seemed like someone you couldn't . . . come out to. The kind of parent who wouldn't be okay with you loving whoever you want." She laughs. "Well."

I put my hands back over my face, but I can't help laughing, too—after almost going down with the island over it, the idea of my mom kicking me out of the family because I'd made out with her boyfriend's daughter now seems almost comical.

"Sorry," I say.

"I mean, if I had fostered any kind of atmosphere where you could've realized who you were earlier, I would've known not to make you two share a room," she says. "That was my, uh, my blind spot as a heterosexual." She pronounces every syllable, like the word is crispy. "You're both young and attractive—"

"Moooooom!" I wail.

"I'm just saying it makes sense now that I know more about you!" She masters herself and grows serious. "Dell, you will have feelings for many people in your life. Some things will work out and some won't. I know everything feels so intense when you're a teenager, but you have so much life ahead of you."

I nod, keeping my hands over my face. I don't really want to hear this part. I want to pretend I can have everything.

"I think you know what I'm trying to say here," Mom continues.

"Yeah. But can we not, just right now?"

"Okay," she says. She pauses and then continues.

"But I want to apologize also for having Ivy stay with us out of the blue and trying to push a friendship between you. I was so focused on the idea that a friend your age might be able to help in a way I couldn't—or was uncomfortable with trying—that I didn't really think about the fact that I was essentially pushing my new partner's family on you. That must have been jarring, especially at a time when you needed familiarity."

"Yeah, it was a lot," I agree. "I'm sorry."

"What on earth for?"

"I don't know. Making your life difficult. I'm already not like the good daughter you probably wanted, and now I'm"—I waggle my arms—"bi, I guess." Saying it is still weird. Precious and frightening all at the same time.

"How would you being bisexual be something that made you not good?" my mother says. "Yes, I would've preferred you learned about yourself with a different person, but you knowing who you are? That doesn't make you difficult. Actually it—it feels like I've been given a second chance, in a way. I didn't react so well when I caught Julie with her girlfriend when we were teenagers."

I gape at her and then feel like an idiot. Julie had as good as told me! I think of cursive writing, Jules Verne, letters and love and conservative parents—and the world abruptly rights itself.

My mother smiles at my expression but sobers quickly. "I was hurt she hadn't trusted me and told me about her and Lucy. It was a childish response, and I understood that later, but I never got the chance to really explain myself to her before she died. I tried to tell your grandparents about that regret a few months into the grieving process, and it just set my mother off. Your gram was not the most tolerant person."

She sighs.

"I hate the idea that some of that viewpoint came out in me. I didn't mean for my issues to affect you. I didn't mean to become my parents." She scrubs under her eyes. "Everyone swears it when they're younger—that they won't end up like their parents."

I want to tell her that she wouldn't be bad to end up like, but my anger isn't completely gone. For a moment, we sit in silence, listening to the ambient buzz of the forest.

"Anything else you want to ask or say to me?" my mother says quietly.

Do I tell her? That Julie spoke to me when I was hanging at the edge of everything?

I reach for the chains of the necklaces at my neck—although I had exhaustedly changed into pajamas last night and then a fresh T-shirt this morning, I was sure I hadn't taken them off—but my hands only strike one chain. Had I lost the new one? Had Julie just been a dream? I pull the chain out from under my shirt, and there, in the palm of my hand, sits not a half of a heart, but a full one, shining gold and whole. There are no faded letters on it, just a very faint imprint down the center of a jagged split now mended.

"Where did you get that?" Mom says. I can see in her face that she already somehow knows, even if she can't wrap her head around it.

"It's for you," I say. I take it off and watch her clasp it solemnly around her neck. When her hand settles over the tiny golden pendant, I think I can almost hear a sigh on the breeze coming off the lake.

I'll tell her about my whole conversation with Julie someday, I decide.

"I'm sorry," my mother says after a moment, still clutching the heart. "I wanted to be strong for you, always. I wanted to be superhuman."

"I didn't want you to be superhuman," I say. "I wanted you to love me."

My mother crumples, arms out.

"Oh, I did. I do, I do love you. I promise."

I crumple, too.

*

I go looking for Ivy after a while, after the voices inside have died down, and my mother and I have cried and cried together. I find her in the forest. Ivy is sitting on a rock, turned toward what is visible of the lake through the trees. Her head is bent, hair swept to the side, a couple strands curling in the sweat on the back of her neck. My stomach drops at the sight of her, warm and wistful. For a second, a wave of sadness threatens to pull me under, but I fight to the top.

My camera is in my hands, and the moment is perfect. I snap a picture.

Ivy looks up.

"You can burn it if you want to," I offer, holding out the photo.

"Keep it," Ivy says. "If you want to."

I pocket it and sit down on the rock beside her. She has a sketchbook in her lap, and she's drawing a man whose legs turn into tree roots, pencils and chalk pastels scattered around her. It's nothing like the delicate, precise way my mother draws—Ivy makes her father's face in thick, sharp lines. It looks alive. I wait for Ivy to hide the sketchbook or lean away. She does neither.

"Your Paul is funny," Ivy says at length. "He called my dad again this morning to check in, and I was awake to talk to him."

"Again?"

"He was the one who called Joe last night after you hung up on him. Apparently, he got my dad's cell phone from my high-school website? That's why our parents and Jamie came back last night. And my dad just happened to have our rowboat with him in the back of his truck, 'cause he didn't know we'd gotten one from the island—he'd been planning for us all to go check out the island in a couple days, ironically. I chewed Paul out for getting me in trouble over the party, but he took it well. He said his parents offered to bring him up tomorrow to visit."

The smile comes to me slowly. Ivy is warm beside me, a comforting glow. The lake is a flat sheet, lighting up in the sun. The forest feels like an open hand, and I am comfortable in my body; I can't feel the pull of any wounds.

"We need more help here anyway," I say. "There's still a lot left to clean up."

"Do you still have that picture of the five of us?" Ivy asks. "Anne, and my dad, and Jamie, and me and you."

"Yeah."

"Thought it would look good in the frame I found."

"Yeah, I still have it."

"I missed my dad this summer, I think," Ivy says, looking down at her drawing. "Almost as much as Jamie."

She sounds surprised.

"Your drawing looks cool," I say. "Is Jamie allowed to come with?"

"What?"

"When you and your dad go on that trip to meet your family."

Ivy smiles. "Yeah. Yeah, he's going to come."

She's looking at me in a new way then.

"Did I ever tell you," she says slowly, "that I actually like you?"

The trees shift above; a coin of light slides from Ivy's hand to mine, braced close together on the rock.

"No."

"Well. There's that."

I want to touch her, and I know I can. No one will throw me in the lake if they see, and I won't bring myself there anymore. Looking at her, I have this sudden sense that I have known her for years, that she has been important to me in every way a person can be important to someone. That she will always mean something to me no matter what form our relationship takes—friends or family or something else, in a universe where my mom and Joe split up, and she and I run into each other again in a city neither of us comes from, older and wiser and grown into ourselves in a way we haven't yet.

Just knowing that in some world I do reach out and touch her is enough. I sit beside Ivy and watch her draw. I remember reading a book on classical art as a child, pausing to pore over young women in soft, muted colors, sitting together in gardens and fields and forests—I can imagine how we must look together on this rock, and it looks like art in my head.

None of this is new, and realizing that feels like rain after a drought.

"I'm still not a lesbian," I say softly. "But I'm not pretending anything. I think I'm just—I'm bisexual. I wasn't lying about liking you and Christopher. It's a real thing."

"Okay," says Ivy. When I stare, she shrugs. "I talked to Paul for a while this morning. If I can be more than one thing and still be one whole person, so can you."

Ivy is using her mother's picture as a bookmark, I realize. Her eyes stick out between the pages, just above Joe's head, pale and faded. Ivy taps at the top of her until she slides back between the pages and then shades in Joe's skin with the side of a pastel until the hue is as deep as her own.

There is still a trace of makeup left smeared on her neck. I thumb it off without thinking, and Ivy goes still, pulse stamping out against my fingers.

"I was an asshole, wasn't I?" she says.

"A bit. You were the one who told me words were important, but you didn't want to let me have my own. That sucked."

"I just didn't want you to make me like you if you were going to go back to being straight like none of this mattered. I didn't get it, I didn't listen to you, I—"

I can't help it—I kiss her, taking the rest of the apology directly out of her mouth. She melts into me like sunshine. I memorize the details so I can carry them with me no matter what. When she pulls away, she stays close.

"I like you, too," I whisper.

"I know." She smiles. "As last kisses go, that was pretty good."

"Don't say that."

"Dell, come on."

My eyes are still closed. I feel Ivy's thumb against the soft skin at the top of my cheek, gathering tears.

"I have to leave for school in a few weeks anyway," Ivy says. "We knew this couldn't last even if our parents weren't dating."

"Now who's acting like none of this mattered?"

"Are you kidding? If things feel intense to you, and you just realized you can like girls, imagine what it's like for me. I wanted you from the start; I just stopped fighting it when I figured everything was going to implode anyway."

And it had, hadn't it? And yet we are still both here. We hadn't been shunned or screamed at by our families, and no one had told us we were sick. Even now, no one was breathing down our necks, watching us to make sure we did the right thing.

"I was kind of obsessed with you from the start, too," I confess.

"I know!" Ivy cries. "You were driving me crazy because you stared at me all the time, but I couldn't tell whether you wanted to murder me or make out with me!"

"Both? Can I say both?"

We're laughing then. Her eyes are wet, too.

"You don't want to run off together?" I ask. "Kidnap Jamie, make a go for it?"

"Nah," she says. "We should probably try, just for a little while, not screwing things up for each other."

"It wasn't all like that."

"No. It wasn't."

She reaches out slowly to brush the corner of my mouth with a knuckle.

"Can we just have one more second like this?" I ask.

"One more second."

A bird calls from somewhere deep in the forest. The wind catches a trace of sweetness off the top of a flower, something it'll carry for miles. Two girls sit together in eternity.

"One more."

"One more."

✳

Camera in hand, I move down through the trees, following the urging of the earth toward the water. When I come out onto the shore and turn my face back to the incline behind me, I can't see Ivy anymore, but I know she's up there. I know where everyone I care about is, myself included. I look at the lake spread out before me, no islands, no ghosts, and I take a deep breath.

I kick my shoes off, remove my shirt, my pants, and everything underneath. I step into the water, and a face appears in the lake below me. It is familiar but not because it looks like my mother's face, or my aunt's face, or any other person in the world.

It's just my face. It's just me.

I stand there for a moment, feeling the air on my skin, and the grit of sand under my bare feet, the water around my ankles. Then I wind up and throw the camera as hard as I can.

It flashes once in the sky, and then it's falling into the water, down out of sight, down past the light to a hidden refrigerator and the cab of a truck and a broken table, down to the letters a teenage girl named Julie once wrote and received. There are four more pictures left on the roll of film inside, but the girl above the water does not need them; she has stepped out of the four walls of a photograph. She knows now how to swim.

Hey, Ivy!

How is second semester going? Is it hell? Do you have to do a thousand paintings every week? (Yeah, I still don't understand exactly how art school works, sue me.)

I know I can just text you now you have a phone, but I kind of like the pen pal thing we have going! I can send you photos better this way.

Did your dad tell you he's started showing me how to use a dark-room? Before you get excited, no, I'm not going to come to Emily Carr for photography or anything, lol. I'm looking at doing some sort of environmental science in university actually. Maybe in a couple years I can be one of the people assessing whether the lake by the cottage is truly safe for people to swim in again. I still don't know how Mom's plan to give the lake back to the town is going to work (are they going to cut a new driveway into the forest so people don't have to park by the cottage?) but we can't start really sorting it out until spring. I'm glad we went ice-skating on it when you were here for Christmas at least.

Mom joined PFLAG. I think she's trying to run for "most progressive mom of the year." It would be annoying if it wasn't so cute.

GSA drama is still a thing. I kinda threw something at Gary 'cause he said something biphobic again. I also think the new girl, Bethany, might have a crush on me, but I may have confused her by telling a story about you. Paul and Daysha think it's super weird that I make jokes about us having been a thing, but honestly, if you can't say "the first girl I kissed was my mom's boyfriend's daughter" and freak people out, what's the point?

You know, sometimes I still dream about the island. But never about that night I swam out there. I always dream just about you and me sitting on the edge of that truck frame, talking. About anything.

I miss you.

Send me more photos! Or drawings of your life or something.

Love, Dell

P.S. Your girlfriend looks really nice. Tell her I'm a fan of the kingfisher tattoo. Shoulder tats look so cool. (Don't tell my mom I said that, though—she'd freak!)

Author's Note

In the first draft of this book, Dell didn't hear or even think the word "bisexual" until Paul brought it up in their final conversation. It was framed as her suddenly discovering that there was a word for who she was, and how freeing that could be.

For a long time, that's how I thought of my own experience. I told myself that when I first heard of bisexuality at eighteen years old, I felt relieved and understood all of a sudden, as if the word had flung open a new door. But the stickier truth was that I didn't hear it for the first time when I was eighteen. I had heard the word "bisexual" while growing up but only in the context of a joke. It was a punchline in TV shows or movies, a slice of sexual humor to be referenced occasionally for shock factor and nothing more. So it felt like I heard the word for the first time when I was eighteen because I had finally come across others who told me it was real and who allowed me to seriously consider that it was something I could be, not just something to be mocked.

A lot of the discussion of bisexuality in this book—including the biphobic assumptions that Dell so confidently holds earlier in the story—is based on my own experience growing up in the 2000s in Ontario, Canada. I grew up in a rural area, but in my early twenties, after I had moved to Toronto and made a whole host of queer friends, I discovered that it wasn't just a "small-town problem." Many of my friends my age who grew up in the city also had very little knowledge of what it meant to be bisexual, pansexual, asexual, or transgender when they were children and teenagers. The world we grew up in was split into binaries: gay or straight, boy or girl, virgin or slut.

While some positive representations of bisexuality did exist during the 2000s, the popular media perception was a myriad of stereotypes, and I couldn't see myself in any of them. Compounding this was the fact that sex ed was very limited during my childhood, and my parents lacked the language to have the conversations with me that I desperately needed.

Thankfully, things have changed since I was a teenager. There is better education now on sex and sexualities, as well as positive and diverse representations in the media of different sexualities and genders beyond the binary.

This book is a claustrophobic look at a few people, and it isn't meant to represent the entirety of the queer community, or even the entirety of the bisexual community. Dell's story is just one bi person's story. And while her journey involves coming to terms with having (what she feels is) an abundance of sexual desire, her sex drive isn't connected to her sexuality itself. Bisexual people can be on the ace spectrum. Bisexual people can have had lots of partners or very few partners—and if a person realizes they're bi before they've had any partners at all, that doesn't make them any less bi! This book is also limited in that its portrayal of bisexuality is very tied to sex and bodies, and those bodies are cisgender ones. Dell's understanding of gender and gender roles is very much informed by the time period the book is set in.

Placing the book in the past also informed some other language choices, such as referring to Indigenous people as Native people, a term that was still in general use in Canada in the 2000s. The book also contains a lot of negative framing around sex and a lot of "slut-shaming," which was, unfortunately, a very common viewpoint in the 2000s.

When I talk to people about this book, I often tell them that this is the book I needed when I was sixteen. And that's a big part of why I wanted to set it in my childhood: so I could reach a hand out to that sad girl and let her know that it's all okay. But I also hoped that a teenage reader encountering the book today might see something of themselves in the pages as well. That they might find some comfort in knowing that they are not alone, that other people have felt this way before, and that previous generations have gone through these struggles and still come out the other side safely.

That's the takeaway I hope for the most. The message that love is out there for you, that even when you have spiraled down to your lowest point, there is a happy ending somewhere.

Acknowledgments

Since I started this book in 2015, I've accumulated a lot of people to thank!

First of all, thank you to Claire Caldwell, my editor at Annick Press. You believed in this novel before I had even graduated from my MFA. Thank you for that first coffee shop meeting, and thank you for your sustained faith in the book months and years later, through countless rewrites and late-night emails. I also want to thank Nikki Ernst for the cover art, Paul Covello, Kaela Cadieux, and the whole team at Annick Press! Particular thanks go to Adrineh Der-Boghossian, Mary Ann Blair, Doeun Rivendell, and Elijah Forbes for your extra eyes.

So many writing professors and mentors helped me with this book. Thanks go to my classmates in the novel-writing class at the University of Toronto where this book was born: you helped me get through the most depressing period of my life, and still keep writing. Djanet Sears, when I was at my lowest, you listened to me blubber about my writing. Then, during my MFA at the University of Guelph, Cherie Dimaline, your advice over that summer helped me hone these characters and love this story again. Dionne Brand, thank you for giving me the push I needed to rewrite the whole manuscript into first person. Shani Mootoo and Catherine Bush, your advice during the thesis process became essential to the finished book.

I have to thank the friends who listened to me talk about this book for hours. Zara, thank you for a conversation that helped clarify the heart of the book when it was still in its infancy. Grace, as one of my first readers, you gave feedback that reworked the book for the better. Tara, remember when Craven House was just Writing House? You changed my life and you know it. And Taryn, my very first reader of the finished first draft, and my personal Paul—thank you for being exactly who I needed at fourteen. Other invaluable friends who kept me going: Emily, Rhianna, Kaitlin, Riley, Jenna, Claire F.—and all of the online friends and communities who were, for some years, my biggest reason to keep waking up.

I also want to mention some of the teachers and mentors who believed in my writing across the years: my gifted teacher, Mrs. Carlson, who let me ignore class to write novels; my Grade 6 teacher, Mr. Killik, who had me write my first play; and Julie Carl, who opened the door to journalism for me.

To my family: Mom and Dad, you guys believed I would go places ever since I was a kid, and never missed an opportunity to tell me how talented you thought I was. Catherine, Alyssa, Tristan, look, I finally got a book published after I dragged around all of those notebooks when we were kids! (Your turn next, Catherine.)

And Fraser, of course you were going to get your own paragraph. You were the love I didn't see coming. Thank you for being this book's biggest cheerleader, and for, well, everything.

ALEXANDRA MAE JONES is a queer writer based in Toronto who spends her spare time knitting, making art, and playing the ukulele. Her short fiction has been published in several literary magazines, and she won first prize in *Prairie Fire*'s 2020 fiction contest. As a reporter, she has written for the *Toronto Star* and CTVNews.ca.